MEN OF THE MEAN STREETS

edited by

Greg Herren & J.M. Redmann

A Division of Bold Strokes Books

2011

MEN OF THE MEAN STREETS
© 2011 By Bold Strokes Books. All Rights Reserved.

ISBN 13: 978-1-60282-240-5

This Trade Paperback Original Is Published By
Bold Strokes Books, Inc.
P.O. Box 249
Valley Falls, NY 12185

First Edition: August 2011

Credits
Editors: Greg Herren, J.M. Redmann, and Stacia Seaman
Production Design: Stacia Seaman
Cover Design by Sheri (graphicartist2020@hotmail.com)

Dedication

This is for Paul Willis.

Contents

ON THE DARK SIDE

Several years ago I was asked to contribute a story to an anthology called *New Orleans Noir*, which was part of the wonderful series of city-based anthologies produced by Akashic Books. This local New Orleans version was being edited by the sublime, award-winning mystery writer Julie Smith. It was an extraordinary opportunity—the other contributors included mystery writers I'd long admired, like Julie herself, Laura Lippman, Eric Overmyer, Ace Atkins, Barbara Hambly, and Chris Wiltz, among others—but it also presented me with a conundrum: What *is* noir, exactly? Because, you see, that was the question Julie gave us all as our assignment—to come up with our own definition of noir, and then write a short story illustrating that definition.

I thought about it for a very long time before I started writing my story.

I realized that, for me, noir was "the endless nightmare"; in other words, a story in which our hero makes a wrong decision—which leads to an endless nightmare of consequences and other choices that must be made—only with each progressive choice the options are bad and worse. An endless nightmare that continues to spiral downward, as the main character slowly loses their moral compass and continues downward, ever downward, until they've lost their sense of humanity. And so, my story "Annunciation Shotgun" was born. The story itself was inspired by a friend about whom I once joked, "the great thing about so-and-so is you can call him and say 'I've just killed someone' and he'll answer, without missing a beat, 'Well, the first thing we have to do is get rid of the body.'"

Always a good trait for a friend to have, don't you think?

When the book was released, I did signings and readings with a number of the other contributors—and the question always came up. "What is noir?" we would be asked, and I would listen, fascinated and humbled by the brilliant definitions my fellow contributors had come up with. I was always rather embarrassed when it was my turn to define noir for the audience.

But all the varied definitions also made me *think* about the term, and the books and films categorized by it—and the influence they had on me as a writer.

I don't remember which noir film I watched first, but I have to say my absolute favorite is *Double Indemnity*. When I watched it for the first time as the afternoon movie, I only knew Fred MacMurray as the perfect father on *My Three Sons* or from his Disney "Flubber" movies. I was stunned to see MacMurray embody the larcenous insurance agent perfectly, with his snide smirk and wise-ass attitude, figuring out how to defraud the company he worked for—and what's a little murder for profit between lovers? The movie profoundly affected me...after that, the Hardy Boys and Nancy Drew mysteries I had previously enjoyed reading paled a little bit in comparison. It was the first film I can remember evoking so profound a reaction in me, and from that point on, I watched any film I could that had "noir" in the description.

I was a teenager when I discovered, with enormous joy, that *Double Indemnity* had also been a book—and the same author had also written *The Postman Always Rings Twice* and *Mildred Pierce*. For some reason, my local library didn't have the books—but a secondhand bookstore did. For about a dollar, I bought almost the entire James M. Cain library. I spent a weekend reading them—they were all, alas, rather on the short side—but Cain's spare prose and cynical characters opened up a whole new world to a mystery-loving teenager who, at that point, had only read Agatha Christie.

Cain inevitably led to other authors who became heroes of mine—John D. MacDonald, Raymond Chandler, Dashiell Hammett—and I like to claim all four of these men as influences on my own mystery writing. And while I write the humorous Scotty Bradley series, I like to think my other series is more noir.

Ironically, in 2010 Julie Smith got me yet another gig writing noir—only this time, it was a radio play. I had never written a radio play before (neither had she), and it was a lot of fun for the two of us. Her contribution to this anthology, "Private Chick," and my own ("Spin Cycle") are adaptations of our radio plays into short stories.

When Bold Strokes Books conceived of doing a gay and lesbian noir anthology, to be co-edited by me and my dear friend J. M. Redmann, I didn't have to be asked twice.

We eventually decided to split the book into two—a gay noir and a lesbian noir. We selected a group of writers—some of them mystery writers, some of them new writers, some of them better known for writing outside of the crime genre—and asked them the very same question Julie Smith asked me five years ago: "How do you define noir? And please, write a story illustrating that definition."

I cannot tell you how pleased I am with the results.

I hope you will be, too.

Now kick back, dim the lights, and pour yourself a nice, stiff cocktail.

And join me on the dark side.

Greg Herren
New Orleans, 2011

KEEPING THE FAITH
'NATHAN BURGOINE

The gray-haired woman at the door aimed a glower at me that would have drawn blood from a lesser man.

"No soliciting," she said.

"I have an appointment with Robert," I replied.

She frowned, probably at the familiarity I was tossing about. "Your name?"

"He has multiple appointments tonight?" I smiled at her. "Busy man."

Silence. Her lips thinned.

I glanced up. "Looks like it might rain soon."

Her frown deepened. "Your name?"

I told her, and she paled. Her disapproving gaze didn't waver. She did cross herself—*subtle*—and raised one finger before closing the door on my face without inviting me in.

No accounting for manners these days. I checked my watch. I was routinely ten minutes early, just for these sorts of delays. My reputation can be handy. Or just a pain in the ass.

She's heard of you. I flicked my eyes to the left, where the transparent figure of a man in priest's vestments regarded me. Still fairly recent to being dead, I figured. Not more than four or five months. He was still getting the hang of things, though he'd managed to make his voice heard—by accident, most likely.

"Something you need?" I asked him. He shivered, surprised that I answered him, and faded away on the next strong breeze, face twisting into confusion even as it broke into mist.

It started to rain.

❖

I wasn't sure what I was expecting inside the old stone building, but it wasn't the comfortable sitting room. Polished, well-kept wood furniture filled the room without looking cluttered. It offered up a cozy welcoming not reflected in the old woman's stare. I wiped some of the rain from my jacket and settled into one of the plush chairs. The gray-haired woman stood near the fireplace with her arms crossed, her eyes locked on me like I would start swiping anything that wasn't nailed down if she so much as blinked.

When my potential client entered, I rose and offered my hand.

He didn't take it at first, but I held it there unmoving. Eventually, he shook it. He had a firm grip, not too large a shake. Just right.

"Thank you for coming," he said. It even sounded honest. I supposed that was a trick of the trade.

"My pleasure," I said.

He gestured to the chair and I sat. He sat across from me, not speaking. This isn't unusual. People need time to find the right place to begin.

I took this opportunity to look at him. He was built lean and tall, with dark hair but soft eyes a shade of blue that was almost too pretty for a man. Had I bumped into him at one of my regular haunts, I'd have offered a gin and tonic and proposed we take ourselves somewhere more comfortable. His bed, preferably, though I'm not known to be fussy with the details. But given Robert Bryce's calling, it didn't seem advisable.

"Father," I said, after the long silence had started to strain my patience. "You gotta open your mouth."

He shifted, frowning slightly. "Of course," he said. He glanced at the gray-haired woman. "Grace, could you bring our guest a glass of water?"

Grace nodded deferentially and left. She frowned again when she met my gaze on her way out.

"I don't think she likes me," I said.

The priest hesitated before speaking. "I require your services."

I nodded. I'd gathered that much from the phone call. I waited, but he seemed stalled again.

"No offense, Father," I said. "But I seem an unlikely choice given your…uh…position."

He sighed, looking directly at me for the first time. His gaze was full of longing and pain. "I need a believer," he said.

Ah. I didn't have to ask why he thought I qualified. Whatever else he thought of me, if he'd heard and believed the stories, then he knew that much. I am many things—many of them darker than he'd probably like—but I am indeed a believer. You can't meet Ol' Scratch and not believe in his boss.

"Okay."

He looked at me a long time, deciding. I waited for him to get over his righteousness and come to practicality. If he'd had other options, he wouldn't have called me.

"Something was stolen from me," he said.

I nodded. "And you'd like it back."

He paused, lips tight. He'd be a lousy poker player.

"I can't find it if you don't tell me what it was." I leaned forward, aiming my gaze up at him. I fixed a smile on my face and tried to appear approachable.

He couldn't meet my gaze. He looked away, a flush creeping up his neck. "It's not…a traditional…" He sighed. "It sounds impossible, but I know it was stolen."

I nodded, waiting for him to blurt it out.

"My faith," Bryce said, almost breathing the word. "Someone stole my faith."

"Your faith," I said. It wasn't the strangest thing I'd been asked to recover.

"Yes." He seemed buoyed by my lack of reaction.

"Is it bigger than a breadbox?" I asked, smiling.

He scowled.

"Sorry," I said, raising a hand. "Just trying to take the edge off."

The door opened, and Grace returned, with the smallest glass of water I was likely to see outside of a child's tea party. She put it onto the table next to me, even though I held out my hand for it.

"Any thoughts," I said, picking it up and taking a swallow—it was lukewarm tap water—"on who might be…" I decided to go for a more subtle word than "thief." "Likely?"

Bryce sighed. "I counsel the locals when I can, and sometimes there is resistance. But no, not really." He looked out the window, watching the rain hit the glass. "There is a young man at a local bar. Rusty. I thought perhaps I'd been making headway, but he recently closed the door. It was unfortunate. His mother hoped I could help. His father doesn't speak to him."

I finished the water and handed the empty glass back to Grace. "Thanks," I said. "It really hit the spot."

Her smile was false and showed too much teeth, like a dog angry at everything and far too old to change its ways. Her eyes flicked down. She wanted to get away from me.

I have that effect on people.

"That will be all, Grace," the father said. She left.

"What do you mean 'closed the door'?"

Bryce looked back at me. "Russ—that's his given name, Russ Maxwell—canceled a discussion we'd scheduled and then simply didn't show for the next one."

I thought about that. "Have you asked Rusty yourself about your loss?"

The father regarded me with a pained expression. There was so much misery in his eyes that I actually felt sorry for the guy. For a second.

"Without my faith? I don't dare…" He blushed.

Ah. Temptation. I smiled at him. "Got it."

"I require discretion." He swallowed.

This was familiar territory. "I'm used to that. It's two hundred a day, plus expenses. Your vow of poverty isn't my problem. I can't pay the rent in goodwill."

The priest nodded. "Of course."

I rose, and so did Bryce. I offered my hand again, and this time squeezed just a little longer than was polite, wondering. He shivered, and let go.

"Please don't," he said, clearly uncomfortable.

I regarded him. "If you've lost your faith, why are you so eager to get it back? Why not find a new way?" I had a few ideas on several new ways he could try, if he was willing.

He looked at the ground for so long I wondered if he was going to speak.

"I didn't lose it," he said. "It was *taken*. I remember my faith, what it was like when I had it. There's something missing…" He tapped his chest over his heart, and closed his eyes for a moment. He looked up. "Have you ever felt completely at peace?"

"Not even once," I said, winking.

He smiled, but it held no joy. "Then I would say we're both looking for something irreplaceable."

"I ain't looking for peace." I smiled.

Bryce regarded me. "Is it…true? What they say about you?"

My smile grew. "Which part?"

"Please," he said. The weight of the world rested on that one syllable.

"I can find it," I said. "And yes, I met...him." Bryce shivered. I nodded. "I'll call you if I need any more information."

He nodded. I left.

❖

A little research time in my office told me Robert Bryce had made quite the name for himself, entirely by virtue of his honesty. Newspapers liked his story, especially the same rags that warned us of the dangers of Liberals, equality, and gin. Robert Bryce had known he was gay since he was fifteen and had spoken openly of his "affliction." He had "resisted the urges of the flesh" and though it was controversial—to say the very least—the church had definitely approved of his abstain-and-pray response to his sexuality.

It hadn't hurt that he was so charismatic and handsome. He looked—in his pictures—like a man wholly at peace.

So who'd taken that from him?

I didn't question the theft. I'd only had to be in the same room with him to feel the crack in his spirit. He'd been busted open like a boxer in a fixed fight, and those sorts of things didn't happen to a man's soul by accident.

But the motive...

Well, that's always the rub, isn't it? I made a short list of names of those who'd spoken out against him, but nothing jumped out.

Plenty had decried him, both within and outside the church. His largest supporter had been a seventy-four-year-old priest, Father Raymond Clayton. I instantly recognized his small photo as the soul I'd seen outside Bryce's church residence. Bryce had taken over his role at the church when Father Clayton had passed away four months earlier. It had been Father Clayton's wish that the young Robert take over his flock, and the bishop had fulfilled that request.

I had a harder time with Rusty at first, but found ads for his "dancing" and "private performances" at the Brass Rail once I scraped the bottom of the periodicals. Here was someone easier to understand. Born Russ Maxwell, "Rusty" was blond, muscular, and coolly handsome. It appeared his services were available to all—for a price. He'd come from a pretty religious background himself—he was a minister's son.

I couldn't imagine his family was proud of him.

I added them to the list, under Rusty's name.

I checked my watch and grabbed my coat. The rain was beating at my office window. I didn't want to go back out in it, but if I hurried I could catch Rusty's first "performance" of the evening. Perhaps even get a private session with him, on the church's dollar.

Sometimes my job has unusual perks.

I tossed a drenched parking ticket off my windshield and into the gutter, and drove off.

❖

The Brass Rail was a dive with a half-dead neon sign flickering over the front door. It was buried far enough off the Market that the streets were nearly empty and the parking lot beside it actually had a lot of spaces available. For the owner's sake, I hoped this wasn't a typical night. I pulled into a spot and idled, waiting futilely for the rain to die down. Eventually, I gave up, got out of my car, and jogged to the front of the bar.

I went inside.

The place stank of cigarettes and sweat. Every third lightbulb was dead. The bar was full of grim men nursing watered drinks and grudges with equal determination. On the stage, a young redhead with freckles and a vacant expression gyrated in front of three stocky men who watched him without blinking. The kid had more than enough between his legs to keep their attention tight and their wallets loose.

I went to the bar, and the bartender glanced up at me.

"Get you something?" he asked.

"Is Rusty free?"

The bartender smirked. "He's not busy, but he ain't nowhere near free." The bartender nodded toward the farthest corner, where I saw the blond dancer from the photos standing near a table of four men. Rusty was wearing leather pants and nothing else—I couldn't imagine going barefoot in this place. He leaned over them and said something. The men let out a low rumble of laughter.

"Thanks," I said to the bartender. He nodded, already forgetting me.

I walked up behind the blond. He had wide shoulders and a nice body. He was a little pale. I wondered what brought someone like him down so low. He could have been somebody's kept boy easily enough—there was no way he needed to work the Brass Rail.

"How much for a private dance?" I said, once I was close enough.

The four men frowned when Rusty turned his back on them. His smile was little more than half a scowl, and his gaze traveled up and down me in a quick measure. I obviously passed, because he nodded and did some mental arithmetic I was sure hadn't come out in my favor.

"Fifty," he said. If it hadn't been the Church's dime, I would have laughed in his face.

I nodded and pulled the bill out of my wallet. He took the cash, tucking it into the front pocket of his leather pants. "Follow me."

I followed him, enjoying the view.

❖

Once the curtain was drawn around the booth, he grinned. "I'm surprised someone like you came here. You're pretty hot for an old guy."

I raised my eyebrows. "Old" probably meant anyone over thirty to Rusty. He started to crawl into my lap, but I held up my hand. He paused, surprised.

"I just want to talk," I said.

He raised one eyebrow. "You want me to talk, big guy?" He grinned. "Want me to tell you how naughty I am?" He trailed one finger down the front of my shirt and flicked his eyes up to meet mine. "What you want to talk about?"

"Robert Bryce," I said.

He sighed, pulling his finger away. "I don't talk to Robert Bryce."

"Not anymore," I said. "But you used to."

He returned his gaze to mine and leaned forward. "That priest never had a good time. If you're checking up on him, all he did was talk."

I shook my head. "I'm not checking up on him."

"Oh?" he said. One finger pulled the chain out from under my shirt collar. My silver cross glinted in the dim light.

"I was a Catholic," I said. "I got better."

"You still wear a cross."

I tugged the chain off his finger and tucked it back in. "It's not a cross, it's a plus sign. Reminds me to stay positive." It had been a cross at one time, but about half of the bottom had frozen and shattered.

It reminded me of a lot more than staying positive.

Rusty laughed.

"Robert Bryce," I said again, this time pulling a twenty from my wallet. His eyes flicked down at the money. He leaned against the wall of the alcove and tugged a cigarette case out of the tight leather pants. He lit one, watching me, and took a drag. He held out his hand. I gave him the twenty.

"I liked him." Rusty shrugged. "It was interesting." He couldn't look at me while he said it, and I could hear the sadness in his voice.

It made sense. His own father had shut him out, so having a handsome young priest come talk to him would have felt like another chance.

"You loved him," I said. Rusty's smile didn't falter but the cigarette shook in his hand.

I waited his silence out. He was far too young to win at that game.

"I'm a whore, stud," Rusty said, giving in. "I get paid to love them."

"You get paid to fuck them," I said. "And he didn't fuck you."

Rusty flicked his cigarette. "You're cold."

"And you're a cocksucker. When did you fall in love with him?"

"I'm pretty sure you've sucked a cock or two yourself." He grinned. There was no mirth in his eyes. Instead, there was a hollowness, an emptiness I imagined got deeper every time he spread his legs for some rich closeted bastard. He dragged on the cigarette, burning through it nearly to the filter.

I leaned forward. "When did you fall in love with him?"

He sighed and stabbed out the cigarette. A moment later he lit another, taking another deep drag. He glared at me.

"Oh gosh. You're right. I completely fell in love with him. Maybe fifteen minutes after I met him," he said, exhaling. "Might have been twenty. Must have been his blue eyes. I swooned completely." His smile twisted. "You're wrong. He didn't even kiss me. Not once. I was just another sinner to save."

Was that regret I heard?

"Are you trying to fleece him?" I asked. If Bryce was wrong, and Rusty hadn't been a part of the theft, I wasn't going to supply him with any details.

"What?" For just a moment there was an honest expression on his face: confusion. It vanished quickly, replaced again by the haughty façade of arrogance. "If someone is bothering Robert, it's not me. Why would I end a good deal? He pays me for my time, and I don't have to do anything but listen."

"But you did turn him down. You stopped meeting him." His mask faltered again. This time he looked afraid. "We both know blackmail pays better."

He laughed. "Oh, honey. Make up your mind. If I love him, why would I try to ruin his life?"

"Love hurts." I rose, taking the cigarette out of his hand.

"These'll kill you," I said, twisting it out in the dish.

He flashed his eyes at me. "Your time's up," he said.

I heard his cigarette case click open as I left.

As far as I could tell, Rusty hadn't had a thing to do with it. I figured someone had told him to back off from Bryce. Outside the bar, I took a second to light my own cigarette before stepping out into the rain. I cursed the blond for wrecking yet another attempt of mine to kick the habit. I'd not gone more than three steps before the translucent figure of the old priest appeared beside me. I pulled up my collar.

"Hello again," I said.

The ghost regarded me. *You see me.*

"I can," I said. His voice was barely a whisper, hard to hear over the rain. He wasn't very good at this.

Why were you speaking with Russ?

"That's confidential," I said. I turned, heading to where I'd parked my car. "What about you? Why are you hanging around?"

The old man's face fell. *My flock. I worry.*

I smiled around my cigarette. It was getting wet. "And what do you need?"

My flock needs you. Not I. He was fading again, from the effort of talking to me.

I flicked my ash. "Well, I'm sure Father Bryce will be a good influence," I said.

The priest looked at me so intently the hairs on my arms stood up.

Deal with the Devil. His voice was barely an echo in my head. The rain was starting to break his form apart. There was no disguising the disgusted look on his face.

I was used to that. Comes with the reputation. I took a final drag, and tossed it aside. "I think we're done," I said.

His eyes were beseeching as he faded from sight. I've had a lot of people try to save me. This was the first time a ghost had stepped up to the plate.

I got into my car. There was a bottle of gin at home with my name on it, but first I needed to go over that list again. I drove back to my office.

❖

Russ Maxwell's parents had been out of town for a week, and at this time of night no one else was interested in either taking or returning my calls.

A couple of wasted hours later, I left my office and went home. I'd almost made it to the top of the stairwell when I saw Rusty. He stood outside my apartment door, watching me. He was still wearing just the tight leather pants, and yet not a single blond hair was wet from the rain. I sighed. I could see through his flat stomach, make out the cracks in the paint on the wall behind him.

"I'm sorry," I whispered, even as I reached for my gun.

Russ shook his head and pointed at my door. It was slightly ajar, the lock busted. His fingers were turning translucent at the edges.

I nodded, understanding. Discretion and all that. I started back down the stairwell, hand on my holster under my jacket, but had barely made four steps when I heard someone coming up from below. I peeked over the edge of the railing. Two large gentlemen were coming up the steps, both in blue work shirts and plain trousers, clean-shaven and without a trace of a smile on their faces. One had a scar that crossed his chin.

I started back down the steps. When they saw me, the two men shifted, blocking the stairwell. Above, I heard my apartment door squeak.

"Fellas." I nodded.

"We just want a word with you," the scarred man said.

"Is that what you said to Rusty?" I asked.

That surprised them. I took that moment to glance behind me. A third man stood at the top of the stairs, sporting a close-cropped beard and a pair of meaty hands. Three to one. Not good odds.

"Don't touch that gun," the scarred one said.

"Don't really want to," I said. "Every time I kill someone, there's hell to pay at the police station."

The two men below me frowned. The one behind me took a step down.

"Russ Maxwell," I said, and felt my senses shake with the name. His faded soul was almost gone, flickering and washed out, floating higher up the stairs. My words brought him back.

The two men below me exchanged glances.

The second man spoke for the first time. "A filthy sodomite." Big word for a working man. I wondered who'd taught it to him.

"I wasn't talking to you," I said. Russ approached, his form flickering into existence behind the men. I pulled on him with my mind, and his ghostly face looked startled and afraid.

The two men tensed. The one behind me took another step.

"Now, Russ," I said, and *pulled* him into the second of the two bruisers in front of me.

The man's body jerked. The scarred man gave to his companion a worried look just as the possessed man slammed a fist into his face. Russ was a quick study and seemed happy to have a chance to dish out some vengeance.

I bolted toward the two men, squeezing past. I made it to the bottom of the stairs before the bearded man slammed into my back. My face hit the door, and white pain flashed in front of my eyes as my nose took the brunt of the collision. I swore and got my feet back under me. He had one of my arms tight in his hand.

I twisted out of his grip and kicked at his knee, making him howl and step back. I braced myself for his rush. When he came at me again, I ducked in low under him. I lifted, rolling him ahead with my shoulder and letting his own momentum carry him head-first into the door. He crumpled to the ground.

I glanced up and saw the scarred man was curled up on the floor. Rusty was still kicking him with the borrowed body. The scarred man groaned with every kick that landed.

"Enough," I said, and *pushed*. Rusty's startled outline wavered behind the bruiser for a moment before fading away, apparently too surprised to hold himself together. Freed of the possessing spirit, the big man shuddered. His skin went white. His eyes rolled back in his head. He collapsed on top of the scarred man, who had stopped groaning.

Amateurs.

I spat some blood from my mouth and left my building. I stopped at the payphone and grimaced as rain trickled down the back of my neck. Blood continued dripping from my mashed nose. I dialed.

Detective Carter didn't preamble when he heard my voice. "What do you want?"

"There'll be a dead body at either the Brass Rail or the home of one of their dancers, Rusty, real name Russ Maxwell."

"Damn it. Why do you always call me with these?" The man had three priorities: justice, baseball, and his old man—in roughly that order. I hoped there wasn't a game on and that his father was well.

"Fond memories of our drink together. The guilty party of three are at the bottom of my stairwell, full of remorse and kicked to crap. They also broke into my apartment."

Carter swore. "I'll send a car."

"Do it quickly. Not sure how long until they wake up."

"Don't suppose you'll come to the station to press charges on the B and E?"

"Only if I can buy you another drink after."

"Didn't think so." He hung up.

I got into my car, not wanting to be around when the cops arrived. I drove for a while, rolling the case around in my head while my nose stopped bleeding. Then I got it. Damn. Who knew I was going to visit Rusty? Short list. This was why I didn't think better of people. I aimed my car back to where it had all started. Time for answers.

❖

This time I didn't ring the bell. The door wasn't locked so I let myself in, moving quietly through the small stone building and listening for the housekeeper. She seemed to be busy in the kitchen. I went past the cozy sitting room and climbed the stairs, hearing a shower. A bedroom door was open, bed sheets turned and ready, and a Bible sat on the nightstand. I went in and found a comfortable chair at a small desk. I turned it to face out and sat down, waiting.

Father Bryce came into the room without noticing me, in a pair of plain cotton pajama bottoms. He was fit and smooth, his hair still damp.

"I see what Russ saw in you."

"Jesus!" Bryce jumped and whirled, seeing me. "What are you doing here? Is that blood?"

I nodded. "It's mine." I tapped my swelling nose. I let my eyes drift over the man's chest. He kept himself in good shape.

Bryce flinched, moving to his dresser and pulling an undershirt from the second drawer. A flush was creeping up his neck as he tugged it on. "Did Rusty…did Russ do that to you?"

I shook my head. "No. Russ Maxwell is dead."

"What?" It came out of him in a rush, and he sat on the edge of the bed heavily. He stared at me.

I stood and went to the bedside. Bryce leaned away from me when I got too close, and I felt my lip curl in a slight smirk as I reached past him for the small silver bell on his side table. I rang it.

Bryce looked at me, confused, but I held up one finger.

"Yes, Father?" Grace appeared a few moments later. She blinked when she saw me.

"I know who stole it," I said.

"You do?" Bryce said, surprised, but I wasn't looking at him. Grace's eyes widened and she took a step back before she could take hold of herself.

"Well, now I do," I said and regarded the housekeeper. Three people knew I was going to see Rusty. Me, Father Bryce, and Grace. "I'm guessing you called those men who killed Russ and tried to give me the same courtesy after I left here, right? The only question I have is why."

Grace glared at me. Bryce looked between us, sinking even farther on the edge of his bed. The blows were coming too fast for him.

"Grace?" he said, his voice barely above a whisper.

"You've no business wearing the collar!" Grace exploded. "Your sort! It's against His will!"

Bryce surprised me by rising. "I have never fallen prey to my sinful urges, and God—"

"Don't you speak of God!" Grace snarled. "God don't forgive you your sickness! Do you know what people are saying about our church? We're a laughingstock!"

"How'd you do it?" I asked, keeping my voice calm.

Grace aimed a spiteful grin at Bryce. "We asked God! We all did. The bishop himself led our prayer circle, he did. It was God who struck you down!" She was panting for breath.

"Did it feel cold?" I said.

She turned to me, startled. The surprise on her face was confirmation enough.

"Like winter against your skin?" I asked.

"Shut up!" Her voice trembled. "You're worse than he is! You've walked hand in hand with the Devil, you have! I've heard about you!"

I didn't react to her ranting. "When you all prayed, it felt like the room was going to freeze."

She shivered and crossed her arms over her chest.

I nodded. "I thought so. That wasn't God." She glanced at me, wary. "God isn't the sort to steal faith away. That'd be somebody else you were talking to." I smiled. "Trust me. Like you said, I've met the gent."

She went pale and started shaking her head.

"Where is it? Where did you all pray?" I asked her, but she didn't answer. She leaned against the wall of the priest's bedroom, and slid down to her knees, a marionette with all her strings cut.

Her head bowed against her knees, Grace began to pray. "Our Father...who art in...who art..."

Bryce took a step away from her, shivering. "She said prayer circle," he said. "The bishop..." He shook his head. "They hold prayer circle in the Sunday School room."

"It'll be there," I said. He looked at Grace, swallowed, and then nodded at me.

I followed as he led the way. Grace kept trying to find the words for her prayer.

❖

Robert Bryce's faith was on the carpet in the middle of the simple classroom.

"Smaller than a breadbox," I said.

"That's it?" he said, looking down at the floor. He hadn't made a move to touch it.

"They wouldn't have been able to move it," I said. For me, it glowed with a golden radiance. To Bryce it was just a small white feather. "The only soul normal folk can touch is their own."

I knelt. When I reached for the feather, Bryce shook his head, and said, "Stop."

I stopped. I wondered if he was worried I'd get it dirty. The priest knelt beside me, and with a trembling hand, he reached out and touched the feather with one finger. It melted away into nothing, and he gasped.

I watched the golden glow surround and permeate him.

And then the glow faded away.

He rose. When he looked at me, his eyes were full of strength and peace.

"Feeling better?" I stood up.

"My own flock," he said, and then swallowed. "It will be hard for them, to accept me."

I stared at him. Hard? They'd tried to ruin him—not to mention murdering Russ Maxwell and planning the same for me. "After what they did to you, you'll still lead them?" I shook my head. "And the bishop?"

Father Robert Bryce smiled at me. "With faith, anything is possible." But there was sadness in his voice. "They'll find forgiveness in God if they repent."

"Some of them are going to go to jail," I said. "For Russ."

He nodded, but took a deep breath. "I have a lot of work to do."

I decided not to say anything. Seemed wisest.

❖

Outside, the rain had finally stopped. I pulled out a cigarette, hesitated, and put it away again.

I felt the soul before I could see it. When I turned, the spirit of Father Raymond Clayton shimmered into being. I nodded at him.

Deal with the Devil. His words were full of sadness.

"Yeah." I nodded. "Sorry about before. I thought you were talking about me."

The priest's soul shivered. I could almost hear laughter. *No. Not you. You turned him down.*

"Don't go spreading that around," I said. "I got a reputation to keep."

The priest nodded, looking back at the church again.

"They're in good hands now," I said. "You should probably... well. Move on."

The priest regarded me for a moment, surprised. I raised my hand.

He nodded.

I *pushed*, and the old priest's soul went wherever souls went.

I checked my watch. If I went to the station I could give Detective Carter my statement about Russ's death—I'd have to think of something plausible—and deal with the break-in. I rubbed my eyes, exhausted by death and faith. At least Carter wasn't prone to philosophy. Come to think of it, Carter also liked gin, and I happened to have a bottle at home with my name on it.

But I could share.

PATIENCE, COLORADO
ROB BYRNES

He wasn't sure exactly where or how he'd lost the highway. He'd pulled off Route 80 somewhere in Nebraska for gas and it had disappeared behind him in the pounding rain, and when he backtracked he'd missed the entrance. But he was in no particular rush to get to wherever it might be he was headed, so he just kept following signs pointing west across the flat, dreary expanse of nothingness.

The radio had been steadily losing the signal of the only station he'd found that didn't preach at him, and as the sky darkened from gray to black he lost it altogether. He listened to the static hiss for a while, then shut it off, drumming his fingers on the steering wheel as he tried to syncopate random tunes in his head to the dull thwack of the windshield wipers.

Now, when he could read the road signs through the rain and darkness, they offered directions to towns that meant nothing to him— Holyoke, Haxtun, Sterling—and a dull pain began to throb behind his eyes. It was time to get off the road for the night. In the morning, maybe he'd drop a few bucks on a map and try to get back on track. Maybe the weather would even cooperate. Maybe not. He really didn't care much either way.

He passed a sign that announced WELCOME TO PATIENCE, and, in smaller letters, "It's a Virtue!" Ahead a telltale blink of red neon told him he'd found his bed for the night.

The car rolled across a twin set of railroad tracks embedded in the asphalt and he followed the neon into an empty parking lot filled only with puddles. The sign—reading only "Motel"—bathed the interior of the car in red as he rolled to a stop in front of the office.

"Help you?" asked the clerk behind the counter as he walked in, a bell attached to the door tinkling to announce his arrival.

"Got a room?"

The clerk jerked his head in the direction of the parking lot. "What do *you* think? Not exactly a boomtown these days." He waited for a reaction and sighed when he didn't get one. "So…just one night?"

"Just one." He looked around the office. At the dusty blinds, the water-stained wall, the faded curtain with a fly strip hanging from one end of its rod. He figured no one stayed more than one night if they could help it.

"Forty-five, plus tax."

He pulled some crumpled bills out of his pocket and the clerk pushed a registration book and pen in his direction.

"So where am I anyway?" he asked, taking the pen in his hand.

"You're in Patience."

"I saw the sign. Am I still in Nebraska?"

The clerk chuckled. "Colorado, Mr…" He looked at the upside-down signature. "Mr. Laughlin. If you want to be in Nebraska, you overshot it by about forty miles."

"Then it's good I don't want to be in Nebraska." The clerk handed him a key with "19" etched into the metal. "So if this is Colorado, where are the mountains?"

"Couple of hours west. You're still in the eastern plains."

"I guess I had the wrong idea of Colorado."

"Well…now you know."

He took a battered suitcase from the backseat of his car and found Room 19 at the other end of the motel from the railroad tracks. A small placard on the battered nightstand read "Thank You for Not Smoking," but the room already smelled of stale smoke so he tapped a cigarette out of his pack and lit up, using a plastic cup from the bathroom as an ashtray.

He glanced at the clock keeping company with the placard on the nightstand. 8:32. Too early to try to sleep. Maybe there was a bar nearby where he could kill a few hours. He picked up the phone to call the office, and wasn't surprised when it didn't work.

A few minutes later he was back in the office.

"The phone in 19 doesn't work."

"The phones go down a lot around here when it rains like this. If you need to make a call…"

"Not really. I was just wondering if there was a place to get a drink around here. A bar or something."

"Last real bar closed about five years ago. But if they haven't closed up for the night, you might be able to get a drink at the bowling alley across the tracks." The clerk halfheartedly nodded in the direction.

"Guess that'll have to do."

Holding his collar tight in a vain attempt to stay dry, he made his way across the motel parking lot and over the railroad tracks, walking in the deserted roadway for a few yards to avoid the larger puddles. The bowling alley sat back from the road, interior lights almost invisible in the gloom, with only a few cars in the muddy, unpaved lot in front. He hoped they were still serving, or at least that they'd open up again for him.

He pushed the glass door open. A sheet of rain followed him inside before it closed again. At one far end an older couple looked up from their score sheet, giving him only the quickest once-over before returning their attention to their strikes and spares. At the other end, he saw the darkened bar tucked next to an unattended shoe rental counter. He squinted, trying to find anyone on the premises besides the older couple, but saw no one.

"Excuse me," he said, approaching the couple. They wore matching green sweaters. "Either of you work here?"

"No," said the woman. The man shook his head in silent accompaniment. "You want Tay. He's around somewhere. Probably in the office."

"Thanks. I'll wait."

He walked to the unlit bar and took a seat in what he hoped was a noticeable spot. A few minutes later a door behind the bar opened and a very young man walked out, spilling light into the dark corner of the bowling alley. He seemed surprised to see a customer.

"Sorry. Didn't know anyone was out here." He offered up a shy smile. "Can I help you?"

"You can pour me a drink."

He closed the door behind him and approached slowly, wringing a bar towel in his hands. He wasn't much more than a kid, probably barely out of his teens. Not bad-looking, really. A bit on the scrawny side, and in need of a decent haircut, but otherwise more attractive than anyone wandering into a bowling alley in the middle of nowhere should expect.

Their eyes met for a few seconds until the kid broadened his smile and looked away.

"I was just closing up," he finally said. "But there ain't nothing going on, so I suppose no harm in serving a man."

"You're a saint, kid."

"Tay. Call me Tay."

"Tay?"

"Short for Taylor." He set down the towel. "So what can I get you?"

"Vodka and anything."

The kid made the drink and set it on the bar, squeezing a lime over it and dropping the fruit on top of the ice. "Vodka tonic. That work for you?"

"It does. Thanks." He took a sip. It was strong. That was good. He looked up at a small chalkboard on the wall, where someone had once scrawled TODAY'S SPECIALS and nothing else. "Any chance of getting food?"

"Food?" The kid followed his eyes to the chalkboard, and he laughed. "Kitchen's been closed for…well, let's see, I've worked here two years, so at least two years. If you want, I can see if we've got any chips or pretzels in the back."

"Never mind. Won't be the first time I drank my dinner."

The kid leaned forward from his side of the bar, grinning. His voice was soft, almost a purr. "You've got a three-course meal in front of you."

"I do?"

"Vodka, tonic, and a lime for dessert." He laughed at his own joke.

"In that case, I guess I don't need dinner after all." Tay laughed at *his* joke, too, even though he wasn't really joking.

"So, got a name, mister?"

"Conor."

"Nice to meet you, Conor." He smiled again. "Sorry if I'm acting a little funny. Just not used to customers at the bar. Not many, anyway. But it's nice to have some company." He glanced around the bar. "So not used to it that I forgot to turn the lights on. Excuse me for a second." Tay ducked back behind the door and flicked a switch. A single light suspended over the bar came to life, enhancing shadows more than visibility.

He was back seconds later, still grinning.

"So this is Patience, Colorado, huh? Is it really a virtue, like the sign says?"

The smile vanished from Tay's face. "Ain't nothing virtuous about this place. Every day it dies a little bit more." He furrowed his brow. "Hope I'm not scaring you, mister."

"Conor."

"Right. Conor. Got a last name?"

"Yeah."

Tay smiled. "That's cool. This is a town where no one needs to know your last name. They want to know everything about you, but they don't need your last name." He paused. "Anyway, I hope I'm not giving you the wrong impression about Patience. It's just…"

"Don't worry about it. Just passing through."

Tay sighed with relief. "Good to hear. I really got to watch myself when I'm bad-mouthing Patience. Got to live here, after all." He started wiping glasses with the rag, and Conor figured it had to be to remove dust, given the lack of patronage.

"I hear you."

"So…just passing through, huh? Where you from? Where you going?"

Conor smiled. "Lots of questions tonight." He looked at his glass—suddenly almost empty—and added, "Get me another drink and maybe I'll tell you about it."

As Tay poured, Conor continued. "Without getting into all the dirty details, let's just say I had to get out of New York in a hurry. Not sure where I'm going. Probably San Francisco."

Tay brightened. "I knew you must've come from a big city. You don't look like you belong around here."

"I don't?"

"It's just…I dunno. The way you carry yourself."

Conor smiled. "The way I carry myself. All right, I guess."

"Maybe I'm not explaining myself…"

"No, that's fine. I think I know what you mean."

"So you're traveling. Got a wife?"

Conor gave his well-rehearsed non-answer: "Nope. I can barely take care of myself. How about you?"

"Ah, heck no." Tay looked up as the older couple in their matching green sweaters slowly walked toward the door. "'Night, Lester. 'Night, Doreen."

"'Night, Tay," she said, and he, again, mutely nodded in agreement.

Once they were gone, Tay looked at Conor for more than a casual amount of time. It was a look Conor had seen before. Once it was the sort of look that made him uncomfortable. But he was much older now.

"I've always wanted to see San Francisco," the young man finally said. He gave a toss of his head, and his hair shimmered under the light of the fixture. "People around here, well…you can probably guess how they are. They hear San Francisco and all they think is, well…" He looked away. "You know."

Conor understood. "They're the same kind of people who'd probably think you and me sitting here alone in a dark bar is leading up to something, right?" He caught Tay's stare and lowered his voice. "One dim light…no one around…"

"Ol' Lester and Doreen are probably already talkin'." Tay laughed and added, "You make it sound like a setup for bad gay porn."

Conor smiled. His instincts were on target. He cocked an eyebrow. "I never thought I'd hear someone say something like that in a place like Patience."

Tay leaned against the bar, his hands spread palms-down in front of Conor, looking into his eyes. "I never thought I'd say something like that in Patience."

Conor brushed the back of one of Tay's outstretched hands, a brief connection that could have been accidental. Tay didn't react. He just kept staring until he finally said, "Guess you probably figured out I don't belong around here."

"I did. So what's keeping you? Hit the road. See the world."

He shook his head. "No money. Unless I rob the place and run, I ain't never leaving Patience. And even *that* wouldn't get me very far, as you probably figured from all the activity here." His gaze swept across the now-empty bowling alley. "I'll die here. I'll die in Patience."

"A bit melodramatic, aren't you?"

"You call it melodramatic, I call it realistic." He took one of Conor's hands in his. "You're gay, too, right?"

"As a matter of fact…"

"I figured. I felt that…*connection* when I saw you. I knew you were like me. And then not being married…"

"Lots of people aren't married."

"Yeah, but you and me aren't *those* people." He paused. "Ever since this kid—used to live in Haxtun and come bowling every now and then—since he left, you're about the first gay person I've seen in the flesh." He paused, and looked away. "I don't suppose…"

Conor took a gulp from his glass. "So how old are you, kid?"

"Old enough."

"Meaning…what? Nineteen? Twenty?"

Tay laughed. "Close enough. Close enough to earn you another drink on the house."

"I won't fight you over that."

Tay smiled warmly as he poured the clear liquid, only looking up when the front door snapped open, interrupting their privacy with the sound of rain and wind. It closed again, and heavy footsteps approached, led by a booming voice.

"Tay Harkness, why in hell's name is this place still open?"

Tay's hand had been hovering near Conor's but was quickly retracted to his side of the bar. Conor half spun on his stool and saw a beefy middle-aged man enter, slick from the rain. His untucked plaid shirt was plastered to his bulging stomach and hung limply over shapeless jeans. The man's eyes peered at Conor, went to Tay, and back again. He took two staggering steps forward before steadying himself against a paneled wall.

Still looking at Conor, he said, "You ain't from around here."

"Passing through."

"Good." The man regained his balance and walked behind the bar, continuing into the office. "Close it up, Tay," he snapped, slamming the door behind him.

"Charming fellow," Conor whispered.

"That's Pat. Pat Thursby. He's the owner. Listen, I hate to rush you, but…" He cocked his head toward the office door.

"I hear you, kid." Conor stood and dropped a ten on the bar as the light was extinguished. "Keep it."

"You sure about that?"

"I am."

"Time to close up, Taylor," growled the voice from behind the door. Tay frowned, but busied himself under the bar before handing Conor a paper bag with a bottle in it.

"What's this for?" asked Conor.

Tay smiled. "Thanks for the tip. Sorry I can't slip you some mixer, but it's all on tap."

"I'll manage." Conor chuckled under his breath and felt for the key in his pocket. "And listen: after you close up, if you're bored… want to talk some more…I'm in room nineteen over at the motel."

"Klein's?"

"I guess. The one next door."

Tay nodded. "Klein's. Sure, I'll try to stop by. I can't make any promises."

"Good for you. I never make promises anymore. They can be dangerous."

❖

The television got three channels, but two of them were only showing infomercials. Conor Laughlin sat on top of the still-made bed, drinking straight vodka out of one plastic cup and tapping ashes into another, not really watching the dated sitcom on the screen and wondering what he'd do if the kid showed up.

Small-town gay kid, desperate to get out of a dying town…willing to throw himself at the first stranger who passed through. He knew the need to connect with another human being, to feel warm flesh and experience passion. It had been a long time for *him*, too. But there was a fine line between that and taking advantage of a kid barely out of his teens, a good fifteen years younger.

"But if you were that moral, maybe you wouldn't have had to leave New York," he told himself aloud, and the sitcom laugh-track punctuated his sentence.

A little more than an hour after he'd left the bowling alley, he heard a cautious tap on the door. He almost missed it under the sound from the TV and the rain cascading from the roof through the broken drainpipe just outside the door.

"Just a minute," he hollered, dropping his cigarette butt in the plastic cup and crawling off the bed to turn off the television. By instinct, he gave himself a once-over in the streaked mirror before opening the door.

Tay stood to the side to avoid the splatter from the drainpipe although he was already soaked and shivering from the short walk across the railroad tracks. Even though the door was wide open, he still asked, "Can I come in?"

Conor nodded. When the door was closed, Tay looked at him warily. "This was probably a mistake."

"Have some vodka and sit down," said Conor, handing him the plastic cup. "Sorry, we're gonna have to share the last cup. You okay with that?" Tay nodded. "So why do you think this was a mistake?"

"'Cause someone might've seen me coming here."

"And they don't know you're gay."

"Some do. Pretty sure people here at least know I ain't like them. Hey, can I get a cigarette?" Conor offered him the pack. "Mostly I didn't want Pat to see me come over here." He lit the cigarette, then walked to the window, parting the heavy curtains slightly. "Don't think he did, but…"

"So your boss…he doesn't know?"

"He knows." Tay took a drag from the cigarette, blowing out the smoke slowly. "Look, can we talk about something else?"

"Whatever makes you happy, kid."

"For one thing, you can stop calling me kid." There was steel in his voice.

Conor took a step back. "Sorry. I didn't mean any offense."

Tay tapped his cigarette on the edge of the other plastic cup, and the ash dropped into the yellow-brown water.

"I know you didn't. It's just…I'm just…I…" His voice cracked. "Everything about this damn town is just…I have to get out of here." Tay closed his eyes so tight the flesh in his cheeks turned red.

"Are you all right?" Conor asked. The room was silent, the only sound the water gushing outside the door.

"There are things you don't want to know about me," Tay said finally; his eyes still closed, a catch still in his voice. "And things about Pat Thursby *no one* wants to know."

"Did he hurt you?"

Tay opened his eyes a sliver. "I told you, you don't want to know. Just…can you take me to San Francisco with you?"

Conor smiled sadly. "You know I can't do that, Tay. I don't even know you. And just jumping into a big city like that from little old Patience, Colorado, well, they'll eat you alive."

The cup of vodka again rose to Tay's lips and he drained it. When he was done, he looked away and said, "You think I can't take care of myself? Let me tell you something, Conor. Once you get a reputation as a sissy-boy in a place like this, there's plenty of guys that want a little action. The wife's dead or out of town…the migrant workers…maybe they're just bored or something…so they go find Taylor Harkness, 'cause everyone knows they can get a piece of *that* action. And one mouth's as good as another, right?" He took a drag on the cigarette and dropped it in the cup. "And the worst one of all is Pat Thursby. Ever since his wife died last year… It's just…" He lost his composure and lifted one hand to shield his face.

Conor could think of nothing to say except, "I'm sorry."

"That's my life here. That's why I gotta get out of here." He looked up at him, his eyes glistening. "You probably want me to go now, don't you?"

"No. I want you to stay."

"After all that?"

"*Especially* after all that."

"And San Francisco?"

"I'd like to help you, Tay. Really, I would. But I can't. As it is, I've got maybe three hundred dollars left in my pocket, and San Francisco isn't a sure thing, so that three hundred's gonna probably have to stretch for a long time. I don't think it's enough for one, let alone two people."

"If money's the problem…"

"Gonna tell me you've got money stashed away? 'Cause the answer's still no."

"I ain't got a pot to piss in. Room and board with Thursby, as long as I work at the alley and…*you know*. But I know where enough money is stashed away that maybe you'd change your mind."

"Is that right?"

"Thursby's got a couple thousand bucks he keeps in a cashbox in the office. Rainy day money. We could grab that and we could hit the road. Be in San Francisco in two days, especially with two of us driving."

Conor thought about it. And thought better of it. "You don't know where I've been, Tay. There's a reason I left New York, and I'm not going to keep repeating my mistakes. You want that money, I can't stop you. But I don't want to know about it."

"Okay, let the old bastard keep his money." Tay poured some more vodka into the cup without asking and sat on the edge of the bed. He wouldn't look at Conor. "Sometimes when I hear the train come through town, I dream of getting out of here. Like going to San Francisco…or New York City…or even Denver. Every night I wait to hear the whistle. It's the sound of freedom to me." He turned to Conor. "I wonder if you can hear it from this room. Probably."

"Why don't you stay for a while and find out?" Conor said, and he began unbuttoning Tay's shirt, slowly exposing his pale, thin torso. Their mouths met, and—as Conor had expected—Tay's lips were hungry for those of another man.

The rest of him was hungry, too.

❖

The first thing Conor heard in the morning was water pouring out of the drainpipe. He turned to the nightstand and looked at the clock. 7:30. Early morning by his standards.

He lay back in the tangle of sheets while dim memories of the night bubbled to the surface. Tay had been there; now he wasn't. Must have slipped out during the night, anxious to get home before Pat Thursby discovered he was gone. All for the best. The kid was probably all right, but Conor was trying to rescue himself from drowning and it wouldn't do any good to drag someone else down with him.

He showered in the bathroom that smelled of smoke and mildew, dressed and prepared to drive as far west as he could manage. Maybe if he could get a second wind he'd even be able to make it to San Francisco in the middle of the next night. First, though, he had to find coffee. He hoped the good citizens of Patience had somehow managed to keep a coffee shop in business, but doubted it.

He was about to leave when he finally saw the note on the dresser.

"I stayed until I heard the train. Freedom."

It made him smile.

He grabbed his suitcase and left the room, sprinting between gushers from the roof to the space near the office where he'd left his car the night before. He'd kept his head down against the rain so he didn't realize anything was wrong until he was reaching for his keys and saw the front left tire was flat.

"Son of a bitch," he muttered under his breath, hoping he had a spare.

He stepped back from the car and realized the rear tire was flat, too. And there was no way he had two spare tires. He made a circuit around the car to check the passenger side, and discovered the other two tires were also flat.

Four flat tires.

This was no accident.

"Are you Klein?" he asked angrily as he walked into the office, grateful that Tay had told him the name of the motel. It somehow made for a more personal connection, and he was taking things very personally at the moment.

"One of 'em."

"Listen, Klein, my car's in your lot with four flat tires. How are you gonna fix that?"

The clerk shook his head. "Sorry, Mr..." He looked at the registration book. "Laughlin?" Conor nodded. "Sorry, Mr. Laughlin, but you signed a waiver when you registered sayin' the motel isn't responsible for damages to the vehicle or things left in the car. Would you like me to get a copy?"

"Not necessary."

"Probably those punk kids from Sterling," said the clerk, shaking his head. "I don't know which are worse: the ones with parents in the prison, or the ones whose parents work at the prison. Anyway, I can call Luke at the garage and have him take a look."

"Do that," Conor said, figuring he wasn't obligated to add "please."

Tay must have been right about the town dying. How else to explain that Luke pulled up no more than four minutes later, in a white tow truck so dusty even the constant rain had only smeared it rather than cleaning it.

"Four tires. And all you got is that donut in the trunk," Luke said, a chaw of tobacco bulging behind his lower lip, repeating what Conor already knew. They were standing with Klein under the motel's canopy in front of the door to Room 10, next to the office. Conor's was the only car in the lot.

"Okay," grumbled Conor.

Luke said, "This should run you about five hundred."

Conor wrinkled his brow. "Five hundred? That sounds steep."

"Tires plus labor."

"What about retreads?"

Luke scowled, worked his chaw, and began calculating again in his head. "More like three, three-fifty, I guess."

"I don't have that kind of money on me."

Luke eyed him. "Can you get it?"

"Guess I'm gonna have to," said Conor, but he couldn't think how.

"Might take me till tomorrow to get the right retreads."

Conor sighed. "Just get it done as soon as you can."

"Okay, then," he said, wiping his hands on his shirt. "I'll get your tires, check your oil..."

"Just the tires. Just the absolute least amount of money it'll take me to get out of this town."

Luke smiled, but it wasn't a happy smile. "Impatient, Mr. Laughlin?"

"That's a Patience, Colorado, joke, right? I get it."

"Okay, then. I'll take care of your car." He grinned. "When you get the money together, you get it back."

"Fair enough."

The truck backed up and Luke hoisted the car onto the flatbed. Conor had an unsettling feeling the punk kids from Sterling had sentenced him to a stretch in Patience that would make their incarcerated daddies feel like day-trippers.

When the tow truck pulled out of the parking lot, the motel clerk—one of the Kleins—asked, "So you're running low on cash?"

"A little bit. Got any ideas?"

"No, but…" He looked off into the rainy, misty sky.

"I read you, Klein," said Conor, peeling a handful of bills off his diminishing stash. "This should keep my room for a few days."

The man looked at the cash. "Two days."

"If I'm still in Patience two days from now, just shoot me."

Klein nodded and walked away. Conor was afraid for a moment that he'd sealed his execution. No one in this town had much of a sense of humor, and he was starting to join them. Had it really been just a few days ago when he was in New York and everything seemed so much better? Not necessarily good…but better.

He heard a whispered "Conor" that was almost drowned out by the rain. He turned to see Tay, his head just peeking out from the far edge of the building.

"What happened?" Tay asked, when Conor reached him.

"Apparently my car was attacked by some punk kids. You see anything last night?"

"No way! The car looked fine when I left."

"Know who those punk kids might have been? Maybe I can make them pay for this."

Tay shook his head. "Sorry, but I'm the outcast, remember? The punks don't want anything to do with the sissy-boy, and…well, I don't want anything to do with the punks. If I can help it." He paused. "You don't think…well, what if one of them saw me come to your room?"

Conor took it a step further. "What if Thursby saw you come to my room? You think he might have done this?"

Tay kicked the soggy gravel. "Shoot. But…no, Pat was out cold when I left, and he was out cold when I came back."

"Okay then."

"So how much is this going to cost you?"

Conor shook his head. "More than I've got."

Tay shook his head. "Sorry." He paused. "Sorry about sneaking off last night, too. It's just, well…you knew I couldn't spend the night, right?"

"I know. We're fine."

"Good." He offered Conor a slight grin, which sort of complemented his bad haircut matted down by the rain. "Listen, I got to get back to work, but let me know how things work out."

"I will."

"And if you change your mind about taking me with you…"

"I won't."

"Okay, then, but remember what I said about the cashbox."

Conor frowned. "Listen, Tay. Please don't ever mention that again. I'll figure this out. Okay?"

Tay puffed out his lower lip, but more in play than protest. Even with the rain and gray skies, a new day seemed to have brightened his attitude.

Although who knew what the night would bring.

His room paid up for another few days, Conor asked Klein for directions to the nearest coffee shop. Klein told him there was one a ten-minute walk away. He found it and took his time trying to wrap his head around Patience, Colorado. He went back to his room and sat on the bed through the late morning and afternoon, trying to figure out where he'd get the money to get his car back.

Because, he thought, the problem with pretty much burning all of your bridges is that it proved a man *could* be an island.

Especially when Patience, Colorado, was flooding around you.

❖

Before he left New York, he'd borrowed some pocket money from Artie Green. Maybe Artie could make him another loan. He managed to get a signal on his cell phone and punched in the 212 area code and seven other digits. His call went to voice mail, so he left a brief message and prayed he'd call back.

A few hours later it finally stopped raining. Or at least took a break. Artie still hadn't returned his call. He'd had quite enough of talk shows and game shows and TV judge shows while he'd sat in bed and tried to think how he could score a few hundred dollars—and quickly—if Artie couldn't or wouldn't come through.

The only thing he was sure of was that he wasn't going to get it from Pat Thursby's cashbox. Not that he had other options, but he wasn't going to compound the mistakes that had turned his life into… this.

But if Thursby's cashbox was off-limits to him, his bowling alley wasn't. He downed the stale sandwich he'd picked up that morning at the coffee shop and, around seven, decided he was thirsty and frustrated and unhappy, and a trip to the closest bar in probably three towns was in order.

Thursby was sitting on a bench outside the front door and frowned when Conor approached, sidestepping the puddles and mud outside the bowling alley.

"Evening," said Conor.

"Leave the boy alone."

Conor, almost past him, stopped and turned slowly. "Excuse me?"

"I told you to leave the boy alone." Even from several yards away Conor could smell beer and cigarettes on Thursby's breath. For a moment his temper flared—maybe even enough to match Thursby's—but he swallowed it down. He wanted to tell Thursby that if anyone should leave Tay alone, it should be Thursby. But he'd be leaving Patience soon enough…as soon as he could find a couple hundred bucks to pay for the retreads. Tay would be left behind. No sense in giving Thursby more reason to make the kid's life even more hellish than it was. He left Thursby sitting on the bench.

Inside, a few people bowled. The old couple was there again, wearing matching blue sweaters. He watched a solidly built teenage girl sling her ball almost immediately into a gutter, and walked to the bar. Tonight Tay was waiting there, as if expecting him.

"Oh, hey," he said, as Conor took a seat. "Vodka and… something?"

"Sure. Surprise me."

"Don't say that. You never know what you're gonna get with me. I'll make the usual."

"It's like I'm a regular."

"In this place? You are."

He started to make the drink, pausing only to grab a Coke for the Solid Girl, finished and set it down in front of him.

"Any luck finding money to pay for your car?"

"Not yet. But I've got a call out to a friend who might be able to help me out."

"Hope it works out."

"Thanks."

Tay absentmindedly wiped a glass, one hand repeatedly twirling the bar towel without inspecting his work. As he rubbed, he said, "I ever tell you how Flo died?"

"Flo?"

"Florence Thursby. Pat's wife. She died last year, right there behind lane three."

"You don't say. What happened?"

Tay first looked to the door to make sure his boss wasn't coming, and then out over the lanes, making sure the bowlers were preoccupied.

"Got crushed by the pin-setter one night."

"I didn't know that could happen."

"Doesn't happen often, but it happens." He cast another glance around the room, then returned his attention to Conor. "I guess she was cleaning up and spotted something wrong. Went back to the equipment room to take a look, got too close, and then, well…" He paused. "That's what the coroner said, at least."

"You think maybe something else happened?"

"All I know is the only other person here was Pat. He says he was taking a nap in the office, but you really think he slept straight through while all that happened? I figure she must've at least had time to scream."

"You think he killed her?"

"Maybe. Or maybe he didn't care enough to help. Thing is, Flo had been in the business a long time. This was her family's, not his. She knew enough to treat the equipment with respect."

"Maybe she just got careless."

"Maybe." Tay kept his hands busy. "Wish I'd have been here, though, 'cause Flo was a good woman. After my parents died she treated me like her very own. A lot better than *he's* ever treated me. That's for sure."

Conor might have said something—although he had no idea what—but he felt his phone vibrate in his pocket, so he excused himself.

It was Artie Green. It wasn't good news.

"Sorry, Conor," said his voice, fading in and out from the bad connection. "I'm tapped out. Have you called anyone else?"

"You know there's no one else, Artie. Not anymore."

Artie sighed. "Wish I could help you, pal. But it's a bad time."

"All right, I'll think of something." Conor tapped a button and disconnected the call without saying good-bye.

When he was back at the bar Tay asked, "Was that your friend?"

Conor didn't answer, and Tay didn't ask any more questions. Instead, he poured him another drink before walking out to the seating area to collect glasses the handful of bowlers hadn't bothered to bring to him. He looked out the front door on his route back to where Conor sat, deep in thought.

"Pat's gone," he said quietly, setting the glasses in the small sink under the bar. "Must've taken a walk or something."

"Good," said Conor. "He's not exactly someone I feel like dealing with right now."

"Sorry it didn't work out."

"Me, too."

"So what are you gonna do?"

"I don't know. Guess I'll figure something else out."

"Yeah, well…" Tay leaned close. "Remember the cashbox."

Conor shook his head and focused his eyes on a worn patch on the carpet. "That's tempting, kid. Especially right now. But I'm not a thief."

"Well, there goes one of my theories."

"What's that?" He looked up and caught light dancing in Tay's eyes.

"My theories about why you had to leave New York. I figured you either stole from someone or killed someone. Now I guess it's down to murder."

"You're funny."

Tay leaned across the bar. "Seriously, Conor. Probably two thousand dollars. Maybe more. We could split it. Then we'd both have enough to get to San Francisco."

"You know, even if I stole the money—which I won't—you couldn't go with me. We both disappear at the same time Thursby's money disappears, we'd be arrested before we made it to Denver."

Tay nodded. "Yeah. I guess so."

"So just put that idea out of your head. I don't know where I'll get the money to get my car out of the garage and out of Patience, but I'll do it somehow."

Conor had a few more drinks at the bar, but Thursby returned and it was time to get back to the motel. Under the watchful eyes of the owner, Tay couldn't even slip him a bottle for the room.

"See you around," Conor said, standing.

"I'll stop by later," Tay whispered, and even though Thursby couldn't hear his words, his expression made it clear he didn't like them.

❖

Room 19. Conor sat on the bed and tapped ashes in the plastic cup and tried to figure out where he was going to get enough money to get his car out of the garage.

There were some relatives he hadn't spoken to in years who might be able to help, but it would take a few days to track them down. And every extra day he would have to spend in Room 19 was another forty-five dollars—plus tax—out of his pocket. It came down to a question of whether or not he'd find enough cash to get out of Patience before he completely ran out of the cash he *did* have and was stuck in the town for the rest of his life.

He had pretty much decided to stop thinking about it for the night when Tay's knock sounded at the door. He opened it and let him in.

"I did it!" he said, a broad smile on his face.

"Did what?" Conor asked, then saw the rectangular metal box in his hands. "What's that?" he asked, although he knew exactly what it was.

"A present."

"It's the money from the bowling alley, isn't it? How'd you get it?"

"Pat passed out in the office, so I just took it."

"He's gonna miss it."

"Not till the morning." Tay leaned forward, grazing Conor's cheek with his soft lips, and began unbuttoning his shirt. "Proud of me? Now you've got the cash to get out of here. And I can start a new life, too! Maybe meet up with you in San Francisco."

The shirt fell to the ground, exposing Tay's smooth, slim body. Conor would have liked to look at that, but couldn't take his eyes off the cashbox.

It would be so easy—too easy—to pop it open, drop a few hundred at the garage in the morning, hit the highway, and never look back. Never again think of Patience, Colorado. Maybe he wasn't a thief, but he'd done worse things in his life.

"I can't do it," he said finally after long seconds of thought, looking up to see Tay unsnapping the front button of his jeans. The pants began to slide over his slender hips, but the younger man quickly clutched them at the waist with one fist, exposing only a hint of the soft flesh beneath them.

"But...our lives!"

"You're gonna have to take the money back. I can't be part of this."

"I won't." He looked away from Conor and hiked his pants back up, snapping the button. "I don't know why you're treating *him* better than you treat *me*! He probably killed his wife! He treats me like his slave! And you're afraid to steal a little money from him?"

"This isn't a game, Tay. I want to get out of here more than you do, but this isn't the way to do it. I'm not gonna sit in jail for years over a lousy couple thousand dollars. You, either."

Tay crossed his arms defiantly across his chest. "I'm not taking it back."

"Then I'll do it. You think Thursby's still asleep?"

Tay didn't answer.

"I asked if he's still asleep."

"I'm sure he is," was the sullen reply. "Usually sleeps for a few hours after he passes out."

"Okay, then," said Conor, and he opened the door, grateful to see that the rain was still holding off. "Let's hope you're right. And let's hope he hasn't already missed this."

"I figured you'd appreciate it."

"You figured wrong." Conor stroked Tay's face with his thumb and forefinger. "And you know that, too."

Inside the room, Tay asked, "And what am I supposed to do?"

"Wait here. Or go home. That choice is up to you."

Conor left the door ajar, taking one glance back to see that Tay—still defiant, still angry—hadn't moved.

❖

A few minutes later he was at the bowling alley. The door let out a moan as it arced inward, revealing the now familiar dim interior.

He took a few steps toward the bar but paused as a voice called out: "Just a minute, just a minute." And then Pat Thursby stumbled through the doorway and into view, a beer bottle in one hand, and Conor had to think fast.

"Thought you was Tay," Thursby muttered. "Bar's closed."

Conor gingerly held the cashbox in front of him. "Found this outside the door. Figured it might belong to you."

Thursby tried to focus his eyes, taking a few unsteady steps toward him to get a closer look. Then he realized what he was looking at. "What are you doing with that?"

"Like I said, I was passing by…"

"Passing by? This time of night?"

"I thought maybe your bar was open."

"Looking for the boy, were you?"

"Listen, Thursby, I don't want any trouble…"

"Give me that box." He lunged forward, ripped it from Conor's hands before retreating. "It better all be in here."

"I don't know what you mean."

Thursby took another few steps forward, backing Conor into a rack of bowling balls that clunked solidly at the impact. "Never liked the look of you the minute I seen you. I'm calling the cops."

"Now calm down…"

"Nothing but a good-for-nothin' criminal. Just like I thought." He waved the beer bottle at Conor. "Don't move. I got a gun and I know how to use it."

"Thursby, you're out of line here. I haven't done anything to you…"

His words fell on deaf ears. The older man took a few ungainly steps backward, reaching for the phone at the edge of the bar…

And Conor Laughlin saw his future. The cops would come. They'd believe Thursby—the responsible local businessman—not the drifter he'd found with his cashbox. If Conor was lucky enough to get a trial, it would be the good citizens of Patience, Colorado—not a jury of Conor's peers—that would hear the evidence. And that would be it. The end of the road.

Exactly what he'd hoped to avoid by returning Thursby's cashbox. The irony wasn't lost on him.

Thursby reached for the telephone, and Conor's self-preservation instincts kicked in. There was no rational thought involved, just an animalistic reaction. Fight or flight…Kill or be killed.

Just like in New York, really. Except quite a bit worse.

❖

Conor stood over the prone body of Pat Thursby, watching blood ooze from his head. The bowling ball he'd used to crush Thursby's skull had rolled a few yards away. The cashbox was tucked under his arm. The bottle he'd been holding was spilled across the carpet. The receiver dangled by its cord from the telephone, swaying slightly in the silent air.

And he kept staring, only starting to comprehend what had happened.

"Oh my God!" he heard Tay say. He hadn't realized Tay was there, or for how long. "What did you do?" When Conor didn't answer, Tay repeated himself. "What did you do?"

Not taking his eyes off Thursby's body, Conor said, "He was gonna call the cops."

"This is bad. What did…" Tay saw the weapon. "You hit him in the head with a bowling ball?"

"I don't remember it," Conor said, slowly coming out of his daze. "He was gonna call the cops and, well…then it happened."

Tay shook his head. "There's no turning back now, Conor. For *either* of us." While Conor stood silently, still staring at the remains of Pat Thursby, Tay locked the front door and extinguished the light. In the dark, with Thursby now no more than a shadow on the floor, it was easier for Conor to regain his composure.

"That's it," he said with a prolonged sigh. "Life ends in Patience."

Tay shook his head. "We can say it was an accident."

"Accident? How do you *accidentally* get your head caved in with a bowling ball?"

Tay motioned at the door. "We drag him outside. Drop his body in the culvert next to the tracks. Make it look like he got hit by the train."

Conor thought it over. His stomach churned. "Is there a train tonight?"

Tay was silent for a while. Finally, he said, "Every night, around two o'clock."

"Ever see anyone hit by a train before? I mean, is this gonna make sense to anyone?"

"Sure. He leaves the bar. Drunk, stumbling. The train is passing by. He trips and smashes his head into the train. It's gonna make sense."

"I dunno…"

"You've got two choices, Conor." Tay was pacing, thinking out loud. "Make this look like an accident, and you'll probably get away with it. Hell, you'll probably be in Denver before they find the body. Leave him here, though, and it ain't gonna be hard for them to figure out this is murder. Like it or not, you're gonna be a suspect. You needed money, you've been hanging out at the bar… Even the cops in *this* town are gonna be able to put these pieces together."

"You could vouch for me."

"And I would. But even if I do, the sheriff's just gonna make it sound like we had some sort of gay sex thing going on. Say you killed Pat 'cause you were jealous, or say we killed him together. The locals will eat that up, and it won't end up helping you." Tay looked at Conor's face, pale in the dreary light that fought its way through the window. "You don't look good, Conor."

"Well…I've never killed a man before."

"That'll do it, I guess. So are we gonna move this body?"

Conor bent down and grabbed Thursby around his shoulders. "You get his feet," he said. He began to pull the body up…

Thursby coughed.

"Jesus!" yelled Conor, dropping Thursby to the ground as he jumped back, barely keeping his balance.

There was silence for a few moments, then Thursby groaned from the floor below them and choked out, "P-police."

"Hit him again!" Tay yelled, as Thursby's hand grasped his ankle.

Thursby gurgled. "T…Tay? Tay, w-what's happening…?"

Conor found the bowling ball and again brought it down on Thursby's head. There was a dull thud as it hit its target and rolled off into the shadows.

This time they stood in the silent darkness for a long time, tensely waiting for another breath…another grasp…another sign of life.

Eventually, Conor took a deep breath and again grabbed Pat Thursby's shoulders.

❖

They made their way down the side of the building, away from the road and next to the tracks, careful not to drag the body although Thursby's bulk made carrying him a chore. They reached the edge of the culvert and slogged through mud until they could drop him, letting Thursby's frame fall naturally to the ground. Panting, they crawled back up to the parking lot.

"I don't know," said Conor, bent close to the ground to examine their handiwork, looking for something they did wrong. "You really think this will work?"

"I'm sure of it," said Tay, crouched next to him. "Blind drunk… maybe he thinks he can beat the train…then, *wham*! It clips him and he ends up in the ditch. Doesn't happen often, but it happens."

That sounded eerily familiar to Conor but he shrugged it off. "You'll clean up the mess inside?"

"Sure will."

They walked back to the building. Conor had no intention of going inside…of reliving the unthinkable act he'd just committed.

"I should get back to the motel."

Tay nodded. "Yeah. Wait here a second." He disappeared inside, and Conor heard a half dozen muted bangs before Tay returned. "The box was harder to open than I thought it'd be. Guess it's good that bowling ball was still around."

Conor didn't smile.

"I know you don't want to take this, but I figure now, well…"

"Right."

Tay counted out the bills and handed Conor just over one thousand dollars in a variety of denominations, none larger than a twenty.

"So now you can get your car and get out of here."

"Yeah."

"And…well, how am I gonna find you? You know, when I get to San Francisco?"

"You think that's a good idea?"

"By the time I get out there, it will be."

"Then look for me when you get there. I'll be around."

❖

Conor didn't sleep that night. The memories—of Pat Thursby's bludgeoned head, the blood-spattered bowling ball, Thursby's gurgles—

were far too vivid. He was even more afraid of what Thursby might do in his dreams.

Instead he washed the mud off his pants and shoes and inspected his clothes for Thursby's blood. He couldn't find any, but that didn't mean it wasn't there. He'd have to remember to get rid of the clothes as soon as he got the chance. He wasn't as confident as the kid that everyone would just accept that Thursby'd been clipped by a train.

Around two in the morning he listened for it, but the rain had come again—torrents soaking the town of Patience and Klein's Motel, rumbling through the drainpipe like a waterfall outside his window—and he couldn't hear anything else. It was just as well. Whatever time that train rumbled through, it would have only brought the reality of what he had done into sharper focus.

It was still raining early in the morning, and when he looked out the window everything—town as well as sky—was a dismal gray. He spent a long time in the shower, willing the hot water to wash away his sins. If not his sins, his memories.

Conor put the last of his damp, dirty clothes in the suitcase when he heard a siren. Holding his breath, he crept to the window and parted the curtain in time to see a patrol car pass. It seemed to slow as it approached the railroad tracks, and then he lost sight of it.

A few minutes later, he left the hotel without checking out with the motel clerk; whichever Klein was working the desk.

He turned the corner of the motel, walking toward town, and saw the patrol car parked in front of the bowling alley, its lights still throwing a pulse of red onto the gray sky. His heart raced and a cool sweat beaded on his brow, despite the rain. He passed the scene of his crime—barely looking at the sheriff's deputy who stood at the edge of the culvert, his attention mercifully drawn away—and quickened his pace.

At the garage, Luke eagerly took his cash and handed him the keys. He played with the chaw of tobacco hidden under his lower lip and said, "I was wondering if you'd be able to come up with the cash."

"A friend in New York helped me out."

"You've got good friends, Mr. Laughlin."

Conor shrugged. "I guess. So how do I get out of here?"

"Which direction?"

"West."

Luke pointed. "Go down here and make a left on Route 6, then when you get near Sterling you'll see signs for 76. Can't miss it."

"Thanks," said Conor, and he began to walk to his car.

He had his key out and was about to unlock the door when a sheriff's cruiser pulled into the lot and drove up to him.

"Mind if I ask you a couple of questions?" asked the deputy, still sitting behind the wheel.

Conor frowned. "I really need to get on the road. Late for an appointment."

"This will only take a few minutes."

"It doesn't sound like I have a choice."

"You don't."

Play it cool, he told himself, and he walked back to the garage. The deputy angled his car behind Conor's and followed, nodding at Luke as he passed, telling him he needed to borrow the office.

The cluttered room smelled of motor oil. Last year's Miss April winked at them from the calendar on the wall. Conor took a seat and the deputy leaned against Luke's desk.

"Checked out of Klein's in a hurry, didn't you?"

"Like I said, I wanted to get on the road."

"What's the matter, Mr. Laughlin? You don't like Patience?"

"It's a lovely town."

"Okay then. Just checking." The deputy chuckled. "So where you headed?"

"Out west. San Francisco."

"Oh. Fancy city."

"Not necessarily."

"It's just that we don't get many visitors in Patience. Makes you stand out."

Luke walked into the office from the garage, wiping his greasy hands on a towel. "So what's going on, Tom?"

"Got ourselves a little situation over at the bowling alley, and I'd like to know if this fella knows anything about it." He turned back to Conor and asked, "Did you happen to meet a man named Pat Thursby while you were in town?"

Conor held back a shiver. "I met him. Why?"

"Something happen to Pat?" asked Luke.

"Sorry, Luke. I know you were close, but Pat's dead. We found his body on the side of the tracks about a half hour ago."

"That's too bad," said Conor as Luke shook his head sadly. "He seemed like a decent guy. But he was pretty drunk when I saw him last night."

"Pat did like his drink," Luke agreed.

Conor asked hopefully, "So...tracks? Was he hit by a train?"

The deputy raised an eyebrow and said, "I highly doubt that, Mr. Laughlin. See, the railroad only runs one train a week down those tracks nowadays."

It took a moment for those words to register in Conor's brain. "Are you sure? I mean, I'm sure I heard a train last night."

"I don't know what you heard, sir, but it wasn't a train. Not last night, at least. And anyway, no train broke into the bowling alley and smashed open Thursby's cashbox."

Conor couldn't speak, but Luke could. "Someone robbed the place?"

"Looks like they robbed him, hit him in the head with a bowling ball, and dumped the body by the tracks."

Everything was wrong. Tay told him there was a train. Tay said he'd clean up.

But there was no train. No cleanup. Which meant...

"Klein at the motel said you were running short on cash. Is that true, Mr. Laughlin?"

"That's true," said Luke, answering for him and eyeing Conor with a look that bypassed suspicion and went straight to unquestionable guilt. "I've been holding his car while he raised the money for new tires. Didn't have three-fifty yesterday...but this morning he does."

"And I suppose he paid in cash?"

"Yeah."

"The morning after this robbery and murder?"

"Yeah."

"Mr. Laughlin, I think you'd better come with me."

❖

Months had passed, but the time had finally come, and so the lawyer welcomed the young man into his office.

"I know you've waited a long time—too long a time—but now that the legal issues have been finalized..."

"I didn't mind the wait," said Tay, taking a seat in a slightly uncomfortable leather chair and pulling it close to the lawyer's desk.

"I know this has been hard on you, Taylor. First murder in Patience in twenty-seven years. It's been hard on all of us, but especially you.'

"Thank you. I'm trying to get past it."

"Well..." The lawyer shuffled through some forms, found the ones he wanted, and carefully arranged them on his desk in front of Tay. "If it's any consolation, Patrick Thursby was very generous to you in his will."

Tay looked to the floor. "He was always generous to me. Like a father. And after Flo died, I was as close to family as he had."

The lawyer sighed. "First Flo, then Pat. Just tragic all the way around. He never really got over her death, did he?"

Tay shook his head sadly. "Neither of us did. You think you're prepared after months of illness, but..."

The lawyer shook his head. "So sad."

They sat in awkward silence for a moment until the lawyer got back to business.

"He left you the bowling alley, you know," he said, pointing at one piece of paper. Tay didn't follow his finger. "Along with the life insurance and his savings. And, of course, whatever he'd inherited from Flo's estate. Although I suspect you just want to get out of Patience at this point, so you can probably sell the building for another fifty thousand or so. If you can afford to wait."

Tay finally looked the lawyer in the eye. "I can wait. But you're right, I need to leave. You can handle the sale for me?"

"I'll take care of it." He looked at Tay, not unsympathetically. "When that Laughlin fella tried to implicate you in the crime..." Tay sighed and looked at the floor. "I know, I know, he was trying to save his own skin. And hardly anyone believed him. But still, well..."

"Yeah, the gay thing. I guess it was sort of an open secret, but now it's just plain open, which is why I really need to get out of here."

"God bless you," said the lawyer. "And I hope someday you find the Lord." When Tay didn't respond, he uncomfortably added, "So where will you be going?"

Tay stood and brushed a trace of lint off one sleeve before answering.

"San Francisco. I hear it's a lovely city."

❖

The following day Taylor Harkness filled the trunk of the car with what amounted to his worldly possessions and began driving. Once— and not too long ago—he'd dreamed of leaving with maybe a thousand dollars. Now he had hundreds of thousands of dollars in the bank.

Patience, Colorado, had treated him well. As he sped west toward a new life, he blew a kiss as he passed a familiar sign:

LEAVING PATIENCE
It's a Virtue

MOUSE
JEFFREY ROUND

Not everyone has the luxury of throwing his life away, Colin reflected, reaching gingerly through the broken window and tripping the latch. He pushed the screen door open and stepped into darkness. He could just barely see Jon's crumpled form in the shadows.

"Hello, Mouse," he said, stepping closer.

Jon stirred and looked up from the armchair. He seemed to be trying to make out Colin's face, to place him in some internal landscape—that part of him that still recognized people. His expression darkened. "Don't call me that," he said, at last recognizing his brother. "I told you never to call me that."

"Okay, Mouse," Colin replied. "But you really need to let some light in here."

Jon watched warily as Colin went around the room lifting the blinds one by one. He brought a shaky hand up to shade his eyes as the room took on contour.

"Jesus! You'd think you were a bloody vampire," Colin said.

Jon sank deeper into the armchair, almost disappearing into it. The fabric was worn, the stuffing springing out at the seams.

Colin looked around. The place was even worse than the last time he'd been here. Flyers and junk mail lay scattered across a bare wooden table. Socks and T-shirts were draped across the back of a sofa. An empty pizza box had slid off the sofa cushion and come to rest, cover open, on the floor beside it. At least his brother remembered to eat now and then.

"How'd you get in?" Jon asked suspiciously, running a hand through his uncombed hair.

"I reached through the broken window and lifted the latch—same as always."

Jon nodded. The wary look receded. "Landlord still hasn't fixed it. I called him a while ago."

"You haven't had a phone for months. At least that's what you said the last time I was here. Are you hallucinating conversations now?"

Jon shrugged. "Maybe. What do you want?"

"I came to see if you were still alive."

"And…?"

"The verdict's not in yet, even though I hear you talking."

Jon's skin was gray, a lighter version of the color of the room before Colin lifted the blinds. A syringe and rubber tourniquet lay on the table beside the sofa. Jon made no effort to conceal them. Obviously, he'd forgot Colin was coming. Or maybe he was past all pretense.

Colin felt sickened by the sight, but he'd long since given up preaching or trying to make Jon change. There was nothing he could say that would alter Jon's need, nothing he could do to quell his urge to destroy himself or make him become again the gentle boy he'd once been. That Jon was gone forever.

Jon had once been pretty, but now he looked worn, the skin stretched taut over his features like something wrapped up too tightly. His head was large for his body, but his skull was beautifully formed, especially in profile, so that the effect was that of a boy with a man's head, both young and old at the same time. As he grew older, the boyishness remained, as if he had willed his body to stay young and childlike. As though he'd lost something and was trying to age back to whatever he had lost.

"Want to go for a walk?" Colin asked, hoping to escape the mess.

Jon turned his head to the window. He seemed to be contemplating the question. "What? Outside?"

"Yeah, outside. Trees. Grass. Sky. That would be the one."

Jon slowly shook his head. "Not in daylight, Colin—please."

"It's late afternoon. I could wait a couple of hours. Get a cup of coffee down the road."

Jon shrugged. He seemed to be trying to focus. "Maybe," he said, then seemed to drift again. He struggled for a moment. "When were you last here?"

"Thursday week, same day as today," Colin replied.

Jon nodded, as though coming to some conclusion about this. "I thought you would have given up on me by now."

"Actually, I have," Colin said. "I have given up on you. You're a self-pitying waste of a human being. I just come around because it gives me something to do."

Jon laughed a sudden, raucous laugh that turned to a rasping cough before it died.

"Mom and Dad send their love," Colin said, wielding the words like a knife.

"They would, wouldn't they?"

Colin shook his head. "Do you need to be so bitter?"

Jon had been a sunny child, bright and eager to please, while Colin had been the sullen one, drawn to the dark excesses of rock music, sporting the long hair and outrageous fashions of the day. "Antisocial behavior," their mother called it, as she watched him mimic the rages against the established norms of the time. But he'd outgrown it, while Jon had slunk deeper into the shadows.

Despite their different temperaments, the boys had been close. Colin was popular at school and that made things easier for Jon, who, being small, would otherwise have been picked on. Whenever any of the older boys bothered him, Jon would say, "My big brother is Colin Timmerman. He's my best friend in all the world. You better watch out for him." That usually stopped anything bad from happening.

Jon loved his older brother, but never stopped to ask if he, Jon, was lovable in return. The question never occurred to him. Such things just seemed a fundamental quality of loyalty: You are my brother, therefore I love you and you love me.

By the time Jon was twenty-four, he'd been through three different substance abuse programs. His parents, Lucille and Roger, had never given up encouraging him, taking him to enroll each time. In return, they'd had their hearts broken over and over again, as Jon promised to do better and eventually fell through the cracks once more. It seemed there was no hope.

Meanwhile, Colin married and brought two beautiful girls into the world. He, not Jon, became the apple of his parents' eye, though they took pains not to show favoritism in front of the boys. As far as Lucille and Roger were concerned, they loved both sons equally, no matter what cross one or the other had to bear.

"Colin just met the right girl, is all," Lucille would say on the few occasions she talked about the course their lives had taken. Colin was lucky, it seemed, while Jon got caught up in the drug scene. There was no telling what made people do the things they did—they just did them.

Therapists asked about Jon's background and family history; they spoke of nature versus nurture, of the brothers' relationship. The questions, like the theories, seemed endless. It was all over Lucille's head, really. All she knew was that she'd cared for both boys equally and treated one just like the other. She wondered if it had been because the family had strayed from the church, though neither she nor Roger had ever been a strict adherent.

Both she and her husband came from unexceptional backgrounds— Roger was the progeny of three generations of miners working out of northern Ontario's Nickel Belt, while Lucille had grown up the only child of Dutch immigrants who came over after the war, hoping to make their fortunes in a more peaceful and prosperous land than the one they'd left. It had been a time of new beginnings, despite the shadow of the Cold War, and many had followed the same star across the ocean, hoping both to prosper and forget.

Roger and Lucille met at a church function. They belonged to the Calvinist Church. While it had seemed a strict fundamentalist sect, socials had been the main reason for their participation. Fund-raisers and bazaars ensured an active association. In time, they married. Before long, Colin was born, followed by Jon four years later.

"Two is enough," Roger decided for them both. "We're not rich."

Lucille hadn't minded. Carrying Jon in the dead of winter in that bleak northern town had been a trial. She'd caught a terrible 'flu and nearly died in the spring a month before he was born. But she recovered and Jon was born on time and it seemed a blessing. Even his sunny temperament had seemed a gift as they struggled to make ends meet.

By then it was the crazy days of the sixties, when old habits and prejudices seemed to melt away overnight as the world went on a roller-coaster ride of changing values and social orders. It was around this time that Philip came into their lives. No one knew for sure who introduced him to the boys, being older. He lived in a squat bungalow a few houses down from the Timmermans. His parents were never around. Few of the neighbors could recall seeing them.

Philip's hair was long, but never shaggy and unkempt like Colin's. At seventeen, he dropped out of high school and went to work in a grocery store as a stock clerk. Sometimes he would bring his records over after work: the newest Beatles album, or the Rolling Stones. Sometimes there were other voices: the Mamas and the Papas, Joni Mitchell, or Donovan. You never knew what he'd bring next. Once he showed up with an album with blue geometric designs. It was a rock opera, he declared, as though it were the newest thing. And it was.

While the Timmermans played cards, the strains of the Who's *Tommy* wafted out into the street. They began to take on the sheen of brave new explorers as Philip's music grabbed the unsuspecting ears of neighbors who wondered at the strange sounds. The Timmermans had the best stereo in town and Philip had the best records. It was a match made in heaven, even if Philip never played cards.

"I'm not a gambler," he'd argue, waving away their protest. "Lucky at cards, unlucky at love. I prefer love."

It was the age of the hippie, after all. First had come the Summer of Love, and then Woodstock. It seemed the world was on the verge of new things, a brand-new order. It was a heady time.

Once, Philip brought over a joint and offered it to both of the older Timmermans, taking care not to do it in front of Colin and Jon. Lucille tried it, but just ended up coughing. Roger shook his head—some things were a bit too much—though he hadn't been offended by Phillip's offer and greeted him just as affectionately the next time he came over.

The first time the boys went over to Philip's house, Colin looked around in envy at the cozy basement apartment. It was perfectly set apart from Philip's parents' living space above. Jon, for his part, became mesmerized by a cage containing a live mouse. Philip took his pet out of the cage and let the small furry creature run over Jon's hands and up his arms to his shoulder.

Philip's world was magical, unlike any other the boys had known. Philip showed them other things: love beads, sticks of incense, and a tie-dyed T-shirt that seemed to be a cloak of many colors, like the one worn by Joseph in the Bible.

He promised one day to show them the secrets of the universe. The next time they came over, he produced a kaleidoscope, instructing them how to twist and turn it in their hands while peering through its lens, where it dazzled the mind. Another time he amazed them with card tricks, and once he showed how a jar filled with crayons held close to an ordinary lightbulb would bleed in a plethora of colors, the wax melting down its sides, almost in imitation of the kaleidoscope's magic world.

These were heady days for the boys, too. For a while, Jon became obsessed with the kaleidoscope. At any mention of Philip, Jon would ask, "Can we go over and play with his kaleidoscope?"

Colin would look at him shrewdly. "Are you my best friend?"

"Yes," Jon would answer. "You know I am."

"All right, then. I'll ask him for you."

❖

It wasn't until he'd known them for several months that Philip told Colin and Jon how he came to have so many of the newest records. He and another friend, who went unnamed, had a little shoplifting gig they operated on the weekends, keeping the best of the music for themselves and selling the rest at a considerable discount to friends from out of Philip's basement apartment.

Philip looked Jon in the eye and said, "But it's a secret, right? I trust you not to tell on me, buddy."

Jon nodded with a worried expression, as though he scarcely dared hope he could keep Philip's secret to himself. Colin made him swear not to tell. It would be a secret, they agreed—a secret shared by just the three of them.

Later came other secrets—lewd stories about girls and late-night seductions, filled with crude humor and exaggerated details. Colin smirked, while Jon tried to look as though he knew what the older boys were on about.

"What does this remind you of?" Philip asked one day, brandishing the kaleidoscope's smooth black tube aloft. "Hey?"

Colin smirked.

"You know, don't you, Colin?" Philip said.

"Yes," Colin said. "I know."

"Smart boy," said Philip.

Once they tried the kaleidoscope under a red light, and it seemed even more magical. And once the kaleidoscope was passed around in the dark, where they didn't even try to see out of it. They told Jon just to hold out his hands and grab onto it, but it felt different then, and Jon thought the older boys were playing a trick on him.

❖

After his first failed attempt at rehab, Jon moved to a ramshackle bungalow on the outskirts of town. When Colin came to visit, he saw the broken window beside the front door. He knocked and tried the handle—locked. Without thinking, he reached in through the jagged glass and lifted the latch, wondering how his brother could live in such desperate conditions, before it dawned on him that his brother lived with a much bigger risk every day of his life.

Jon was sitting at the kitchen table smoking a cigarette when Colin entered. He didn't express surprise that his brother had just walked in on him unannounced.

They talked for a while. Colin couldn't remember ever feeling so distant from his brother. Whoever this person was who claimed to be Jon, Colin didn't know him anymore.

"How are things with you and Viv?" Jon asked.

"Fine. Just great."

"That's good."

Colin watched him sitting there for a moment. "You should get yourself a girlfriend."

Jon just looked at him.

"You've got to do something, Jon."

"Why?"

"Because…because it's wrong." His face clouded. "It's disgusting. I don't approve of what you've done to yourself."

"So I should change because you don't like it? Will you stop being my friend if I don't?"

"Don't say stupid things. This isn't my fault."

"No, of course it isn't."

Jon seemed to have drifted off again then said, "I'm thinking of getting a job." He shrugged. "Maybe that will help."

But of course, the job never materialized, if he even started a search for one.

❖

The year Colin started high school, their parents began to quarrel. Colin heard a rumor that his father was having an affair with one of their neighbors, Miss Lavoie. He started a fistfight with Steven Bailey, the boy who'd told him, screaming in the hallway outside his locker that it wasn't true. Steven wouldn't take it back, however, and he and

Colin never spoke again for the rest of their high school years. Colin also avoided Miss Lavoie and refused even to walk down the street she lived on, as though it had been forbidden to him.

The quarreling usually began when their father got home from work at night. Sometimes, if he'd stopped after work for a drink, it might escalate into yelling. Colin and Jon would sneak over to Philip's house for some relief, returning after their parents had gone to bed.

If their mother protested, Colin would argue that it was better than sitting around listening to his parents scream at one another. Anything, he said, was better than that. His mother would lapse into silence or the tears that seemed to come more frequently as time wore on.

It was Philip who explained the nature of sexual affairs to the two brothers, saying they were quite common now, as though he'd had a lot of experience with such things. On the way back from Philip's that night, Jon was silent till they returned home.

"I hate him," Jon whispered to Colin.

For a moment, Colin wondered if he meant Philip or their father.

❖

One night Colin overheard his mother on the phone with her sister Margery after everyone had gone to bed. She was talking about divorce. It never came to that, however. The fighting seemed to end one day as suddenly as it began, restoring peace to the home once again, though by then a coldness had set in, like the Cold War the world was going through. It was hard to say exactly how it manifested itself, but there was a menacing chill in the air whenever his parents spoke. Something had shifted, bringing in a less favorable climate with it.

Colin could feel it, even if he couldn't put his finger on what, exactly, had brought about the change. By then Philip, too, seemed to have receded into the background of the boys' lives. Jon was eleven by then, and Colin nearly fifteen. Philip was already twenty-one. So, too, the kaleidoscope came out less and less often, like a joke no one spoke about anymore.

"He's too old for you," their mother once said, when Jon said he and Colin would be seeing Philip on the weekend. "It's not natural for a boy so much older than you to be spending so much time with you. Find some friends your own age."

And then the day came when they stopped seeing Philip altogether. He suddenly joined the army and they almost never saw him, except for brief glimpses on the street at Christmas when he came home from his base, his hair shorter and his expressions harder.

❖

Later, there were girls in their lives. Roger seemed especially happy that his sons were dating. Colin was popular and had his pick. He was getting a reputation around the neighborhood. Jon's relationships were fewer and less easily defined. First, there was a short redhead named Maisy or Daisy—his parents were never sure, just as they could never tell quite what her relationship with Jon was. She disappeared suddenly, never to be mentioned again. She was followed by a pretty blonde who seemed more interested in Colin than in Jon. She eventually disappeared as well.

What his parents never knew was that all the girls Jon dated left him saying he was weird or even cruel. At school, Colin heard more rumors, this time that Jon had asked them to do strange things. Things that disgusted them. None of his relationships lasted long, and most of the girls pretended not to know him or acknowledge him in the hallways afterward.

❖

Times changed. The old sounds were gone. The upbeat optimism of the sixties had been replaced by harsher sounds—heavy metal, glam, punk. By comparison, the seventies seemed duller, angrier. The Beatles had broken up, the Rolling Stones cut a disco record, and all that goodness seemed forever behind them. Whatever it had been, whatever it had touched, seemed lost.

Colin moved forward with the age, embracing punk rock and then New Wave. He seemed to surge into life, while Jon seemed to have got stuck, listening to the same old records he'd listened to in his childhood.

"Some people never grow up," Colin once told his mother when she expressed concern about Jon's seeming lack of development or interest in anything outside the home. "Mouse is one of them," he said, the nickname having stuck by then.

"Wherever did he get that horrible name?" Lucille suddenly asked, after having heard it used for years. It was as though she'd just woke to the reality of Jon's life for the first time.

Colin shrugged. "Some guys gave it to him," he said, as though it were of no concern.

❖

Colin had just turned thirty when their father had the stroke that confined him to a wheelchair. They could hardly understand him when he spoke. From that time on, he ceased to be an active force in the family. Lucille relaxed a little, though there was still the problem with Jon.

A legacy from a benevolent grandmother was the final touch that contributed to Jon's unending descent into his hell of drugs and otherworldliness. It provided him just enough money to live on and buy his drugs without having to interact with the world, unless he so chose. Severing that last lifeline of necessary contact with others was what killed him, Colin would say in later years, perhaps with more than just a little sense of his guilt implicit in the statement.

They never saw Philip anymore, though his mother still lived down the street. She and Lucille had struck up an unexpected friendship. The latest news was that Philip was on his third marriage in only ten years. He just seemed to have rotten luck with the girls he met, his mother would tell Lucille, shaking her head in bewilderment.

❖

It wasn't clear when their parents first understood the seriousness of Jon's situation. Like many things difficult to accept, the knowledge seemed to dawn on them gradually. Colin expressed bewilderment whenever his mother pressed him for reasons why his brother would turn to drugs to the extent of closing off the rest of the world around him.

"What happened between you?"

"Nothing," was all he said. "Just boys—you know."

She shook her head sadly. "He so looked up to you, you know."

Colin turned away.

Lucille blamed herself for not having paid enough attention to her youngest son; she blamed her husband for the affair that had turned love to anger and finally to a lasting resentment. She blamed herself yet again for staying with Roger rather than divorcing him, as she'd once threatened to do, thinking that had she done so she might have expelled the demon from their lives that had turned their son against himself.

There was no answer and nothing that could console her for what Jon had become. Nor could she share the guilt with her husband; since his stroke he had all but turned inward, only banging his cane against the side of his wheelchair at times and screaming in nearly incomprehensible rage that he hated her for what she'd done to him, that she'd denied him any lasting happiness with her frigidity and her willfulness in making him give up the one love he'd found in life. She had wanted to spare her sons such uncaring anger, but now here it was.

By then, both Colin and Jon had moved out, however, so neither of them had to deal with it directly. For that, she was grateful.

Not surprisingly, Lucille finally turned to the religion she had once forsaken. She recalled the Calvinist Church's doctrine of total depravity, how every person was born into the service of sin, and of its opposite, the doctrine of irresistible grace that could be applied by God alone to those whom He is determined to redeem, bringing them to a saving faith. She was counting on the latter to see her through it all.

❖

Colin stopped dropping by Jon's place. Sometimes more than a month separated the visits. One day, however, he felt a sudden urge to go. He drove over and knocked. The broken window had finally been replaced after years of letting the air into the interior gloom.

Colin's knock reverberated with a dull certainty. There was no answer, no stirring to say that Jon had heard his knock. The screen door was unlatched, but the wooden door was locked. Colin brought out the key from his pocket, the key he'd never used before, and let himself in.

He didn't want to be there. He was in a mood. The day before, Viv had told him she wanted a divorce. She wasn't interested in keeping up the pretense of a marriage any more. She'd known all along, she told him. Colin felt panic at the thought that he would shadow Philip in such things, this marriage not the last in which he would try to hide.

He wandered about, getting used to the dark, tripping over a bag of garbage left inside the doorway. He sniffed the air. How many pick-ups had passed while it sat there?

He delayed raising the blinds, as though to ward off the light—and the inevitable—a few moments longer. He wanted to hold onto the world-as-it-was before he let in that final, irrevocable fact that could never change, could never be reversed.

Jon lay sprawled on the couch, his body scrawny and shrunken, wearing only a T-shirt and socks. It was as if he'd fallen asleep watching TV, except the TV was turned off and he was staring slightly off-center at a shelf of books. What was it, Colin wondered, that had caught his attention in those final seconds of fading away? He followed Jon's gaze to the shelf and the tip of a long, black tube just visible behind a pile of books.

It was the last thing Jon's mind had had any conscious awareness of as he slipped away into whatever region he'd gone to. Colin went over to the shelf and plucked down the kaleidoscope, twirling it in his hands. How had his brother come to have it after all these years? Had he stolen it or had Philip secretly given it to him all those years ago?

For a moment, standing there, he felt like an insignificant figure in this drama, rather than its chief perpetrator.

"Poor Mouse," he said, shaking his head. "Poor, poor Mouse."

He remembered Philip's question: "What does this remind you of?" and Jon's sobbing when they made him hold out his hand.

For a moment, nothing happened. Suddenly the emotions came surging up. He smashed the tube against a wall, shattering it and sending the pieces flying in all directions. He began to sob. The feelings took a long time to die out, the sobs coming a little less frequently until finally they stopped altogether. Colin wiped his hand across his face, rubbing away the tears.

He thought of Philip then, and all the hours spent at his house, away from Philip's parents, who had left them on their own downstairs without enquiring what their son could possibly be doing with two boys nearly half his age. They never asked. Nor had Colin's parents asked why he suddenly had so much spending money when he didn't even have a job.

"It feels like a mouse, doesn't it?" Colin could hear Philip asking, and waiting for them to reply.

"Yes," Colin had spoken up, the older of the two. "And Jon likes it."

Jon glanced up at his older brother with a questioning look.

"Go on, touch it," Colin encouraged him. "You like it, don't you, Mouse boy?"

Jon looked up at his brother with something like love in his eyes. Love and trust. "No, I don't like it."

"Sure you do. You like it, Jon. Pet the little mousey."

"I don't want to do it."

Philip's laughter drowned out Jon's words. Colin joined in as the tears began to well in Jon's eyes. A hard look came into Colin's face. "Don't cry," he commanded. "Don't cry or I won't be your best friend anymore."

FAITHFUL
MICHAEL THOMAS FORD

I knew when Jake came in and sat on the edge of the bed, not moving, that it had gone wrong. He didn't say anything. He didn't touch me. He just sat there, his hands in his lap, swallowed up in the darkness while I waited for him to speak.

Usually he was the hardest after a hit—shedding his clothes as he walked in the door and slipping into bed next to me so I'd feel the length of his cock hard along my ass, his balls heavy against my thigh.

"Come on, baby," he'd say in his low, throaty voice as he moved his mouth over my neck. "Come on. I need to fuck you."

Before I could even wake up, his fingers would already be squeezing my nipples as he pushed inside me, a man possessed. His prick on those nights was strangely hot, like steel radiating heat from the inside, and as he thrust fiercely against me he seemed to be trying to outrun whatever fiery demons held him in their grip. It was as though everything he felt from seeing some man fall under his bullets needed a place to explode, before it burned him up from the inside and sent his soul scattering across the sky. He'd fuck me hard and quick, and I'd come just from the touch of his fingers on my tits, knowing that the last thing those hands had done was kill.

But this night was different. This time, there was only silence. I felt my heart beating, and the familiar rush of blood to my cunt that accompanied his return. But I knew from his stillness not to touch him, and I lay in the darkness, the sheets bunched coldly between my legs, as I waited for him to return to me.

"We made the hit," he said finally, his voice quiet as a stream of chill air.

The hit. Richie Marotta. They'd been planning it for a long time. "So, what's the problem? You guys have been after Richie for months now."

He rubbed his hands through his hair. "Yeah, well, this time someone got in the way."

I sat up, pulling the sheets around me. I could feel the coldness of Jake's mood against my skin like rain, and it made me shiver. "Who?"

"Corelli," he said softly, as though speaking the name any louder would invoke some kind of evil spirit.

Corelli. Jimmy Corelli. Head of the biggest syndicate on the East Side. He'd been in power longer than anyone else in the city. No one dared touch him. He let the smaller guys do their business uninterrupted while he looked after the big operations. In exchange, there was the unspoken agreement that none of them would try to get too big. Killing him was like spitting in the face of God.

"Corelli? Jesus Christ, Jake."

"We weren't even after him," he said, his voice close to cracking. "I mean, Jesus Christ, who the fuck would go after Corelli? We were just supposed to take out Richie. It was an easy hit. He was meeting with his guys over at the docks. All we had to do was bust in, blow their fucking heads off, and get the fuck out of there. Who the fuck knew he was meeting with Corelli?"

"What happened?"

"What happened? We stormed through the fucking door and started firing, that's what happened. Then when it was all over, we saw there were three more bodies than there should have been lying there with holes through them. Corelli and his goddamn sons. Both of them. Dead as shit. When Eddie rolled them over I just about pissed myself like a baby. All I could see was Corelli's face looking up at me with his goddamn eyes still wide open."

He started to shake. "We killed the whole fucking family," he said, his voice hysterical. "The whole goddamn fucking Corelli family. Do you know what the fuck that means? It means every one of our fucking asses is history, starting with mine."

Putting my arms around him, I held him as he wept. His large body fell back against mine, and my face was buried in his neck, surrounding me with the scents of his skin—sweat, excitement, and fear. Closing my eyes, I thought of Corelli lying dead, his blood pooled around him like a halo, and felt a familiar ache in my pussy. I undid the buttons of Jake's shirt and ran my hand inside. His heart was beating so fast I thought it might give out from fear. But still I couldn't help pushing my fingers down his belly, past his belt, and into his pants, where I wrapped my hand around his dick. It was rock hard.

Without a word, I pulled him back on the bed and unzipped his pants. Freeing his cock, I straddled him and worked the head of his prick into me. His eyes remained closed as I began to ride him, and I knew that he, too, was thinking about the way Corelli's eyes had looked up at him in wonder. After a few minutes, his hands closed around my ass and he shot deep inside me.

❖

We knew running was useless. They always find the ones who run, and looking over your shoulder gets uncomfortable very quickly. Besides, it just wasn't the way things were done. Everyone who got into it knew that from the outset. The rules were bred into us from birth. All we could do was wait, wait and see what Corelli's men would do.

We didn't have to wait long. The phone rang less than an hour after Jake came home, while he was pacing the room and smoking and I was sitting on the bed, my cunt still sore from Jake's pounding. He grabbed it on the first ring, not even bothering to say hello. He was silent as he listened for a minute to whoever was on the other end, then he hung up.

"What?"

"That was Joe, Corelli's second," he said, his voice tight. "They want to see me."

"What do you mean they want to see you?"

"He said they know what happened, and they want me to come up to discuss it."

"Discuss it? You can't go there. They'll just kill you."

"I don't think so," he said. "If they wanted to do that, they'd just come over here and do it."

"I don't like it," I said. This wasn't the way things happened. Not in our world.

"There's something else," Jake said. "Joe said to bring you with me."

I looked over at him. "Me? Why?"

He sat down next to me. "I don't know. Look, you know you don't have to. I'll go alone. You can get the fuck out of here…"

"No," I said. "I'm going. You go alone, you're good as dead. With me there, at least you have a chance. You know I'm off-limits to them." Rule number two—women don't count for shit, unless they're pushing out more boy babies to add to the ranks. They wouldn't off me because it wouldn't get them anything except another body to get rid of.

We argued about it for fifteen minutes, but in the end I won, mainly because Jake was scared of being late and pissing off Corelli's guys. While he pulled on some clothes, I got dressed. Despite my fear, I sensed somehow that looking my best might be to our advantage. I pulled on a black velvet dress that Jake had bought me to wear to the opera. Sleeveless, it hugged my body tightly, pushing my breasts up and out. The black looked good against my pale skin, and with my long black hair pinned up, I looked like any other woman on her way to a performance of *La Bohème*.

We arrived at the house a few minutes before the time Joe had told Jake to be there. Befitting his status, the seat of Corelli's empire was an imposing brownstone in one of the city's older neighborhoods. Surrounded by a heavy iron fence, it sat back from the street like a watchdog guarding its territory. I'd passed it many times on my way to and from different places, and every time I'd wondered what went on behind its curtained windows, what it would be like to walk its halls. Now, standing on its steps, I stared at the red lacquered door and wondered how I would get away.

Jake rang the bell, and a moment later it was answered by a young man in a white suit.

"We're here to see Joe," Jake said, the hand that held mine shaking so hard I had to squeeze it to make him stop.

The young man gestured for us to enter. Without a word, he led us up a staircase, then down a long hallway to another door. When he knocked, it was opened by another man, this one older, with graying hair.

"Joe," Jake said, nodding to the man as though we were meeting him on the street.

Joe nodded in return. "Come in." He didn't look at me.

We entered the room, and Joe shut the door behind us. To my surprise, I saw that we were in what seemed to be a bedroom suite. A large bed was in one corner, and across the room from it were several armchairs. In one chair sat a man in a dark suit, while two other men stood behind him.

Joe led us over to the man in the chair. When we neared, he stood and held out his hand to Jake. Jake took it, and the man shook. "Hello, Jake," he said, his voice low and pleasant.

He then turned to me, and again he held out his hand. When I took it, he closed his fingers around mine firmly. "And this must be Sofia. It's nice to meet you."

Not sure what to do, I smiled and nodded slightly. The man smiled back, and I was struck by how young he looked. His face was thin and handsome, with dark eyes and a mouth I couldn't help but think of as beautiful.

"Please," he said, indicating the chairs. "Sit down."

Jake and I sat, and the man resumed his place. He reached into a box sitting on the table next to him and pulled out a cigar. Taking great care, he trimmed the end, lit it, and drew in his breath until the end of the cigar crackled with heat. Taking a puff, he leaned back and let the smoke exit his lips in a dreamy, sensual cloud that drifted in the air between he and us. Then he turned to Jake.

"First," he said. "I should introduce myself. I am Nick Corelli."

Jake looked confused. "Nick Corelli?" he said.

The man nodded. "Yes," he said. "I know most people thought my father had only two children. But there are…were…three of us. My mother died when I was born, and I was sent to live with her sister in Milan. I then spent many years in school. I only recently came back to the city."

"Your father," Jake said. "You have to understand, I didn't mean to…"

Corelli raised his hand. "I have been told what happened," he said. "There is no point in discussing it."

Jake glanced at me, then looked back at Corelli. "If there's anything I can do to…"

Corelli laughed, his voice filling the room. "Jake, my friend, you know how it is. We all know how it is, don't we? I cannot just let you go without some kind of reparation. My father was the most feared man in this city. As the last of my family, I inherit what he created here. I think you agree that it would not be a fitting start to my reign to simply forgive the man who killed my father and brothers."

Jake was silent. I looked at him, waiting for him to speak.

"What is it you want?" I said, when I saw that he wouldn't.

Corelli turned his eyes to me. "A game," he said.

"I don't understand."

"My father was very fond of gambling," Corelli said. "Horses. Cards. Women. He would often settle outstanding debts with a game. If his opponent won, the debt was forgiven. If not, then my father… collected what was owed to him."

"You want to play cards for your father's honor?" I said.

Corelli laughed again. "Oh, no. I have something much more amusing in mind." He took another drag on his cigar before speaking again. "Do you love your husband, Mrs. Anthony?"

I looked over at Jake. "Of course I do."

"And does your husband make you come?"

"Excuse me?"

"When he fucks you. Does he make you come?"

I looked into Corelli's eyes defiantly. "Of course he does."

"That's very good," he said. "A man should know how to please his wife." He gestured toward the three men who remained behind his vacant chair. "Now look at these men. Would you say they were attractive?"

I looked at the men for a moment. "Yes," I said. I didn't know what Corelli was up to, but I figured lying wasn't going to get me anywhere.

"Good," Corelli said. "And would you say that you would enjoy making love with them?"

"Perhaps," I said after a moment. "It would depend on whether or not they were good lovers."

He smiled. "Do you think they would make you come, as your husband does?"

I stared into Corelli's eyes. "I don't know."

Corelli looked at Jake, then back to me. "The game I have in mind is a game of love," he said. "I would like to see you make love with these men."

Jake looked at Corelli. "What the hell do you think—"

I interrupted him. "And if I do?"

"If you do, then your husband goes free. If not, then I will have to take my payment."

"A man's life for watching me fuck?" I said, angered. "If you want a whore, Mr. Corelli, I'm sure you can easily find one."

"Very true," he said, smiling. "I'm sure there are some in this very house even as we speak. But it's not just about fucking, Mrs. Anthony. As I said, this is a game of love. My father always said that a woman would come only for the man she truly loved. I've wondered for a long time if that's really true."

"I wouldn't know," I said. "My husband is the only man I've ever been with."

The corners of Corelli's mouth rose up. "Then this should prove very interesting. If my men can make you come, then your husband dies. If not, then true love wins, both of you go free, and all of this is forgotten."

"I haven't agreed yet," I said.

Corelli raised one eyebrow. "Then perhaps I should order my men to kill your husband now." He nodded, and one of the men ran over and grabbed Jake's head, putting the barrel of a pistol to his temple.

"It's up to you. Mrs. Anthony," Corelli said, watching my face intently.

"Sofia, no," Jake whispered. "Don't do it. Don't."

I looked into Jake's frightened eyes. It was true, he was the only man I'd been with. He knew my body inside and out, and just thinking about his cock inside me made me wet. I turned back to Corelli.

"It's a deal," I said.

Corelli clapped his hands. "Very good, then. Alex, make Mr. Anthony comfortable here."

The man holding the gun to Jake's head produced a length of rope, which he tied around Jake's arms, securing him to the chair. He then gagged him with a cloth. I looked at him and saw that his eyes were fixed on me, pleading with me.

I love you, I mouthed to him.

Corelli remained in his chair. "Oh, and one more thing. I think perhaps we need an audience for our little performance. Joe, if you please."

Joe walked over to the door, opened it, and went into the hall. When he came back, he was accompanied by Eddie and five of Jake's other main men.

"What the fuck is going on?" said Eddie when he saw Jake tied to the chair. "You said we were just talking here. What kind of shit is this?" He attempted to turn and knock Joe to the ground, but Joe punched him hard in the stomach, dropping him to his knees.

"Mr. Annarotti," said Corelli. "Thank you for coming by with your friends. I wanted you all to see that I am indeed a fair man. I know how stories can become…distorted…in the telling. This way, you can see for yourself, so that there are no misunderstandings afterward."

The same young man who had shown us in entered with six chairs, which he set up, three on either side of Jake's chair. The men sat down, Eddie holding his hand to his stomach.

Corelli turned to Eddie. "I have made Mr. Anthony an offer," he said. "His wife has chosen to accept it. If she succeeds in the task I've set before her, your boss is free to go about his business uninterrupted by me or anyone else. Should she fail, then all that he has will belong to me. That includes you, Mr. Annarotti, as well as your men. Do we understand each other?"

Eddie looked over at Jake, who nodded slightly.

"Yeah, we understand," Eddie said. He looked at me then, his eyes dark with fear. I knew he had no idea what was about to happen, but he was too frightened to ask any questions.

"Tony," Corelli said. "Perhaps you'd like to be the first to tempt Mrs. Anthony."

Tony nodded. Walking over to me, he took my hand, and I stood. He led me across the room to the big bed. The chair with Jake strapped to it was directly opposite the bed, and he could see everything that was going on. Corelli, settled into his chair, watched as I turned to Tony and looked into his face. He was handsome in a rough way, but his eyes were the cold eyes of a man used to taking what he wanted.

Before I could think about what was going to happen, Tony grabbed me and kissed me. He was a big man, and his powerful arms encircled me tightly as his tongue forced its way into my mouth. His hands crept to the hem of my dress and pulled it up over my ass. I felt him tear my panties away easily, and then his fingers were gripping the mounds of my cheeks.

He pushed me so that I fell onto my back on the bed. Removing his suit coat, he quickly undid his tie and his shirt, tossing them onto the floor and revealing a well-muscled chest and stomach covered in a thick swath of dark hair. Another few tugs, and his pants followed. He stood looking down at me, his cock swelling between his legs as he stroked it to its full length. Then he climbed on top of me, his hands pulling my dress over my head. When my breasts were bared, he immediately began to pinch my nipples hard.

My body rose up against him as I jerked in surprise, and my pussy pressed against his balls, his hard cock slapping my stomach. Tony continued to pinch my nipples as he slid his body down mine, spreading my legs with his knees. Pushing his cock into my cunt, he slid all the way inside in one long thrust, making me cry out.

"So soon, Mrs. Anthony?" Corelli's voice came from across the room, taunting me. "Is Tony so much bigger than your husband that he can make you come just from being inside of you?"

I looked into Tony's face. He was half smiling, and I could tell he was enjoying his part in the game.

"Give me your best shot," I hissed as I put my legs around his waist and tightened myself around his prick.

Tony groaned as he began to pump in and out of me. His big fingers worked over my nipples as I ran my nails up and down his broad back, scratching the hell out of him. I knew I'd be able to outlast him if I concentrated on making him lose his load. Every time he thrust into me, I pushed up to meet him, driving him as deep as he could go.

As Tony fucked me, I looked over to see how Jake was. His eyes were on me, and I could tell that despite the gun that Alex was holding against his head, he was hard inside his pants. *Good old Jake*, I thought as I pulled Tony's cock into my cunt.

Tony fucked me mechanically, like a machine bent on beating my pussy into submission. Over and over he slammed into me, his breath coming in hot blasts against my face as he grunted in time with his thrusts. When his eyes shut and he began to groan, I knew I had him. He pumped into me a few more times, then I felt him explode inside me. He buried himself so that his balls were slapping my ass as his prick throbbed, spewing its load. When he was done, he pulled out and looked down at me.

"Nice fuck," he said, wiping his dick on my ass.

"Not nice enough, apparently," said Corelli. "Mrs. Anthony barely broke a sweat over you, Tony. Perhaps Joe can do better."

Tony got off the bed as Joe came over. In his forties, Joe looked like any number of Italian men of that age. His gray hair was thinning, and his stomach was less than tight from all the pasta he'd crammed down his throat over the years. As he removed his clothes, I thought of the times when, as a little girl, I'd watched my father undress after he came home from work. Like my father, Joe carefully folded his clothes and placed them on a nearby chair.

When he pulled his T-shirt over his head, I saw the scars. Three small, ragged holes near his navel. Bullet wounds. He saw me looking, and turned around as he removed his underwear.

"On your stomach," he said harshly.

I rolled over, and only then did he get on the bed. I felt his hand come down, slapping my ass hard. "Up on your knees," he ordered.

I pulled myself up so that my ass was in the air, my face lowered onto the pillows. Joe moved in behind me, and I waited for his cock to enter my pussy.

Instead, he slammed into my asshole, shoving his cock past the tight ring of muscle with no warning. I screamed into the pillows as he pressed himself tight against my butt. Before I could adjust myself to him, he pulled back, almost all of the way out. Just the head of his dick was inside me, and he began to fuck me in short movements, teasing my asshole until the pain subsided and I began to feel fingers of pleasure creeping up my cunt. Jake had always wanted to fuck my ass, but I'd never let him. Now, as Joe took my virgin hole, I began to groan into the pillow.

"Sounds like Joe is giving your wife a real ride," I heard Corelli say to Jake. "Perhaps our game will end sooner than expected."

I bit my lip, determined not to come. Even though Joe's cock was bringing me closer and closer to the edge, I wouldn't let him push me over. The harder he fucked me, the harder I bit down, until my mouth was filled with the taste of blood and I heard him breathing harder.

"Good girl," he said, slapping me with his hand as his cock buried itself in my hole. "You're giving daddy just what he wants."

"You fuck real good," I said through my teeth. "Bet you like ass a lot. I guess you've had a lot of practice with a lot of guys."

Joe slapped me hard on the ass, making me jump. He thrust harder against me, filling my ass with his cock as he continued to spank me. The combination of his rough hand hitting my skin and the pounding of his prick was making me crazy. Then, just as I felt the first small waves begin to shudder within me, he came. Pulling out, he let his cum spray over my back in thick drops. I collapsed against the pillows, panting, and willed the stirrings in my pussy to subside.

When I opened my eyes, Alex was standing beside the bed. He didn't seem to be much older than nineteen or twenty, his body thin and almost hairless. But in his hand was a long, thick cock. Already a string of precum was dripping from the engorged head, and the more he pumped himself, the more it oozed.

"Suck it," he ordered, grabbing me by the hair and pushing his dick between my lips.

I took as much of him in as I could, attempting to breathe. The thickness of him was choking me, but he kept shoving more and more into my mouth. I grabbed at his balls, trying to stop him, but he held my hands out of the way as he forced himself all the way in.

"Get it good and wet," he said.

I did as he said, slicking the length of him with my mouth until his shaft was covered in a mix of lipstick and spit. I was hoping I could make him come just from sucking him, and tried to keep him in my throat. But just as I thought he would lose it, he pulled out. Still standing at the side of the bed, he jerked my legs over his shoulders and impaled me on his shaft. My ass was still sore from Joe's pounding, and my tits ached from Tony's fingering. Now Alex worked on my cunt, spreading it wide with his thick cock.

Then both Tony and Joe were there again, their cocks hanging over my face. As Alex fucked me, they took turns sticking their pricks between my lips and making me suck them hard. As my mouth filled with cock, my pussy was being pounded by Alex's steel-hard dick. All around me I felt heat and skin and hard flesh.

"Come on," Alex said. "Come for me. Come for my big cock. I want to hear you come."

I slipped Joe's prick out of my mouth.

"You'll have to do better than that, little boy," I said. "I can't even feel you in there."

Pulling my legs tightly against him, Alex fucked me as hard as he could, his balls slapping against my ass. I knew that if I survived the night I'd be black and blue the next day. Even worse, my cunt was starting to ache like it did before I came. Every muscle in my body was tense, and I was on the verge of being swept away. Next to me, I could see Joe and Tony jerking off over my breasts. I started to moan.

"She's almost there," I heard Tony say. "Fuck her, man. Fuck her good. Make the bitch come."

I looked Tony in the eye. "Never call a lady a bitch," I said, and wrapped my hand around his cock. With three quick jerks, I felt him twitch, and his cum splattered against my tit. "You lose," I said.

Seeing Tony's cum dripping down my breast, both Joe and Alex lost it. They came together, one covering my chest with more jism, the other bucking against my cunt as he gasped for air.

"Very good, Sofia." Corelli was walking across the room toward us, his cigar filling the air with smoke. "You managed to outlast my best men. Your devotion to your husband is admirable."

"Looks like I win," I said.

Corelli smiled. "Not quite. You still haven't given me a chance."

The three men got off the bed, making room for Corelli. Alex went back and resumed his guard over Jake, while Joe and Tony stood watching. Corelli wiped his finger through the mixed puddle of cum on my chest. He brought it to my lips, smearing it across them.

"You look lovely in this," he said. "It's very becoming."

"Fuck you," I spat back.

Corelli laughed. "Why, that's exactly what I had in mind."

Removing his shoes but keeping his clothes on, he stretched out on the bed with his head at the bottom of the mattress. "Come here," he said, patting his chest.

I turned around and straddled his chest. I was looking right at Jake as Corelli put his hands on my ass and pulled me forward. His mouth covered my pussy, and his tongue slid between the bruised lips. I put my hands on his shoulders to steady myself as he pushed up into me, eating the cum left behind by his men.

Jake's eyes were on mine as Corelli worked on me. I could see the fear in them as he watched my face for any sign that I might be about to come. Alex had the gun pressed tightly against his head, and I could see that he was sweating nervously.

I could also see that he was still hard. I doubted that he'd lost his erection throughout the whole thing. It struck me as funny, and for some reason I almost started to laugh. But then Corelli found my clit with his teeth and began to nibble softly at it. Unable to help myself, I ground against his face.

Reaching down, he unzipped his pants and pulled out his cock. Pushing me away from him, he looked into my face. "Sit on it," he said. "Feed my cock to your hungry cunt."

Crouching over him, I slipped his head inside me. Still keeping my eyes on Jake, I pushed down, swallowing Corelli's cock until I was sitting against his stomach. I watched my husband's face as I rode the prick of the man who wanted to kill him. I could tell that in spite of his terror, Jake was getting off on seeing me fuck another man, especially one who held his life in his hands. It wasn't about sex or even love. It was about power.

The truth was, I was getting off on it, too, and watching Jake was making me horny as shit. Looking into his eyes as Corelli's cock filled me, I knew that he longed to free his hands so he could jerk off. I imagined him sitting in the chair, his big prick gripped in his fist as he beat off. I pictured the head swelling, turning dark red as the blood filled it. I saw his balls pulling up as he came closer and closer. I saw the rain of cum splatter his belly as he went over the edge.

I couldn't help it. As Corelli pushed into me one last time, my throat opened and I began to cry out. My voice filled the room, and as I came in great, heaving gasps, my moans were echoed by the muffled sounds of a gunshot.

When I looked up, Jake was slumped forward in his chair. On the wall behind him was a red stain, as though someone had come in a great crimson splatter across the white surface. There was a smaller stain, darker, against the front of his pants.

"I win," said Corelli, pulling his cock out of me and pushing me away.

❖

I lay on the bed, watching as Corelli zipped his pants and got up. He walked over to the mirror on the wall and looked at himself as he straightened his tie.

"Well, gentlemen, it looks like our little game is over. From now on, you report to me. If any of you don't like that arrangement, I'd be happy to give you the same chance Mr. Anthony had."

He turned back to the bed. "As for Mrs. Anthony, I think she showed us all just what it is she needs. For now she'll be staying with me. After all, a grieving widow needs all the comforting she can get."

Walking over to Eddie and the boys, he stopped before the blood-covered wall. "Any questions?"

Eddie nodded. "No, sir." Jake's blood had speckled Eddie's shirt, as well as the shirts of the other men, and none of them could bring themselves to look at the body sitting between them.

"Good. Now why don't you boys go home. Joe will call you all in the morning to discuss your new positions."

He nodded toward Jake. "Get that piece of shit out of here."

Eddie and the other men left. None of them looked at me. Corelli's boys grabbed the chair with Jake's lifeless body still strapped to it and hauled it out of the room, leaving us alone. Corelli locked the door, then came back to the bed. Bending down, he kissed me deeply, his tongue as gentle as it had been cruel only moments before.

"You were good," he said, slipping the buttons of his shirt open and sliding it off. "I knew you would be."

"I had the easy part," I said, reaching behind to release the binding that held Nick's breasts in place. When they were free, I took one in my hand and ran my tongue lightly over the nipple. Nick jumped, drawing in a sharp breath.

"That's for making me wait so long," I said. I took the nipple in my mouth again, sucking gently this time and then releasing it. "You're so beautiful."

Nick laughed. "My father didn't think so. He never wanted anyone to know he had a daughter. He blamed me for my mother's death. That's why he sent me away. As far as anyone knew, there never was a Nicola Corelli. When I came back wearing suits instead of dresses, he didn't say a word to anyone. I think secretly he convinced himself that I'd been a boy all along. Even my brothers pretended."

"I knew the first time I saw you walking down the street that you'd be my lover," I said. "I went home and made myself come, thinking of kissing your face. When Jake fucked me that night, I thought about you holding me. It was the only time I was ever unfaithful to him."

"You mean the first time," Nick said teasingly.

She was right. After that day, I had looked for Nick everywhere. Sometimes I would see her on the street, or walking through the park. Each time, I would feel the dampness spread between my legs. Once, after catching a glimpse of her sitting a few tables away from me in a restaurant, drinking coffee, I had begged Jake to finger me under the table until I came watching her blow the smoke from her cigarette into the air.

We met, finally, at a New Year's Eve party held by a mutual associate. Shortly before midnight, I was going up the stairs to the ladies room, and Nick was coming down. She was dressed in a tuxedo, and when our eyes met, I held her gaze. She followed me to the bathroom, where she pushed me up against the wall and kissed me. Lifting me onto the edge of the sink, she fucked me for the first time. As the clock downstairs struck twelve, I came, moaning in Nick's ear as Jake looked around the room, wondering where I was.

After that, we saw one another whenever we could. It was as though Nick had entered my blood and flowed through my veins, filling me with her heat. I needed her every minute, and she needed me just as badly. All that stood in our way was Jake and Nick's family. One hot, wet summer night, while Jake was away on business and the thunder crashed around us as we lay in Nick's bed, we'd come up with our plan. Now, a few months later, we were together as we'd dreamed of being.

"I remember seeing you at that party and asking my brother who you were," Nick said. "He laughed at me, telling me no woman would ever want me because I couldn't give her what she needed."

"But now your brothers are dead," I said, running my hands through Nick's hair and down her back. "And you're just what I need." I slid my hand into her open pants and felt the cock inside, the straps of the harness curving over her beautiful ass. "Jake used to be as hard as this after he'd killed someone."

Nick straddled me, pushing her cock against my belly. "But now

Jake is dead, too, and you're mine. Poor Jake, he never should have told you where he was making the hit on Marotta."

"And you should never have told your old dear papa that Richie was trying to take some of his business away from him. Otherwise, he'd be safe and sound in his own bed."

Nick kissed me. "They knew the game was a dangerous one when they started playing it," she said. "They just didn't count on the players changing. But from now on, we're in control."

"Do you think we'll be able to pull it off?"

In answer, Nick entered me, and I enfolded her in my arms, drawing her deeper. As she began to fuck me, I knew that the game was just beginning.

Spin Cycle
Greg Herren

My alarm woke me from the dreamless sleep of the truly content.

I smacked my hand down on it—it was a reflex. I opened my eyes and sat up in my bed. I could smell brewing coffee from downstairs. I yawned and stretched—I couldn't remember the last time I'd slept so deeply, so peacefully. I reached for my glasses from the little table next to the bed and slipped them on. Everything swam into focus, and my heart started sinking the way it did every morning when I started coming to full consciousness.

Still in the goddamned carriage house, I thought, getting out of bed with a moan, *and no commutation of the sentence in sight. Stupid fucking Katrina.*

But there was silence outside, other than birds chirping in the crepe myrtles.

No hammering or sawing. No drilling.

I smiled.

I slipped on the rubber-soled shoes I had to wear upstairs. I avoided the carpet nails jutting up from the wooden floor on my way to the bathroom. The floor slanted at about a thirty-degree angle to the left. It used to disorient me, but I'd gotten used to it in the nine months I'd been sentenced to live in this pit. I looked at the bags under my eyes while brushing my teeth and washing my face. No need to shave, I decided. I wasn't going anywhere or seeing anyone today.

In fact, I'd finished a job and didn't have to start the next for a few days.

I was at loose ends.

I pulled on purple LSU sweatpants and a matching hooded sweatshirt before heading downstairs to get some coffee.

I was on my second cup, surveying the stacks of boxes piled in practically every available space. It was the same routine every morning. Drink some coffee, look around and try to figure out if there was some way to make this fucking place more comfortable, more livable. I had yet to figure out a way, without renting a storage space and getting everything out.

And every morning I came to the conclusion there wasn't a way.

I closed my eyes, and took deep, calming breaths.

Maybe I should just rent the storage unit and be done with it, I said to myself. *You don't know how long you're going to be stuck in here before the work on the house is done. Imagine not having all these towering stacks of boxes collecting dust in here. Imagine not having this soul-deadening reminder everywhere you look—*

A knock on the front door jolted me back into the present. I crossed the room and opened the door. "Yes?"

The tall black woman in a gray business suit flashed a badge at me. "I'm Venus Casanova with the NOPD. I'm sorry to disturb you, sir. I was wondering if I could talk to you for a few moments?"

"Sure, come on in." I stepped aside to let her in. "Have a seat. Would you like some coffee? I just made some."

She flashed me a brief smile as she sat down on my rust-colored love seat. "No, thank you. I've had more than enough this morning already." She slipped a small notebook and pen out of her jacket pocket. "The label on the buzzer out by the front gate said J. Spencer. Is that your name?"

"Joe Spencer, yes," I replied. "What's going on?" I sat down in a green plastic chair. There were two of them on either side of a matching table. They were patio furniture, meant for the outdoors. Before the flood, I would have never had such things inside my house.

But as I kept telling myself, it was only temporary.

If you could call nine months and counting temporary.

"How long have you known Mr. and Mrs. Dufour?"

"Bill and Maureen?" I thought for a moment. "Just a few months— he started working on the house back in March. Nice couple, a little odd. I thought Bill was a little old to still be doing this kind of work by himself, but then I'm not paying them." I laughed, to take the sting out of the words. "So, what's going on? Why are you here, Detective?"

"I'm afraid I have to tell you Mrs. Dufour is dead." Her voice was calm, her face without expression.

"Oh, no! Bill must be—oh, how awful. How absolutely awful." I shook my head. "I assume it was her heart?"

She tilted her head slightly to one side. "Why would you assume that? Did she have a bad heart?"

"Well, I don't know about that," I replied. "But she was pretty old. Older than Bill, but I'm not for sure how old he is, to be honest. But she told me she was in her late seventies...and since he's doing construction work, I figured he couldn't be much older than sixty-five. But I do know she's his fourth wife."

Her right eyebrow went up. "His fourth wife?"

I shrugged. "Yes, he told me once he'd buried three wives and would probably bury Maureen, too. He laughed about it—which I thought was kind of creepy, frankly. I mean, I guess when you've had three wives die on you—I don't know. It's just not something I'd think you would laugh about."

"So, did you know them well?"

"Not well. I mean, I talked to him more than her. Mostly about the house stuff, how it was going, things like that. He'd stop by every once in a while and give me a progress report, and of course he's always outside working whenever I come or go, you know?" I took another drink from my coffee mug. "They're a little odd."

"Odd?"

"Odd. I mean, they're friendly enough, but I always got an odd vibe from them. I didn't like to be around them, they made me uncomfortable. It's nothing I can put my finger on and say for a fact... but yeah. There was just something about them." I shivered a little. "Something not quite right, do you know what I mean?"

Before she could answer, there was another knock on the door. I smiled and got up. "Let me get that." She smiled and nodded. "Yes?" I asked.

The man standing there was handsome, and I couldn't help the involuntary smile. He smiled back at me. "Excuse me sir, but I need to speak with Detective Casanova." He flashed a badge at me.

She came up beside me. I stepped away from the door, but could still hear them as I refilled my coffee. "Yes, Blaine?" She asked, lowering her voice.

"We're going to take Dufour down to the station while the lab finishes processing the apartment. Do you want to talk to him before they take him?"

"No, have someone take his statement. I'll finish interviewing Mr. Spencer and head down."

"All right."

She shut the door and sat back down on the love seat. "Sorry about that, Mr. Spencer." She flipped through her little notepad. "Where were we? Oh yes, you were saying there was something about the Dufours you didn't like?"

I took another drink from my coffee. "I wish I could be more specific, but I really can't. I remember when Mildred—the lady who owns the property—hired him, and they were moving into the house… he worked on gutting my side of the house during the day and was fixing up a few rooms for them to live in on Mildred's side…"

"So you're a renter?"

"Yes, I've lived on the 1367 side of the house for about six years. The property owner, Mildred Savage, lives on the other side. Well, not now, obviously. She and her husband are living with some friends down on Jefferson Avenue. And I'm living here in the carriage house, until the house is done. Bill's doing my side first." I gestured around the small room, the piles of boxes. "This place is kind of cramped, as you can see." I gave her a small smile. "I know I shouldn't complain—at least I have a place to live."

"This neighborhood didn't flood, did it?"

"No, our roof came off." I laughed, shaking my head at the irony. "Unlike most people, we had water from above, not below. I lost everything on the second floor—all the furniture and everything was ruined, my clothes—my bedroom was upstairs." I waved at the piles of boxes. "Everything I was able to salvage is in these boxes."

"You evacuated, I gather?"

"Yes. I went and stayed with my sister up north. Indianapolis—a horrible place." I made a face. "I couldn't wait to get back here as soon as possible. And the carriage house was open, so Mildred let me move in here while the house is being worked on. It was very kind of her. Otherwise I'd have been stuck up there for God knows how long."

"How long have you been back?"

"I came back on October eleventh. There was still a lot of debris from the roof around. I cleaned it all up, and moved whatever I could salvage out of my side of the house in here. It's a little cramped. Cozy, I guess. Are you sure you don't want any coffee?"

"I'm sure."

"Well, excuse me while I get some more." I got up and refilled my cup. "If I don't drink a pot every morning, I'm useless for the rest of the day." I sighed. "And I have some work to do today—a deadline."

"What do you do for a living, Mr. Spencer?"

"Well, I'm a photographer—that's my real passion, but I mostly make my living from doing graphic design work." I sighed. "I work from home, and this place is so small I can't really…I've thought about renting office space somewhere, but…I keep thinking the house will be finished and everything will go back to normal."

She nodded sympathetically. "So, the Dufours moved onto the property how long ago?"

"About three months or so ago." I shrugged. "March? Yes, it was March, I think…since Katrina I can't keep track of dates and things—which is a problem when you work on deadlines." I took another sip of coffee. "But like I said, at first they seemed nice, but you know, I'm not really used to being around people much." I laughed. "I've always worked at home, you know, and do most of my communication with clients over the phone or through e-mail. I didn't really leave the house much before the storm…but since the storm, you know, being the only person here on the property and the rest of the block being deserted, I felt kind of lonely, you know? I never felt it before the storm. Only after."

"I understand what you mean. The storm changed everything, didn't it? The way we look at things?"

"Exactly. I remember the day they moved in…it was a nice, sunny day. Mildred had called and told me they'd be moving in—I couldn't believe anyone was willing to live in the house the way it was—but they did! At that age, they were basically living like squatters while he redid the walls and floors in the back bedroom and the bathroom and the kitchen…"

The sound of hammering drew me out of the carriage house with my coffee mug. It was a gorgeous March afternoon—seventy degrees or so, white wisps of clouds drifting across a blue sky, and a warm breeze rustling the crepe myrtles running along the property line fence.

The Dufours had moved in three days earlier, and my mood was good. After six months in the carriage house, there was an end in sight.

At last.

I walked to the back door to Mildred's side of the house. The door was open, and I could see Bill hammering at the moldy walls in what had been Mildred's utility room at one point. The room was now empty—everything in it had been ruined. He looked up as I climbed the four wooden steps to the door frame, a big smile on my face. "Hey there, Joe, what do you think?" He put the hammer down and put his hands on his hips. He puffed his chest out.

"I just thought I'd look in and see how things are going. Wow." I whistled. "You certainly have gotten stuff done around here."

"I like to work." He preened a bit. He was wearing dirty overalls with a red flannel shirt underneath.

"Where's Maureen?" I leaned against the door frame.

"The Laundromat. That woman sure likes to do laundry."

"She drags the laundry down to the Laundromat?" I gaped at him, not believing my ears.

"Yup, she sure does." He gestured me to follow him into the next room. The sun shone through the windows into what used to be Mildred's kitchen. He pointed proudly at the new plasterboard. "Look at these walls! Now, that's some quality workmanship, don't you think?"

"Yes, yes it is." I touched the wall closest to me and returned his smile.

But couldn't get the image of the old woman dragging a laundry bag down the sidewalk out of my mind.

"This is the kind of work I'm doing on your place. Should be done gutting everything tomorrow, got some Mexicans coming to help haul the shit out. Once that's out, I've got the electrical guys and the plumber coming out to get all that fixed up nice. Then I can start on your walls."

"That's great," I said, my heart starting to lift. *I'll be in my home in no time*, I thought happily, finishing my coffee—and made a decision. "Bill, you know—I'm a little worried about Maureen. She shouldn't have to go to the Laundromat. I mean, that's a long way for her to go, dragging loads of laundry down to the corner. And she's not—" I hesitated.

Bill threw his head back and roared with laughter. "You can say it, son. She's not young. I know that, son, I'm married to her, you know! She's seventy-eight."

"And she shouldn't be dragging the laundry to the corner," I insisted.

"She has a cart, Joe. Don't worry about her. She's fine. She's like my second wife—"

"Your second wife?"

"Yup, that's right, Maureen's my fourth wife. I've already buried three, son, and I'll probably bury her, too." He laughed again. "I'll just find another one when that day comes, I suppose. A man needs a wife, don't you think?"

"Yes, I suppose."

"Why aren't you married, Joe?"

"I was." I stepped out onto the back stairs. "Well, I just wanted to stop by and say hello."

"Stop by any time you like."

He started pounding at the walls again as I went down the stairs.

My mind was made up.

❖

"So, you offered to let her use your washer and dryer? That was kind of you." Venus smiled at me.

"I couldn't stop thinking about her dragging it all the way down to the corner. I couldn't get that image out of my mind all night. She was a seventy-eight-year-old woman, for God's sake, and I couldn't understand why he would let her do that, cart or no cart. She had one—I saw her with it the next morning, bringing in the groceries from her car. You know, one of those old-lady carts with four wheels that you can load up with just about anything? I mean, Mildred's washer and dryer were damaged—I dragged them out to the curb myself. But mine was in the back just beyond the kitchen, and they worked just fine. I used them all the time. And so the more I thought about it, the more it really bothered me…so I decided the next time I saw Maureen, I'd tell her to just use mine…"

❖

The very next day, I ran into Maureen at the front gate. I'd run some errands and had stopped to get some things at the grocery store.

"Morning, Joe!" She beamed at me. Her iron-gray hair was wrapped up in a babushka. She was maybe five-four in her white Keds. She was wearing a pair of jeans and a sweatshirt.

"Good morning—um, I see you're off to the Laundromat."

"Yes, it sure does seem to pile up. I swear, I'm doing laundry every day, it seems!" She laughed. "Good thing Bill bought me this cart. I'd hate to have to carry a basket all the way down there. I mean, sure it's just the corner—I'm sure a handsome, strong young man like you could easily carry a laundry basket all that way, but an old lady like me—well, good thing I've got the cart."

"Yes, well, I've been meaning to tell you—"

She cut me off. "Where've you been? You're usually not out and about this early!" She peered at my grocery bags.

"I had to mail some things, and I had to pick up some things at the Sav-A-Center." I smiled back at her. "Maureen, I've been meaning to tell you—you know, you don't have to take your clothes to the Laundromat."

"They aren't going to wash themselves!" She guffawed loudly at the thought of it.

"There's a perfectly good washer and dryer in my side of the house, just sitting there. You know you can use them instead of going to the Laundromat. I mean, I don't use them that much myself, and well, I just hate the thought of you—"

A smile spread across her wrinkled face. "Oh, thank you, Joe! That's so nice of you! I told Bill what a nice young man you are, and that is so kind! I swear, I won't be a moment's trouble. I won't make you sorry you offered! That would be so much easier—I wouldn't have to sit there and wait for the clothes, you know how they always say at the Laundromat they'll throw unattended clothes right in the garbage, can you imagine that, and I just can't see telling Bill his best shirt was thrown away, you can only imagine the temper that man has, no sir, so I sit there and wait for the clothes. Oh, thank you thank you, thank you!"

I winked at her. "You can start with that load, Maureen."

And I walked back to the carriage house.

❖

Venus perked up. "She told you he has a temper, did she? Did she sound like she was afraid of him?"

"Well, that was the first time I heard about it. But I used to hear him yelling at her sometimes, late at night. Well, late at night for them. They were usually in bed by nine."

"Was this frequent?"

"She didn't have a heart attack, did she?"

"If you don't mind, Mr. Spencer, I'll ask the questions."

"Did he kill her?"

"Mr. Spencer—"

I crossed my arms. "I'm not answering another question until you tell me what's going on."

"Someone killed Mrs. Dufour, yes." She inhaled. "We're gathering evidence, Mr. Spencer, and that's why you need to answer my questions."

"Murdered. Someone killed her. Murdered." I shivered. "My God, the door to their rooms is just twenty feet maybe from my front door... Did someone break in? Climb the fence? Oh my God, oh my God!"

"Did you hear anything last night? Anything out of the ordinary?"

I thought for a moment. "No, no I didn't. But I was upstairs in the bedroom watching television, and I'm afraid I had the sound up rather loud...it was really windy last night...the tarp on the roof was making a lot of noise, and so I turned the television up."

"Did you see either one of them last evening?"

"I saw her, I don't know, around six maybe? I was down here working at my desk, trying to get a rush job done. He was sanding things—you see where he has the sawhorses set up, right near my front door?—so I was having difficulty concentrating, but he finally stopped around four o'clock, I think. I finished the job right around six, and I happened to look out the window and saw her walking around the back of the house—heading for their door. I guess she was over doing some laundry on my side of the house."

"Did you see anything out of the ordinary?"

"No, I pretty much saw her every day around that time. Actually, seeing her come around the house was a regular thing." I laughed. "Doing the laundry—it was like a fetish for her."

"A fetish?" Venus looked puzzled.

"I know that sounds crazy, but it's true. She was constantly doing laundry."

"Surely you're exaggerating?" Venus smiled.

"No, I actually wish I were..."

❖

I climbed the steps to the back door, carrying my laundry basket. I could hear the dryer running, and moaned to myself.

Sure enough, Maureen was turning the dial on my washing

machine. She pulled the dial out, and I heard water start rushing into it. I closed my eyes.

"Why, good afternoon, Joe! Wanting to use your washing machine, I see!"

"Well, um, yes."

"'Fraid I beat you to the punch, there, Joe! I just put in a load!" She laughed, winking at me with her right eye.

"But you were doing laundry this morning…I thought you'd be finished by now." I said slowly.

"Oh, it just piles up when you're not looking, doesn't it? You've got to stay on top of it, you know, or you'll be doing it for days on end!"

"But you were using the washer all day yesterday…I really need to do a load of clothes, Maureen. I don't have any clean underwear or socks."

"It does pile up when you let it go for a while, doesn't it?"

"But the reason it's piling up for me is because you're always using my washer."

She laughed again. "Well, Joe, there's the two of us, you know. We dirty up twice as much as you do."

"But at the rate you're using my washing machine, you and Bill would have to be changing clothes every hour."

"Oh, Joe, you are the funny one! Talk to you later!" Still laughing, she went out the back door.

I bit my lip. I set my laundry basket down on the floor. *What the hell is she washing all day, anyway?* I asked myself. I walked over to the washing machine, and opened the lid. I stared down into my washer in disbelief.

There were two dish-towels floating in the sudsy water.

"What the—" I couldn't stop staring at the towels. I slammed the lid down, and the machine started agitating again.

Is she insane?

I bit my lip and reached for the dryer door, and opened it.

An LSU baseball cap nestled in the bottom of the dryer.

A baseball cap.

"Dear God in heaven, what is wrong with that woman?" I said out loud.

❖

"She was doing a load of just two dish towels? And another load that was just a baseball cap?" She clearly didn't believe me—it was written all over her face. "You're exaggerating a bit there, aren't you, Mr. Spencer?"

"I wish I was, Detective." I leaned back in my chair. "I sat on the back steps until I heard the washer stop, and then I went in and put my load in—I took the dish towels out and left them sitting on the dryer. I was working on a job, so I came back here and lost track of time. About forty-five minutes later I realized my load would be done, and I could put it in the dryer, you know, start my second load. So I walked back over." I sighed. "You'll never guess what I found?"

"What, Mr. Spencer?"

"I heard the washer running when I went in the back door, you know? I was puzzled—it had been almost an hour since I started my load, you know—the baseball cap should have been finished." I shook my head at the memory. "My wet clothes—my *underwear*—was sitting on top of the dryer. I opened the washer and there was another load— two bath towels—not mine—my laundry basket with the next load was still sitting there on the floor. She took MY clothes out, put them on the dryer, and even though she could see I needed to do a second load, she started a load with just two towels. TWO TOWELS!" I took a deep breath, trying to keep the rising anger down.

"That must have been incredibly frustrating for you—"

I cut her off, the frustration and anger bubbling up all over again. "I didn't know *what* to think. I was shocked at the total lack of concern for my needs—especially since they were MY MACHINES, which I bought and paid for—and she just blithely ignored that I needed to do my own laundry, after I had told her—and then took MY stuff out of MY goddamned washer SO SHE COULD WASH TWO FUCKING TOWELS?"

"Mr. Spencer, please calm—"

"I'm so sorry." I interrupted her again, taking a few deep breaths. I smiled at her. "I just don't understand whatever happened to common courtesy. I mean, here I was, doing her a favor, and she was putting me into the position of having to BEG to use my own appliances!"

"No good deed goes unpunished, Mr. Spencer?"

"Exactly. So I decided to try talking to her again."

"And how did that go?"

❖

I hesitated at the back door. I could hear some big band music playing, and Maureen humming along to it. I knocked, but there was no response. I gritted my teeth and knocked louder.

The back door swung open, and Maureen smiled at me, wiping her hands on her jeans. "Oh, hello, Joe. I was just washing up some dishes."

"I'm sorry to bother you—"

"It's no bother at all. Now what can I do for you?"

"It's about the washing machine, Maureen."

"Is there a problem?"

"Well, I need to use them, Maureen."

"Well, go on and use them, then!"

"I've been trying to for the last couple of days."

"I'm afraid I don't understand you."

"Every time I try to do my laundry, you're doing yours."

"But, Joe, you said I could use your washer and dryer whenever I wanted to!"

"Yes, yes I did. But—"

"I'm just doing what you said."

"But, Maureen—"

"First you said I could use your machines whenever I wanted to. I did what you said and now you're acting like I did something wrong. I really don't understand you, Joe. That doesn't make any sense to me."

"Maybe what I should have said was you could use them whenever I wasn't."

"But, Joe, you're never using them when I go over there. They're just sitting there, empty."

I took a deep breath. "Maureen, the point is you're using them constantly. *Constantly.* I went over there this afternoon and you were doing a load that was just a dish towel. So I waited, and when it was done, I took it out and put a load of mine in. When I went back later, you'd taken my clothes out of the washer, were drying the dish towel, and had started another load—with two bath towels, while my laundry basket was sitting there and you could clearly see I had more laundry to do."

"Did you want me to do your laundry? Is that what this is about?"

I stared at her in disbelief. "No, that isn't what this is about. What this is about, Maureen, is me being able to do my laundry."

"Because I'm not going to do your laundry."

"I'm not asking you to!"

"I don't understand."

I counted to ten in my head, trying not to lose my temper. "Maureen. I am telling you that I also need to do my laundry. You and Joe aren't the only people on this property who need to wash clothes. Has it never occurred to you that I might need to do mine?"

"But Joe, like I said, the machines are never in use—"

I cut her off. "What do you think it means when there's a load of my clothes, wet, in the washing machine and a laundry basket with more clothes in it on the floor, Maureen?"

"But you just left the clothes in the washer and I had things that needed to be washed, Joe. I mean, that wasn't very considerate of you especially when I had some things to wash. Did you just expect me to wait around all day for you?"

"Maureen, you had two bath towels. That could have waited until I was finished with mine, is all I'm saying."

"But I can't just wait around for you all day."

"I really don't care, Maureen! IT'S MY WASHER AND DRYER! If you want to use them, you need to be more considerate of my needs!"

"But you said I could use them whenever I needed to!"

"Maureen, if you have a load that can't wait and my clothes are in the washer—and I don't care if they've been sitting there for three fucking days—you can take your load of two towels to the goddamned Laundromat on the corner if they can't wait! That's why I bought a washer and dryer! So I could use them whenever I want to! I don't want you touching my clothes!"

"But it would be silly to spend the money to wash two towels at the Laundromat."

"So if you want to save that money, Maureen, you need to be more considerate of my needs. You use my machines twenty-four seven. They're running practically day and night. You're going to wear them out. Are you going to replace them when you do?"

"You said I could use them."

"Okay, let me explain this to you one more time. I have another load of clothes to do. You are not to touch the goddamned washer and dryer until all of my clothes are finished. Is that understood?"

"It's not fair, but okay."

"In fact, I don't want you using my washer and dryer again today. Tomorrow's fine. But today, no."

"Okay." She nodded and shut the door.

❖

"I'm surprised you were able to hold your temper. That must have been incredibly frustrating."

I laughed. "You have no idea. It was like there was a synapse in her brain that wasn't firing, you know? It was like in her mind I was being an ass by trying to restrict her access, I was being unfair and unreasonable. But I was able to get my clothes washed. Later on that night, I was actually feeling a little guilty about the whole thing, and I decided to apologize if I was rude the next time I saw her."

"That was really nice of you."

"I'm a nice guy. But before I saw her again, Bill stopped by that night to talk to me. He'd been drinking. I'd noticed him walking around outside before with a beer or a drink in his hand, but I'd never thought much about it. It was about nine o'clock, and I was upstairs…"

❖

I came running down the stairs. "I'm coming!" I shouted. Someone was pounding on my door, hard angry knocks. I unlatched the door and swung it open. "Bill! What are—"

He reeked of alcohol, and his eyes were half-closed. "Can I talk to you?"

"Sure, I guess. Come in." I shut the door behind him. He plopped down on my love seat. I crossed my arms and leaned against the door. "What can I do for you, Bill?"

"Hear you had a little run-in with the wife today." He laughed. "You've never been married, have you?"

"I was."

"Me, I always need a wife. They keep dying on me, though. When the last one died—it was kind of unexpected, kind of fast, dropped dead right out of nowhere—I wasn't sure what I was going to do. Then I found Maureen, and I married her. Don't know what I'm going to do when she's gone. Guess I'll find another one."

"I don't really—"

"I know she's a bit much, Joe, but she's old. She's not quite right in the head, you know. It's starting to go on her. And being here while I work on the house is hard on her, you know. Back up in Monroe, she'd watch her stories and *Oprah* all day while I was working. Here she ain't got nothing to do. We don't got a TV here. So she cleans. She don't like to be idle—idle hands and the devil, you know how that goes, don't you, Joe?"

"Yes, I've heard that before. But I don't see—"

"So she's a little bit nuts about the laundry. Can't you cut her a break?"

"Bill, I don't care if she does laundry from sunrise to sundown. Every day, all day, I don't care. But when I need to do mine, she needs to let me. And I don't have a lot of free time—so it's enormously frustrating—"

"I know, Joe. That woman would try Job, I swear to God. There are times when I just want to give her a good smack, see if that'll shake the brains free a little, knock some sense into her. But you got to remember she's an old woman. Her brain don't work like it used to. And doing the laundry—keeping busy—makes her happy. And that makes me happy."

"Like I said, Bill, I don't care if she uses the washer—"

"She can't be hauling the laundry up to the corner. She's old, Joe. And if she can't keep busy she won't be happy here. And if she's not happy here, I'm not going to be happy here. And then we're going to have to go back to Monroe, if you catch my meaning."

"I think I do."

"And then Mildred's going to have to find another contractor. And that ain't going to be easy—there's more work here in New Orleans than there are contractors. No telling how long it's going to take Mildred to find another contractor. And you're not happy living here in the carriage house, are you?" He got up and walked over to me, leaning into me until his face was inches from mine. The sour alcohol on his breath made me a little queasy.

"No, I'm not."

"So that's just going to delay your getting back into your house, isn't it?"

In that moment, I would have gladly killed him. "I understand what you're getting at, Bill."

"Good!" He clapped me on the back, his face wreathed in a smile. "I'm glad we've come to a kind of understanding. You want to come over for a drink?"

"No."

"You sure?"

"Quite sure."

I shut the door behind him.

❖

"So, basically, he was blackmailing you?"

"Exactly. I had to let her do as she goddamned well pleased with my washer and dryer, and just suck it up and not say anything, or he'd quit. And you know as well as I do it could have taken months before Mildred could find someone else to work on the house."

"Contractors are scum."

"They certainly are! Did you have problems with one?"

"I lived in New Orleans East. There was no saving my house. I took the insurance money and sold it as is. But in my line of work— well, let's just say there are a few honest contractors out there doing good work, and a lot of criminals who should be strung up. The stories I could tell you—"

"I'm sure. I read about some of the scams in the paper the other day. Really makes you wonder what the world's coming to, doesn't it? You sure you don't want some coffee?" I got up and refilled my cup, emptying the pot. "I can make more—it won't take two seconds."

"No, I've had plenty today." She winked at me. "Trust me."

I sat back down in my easy chair. "So, no, it really doesn't surprise me he'd kill her, you know. Like I said, she was a pain in the ass. And he drank so much…"

"Did you ever talk to Mrs. Savage about the situation?"

"I did a few times, and she was sympathetic, but she never did anything about it." I shook my head with a sad little laugh. "I can't hardly blame her. I mean, here I was living under my own roof, really, while she and her husband were staying with friends. I know she just wanted to get back on the property as soon as she could…who wouldn't? She just would tell me to be patient, she'd have a chat with them, but nothing ever changed, you know? I even tried setting up a schedule. I sat down with her and told her she could do the laundry every day, but I would do mine on Wednesday and she would have to respect that."

"More than reasonable, I think."

"Yeah, you'd think, wouldn't you? But she was crazy. Absolutely crazy. After we set the schedule, the next Wednesday morning I got up and went over there, and sure enough, she had a load going in the washer. I thought my head would explode."

"You're kidding!"

"I wish I was. I was so angry I was ready to kill them both." I laughed, and gave her a broad wink. "I guess I shouldn't say that to a cop."

"Should I consider you a suspect, Mr. Spencer?" She smiled at me.

"Like I'd kill someone over using my washing machine!"

"You'd be surprised what will push someone to kill…but no, at this moment you're not a suspect. It seems pretty cut and dried to me. Did you hear them arguing last night?"

"No, like I said, I've gotten used to turning the television up really loud, so I wouldn't hear them."

"Do you know what they used to argue about?"

"No, I mean, I never could make out what they were saying. All I heard was the noise—and it was definitely angry noise, if you know what I mean. His drinking and her—well, whatever it was—I always thought it was a potentially lethal combination."

"What time did you go to bed last night?"

"I guess it was around ten thirty, or just after. I always watch *The Daily Show* before I go to sleep. What time did he," I swallowed, "you know?"

She didn't answer my question. "How did they seem yesterday to you?"

"I didn't really talk to either of them…Maureen did stop by for a moment."

There was a frantic look on her face when I opened the door. She was clearly agitated, looking from side to side, shifting her weight from one foot to the other. She was wringing a dish towel in her hands. "Why hello, Maureen." I smiled at her. "Is everything okay?"

"Where is my laundry?" Her voice shook.

"How would I know?"

"I took a load over there half an hour ago and it's not there!"

"Maureen, dear, are you sure?"

"Joe, I took a load of towels over this morning, I know I did. I remember going over there…"

"Then where could it have gone?"

"I was hoping you knew."

"How would I know, Maureen? I haven't been over there since two days ago when Bill showed me how the place was coming along."

"You're sure you don't know?"

"No, I don't, Maureen. Just like the other day when you accidentally put the red dye in with your whites."

"I don't remember doing that…why would I do that?"

"I don't know, Maureen. It doesn't make any sense. I guess you were just a little confused," I said soothingly.

She nodded. "Confused. I've been really confused lately."

"Why don't you go lie down for a little while and get some rest?"

"That—that might be a good idea."

"Why don't you just go take a nap and forget about it?"

"Oh, oh, okay."

I shut the door and smiled to myself. "Stupid bitch," I said to myself as I walked behind a stack of boxes. I picked up Maureen's laundry basket—two towels—and walked back over to my door. It was almost too easy, I reflected, as I opened the door and walked around to the front of the house. Bill was sawing some plywood, set up on two sawhorses. "Bill?"

Bill stopped the saw and smiled. "Oh, hi there, Joe." His eyebrows came together. "Why you bringing your laundry around to the front?"

"It's happened again, Bill." I set the laundry basket down on the ground. "This isn't my laundry, it's yours."

"What happened this time?"

"Maureen just came by, extremely upset, because her laundry had disappeared. She said she took the load over and put it in the washer, but when she went back to put it in the dryer it was gone. She thought maybe I knew what happened to it."

"Go on."

"So I told her to go lie down, and I went over to the laundry room. Bill, the basket was sitting there on top of the washer. If it was a snake it would have bit her."

"Dear God."

"It's getting worse, Bill. I mean, what's going to happen next? Is she going to leave the stove on when she goes to the grocery store?"

"She wouldn't do that," he whispered.

"Well, a week ago she wasn't putting red dye in with the whites, either. I had to run three cycles of bleach through the washer to get that dye out, Bill. She's not getting better, and you know it. She needs help. Aren't you afraid what might happen if you go to the hardware store or the lumberyard and leave her here alone?"

"I—"

"I mean, it was one thing when she was just forgetting things. But this is really serious." I sighed. "Well, I've said my piece. I'll leave the laundry basket where I found it."

❖

"So, she was getting even more forgetful?"

"I guess he just lost patience with her one last time. It's sad, just terrible." I got up to answer the door. I shrugged as I turned the knob. "She really went downhill quickly, detective." I opened the door and smiled. "Detective Tujague, was it?"

"That's right."

"Come in. You want to speak to Detective Casanova?"

"Actually, I want to ask you something."

"Me? All right."

"Did you see Dufour last night?"

"No. I was just telling Detective Casanova about the last time I saw him. It was about two or three yesterday afternoon. I can't be more specific than that, I'm sorry. Why do you ask?"

"Dufour says that he came over here last night and you two had drinks together and talked about the situation with his wife. He got tired and you helped him back to his apartment, and that's the last thing he remembers before waking up this morning next to his wife's corpse."

"I'm sorry, but he's obviously mistaken. I don't drink. So he doesn't remember killing her?"

"Well, that's his story. You're certain he wasn't here?"

"I couldn't be more certain. I don't drink. You can do a blood alcohol test on me if you like. But he was not here last night."

"Okay, thanks. Venus?"

"That's about all I need. Thank you so much for your time, Mr. Spencer."

"If I can be of any help—"

"We will need you to come down to the station at some point and make a statement."

"Just let me know when."

"Thank you, Mr. Spencer." Venus smiled at me as she walked outside. "I really appreciate your help."

I closed the door and leaned against it. I exhaled.

They didn't suspect a thing.

❖

Bill had come over, around nine thirty. I invited him in, and he took a seat on the love seat. He was carrying a plastic go-cup.

"Hi, Bill. How is she?"

"She was almost hysterical. When she gets like that, man, she really drives me to drink. I told her to take one of her goddamned pills and lay down, she was giving me a headache."

"What are you drinking?"

"Whiskey. Tonight's a whiskey night. Man, that was a tough one. After she went to sleep I called her daughter. That one's a real bitch. Didn't want to hear a word I was saying. Wants to fly out here and see for herself. I told her I don't need her permission to put Maureen in a facility, thank you very much, and to try to keep a civil tongue in her goddamned head. Just like her mother, doesn't know her place. No wonder that one couldn't keep a man."

"I'm real sorry about all of this, Bill."

"Well, you know, Joe, that's mighty kind of you to say. I know you had some trouble dealing with the woman, and I want you to know how much I appreciate your going out of your way to keep her happy. You didn't have to do that."

"Well, I couldn't have you quit the job before the house is finished."

"Oh, I would have never done that. I might have sent her back up to Monroe, but I believe a man always finishes what he started. Once I give my word, I don't go back on it."

I stared at him. "Well, you sure had me fooled, Bill!" I somehow managed to keep my voice friendly and light.

All these weeks—all of this frustration and irritation, that I've put up with—for nothing?

He laughed. "Just trying to keep the peace and make the best of a bad situation. I do appreciate everything you've done though in the last few days. She really went downhill fast."

"Went?"

"What's that?"

"Nothing. Here, let me refill your drink."

"I thought you didn't drink."

"I always keep good liquor around—just because I don't have a drink doesn't mean everyone else has to be on the wagon."

"Say, that's some good stuff!"

"I always believe if you're going to get something, get the best." I put his cup down on the counter and reached up for the Wild Turkey bottle.

And right there, sitting on a lower shelf, were the sleeping pills.

They'd been prescribed for me after the storm.

I shook out two of the capsules and opened them, pouring them into the bottom of his cup. I smiled.

It was all falling into place.

I put some ice in his cup and poured the Wild Turkey over it, watching as the granules dissolved into the alcohol. I smiled and carried the cup back over to him. "There you go, Bill."

"Thank you." He took a long drink. "Ah, that's some good stuff. I never get much chance to drink the good stuff."

"So, you think she's going to have to go into a facility?"

"Like you said, I can't watch her all day." He sighed. "I can't be without a wife, Joe."

"But—"

"I don't know what to do. I guess I'll have to divorce her. Damn. I never thought I'd see the day come when I'd be getting a divorce."

"All your other wives have died?"

He yawned. "Yes, I've put them all in the ground. I figured I'd be burying Maureen, too—but this? Sorry," he yawned again, "I don't know why I'm so sleepy all of a sudden."

"You've had a draining day—all that work on the house, and Maureen…"

"Yeah. I'm sorry, Joe, I guess I'd best be getting to bed." He fell back against the back of the love seat. "I don't know what's wrong with me."

"Let me help you up." I helped him to his feet and put his arm over my shoulders. He reeked of whiskey and sour sweat. "Just lean on me, Bill, and we'll just get you to bed."

"I…don't…understand…why…that…whiskey…hit…me…so…hard…"

"Don't worry about it. It happens to everyone."

"I can…barely…keep…my…eyes…open…"

He was practically dead weight by the time I got him back inside the main house. I eased him down onto the sofa. His mouth fell open and he started snoring.

I stared down at him contemptuously.

"Idiot."

All I'd wanted was for her to be put away. I wanted her and her insane laundry fetish gone, out of my life for good.

It would be so easy, I thought, looking down at his open mouth, to just put a pillow over his face—

In the other room, Maureen gurgled in her sleep.

I turned away from him and walked over to the bedroom door.

She was on top of the covers, sleeping on her back in a floral nightgown. Her glasses were on the nightstand next to the bed.

I looked back at Bill on the couch.

I never go back on my word, I heard him saying in my head again.

I smiled.

I walked over to the bed and looked down at her.

"Maureen? Maureen? Can you wake up for a minute?" I said softly, reaching down to shake her shoulder. "Maureen? Can you open your eyes?"

She shifted on the bed. "Go 'way, leave me alone." Her voice was drowsy.

"Can you open your eyes for me?"

They fluttered open, and she blinked at me, squinting. "Joe? What?"

"Bill had a little too much to drink and I had to help him home."

"Okay, thanks."

"Good-bye, Maureen."

I reached down and my hands closed around her throat.

She thrashed against me, but I put my weight behind my hands.

And finally, she stopped.

I let go of her throat and smiled down at her. "You look so peaceful, Maureen." I went back to my own apartment.

❖

From my living room window, I watched them lead Joe away in handcuffs.

He looked upset, confused.

They always say that criminals are stupid. I like to believe only stupid criminals get caught.

I hadn't planned on killing her. No, all I wanted to do was get rid of her, have her locked up in a home someplace where she'd never bother me again.

But it all just fell into my lap, and who am I to say no to opportunity?

And he was just as bad as she was, wasn't he?

All that time, he knew she was making my life hell and didn't do a fucking thing about it—actually, he *helped* her.

But to give him credit, he'd been bluffing and I'd been afraid to call him on it.

But I won the hand, didn't I?

A strangled wife, a hungover husband reeking of whiskey? And the sad neighbor, telling the terrible story of how they fought almost every night, yelling and screaming at each other? "No, Officer, he was never here." His word against mine—and really, what motive did I have for killing his stupid old wife? Like I told Detective Casanova, no one would kill someone over a washing machine.

Stupid annoying old bitch.

And that's that. They have him dead to rights, anything he tries to say will just be seen as a lie calculated to get him out of a murder rap.

Stupid, stupid people.

Note to self: Never, ever let someone use your washing machine again. Ever.

MURDER ON THE MIDWAY
JEFFREY RICKER

Summer in St. Louis was three months of misery. During the day, the sun tried to burn you to a crisp. If that failed, at night the humidity tried to steam you alive. It was like the city wanted you dead.

The weather didn't kill Jacob Anderson, but he was still just as dead.

He was lying face-down in the middle of the carnival that had taken up residence on the parking lot of the Unitarian Church. They'd done this for the past several years, raising money for Building Our Youth, the local gay support group that was Jacob's primary mission in life.

Cause of death: blunt force trauma to the back of the head from the mallet used in the Test Your Strength booth. Whoever killed Jacob probably could have made the bell ring.

It was an undignified end for someone always trumpeted in the media as a pillar of the GLBT community, always willing to lend support and hard work for a good cause—especially if it involved helping rejected gay teens and young adults. It didn't take long for the phrase "hate crime" to get tossed around. The city wasn't exactly known for its tolerance.

Sam Page was surprised when Milo Leveque came into his office two days later to discuss the case.

Milo was one of St. Louis's A-list gays. Independently wealthy and semi-retired after making some incredible—and incredibly well-timed—real estate deals a few years earlier, he now devoted himself to civic life. He was seen at all of the right art gallery openings, served on the boards of Food Outreach and Effort for AIDS, gave money to the cultural bulwarks of the city, and helped plan A Tasteful Affair every year. He helped raise money for Pride St. Louis even though he never set foot in the park for the sweltering summer festival.

Maybe he didn't want the heat and humidity of St. Louis to kill him.

He was also blond and fit, and Sam would have paid attention to him even if he wasn't a potential client and loaded to the gills.

"Someone is threatening me," Milo said, sitting down in Sam's shabby office. "They think I know something about why Jacob was killed, and they want me to keep quiet about it."

"What makes you think that?"

Milo reached into his front pocket and pulled out his phone. He flipped it open, pressed a few buttons, and handed it to Sam. It was a cheap phone, which surprised Sam. Milo seemed like the sort of person who would be first in line to get the latest smartphone—well, the sort of person who'd pay someone to stand in line for him.

It was a text message, the sender's number blocked. *Keep your mouth shut. I've still got a few swings left. Just ask Jacob. Oh, wait…*

Sam snapped the phone shut and handed it back.

"Any idea what they think you know?"

Milo shook his head. "I have no idea."

Sam narrowed his eyes. "If you know something and want me to help you, you'd better tell me. I don't like it when clients only tell me half the story."

Milo leaned forward. "So you'll take my case?"

Sam waited long enough to instill a hint of doubt. "Nicely played, Mr. Leveque. And yes, I'll take the case."

"Do you think you can trace that text message?"

"Obviously, you don't want to go to the police." Sam shrugged. "If the sender had any sense, he used one of those pay-as-you-go phones. Or sent it anonymously over the Web. Next to impossible to trace."

"But not impossible, Mr. Page."

"I'll give it a shot." Sam picked up a pen and positioned a legal pad in front of him. He was not a note taker, but he found it helped to have props—clients liked that. Besides, putting something in his hand kept him from wanting to reach for a cigarette. "So," he asked, "do you think Jacob's murder was a hate crime?"

Milo shook his head and smiled, but said nothing.

"Spit it out, Mr. Leveque. There's only one thing I require from my clients: complete honesty."

"Please, call me Milo. And how often do you get complete honesty from your clients?"

Sam ignored the question. "So tell me why you think Jacob was murdered."

Milo leaned back again and put his hands behind his head. His biceps flexed impressively. He clearly devoted himself to both civic *and* gym life. "Jacob got his biggest charitable donations by using his best asset: his ass."

"Excuse me?"

Milo smiled. "Turn on your computer."

Sam typed in a URL Milo gave him, and soon he was staring at a profile on a site called rentboy.com. A photo of a lean, muscular, and almost completely naked Jacob Anderson smiled seductively at him. He described himself as being three years younger than he really was at his time of death and a "nonstop pig bottom who'll let you do anything you want."

Charming.

"This still doesn't explain why someone would want to kill him," Sam said.

Milo rolled his eyes. "Jacob specialized in wealthy, closeted clientele. People who had certain tastes, but didn't want them widely known. He saw to it such...*tastes* found expression."

Sam smiled at Milo's delicate euphemism. "Go on."

"Sometimes, he found his clients were prepared to pay to keep their tastes private. Jacob sometimes offered a visual incentive to open their checkbooks."

Blackmail. Now there, Sam thought, was a reason for murder. "Pictures?"

"Videos. Easier to set up and oh so much more persuasive."

"Were you one of Jacob's clients?"

Milo didn't answer at first. "I know what you're thinking," Milo said. "I was stupid to get involved, and would be even more stupid to admit it."

"I don't judge."

"Everyone does, Mr. Page. You'll just have to believe me. Jacob may have been doing a lot of things to me, but blackmail wasn't one of them. I want you to find out who killed him because I don't think the police will." He leaned forward and placed his hand over Sam's. "Please."

Sam stared at their hands for a moment, and turned his over in Milo's palm to end with a handshake. "I'll do my best, Mr. Leveque."

"Please, call me Milo."

"Right. Milo."

❖

Was Milo really motivated by a desire for justice? Sam doubted it. He also couldn't figure out why someone who looked like Milo would have to pay for sex, unless he was into something truly twisted that no one would do for free. Even if that were the case, such things usually found their own level in a way that didn't involve a financial transaction.

That meant something else was the driving factor behind Milo's hiring him, but Sam hadn't yet figured that out. Maybe Milo wanted to hide the fact he was sleeping with a hustler, even if he was a hustler for noble reasons. And yet he'd readily admitted it to Sam, and didn't seem all that ashamed about it. So what was he hiding? All Sam knew was he'd gotten used to people lying to him. Milo was likely no exception.

Still, Sam had to let himself hope every once in a while.

In parting, Milo had given Sam a key to Jacob's apartment. That he *had* one raised Sam's curiosity, but he didn't pursue it for the moment because he wanted to see the place with his own eyes.

Since the murder had occurred elsewhere, the police hadn't cordoned it off as a crime scene. Sam suspected plenty of illicit if not downright illegal things had happened there, if not murder.

It was the upstairs unit of a two-family house in south city, a few blocks south of Tower Grove Park. In this part of town, a nice block might be surrounded by a block or two of sketchville. Jacob's was one of the nice blocks, mostly single-family houses and tall, sheltering trees. The two-family was nestled in the middle of the block. Jacob's downstairs neighbor didn't appear to be home.

Sam wasn't alone, though. He opened the front door and looked up the stairs. A man peered over the landing. He regarded Sam through narrowed eyes, one hand on the railing, the other out of sight. Another face peered around the corner, only this one was about nine inches off the floor, covered in black fur, and had whiskers.

"Who are you?" the man asked.

Unable to see the man's other hand, Sam held up one of his own while he carefully reached for his wallet. "I'm a private investigator

looking into Mr. Anderson's death." Sam climbed the stairs far enough
to hand his business card to the man. "Are you a friend of Jacob's?"

When he took the card, Sam could see what the man was holding
in his other hand. It was just a can opener. The black cat descended the
stairs and proceeded to rub against Sam's ankles.

"Hello, who's this?" Sam knelt and scratched behind the cat's
ears.

"That's Nero. I'm Rick."

"You're Jacob's…" Sam let his voice trail off.

Rick shook his head. "Friend. I figured everyone would forget
about Nero, so I've been looking after him ever since…" Now it was
Rick's turn to let the thought trail off. He rattled the can opener, and
Nero came bounding back upstairs. To Sam, Rick said, "Come on up.
I need to feed him."

Sam followed. At the top of the stairs Sam found himself in the
living room. Nero followed Rick into the small galley kitchen at the
back. In the living room were pictures of Jacob where he showed his
face and actually wore clothing. In all of them he was usually smiling
and in the middle of a large group of people. The apartment seemed
pretty standard for a young—but not *too* young—gay man who didn't
make much money working in the not-for-profit arena: small, tidy,
sparsely but tastefully decorated.

"So, who hired you?" Rick asked.

"Actually, that's not something I can—"

"It was probably that Milo guy, wasn't it? He came around a lot.
Judging by his ride, I'm pretty sure he's loaded, right?"

Sam raised his eyebrows. "You must live close by if you know
about people's comings and goings."

"I live across the street, but Jacob talked about him all the time.
Out of all the guys, I think he liked him best."

"So you knew what Jacob…"

"That he was a hustler-slash-blackmailer for charity? Yeah. And
don't even get me started on how many times we argued about that. I
told him it was dangerous." He set Nero's bowl on the floor. "Wish I
hadn't been right."

"Have the police been by?" Sam was sure they had, but maybe
Rick would know something he didn't. He meandered into the master
bedroom. The furniture was simple, Scandinavian in style but nicer
than Ikea. In other words, how most gay men decorated. The bed was
neatly made.

"Yeah," Rick said. "Interviewed the neighbor downstairs and left after a couple hours."

"They didn't talk to you?"

He shook his head. "I stayed across the street until they left."

"They take his computer?"

"Why do you ask?"

Sam didn't answer. Of course they took the computer. The second bedroom was set up as an office and had a desk, printer, and other peripherals, but no desktop or laptop. He doubted there was much left to find in the apartment. He sat on the bed.

"Ever see any of his other clients?"

Rick shook his head. "Milo was Jacob's only in-call. Otherwise he was strictly out-calls only."

"How much did you know about what Jacob was up to?"

Rick shrugged and sat on the other side of the bed. "I volunteer at Building Our Youth, mostly doing stuff around the office. Data entry, that kind of thing. Jacob was reeling in a lot of big anonymous donations, and I asked him how Building Our Youth managed to get so lucky. He said something about it being more than luck, and eventually the whole story came out."

Finished with his dinner, Nero came into the bedroom and jumped on the bed. Rick petted him absentmindedly. "Jacob introduced me to Milo when he came to pick up Jacob once. Nice car, good-looking, but kind of snobby. I guess you know that since you're working for him, right?"

Sam smiled. "I'm thinking Jacob's killer might be one of the donors he was blackmailing."

Rick frowned. "The paper said it was a hate crime. I mean, the carnival was a benefit for Building Our Youth." Rick smirked and looked down. "The carnival was his idea. Jacob told me once he had a thing for carnies. He said his fantasy was to get taken from behind while playing skee ball."

"Sounds like Jacob was a man of odd tastes," Sam said.

"I *know*," Rick said. "I have no clue why he told me some of the things he did. I can't imagine telling anyone, even my closest friend, some of that stuff."

"Maybe he felt a little safer knowing that someone was aware of what he was up to. In case something bad happened," Sam said.

Rick put his arms around Nero and hugged the cat. "For all the good it did."

"You miss him, don't you?" Sam ventured.

Rick nodded. "He was hard to figure out, though. Sometimes I think he was my closest friend, and other times I think I hardly knew him. I couldn't tell you where he grew up or what his favorite color was, but he told me all this other stuff. It's weird thinking he's gone for good." Rick shrugged. "The least I can do is look after his cat until his family comes to take care of his funeral arrangements."

"Maybe you can still help find out who's responsible for this."

Releasing the cat from his embrace, Rick cocked his head at Sam. "Well, if you want, I could give you a list of Building Our Youth's major donors. That'd help, wouldn't it?"

"I thought they were anonymous donors," Sam said.

Rick scoffed. "Please. They just didn't want to be acknowledged publicly. They might have been getting blackmailed, but if they can get a deduction for their hush money, they'll claim it."

A lead at last. Thank God. "If you can get that for me, it would be a good start. If we knew who his escort clients were, we could compare the two lists of names and see if there are any matches, and we might solve this faster."

Rick narrowed his eyes. "Solve for your client, you mean. Not exactly for justice."

"Justice is the police's job, not mine," Sam said. "That doesn't mean I don't care, but I do have to remember who's paying my fee."

"Just like Jacob." Rick smiled without humor and got up from the bed. "I have something you'll want to see."

The laptop, wrapped in a plastic bag, was hidden in the bathroom linen closet, behind a removable panel allowing access to the bathtub plumbing. Rick took it out of the plastic bag and placed it in Sam's lap.

"He was really paranoid about anyone getting their hands on it," Rick said. "I can only assume he kept records of his clients on it."

Sam could barely resist the urge to tuck it under his arm and run out of the apartment. "The police would shit themselves if they knew we had this."

"Then don't tell them." Rick smiled. "No one knows about this, just you and me."

Sam started to open it, but Rick put his hands on the lid.

"Not here. If you don't mind. I don't want to see anything that would make me remember him differently."

Outside, Sam lingered for a moment on the sidewalk. Rick had given him a bag to carry the laptop, and he shifted it from one shoulder to the other. The heat was relentless, and he broke a sweat just standing there. The trees offered futile shade that gave no relief and made the pavement look bruised.

Sam was missing something. He was convinced of that.

What he wasn't missing: He was standing in the middle of the sidewalk with the only evidence, as far as he knew, to an unsolved murder.

❖

Sam wasn't sure what he was hoping to find on the laptop. It didn't seem like there was a whole lot to be found. The messages in Jacob's in-box were mostly from family—his mother wondered when he was coming to visit. His photos were mostly from work events, the office, or his cat, Nero. *Do all lives look this pathetic and small after the fact?* In one picture, Jacob held the camera out in front of him while with his other hand he cradled Nero, who was at best indifferent to the effort. That was the worst, and Sam almost found himself feeling sorry for the little dead man-whore with the heart of gold who was robbing from the rich and closeted to give to the poor and newly out. Mostly, he pitied the cat.

Then he opened Jacob's Web browser and called up the escort site Jacob had used. Fortunately for Sam, Jacob was either forgetful or lazy: He'd saved the username and password in the browser. With a click, Sam was suddenly paging through Jacob's private photos. If his default profile pic left little to the imagination, these closed the gap between little and nothing. He also had access to Jacob's website messages. Those catalogued his arrangements with a variety of clients.

This gave Sam an idea, and he started looking through the browser's history and bookmarks. By the time he was done, he realized Jacob didn't keep anything at all on the laptop itself, but there was plenty to be found. And he had a pretty good idea of who his suspects were.

❖

Sam met Milo in the café downstairs from Milo's office.

"Have you had any luck yet?" Milo asked. He slid into the booth across from Sam.

"I have his laptop, but so far I haven't found anything of value on it." Sam sipped from his large black coffee. He was not strictly lying. "If we keep poking our noses into this case, we're going to attract police attention. I have a few friends in the department. They don't take kindly to people getting in the way of their investigation."

"I think we've already attracted attention." Milo took out his cell phone and showed the screen to Sam. It was another threatening text message: *A private dick will only get you fucked.*

Sam looked up. "How the hell do they know about me?"

"They must have seen me go to your office. Which explains why I get the feeling someone's following me."

Sam glanced around the coffee shop. "Like the big guy in the corner who's been watching us this entire time?"

Milo looked over his shoulder. "Not him. That's Simon. I hired him for private security with all this going on. I told him he probably shouldn't sit with us."

"He should probably stop staring at us if he wants to be inconspicuous," Sam muttered. Simon looked like he'd just escaped from the ape house at the zoo. "Look, I'll keep trying to find something on the laptop, but if that fails, I may have to start talking to other people. I know you want to keep this quiet…"

"Very. The people Jacob was blackmailing don't want word of this to spread."

"You know the people he was blackmailing are the likeliest suspects, right?"

"Of course. But I know these people. They wouldn't do that sort of thing."

Sam doubted that. People with money eventually pushed the limits of what they could get away with. What was Milo trying to get away with? His own reputation, maybe?

Then Rick called later that afternoon and said he was being followed.

"There was a black car parked out in front of the house this morning," he said. "It was also outside my office when I went to lunch."

"You sure it was the same car?" Sam asked.

"I didn't see the license plate, but it was the same make and model, a Lincoln Town Car."

"Get the plate number next time," Sam said. "If whoever's driving is connected with the murder, we could use that."

Rick laughed. "Thanks, I'm touched by your concern. If I get run down in the street, I'll be sure to write the license number in my own blood."

"Sorry. I'm on the clock."

"I doubt you're ever off the clock, Mr. Page."

"Please. Sam."

"Okay, Sam. I want you to find out who killed Jacob, too. Have you had any luck?"

"Kind of but not really. I know who Jacob's last clients were, but my client's worried about anyone getting wind of what was going on. I don't see how I can narrow down the list of suspects without contacting them."

"Which Milo doesn't want you to do."

"Exactly."

"Come to my apartment tonight," Rick said. "Bring the laptop. I'll have something for you that should make your job easier."

❖

Rick handed Sam a black thumb drive when he opened the door. "It's an Excel file," he said. "Names, dates of donations, amounts. The most recent, highest-level donors to Building Our Youth. All solicited by Jacob. Some of them have donated several times over the past few months."

"I don't doubt it," Sam said. He sat at Rick's kitchen table with the laptop open between them. He plugged in the drive and opened the file. "You know, you could have just e-mailed this to me."

"I know." He sat with his arms crossed and looked as if he were trying to make himself as small as possible. He dropped his chin and spoke into his chest. "It just seemed like something I should deliver in person."

Sam scrolled through the names. There was the married vice president at Steel Financial donating a thousand dollars. A cheap price to pay to keep quiet his desire to be tied up and have Jacob piss on him. There was also the alderman and restaurant owner whose predilections leaned toward hot wax and unsafe sex.

"What I don't get," Rick said after listening to Sam relay some of this information, "is how they all connected with Jacob like this."

Sam shrugged. "Just lucky, I guess."

"Some luck," Rick said. "Do you think there's any chance this won't get out? About Jacob, I mean."

Sam shook his head. "Even if no one figures out for sure who his clients were, someone will eventually find his profile and make the connection. You can't see his face, but someone will connect the dots. You get naked on the Internet, someone's bound to tell your mom."

"Oh, God." Rick rested his forehead in his palms. "Jacob's mother is going to be here this Friday. What do I tell her?"

"Try the truth."

"That her son was a whore?" Rick slumped in his chair.

"Try telling her he was your friend and you cared about him, and he tried to do good and help a lot of people."

Rick crossed his arms. "That's really touching. I don't think you believe a damn word of it."

Sam smiled. "The question is, do you?"

Suddenly, Rick leaned over the table, pushing the laptop shut with one hand as he used the other to draw Sam into a kiss. Sam wasn't sure he believed a damn bit of this sudden affection either. It had been such a long time, though, since he'd been with anyone that he was inclined just to go along with it.

He had a feeling he'd regret it later.

❖

The sheets pooled at the foot of the bed. Rick had just rolled off Sam and sprawled next to him. The ceiling fan drew a lazy circle above them.

"I didn't see that coming," Sam said once he'd caught his breath.

Rick sat up and looked at Sam. "I hope that doesn't mean you didn't enjoy it."

"No, you were great. It's just I'm usually not this lucky."

"Maybe luck didn't have anything to do with it."

That's what I'm afraid of, Sam thought. Before he could answer, he heard glass breaking outside.

"What was that?" Rick was the first one out of bed. He walked over to the window and drew the slats of the blinds apart. "Holy shit. Someone's breaking into Jacob's apartment."

I knew my lucky streak couldn't last. Sam was on his feet and into his jeans by the time Rick turned around.

"Where are you going?"

"To see who's breaking and entering. Give me your key."

"Do you have anything you can use as a weapon?"

Sam didn't have a gun. He had a permit, but he didn't like carrying guns. They were loud and heavy and always made a bigger mess than they cleaned up. He did stop at his car for his Maglite. He used the hefty blue baton more often as a blunt instrument than a flashlight.

Sam also noted the black Town Car parked behind his. It hadn't been there earlier. He placed his hand on the hood—still warm. He memorized the plate number.

Whoever broke in wasn't trying to hide that fact. They'd left the front door ajar, the pane of glass above the doorknob partly broken out. Sam nudged the door open wider and crept inside. He took each step with care, trying to remember if any of the stairs creaked.

From the bedroom he heard drawers being pulled open and their contents dumped on the floor. Heavy footsteps moved toward the desk. More random clattering followed. As Sam tried to remember what was on the desk, the intruder clicked on the desk lamp. His back was to Sam, who was now backing toward the kitchen.

He was a big man. The broad expanse of his back blocked Sam's view of whatever he was rifling through on the desk. He paused, his shoulders sagged, and then with a sweep of his arm he cleared everything off the desk. At that point, Nero let out an outraged hiss and bolted from the bedroom, between Sam's feet and into the kitchen. Sam tried to turn but stumbled, tripped over his own feet, and slammed into the floor. Between getting the wind knocked out of him, the screaming pain in his ankle, and the dull crack of his head against the hardwood, he was dimly aware that he'd lost his grip on the flashlight.

Smooth, Page. Real smooth.

Sam lay there and waited for the worst—kick to the ribs, boot to the balls, or bullet to the back of the head. Luckily for him, the intruder bolted downstairs and out the front door. From outside, he heard a voice say, "I've got it. *Move*," followed by a revving engine and tires squealing down the street.

That was when Sam realized the break-in had never been the point.

Nero came out from wherever he was hiding and rubbed his chin against Sam's forehead. He meowed in that way cats have of making a meow sound like a question. Sam groaned and got to his feet.

"I'm okay, buddy," he said, looking down at Nero. "I think. I'm an idiot, but I'm okay."

When Sam got back to Rick's apartment, the laptop was gone. This time, the intruders had the presence of mind to close the front door behind them. Rick's body lay in the middle of the hallway. Blood had started to pool behind his ear, a look of perpetual surprise on his face. If he were still alive, Sam would have told him not to be so surprised at being betrayed. Sam certainly wasn't.

He retrieved his shirt and cell phone from the bedroom. He had to make a call he really wasn't looking forward to.

"Tarrant," a woman's clipped voice said. She'd picked up after the first ring.

"Are you working late or up early, Christine?"

She sighed before answering. "What do you want, Sammy? I'm assuming it's not good, whatever it is, since you're calling at"—she paused—"four thirty-eight in the morning."

Sam smiled. He'd always appreciated his friend's precision. "You're on the Anderson murder, right?"

"I would ask how you guessed, but then you know how my luck goes." A pause. "Why *do* you ask, anyway?"

Sam glanced over at Rick's body. "I think your luck's about to change."

❖

When Sam walked into Milo's office later that morning, he still hadn't slept. The circles under his eyes showed it. He'd showered briefly, dressed indifferently, and hadn't bothered to shave. Even so, he felt like he was holding four aces.

"I just wanted to let you know that the laptop doesn't matter."

Milo, to his credit, didn't miss a beat. "You couldn't find anything on it?"

"That's not what I mean. It was stolen last night. As you know."

"Page, what the hell are you talking about?"

"I'm talking about all the incriminating videos that your friends wanted to make sure disappeared. They're not on the laptop. But you already know that, too, since the police picked up your friend Simon about an hour ago. Guess what he had with him?"

Milo didn't answer. Sam pulled a thumb drive from his pocket and tossed it on Milo's desk. "The videos weren't on the laptop. Jacob used online file storage, which makes sense considering he transacted all his business online. Well, he closed the deal in person, of course. Or maybe he was worried about his laptop and all his files disappearing."

Milo glanced at the flash drive but didn't make any move to pick it up. "So you think I was involved in Jacob's death?"

"I knew you were using me, but I couldn't figure out what you were hoping I'd find. Then when you realized Rick just let me walk out of Jacob's apartment with the best piece of evidence the cops couldn't find, you must have gotten a little panicky and put the screws to him."

"And how did you connect me to Rick?"

"Not too hard, when you talk to people and actually listen to what they have to say. But I want to know what you said to Rick to get him to go along with your plan."

"Considering his main concern was his friend's reputation, it was easy. I told him I'd hired you to help keep things quiet, but I was worried you were planning to go to the police, or worse, the press. So I asked him to keep an eye on you and try to get the laptop back."

"So you had no idea Rick knew where the laptop was all along?"

For once, Milo looked surprised. "He did?"

"Hidden in Jacob's linen closet behind a maintenance panel. Guess Rick didn't trust you too much if he didn't share that bit of information. So was killing him your idea or just an unfortunate accident?"

Milo leaned forward in his chair. "Rick's dead?"

"Judging from your reaction, you're either a really good actor or Simon didn't mention that. Guess everything didn't go according to plan last night."

"I had nothing to do with that." Milo leaned back in his chair and crossed his arms. "And you still don't have any proof that I had anything to do with Jacob's murder."

Sam shook his head. "No, but once they finish dusting the mallet for fingerprints, it should be relatively easy to put the murder weapon in the right hands. Even if you paid him to, which is what I would guess if I had to."

"And why is that?"

"Because you don't have the guts to do your own dirty work."

Sam headed for the door, then turned back toward Milo. "By the way, here's your phone."

Sam tossed a cell phone on the desk. Instinctively, Milo reached for it, then drew back. He pulled an identical phone from his own pocket.

"Never turn your back on a private investigator. I switched them when I met you for coffee yesterday. I didn't peg you as a guy who'd use such a cheap phone. Imagine my surprise to find you sent the texts to yourself."

"I guess you think you're pretty clever, huh, Page?"

Sam shrugged. "I don't know about that. But I do know you're not as clever as you think."

Before Milo could retort, the intercom buzzed. "Sir," his receptionist said, "there's a Detective Tarrant from the police department here to see you."

Milo sighed. "Send him in, Kate."

"*Her*, sir."

Sam grinned. "Oh, she won't like that."

Sam walked out as Tarrant entered Milo's office. Two uniforms waited in the reception area. Tarrant gave Sam the barest of nods, aiming a stony gaze at Milo.

Sam knew he wouldn't get any credit from the police for helping solve either murder. He tried not to mind that. He'd already deposited Milo's check, and Tarrant had his statement about Rick's killing and his work for Milo. If he was lucky, she'd buy him a drink once it was wrapped up.

Meanwhile, he had to get home and feed his new cat.

The Thin Blue Line(s)
Max Reynolds

I didn't expect to kill her. I had thought about it, sure. Who wouldn't? Belinda Sondheim Walsh (and yes, she liked to let people think she was related to *that* Sondheim) was the most difficult writer I had ever dealt with in my fifteen years in the business since I'd landed here at—well, better I not mention where, given the circumstances—with my excessive number of useless literary degrees from superb colleges that had made my family proud, but put me in debt for life. And believe me, I'd dealt with some doozies among the writing class, especially some of the older poets I'd inherited when the ancient Mr. Edwin Godwin (a name straight out of Dickens that always made a fat *Pickwick Papers*–style giggle well up in my throat) had retired, saint that he must have been. *Good Lord.* I wonder how that poor man survived as long as he did. At least he had his cats. All seven named for (to my mind) barely readable poets. Poor man, poor cats.

But Belinda—she could have killed off even Godwin, although he'd dealt with her for a decade before I got her and it's my theory she was the final nail in his coffin that forced him into retirement. Belinda ("You may call me Belinda. Really, dear. It's okay." As if she were literary royalty and I her lowly subject.) was one of those writers who thinks all her words are golden. Their own little Rosetta Stone to *haute* literature. *Don't change a thing.* Not a letter, nor a comma. Don't remove one of the endlessly misplaced semicolons because she single-handedly was going to bring back the semicolon to prominence. In one book, no less—or so it seemed as I was lying on my sofa with my favorite little nub of a blue pencil because I still edit like that—iPad, WordPad, notepad, be damned.

Yes, she informed me when I inherited her (along with the chorus of elderly poets), "I don't get edited." Like my job was suddenly redundant in the truest sense of the term. I remember sitting having drinks with Amelia Watson, my friend over at—well, no need to name names since it's a revolving door in the world of the editorship—and slugging down two dirty martinis (or was it three?) in quick succession because only gin can take away the bad taste of a difficult author, that I was amazed no one had killed Miz Walsh yet.

And now she was dead.

But you need to understand why. She was really the killer, you see—she was butchering the language all over the place and yet, still thought her words were golden and untouchable. And when I say golden, I mean literally so. She expected her collected letters to end up not in one of the great little liberal arts colleges for which we are known nationwide, but to be in Fort Knox, big blocks of shimmery literary bullion or Troy ounces of genius.

Please.

And now there she was, lying on the floor in front of my desk, Auden's letter opener that I had been given by my charming Great-Aunt Tillie (who was straight out of a Capote short story) when I first became an editor up to the hilt just below Belinda's "I'm so perfectly thin as only the chicest of writers who aren't naturally French can be" sternum.

God, I was glad she was dead.

Or maybe not. Because the satisfaction of the deed is never balanced by the unpleasantness of the cleanup.

Now, in addition to my beloved Auden via Great-Aunt Tillie's letter opener, which I loved to use every day and which I regularly just fondled when I was thinking about what needed to be done next, in addition to that prized possession, I was also going to have to give up my gorgeous rug that had belonged to James Purdy (whose purloined paperbacks had helped teach me to be gay back in high school) that I had stayed up a whole weekend bidding for on eBay with God knows how many other gay men and literary obsessives.

Even dead, Belinda was causing me problems.

❖

It's never easy to say when a problem starts—in this case, Belinda Sondheim Walsh. And I am what we call in the literary trade an "unreliable narrator," so make of it all what you will. But here's how it seemed to me to have happened.

As I said, I inherited a lot of Mr. Godwin's authors. Some of

whom were indeed prized. But Belinda was not among those. She had
that kind of fussy yet plaintive literary talent that was still, regrettably,
in fashion. Her characters were wholly unlikable—Jonathan Franzen
and Philip Roth would have been proud—and her plotting was a little
on the rambling side. It's hard to know what had originally made her
famous. Some thought her writing funny. Others said it was "smart" and
had a "highly developed sense of irony"—I'm quoting here, naturally.
She had, one reviewer noted, "her finger on the pulse of the familial
zeitgeist."

Maybe. But I was the one with my fingers on Auden's letter
opener.

If I could have been objective, which I could not be, as you will
discover, I might have been able to see what critics liked about her. But
then, they didn't have to deal with her, did they?

And that was what led to the problems. See, Belinda was one of
those writers who likes her hand held line by line, yet doesn't want
a word changed. Hell—not a semicolon changed. *Listen to my every
word, but do not comment.* A dicey combo, if you ask me. Because I am
an editor through and through, and when I hear a dangling modifier or
a split infinitive or a pause where it doesn't belong or a string of ever-
more-florid adjectives or strained metaphors, my editing finger starts
to itch.

The first day I met Belinda, I disliked her on sight. Now the
rumors that all gay men hate women are nonsense, naturally. People
do know this now, I'm sure, but I feel it must be restated. It's actually
trite but true that some of my best friends are women. Amelia and I are
thick as the proverbial thieves, and Natalie Thompson and I have been
friends since college where we met in a ghastly semiotics class we were
both forced to take and suffered through together. And then there's M.J.
Collins—we used to share an apartment in the Bowery when we both
landed here in the publishing capital of the world and of course could
not afford the rents. She's my middle-of-the-night-sobbing go-to friend
for all seasons.

So, I like women well enough. I don't want to sleep with them,
however—and therein, pardon the pun, lay the problem.

Mr. Godwin had not warned me about Belinda, but then Godwin
was in his dotage, and if he'd ever had a sexual thought it was well
before I was born and Belinda would not have been the one to bring it
out in him, of that I am certain. I have a sneaking—and horrifying—
suspicion that his interests lay in those below the age of reason and that

he had sublimated all his dangerous Lewis Carroll–style proclivities into the language he loved as much as his cats.

But I digress, as they say in all the best nineteenth-century novels. *I digress.*

It's not that Belinda wasn't an attractive woman. She was, in that pinched, ultra-thin, studiously fashionably well-dressed, well-coiffed, well-manicured, and well-made-up kind of way. But my interests were decidedly different. Cam was my man of the moment—a long moment that was turning into way more than a moment—and I was smitten to the point of obsession with him. Cameron Walker was, first of all, British, and I have a thing for accents. Even stupid Brits sound smart—that accent does it every time. But beyond the accent, I am an unabashed Anglophile ever since that junior year abroad in which Natalie and I fucked our way through London, Oxford, Cambridge (oh, *Cambridge!*), and even a few weekends in Bath and Leeds, if you can imagine. Not together, of course—she liked tweedy men with tightly furled umbrellas and I liked a rather rougher trade in those days, E.M. Forster's *Maurice* and Evelyn Waugh's *Brideshead Revisited* having kinked up my early sexuality rather effectively. But my lust for the Brits never ebbed, even if I now preferred them suited as opposed to coveralled.

Anyway, back to Cam, my current drug of choice. We met at a literary event, naturally. He was tall and lanky in that British way, with the almost studied dark hair hanging into his eyes, and he was really right out of a promo page for Eton, except when he smiled he had good teeth; his mother being American, orthodontia had been *de rigeur* in his family.

I was representing my house; he, his. We shared *amuse bouche* and wine and he seemed as taken with me as I was with him and within a day—why did it take a whole day?—we were in his bed in his cramped but gorgeous Upper East Side apartment. And was it grand…and I don't just mean his, uh, *equipment*, although that was indeed grand, as well.

So when Belinda was handed over to me, I was only a month in with Cam, but it was solid. We hadn't said *commitment* per se, but we weren't fucking anyone else, either, and neither of us seemed to want to, which was certainly unusual for me, if not for him. And we had more in common than we had ever expected: books, ambition, we both loved music of all kinds, and we had a raw sexual intensity together that had actually kept us texting throughout the days until we got to the nights. Plus, as Amelia, Natalie, and M.J. all told me—we looked *great* together.

It was almost cozy, how well things were going. We'd met just after Valentine's Day and now it looked like we'd be having a first Christmas together with all the trimmings.

And then there was Belinda.

❖

I realize now, as I am pacing back and forth in what used to be Mr. Edwin Godwin's office here at—no, I won't say; it's such a small world, publishing—that Cameron is why I had to kill Belinda.

Let me say for the record that I am not bisexual. A lot of twenty- and thirty-somethings in New York and London are, of course. Playing the gender field has gotten excessively, even tediously popular. I'm not critical of that fence-jumping, but I have never been one of those. I like men and only men. Women are for friendship, men are for fucking. And it's a hard and fast rule—no pun intended—I have that I don't get involved, even briefly, with men who are testing the waters. I accidentally got a mad crush on a married man a few years back and it nearly killed me when he finally told me he was married and had three kids and an actual house in Connecticut. That was way too Cheever-esque for me. I practically asked for documentation of true gayness after that, even for a quick screw.

But Cam wasn't bisexual. He had female friends, too—publishing is one of the only fields with more women than men—but he didn't cross the fence sexually. So I felt safe. So very safe.

Until Belinda.

Yes, here's the part where the self-proclaimed unreliable narrator becomes the self-proclaimed homosexual stereotype. Brace yourselves.

❖

So there I was, sitting at my new desk, formerly the desk of Mr. Edwin Godwin, when Belinda Sondheim Walsh just breezed in on a cloud of Dior J'adore and sat herself in the odd little Queen Anne chair across from me that Godwin had thought an essential piece of literary paraphernalia.

"I'm Belinda Sondheim Walsh," she stated in a voice that was set at a pitch I couldn't quite place, but which I was certain might drive dogs mad. "You may call me Belinda. Really, dear. It's okay."

She crossed her legs with a studied elegance and tapped a finger on the edge of Mr. Edwin Godwin's—now *my*—desk in a way that made me wish I had one of those hard birchwood pointers that the nuns used to crack across our fingers when I was back in elementary school, my class seeming to have been the last in which corporal punishment was still accepted.

I stood, instead, and came around my desk in the best, most officiously gay literary editor way I could imagine—Maxwell Perkins back from the dead and very gay—and offered her my well-kept metrosexual hand.

"I'm Anthony Perrone, your new editor. You may call *me* Tony. Did we have an appointment I was unaware of?"

She took my hand but did not shake it, rather laid her fingers in mine like an offering from a supplicant. Which she very definitely was not. I withdrew my hand in what I hoped was not too abrupt a fashion.

"Appointment?" That voice again. I shook my head just the slightest bit and walked back around to my chair and sat back down.

"I never made appointments with Edwin," she continued. "I just came by when I needed him. That's how it is, you know." There was a smug, insider-y tone to her oddly pitched voice that set my teeth on edge and I stared for a moment at my computer screen to slake any of my immediate desires to find a weapon from amongst the things on my too cluttered desk. My eyes flitted to the letter opener and then left.

"Perhaps it *was*—and I have no doubt that you and Mr. Godwin have had a remarkably close relationship over the years, but while he had a kind of charming laxness in his dealings with authors," and here I paused, because I could see she was shifting in her chair in that imperceptible way that cats do right before they spring at your face and you lose an eye, "regrettably, I cannot afford quite the same openness because we are now down an editor, and yet up authors. And I am, as you can see…" and here I turned slightly and did an extravagant flourish as I took in the stacks of manuscripts, galleys, ARCs, and other literary effluvia that was the compounded hoarder-ish conglomeration of both my own former cubicle and Godwin's office of the past forty-eight years.

I sat back, somewhat pleased with my presentation of my plight.

Belinda was neither chastened nor amused.

"Well, you needn't worry, Tony," she said. Augh—that *voice*—and continued, "I don't *need* editing, as Edwin can tell you. I just like a little"—here she searched for a word—"gentle *prodding*. You understand, dear. Something to get me moving in the right direction."

Here she crossed and uncrossed her legs in the same way Sharon Stone had done in *Basic Instinct*, and I shifted my gaze just in case she was panty-less as La Stone had been. That was not an image I wanted in my head. Ever.

And yet, looking back, I am now sure she had been. Panty-less, I mean. And purposefully so. And wanting me not to just *look* but take that *prodding* comment to heart.

One hears a lot about cougars these days. And frankly, why shouldn't women at the peak of their sexual arousal and probably acumen (youth *is* wasted on the young; one learns exactly what that means as one gets older) want to have a suitable bed mate with equivalent stamina and passion? I don't fault them for that. But I'm not looking to be anyone's not-quite-a-boy-anymore-at-thirty-five boy toy. Besides which, as I have already stated, I am not a fence jumper. Ever. I don't need to refer to myself as a man who sleeps with men. I am gay. Through and through. It's intrinsic. That leg-crossing event did not affect me one iota except to make me want to find Miz Walsh a different editor, straightaway. Pun implied.

But Belinda took it into her head that I was indeed a fence jumper. Or that I should be, just for her. *Especially* for her. Which made working with her increasingly difficult until the fateful evening of the letter-opener incident, which, I suppose, would best be described as my first murder. Since *The Ox-Bow Incident* was already taken as a title and I hate being derivative.

So—*Tony's First Murder* it was. Sounds like some ghoulish children's picture book—and you can imagine the visual already, can't you?

Here's what happened:

I was supposed to work a little late that night in November, when it's already fully dark before five in the afternoon, and then meet Cam and then we were going away for the weekend to my friend M.J.'s place in Connecticut, because no one who lives in New York can ever fully escape Cheever, no matter how hard we try. Don't get me wrong—I love Cheever. I just didn't ever want to be a character in a Cheever anything: short story, journal entry, novel. And yet, now here I was a Cheever anti-hero, fully fleshed in the office of, well, we established that the name doesn't matter, but an esteemed and estimable publisher of more than a hundred years with a dead woman on my floor—on my *rug*—when I am supposed to be going to Connecticut for a hopefully very dirty weekend with the man who I am pretty sure is the love of my life.

What to do with the body? And what about my rug and letter-opener? I have read enough mysteries and seen enough episodes of *CSI* and *Law & Order* to know that it doesn't take much of a misstep to get caught when one kills. Of course murder is always the first misstep, isn't it? And I've fully made that little do-si-do. Thanks to Belinda.

I know—I am digressing again, all engaged in my own concerns with how to dispose of Miz Walsh now that she is a body, not just a body of work. *You* want to know how she became the late Belinda Sondheim Walsh.

It's silly really, what happened. But then murder is often the result of something frivolous—an argument in the kitchen where butcher knives are handy. Or an argument in an office where Auden's letter opener is just lying there demanding to be used even though the mail has already come and gone.

It was simple: She seduced me. Or tried to. And I said no. Rather harshly. And she refused to take no for an answer and came around the desk and I tried to get away.

The odd part is, had I been the woman and she the man, I could have called the police post–letter opener, cried (as I actually *did* do—the crying, I mean, not the calling of the police), and I would have been taken in hand by some lovely and compassionate policewoman who looked like Mariska Hargitay, and no charges would have been filed. A would-be rapist is, after all, a would-be rapist. Irrespective of gender.

But no one would have perceived Belinda Sondheim Walsh as a threat to me. She was five-three, ratcheted up to five-six in her spiky little Manolos, and she was quite thin. She had a birdlike quality to her that some—those who had never spent five minutes with her—would have deemed *fragile*. Meanwhile, I was six-two with what is generally described as "swimmer's build"—that is, strongly muscular but slender without being thin or wiry or, ever, ever fragile.

Stand the two of us together, Belinda and I, and no one would ever pick me as the potential victim. And of course it was she lying dead on the floor, blood pooling and spreading across her small breasts beneath the silken blouse.

But as I said early on in this recitation, it was she who was the killer. She brought this on herself—truly. I know most people won't believe that, because men are always the villains of the piece and women the perpetual victims, but this is the twenty-first century, not the nineteenth, and women have achieved a level of power that allows for them to be the perpetrators now and again. And she was. And I was her victim. And now she's dead because of it.

It sounds ludicrous even to me, and I was there.

But here's what happened, since I promised to explain. Belinda and I had been working on her latest novel for some months. I say *we* because her opening volley—and that's what the leg-crossing event was—was just that: the first in a series of ever more awkward impromptu visits to discuss her work and the state of her attraction to younger men. By which she meant *me*.

The book had been due in May, for a December release. Tight scheduling to begin with. Belinda did have critical acclaim. I may not have understood it, but that didn't matter. She had a retinue and as such got a good billing from us for holiday release, which usually brought with it good sales.

Except the book hadn't been done until August and the schedules had been thrown. Utterly. I was under pressure to get the book from her and she was withholding it—I felt purposefully—to get me into bed with her. Which was never going to happen because first of all, I am not a fence jumper, and second of all, I was mad for Cam and I was not going to cheat on him with anyone—certainly not a woman I had grown to despise and even fear.

So there we were, in increasingly tight quarters together. She would be in my office until late in the hot evenings throughout the summer when publishing grinds to a halt as everyone is fleeing New York for the Hamptons or anyplace with a breeze. Cam and I were spending most of our weekends in Rehoboth with friends. Except when Belinda needed me to hold her hand. And so Belinda had become a bone of contention in my otherwise blissful romance with Cam. My own complaints about her were echoed by Cam in a way that made me fearful that he did in fact suspect that I was fulfilling her fantasies on those late nights in my office.

Which I most definitely was not.

❖

A book is never fully finished until it's on the shelves. And even then, there is a whole new level of concerns, but my part ended when the book was indeed bound and bound for the bookstores. But due to the delays Belinda had caused, we had to go over edits and changes and galleys and proofs right up until the last second.

Which, regrettably, was when I killed her.

As I explained early on, Belinda refused to be edited. So she had to be cajoled into thinking any given change was her idea. Which was both maddening and time-consuming and driving me to spend more and more of my evenings downing martinis with Amelia and lamenting the fact that I could not escape this woman. I would call M.J. late at night after Cam was asleep and I was sober again. I told her about how Belinda's initial mild flirtations had moved into a sexually aggressive stage that made me so uncomfortable that I was drinking too much and was afraid I might either lose my job or lose Cam or both.

M.J. was a realist of the highest order. "Someone else has to know she's doing this, Tony," she told me. "She didn't just start this with you."

I explained about Mr. Godwin, the closet pederast, and how I was sure Belinda was several decades too old for him and how I couldn't see her dressing up in a schoolgirl uniform. Plus, I knew it was a younger, not older, man she wanted. Everyone wants young. Except the young, who want older. And me—I wanted Cam, who was just a few months younger than me. Not years.

It was a mess, I told M.J. After all, I had just settled into Godwin's old job and didn't want to rock the boat—recession plus the endless mergers in the publishing world meant that no job was secure. I was a valued editor, I knew that. But how valued was anyone, really? Godwin had been there for nearly fifty years and no one seemed to miss him at all.

I couldn't confess my fears to Cam. And I was beginning to feel that my comments about Belinda might sound sexist to Amelia and M.J. Which was when I called Natalie. Because she'd been through something similar with an older male author who was always touching her inappropriately. And she had gotten herself out of it without losing her job or her position or even the author.

Natalie told me to tell Belinda to stop. "Just do it. You've put up with this for way too long, Tony. What the fuck were you thinking? She should have been told right from that Sharon Stone bit that she was totally out of line and that you didn't bat for her team and besides you never mix business and fucking. *Ever*."

Natalie was pissed—*for* me and *at* me. It all made sense when she said it, and I realized that I had thought I was protecting myself and keeping Belinda from being embarrassed all this time, but in reality, I had just emboldened her. She thought we were playing some teasing little sex game and that I would, once I got her book done, give her what she wanted. Capitulate.

I decided to talk to her. We were at what used to be called blue-line stage. The book was done. All that was needed was for her to sit in my office and glance over the final proofs. Most authors weren't accorded this privilege, but Godwin had set a bad precedent based on the old way of doing things pre-computer and digital typesetting, so there we were, on a chill November evening, going over the final proofs of what we both had agreed was indeed her best book.

And that's when she did it. That's when she crossed the line.

❖

I had the proofs spread out in signatures before Belinda arrived. It was Thursday night and Cam and I were leaving later that night for the long weekend at M.J.'s, taking advantage of Veteran's Day—a holiday only celebrated by the veterans themselves, the federal government, schools, and publishing houses. I was stressed beyond imagining and looking forward to the time with Cam, M.J., and her husband, James. We made a good foursome, and now that M.J. was quite pregnant with their first child and working from home, she relished the company as much as we did getting away.

Belinda arrived at just before four p.m. dressed for an evening on the town, so I assumed that the La Perla lingerie that was supposed to be viewed through the sheerness of her blouse was for someone else, not me.

I was wrong. Dead wrong, as it turns out.

We began to work. At 5:45, my assistant, Alana, stuck her head through the partially opened door to say she was leaving and that everyone else was gone from the floor but me. My expression must have reflected my distress at the ever more oppressive closeness of Belinda, because Alana raised an eyebrow and asked if there was anything else I needed, and shouldn't I be leaving soon since I was going away for the long weekend? She looked sideways at Belinda, remarking on how lovely her outfit was, never realizing that she had just tossed gas onto an already raging fire.

I murmured that I would be leaving as soon as the proofs were checked and that I would take them downstairs myself and she needn't worry about them and I hoped she had a nice long weekend herself, and then she was gone with a click of the door latch behind her and the kind of dead calm that falls over an empty office settled in on me and Belinda Sondheim Walsh and really—could something deadly have ever been far off at that point?

We finished the proofs within a half hour and then it was time to leave. Or so I said, explaining about my weekend plans, again, because Cam had called just before Alana had left and she had put the call through to me (I think he had called the office phone and not my cell specifically to check if Alana was still there and thus would know I was not alone with Belinda) and I had told him I'd be leaving seven-ish, possibly slightly later, and that I had picked up the rental car at lunch and it was in the garage downstairs so we could be on the road by nine at the latest.

As I finished up the job, I turned my back on Belinda, who had settled herself in that wildly uncomfortable chair that only she seemed to enjoy. I bent over the desk to put the signatures in order and check once more that each had been initialed and marked for errors. I had just finished scrawling a note to production and was reaching for a rubber band to put around them when I heard a light rustling and before I could turn, Belinda had put her arms around me and slid her hand directly onto my crotch, expertly—or so she believed—seeking out my cock.

I suddenly understood how women must feel when a man they trust or think they know assaults them. The initial response is to be stunned. And because that takes a few moments, the attacker gains the upper hand.

Which is what happened with Belinda. I was thrown off guard by her grabbing at me and was unsure what to do next. And what I did next was totally wrong. I removed her hand and turned toward her. The look on my face was one of pure shock and probably a touch of revulsion. Hers, however, had that look of barely controlled passion that I had seen many times, just almost always on the face of someone I was about to fuck. *Because I wanted to.*

"Shouldn't we celebrate the end of a job well done with—well, a *job* well done?" She had not moved back even an inch when I had turned and now I was pressed back against the desk and I could have just shoved her away and why I didn't, I have no idea, but this is clearly what happens: One loses one's bearings altogether. And I did. Because I felt something I hadn't felt in years: afraid.

How could a man over six feet tall and a muscular 180 pounds be fearful of a woman as petite and seemingly harmless as Belinda? Well, that is the thing about sexual predation, isn't it?—there's no logic in it.

I feared for Cam, for my job, for myself, for my own identity. It all swam together in my head, making me dizzily unsettled. She had already reached for me again; this time her fingers were on my belt and zipper with a fleetness that would have been disarmingly alluring had the man involved sought the attention. But I began to sweat, despite how chill the room had become, and I knew I had to stop her, but my voice came out a garbled whisper which could easily have been misconstrued for sexual desire by someone desperately seeking just that.

But then I found my voice at the same time she found my cock, and it was not a good mix. Her fingers were around me at the same time as I said with all the outrage and fear I felt, "Belinda, you have to stop!"

How can one explain the ineffectuality of language when it is all one knows and all one does? Language was my life and yet here it was, failing me utterly. Belinda Sondheim Walsh took my words not as they were meant—a clear and direct imperative to cease and desist—but as a passionate plea for more. She read my "you have to stop!" as "we shouldn't do this here, but somewhere more private where we can revel in our mutual passion."

She told me she couldn't stop and wouldn't stop and we both knew I didn't really *want* her to stop—not *now*. And so she slipped her hand into my now-open pants and proceeded to search for what she wanted and seemed bemused to find that I was not excited as she'd expected *because of course I was afraid, not turned on*. But she thought she had a remedy for this. I leaned away, back farther against the desk, and repeated my whispered "stop," my regular voice seeming to have left me altogether, and I turned my head away from her as she leaned toward me to kiss me, and that's when I saw the letter opener.

❖

I'm not entirely sure what happened next. As I said from the outset, I'm an unreliable narrator. All I know is that I grabbed the letter opener in the same way Grace Kelly grabbed the scissors in *Dial M for Murder* when she was being strangled by the man Ray Milland had hired to kill her. I felt the same fear she had exhibited on screen—although Belinda was not trying to kill me, but I felt threatened down to the core of my being and all I could think of was escaping. The scent of her—her perfume, her makeup, her hair, her *desire*—it was overpowering. It was overwhelming me, oppressing me, sickening me. My heart was racing with the adrenaline of fear and I actually thought I might faint.

But I didn't. I'm not sure exactly what I did, but suddenly there was a strange sound like a boot in mud—a wet sucking noise that was wholly unpleasant to the point where I thought I might retch, and then there she was—on my rug, the letter opener just below and between her breasts and a look of surprise on her face, her lips just slightly parted, as if she had one more thing to say that had gone unfinished.

❖

I'm not sure what I did next. I found myself sitting on the floor in front of my desk and next to her body. I was crying, which I rarely do, especially not sober. My pants were still undone and my hair was in my eyes and I could feel sweat running down my back, chilling my body. I was shaking, and on the tips of the fingers of my left hand there was just the slightest trace of blood.

Now what?

This was that scene in the murder mystery—novel, play, film, TV show—where the murderer looks around wildly and wonders what to do next. No doubt I had that wild look on my face at that moment when I realized what I had done and that it could not be undone.

I stood, shaky, my legs like rubber, and looked around for something to wipe my hand on. A small stack of napkins lay on my desk alongside the remains of the Greek salad I had had for lunch. I wiped the blood off, Lady Macbeth coming immediately to mind.

What next?

I could not do this by myself. Or so I thought. But who could I ask for help with disposing of a body? And why was I thinking that was the best way to go? I could still call the police, explain, hope for that compassionate Mariska Hargitay character to realize that men get sexually assaulted, too, if not very often. But that seemed a vaguer and vaguer possibility.

Disposal it was. I would have to do something about the letter opener and the rug. And then there was Cam. Did I dare to involve him in this mess? Was there *anyone* I could turn to? Anyone who would understand—and forgive me?

It was right about then that I wished that my mother hadn't died suddenly the year before. She was always good in a crisis, and somehow I felt she would have had some answers for me. But maybe not. I was on my own here. Murder is definitely a very solitary act.

❖

And so I began at the beginning, with the letter opener. I went to the men's room and got a stack of paper towels. The sound the letter opener made when I pulled it from Belinda's chest was disgusting and my gorge rose, but I did not vomit. I wrapped the letter opener in some of the towels and stanched the blood with the rest. I knew I had to bleach the letter opener (I'd learned that from a previous author) to get the blood off just like I knew that the letter opener was such a fixture on my desk that it had to be there when I was there on Monday.

I looked at my watch. How was it possible that killing someone had taken so little time? It was only 6:45, but it felt like midnight. I knew I had to call Cam. *And say what, exactly?* "Hi, darling, this book is just murder and it's taking longer than I expected because it's just a bloody mess?"

The car.

The rental car was in the garage in the basement of our building. Would it be possible for me to put Belinda and the rug in a packing box and take both down in the freight elevator to the luxury SUV I had rented so that we would have enough space for driving M.J. and James around on the weekend, my not wanting her to feel stuffed into the backseat at six months pregnant? Was this even possible?

I looked at the dead Belinda, so petite and so…*foldable.* I had to try. How long would it be before rigor mortis set in? I had no idea, but worried it was soon. Then she'd be stiff as a board and I wouldn't be able to move her. Time was ticking out on me. I had to do something, and fast.

I shut the door to my office, locked it, and headed for shipping.

❖

No one ever thinks they will be packing up a dead woman in bubble wrap in a shipping box usually used for books on a cold November night. No one ever thinks—unless one is a sociopath, of course—that one will ever *kill* anyone. But here I was in the second act of *Tony's First Murder* as if I had been packing up dead people all my life.

I'd been lucky about the rug. There might have been a few spots of blood embedded in the weave that I didn't discern right away, but considering the amount of blood that pooled on Belinda's chest, it was amazing that she hadn't bled onto the carpet. I guess the majority of the bleeding had been internal. I didn't like to think about that, really.

So I left the rug where it was. I had sopped up the blood on her chest with the paper towels from the men's room. I had had the forethought to grab a pair of latex gloves like the kind we used when handling the older books so that I wasn't spreading blood everywhere—or my fingerprints where they shouldn't be.

I lay the bubble wrap on the floor and rolled Belinda's body into it, moving her into a fetal position so she would fit in the shipping box.

Once she was in the box, I called Cam. It was still only 7:15.

He answered on the first ring with a slightly startled hello. "Darling," he said, "I'm so knackered." He had fallen asleep watching the news—he hoped I could drive, he was dead tired and wanted to sleep in the car if that was okay.

His voice reminded me of everything normal—that he loved me, that we were going away for a weekend with one of my best friends, that maybe I didn't have a dead woman in my office.

"I have one more thing to clean up, and then I'll be home," I told him. "And of course I'll drive. You rest. I'll see you soon."

I could do this. It would all be okay.

❖

One never hears birds in the city. Not really. Other sounds mute the sounds of birds. You see pigeons everywhere, of course. That's the requisite city bird. Just like the rats in the subway—they're part of the landscape. But you don't see the other birds much, except in the parks. And you don't hear them.

So I was actually startled awake by the sound of birds at such an early hour as I woke in M.J.'s guest room, Cam still sound asleep next to me. It wasn't quite light yet and the birds seemed unnaturally loud, so unused to hearing them was I.

I had left my office in its usual state of disarray. I had thought about tidying up, but realized that would be more suspicious, not less so. I checked the rug carefully. I saw no blood. There had been a few drops on my desk and a smear on my desk lamp. I wiped those off with the Clorox wipes Alana uses for the phones, since she's a germophobe, and hoped it hadn't had time to seep into the wood. Normal people don't keep Luminol in their desks, so I had no way of checking for sure.

I'd been lucky with the box. It wasn't as heavy as I had expected and the freight elevator had been empty and no one had been near the rental car in the garage. I had been able to leave easily and unnoticed. The garage guy didn't know me—I never had a car except in the summer, and besides, he was new and would likely only remember that I had been there, if asked, but not remember if I may or may not have had a large box in the back of my car that could have held a dead author.

I knew Cam would still be sleeping. I could tell by his voice when we spoke. Now was the time to rid myself of this meddlesome author, to paraphrase Eliot. But where? The river seemed the easy answer, but bodies float and there was likely to be some residue of something that wouldn't wash away immediately and I didn't want Miz Walsh surfacing before I did. Plus, I honestly felt it would be wrong to have her eaten by fish. I was starting to feel some unpleasant twinges of guilt about this whole thing, even though I felt my actions had been both un-pre-meditated and entirely justified. But now it wasn't about the self-defense—it was about the cover-up. *And* not getting caught.

I would have liked to have dumped Belinda in another borough—Queens would be best, I thought—so many *mafiosi*—or someplace ungentrified in Brooklyn—but I couldn't risk driving over a bridge with her. So Washington Heights it was. I'd head up to 171st Street and leave her in DDP territory and hope for the best. The Dominicans didn't deserve her any more than I did, but in gang territory, bodies get found a lot more slowly. I was also hoping the near-freezing temperatures would skew the time of death.

I had to get her out of the box, of course. That was dicey. It meant looking for a side street with a Dumpster. I couldn't risk the box being somehow linked to me. And I didn't want her to be found immediately—or identified quickly.

❖

Killing someone, disposing of a body, and then making a getaway to another state for what was supposed to be a calm and restful three-day weekend takes a lot less time than one would think if one focuses. Cam and I had indeed been on the road by nine, Belinda having been left, finally, in a scraggy little woodsy area near 174th where the surrounding buildings were tagged with DDP signs and the occasional bold Crip tag that had been struck out, obviously by the Dominicans. I was feeling grateful for that gang book I had edited last year and even more grateful for the cold as I laid Belinda carefully under a little plot of bushes that led into what I was certain was an area where sex and drugs would be available in another hour or so. I was fortunate to have missed the traffic—drug dealers and prostitutes and men who have sex with men but can't commit to saying they're gay. It was a fitting place to leave her. She'd always talked about going to "one of the scary neighborhoods" and then writing about it. Now she could experience it without fearing violence. That part had already happened.

I rolled over and put my arms around Cam. The sky was getting lighter, the birds less vociferous. I didn't know if Belinda would be found right away, or if her expensive everything—clothes, jewelry (I had left it, but no doubt someone would strip the body before they called it in), hair, manicure, and of course that La Perla underwear—would make it easier to identify her, since she had been so thoughtful as to leave all her ID sans one credit card (which I pocketed and which would indeed end up in the river) at home, as very little fit in her chic but tiny purse.

Part of me knew I should turn myself in—explain it all, hope for the best, throw my lot in, hoping for mercy from the stock characters of TV police procedurals and murder mysteries. But I just couldn't risk it. Down the hall were M.J. and her husband and their soon-to-be-born baby. Beside me was the love of my life. Back in Manhattan was the job I had loved before Belinda and which I hoped I could love again. In among my things in the duffel in the closet was the now-bleached letter opener that had belonged to W.H. Auden and which had been a gift from my Great-Aunt Tillie.

I hadn't meant to kill Belinda. But I wasn't nearly as sorry as I should have been or might have been if she hadn't been Belinda Sondheim Walsh and if she hadn't imposed herself on me to the point of crossing not just a personal line, but a criminal one. I would have to content myself with that thought—that she had made her choices and so had I. And we'd both been wrong—dead wrong.

I settled in next to Cam to the fading sound of birds and the overwhelming calm—dead calm—of the quiet Connecticut morning.

AN APPETITE FOR WARMTH
NEIL PLAKCY

It was like a vacation driving down to Miami with Red. He was a horny fucker, for sure, and I must have given him a dozen blow jobs over the couple of days it took us to drive from Albany. The farther south we went, the warmer it got. The snow was gone by the time we hit Maryland, and I could shuck my jacket by South Carolina. Somewhere around Palm Beach I stripped off all my clothes and sprawled on the front seat next to Red, letting the warm air rush all over me.

We met at a truck stop where I used to hang out. He was a burly, copper-haired driver for a big transport company, and I guess you could call him my first boyfriend, though he was nearly forty and married, and I only saw him every other weekend when his rig stopped in Albany on a regular route between Chicago and Boston.

"Man, you are one sexy bastard, Sean," Red said. We were barreling down the turnpike when we came to the exit ramp for I-595. I was giving him one last blow job before he had to drop his load when the ramp curved steeply and I heard him say, "Jesus Christ on a stick!" and then the truck smashed through the guardrail and went plummeting into space.

He was wearing his seat belt, company policy, so he stayed in the cab as it crashed to the ground thirty feet below. I went sailing out the window, and I remember thinking this must be what it felt like to fly. I landed in the crotch of a tree, perched above the burning truck, and I felt warmer than I ever had in my life. I thought for a while I'd died and gone to hell, where I'd always known I was going, and then I must have passed out and toppled out of the tree.

❖

I always had an appetite for warmth. Growing up in a small town in upstate New York, I never could get warm enough, except for a few weeks in the summer. My dad left when I was about five, and for the next few years my mom struggled on her own to raise me and my sister. She kept an eagle eye on the thermostat all winter long. Then when she got married again, my stepfather used to knock me around if I so much as looked cross-eyed at turning the heat up.

I started making my own money when I was fourteen, cleaning up at a construction site. One of the carpenters felt sorry for me and showed me how to hang drywall, nailing the big sheets to the aluminum studs, then taping over the seams and sanding them down. In return, I gave him a blow job once a week or so, something he said his wife would never do.

By the time I was seventeen, I was making good money hanging drywall, then spending it getting drunk on Saturday night. Then I'd drive out to the highway rest stop and give blow jobs in the men's room until two or three in the morning.

When I was nineteen, somebody sent my mom a picture of my dad and told her he was dead. Looking back now, I can tell it was AIDS, but then all we knew was that he'd wasted away. "He was so handsome once," she said to me, just before she tore the picture up in little pieces. "You look just like him, Sean."

I figured it was time to stop screwing around and get my life in order, so I got married, to a fat waitress named Donna I'd known in high school, and we moved down to Albany to get ourselves a fresh start. I picked up drywall work pretty fast, and she got a job waitressing at a bar called Your Place. It was probably the only bar in town where I never had a drink.

The beer warmed me up. I'd work all day, and by the time the foreman let us call it quits, I'd be chilled down to my bones. A couple of beers later, I'd start to feel warm again. Donna was good for that, too; I could squeeze up against her, my skinny chest, arms, and legs up tight against her cushiony flesh, and sleep. We even had sex, now and then, and though I could do it, I didn't much like it. Back then, I thought that's the way it was; the sex you were supposed to have was lousy, and only the sex you weren't was any good.

The first time I was arrested at a rest stop I managed to keep it a secret from her, but she found out about the second time because a bastard cop came to our house and told her. He said she had to protect herself against disease, and she made us both get tested and then made me promise not to go out there again.

It took me a couple of weeks til I found my way to a truck stop at the edge of town, a place the big rigs pulled over for a breather before the long haul to Boston, or going the other way, down to New York. There was always a supply of horny truckers waiting out a mandatory rest period.

It was around then that Donna got pregnant. She'd gone off the pill without telling me, and it made me so mad I drank two six-packs of Genesee Cream Ale and then worked my way down the line of trucks, giving one blow job after another, letting the guys do pretty much anything they wanted. One guy took me into the shower at the rest stop, stripped us both down and then peed all over me. I didn't care a bit.

Then I figured I owed it to the kid to sober up and be the kind of dad I never had. For the rest of Donna's pregnancy I hardly drank at all, and only fooled around with Red, because like I said, he was kind of like my boyfriend by then. Hell, I was only twenty-two, and I could see the walls closing in around me for the rest of my life. Sucking his dick and getting plowed up the ass by him was about the only good thing I had going.

Donna gave birth to a little boy, and she wanted to call him Richard. I said okay, only if we called him Ricky—not Dick. I had enough problems without thinking of blow jobs every time I called the kid to dinner.

Donna started to get real distant after Ricky was born. She went back to Your Place, working nights, and I had to stay home and look after Ricky. She wouldn't get home till two or three in the morning, and I'd be shivering under the covers, but she wouldn't let me cuddle up against her.

I was working at this big mall, and somebody had screwed up the drawings for the steel, so one end of it was still open, even though we were working inside trying to fix up the interior. We enclosed the open storefront in plastic and brought in salamanders, these little space heaters, so it was warm enough for us to work, but still, I'd be freezing by the end of the day.

Then one Saturday when I met up with Red, he dropped a bombshell on me. We were sitting back in the little sleeping compartment behind his cab, after sex. He was smoking a cigarette and I was drinking a can of beer, both of us naked, my cold feet pressed up against his shins to try and get warm. "They're giving me a new route," he said. "Chicago to Miami."

His wife and kids lived in Chicago, so he had to keep that as his base. But whatever customers he had in Boston had gone out of business and the company was shifting him around. "I come back from Boston this time, I head straight down to Miami," he said.

"Aw, hell," I said. "I'm never gonna see you again."

"Come to Miami," he said. "I'll pick you up next week when I pass back through. We can fuck our way down the entire eastern seaboard."

"And what do I do when I get there?"

"Exactly what you do here. Put up drywall and suck my dick."

"What about my wife? I've got a kid, too, you know."

He shrugged. "You do what you gotta do," he said.

And just like that, I thought, "I'll move to Miami." It was February, and ass-chilling cold in Albany. I could finally warm up down there, run around in shorts and T-shirts all winter and still feel good.

I decided I was done with women, too. There was no doubt in my mind by then that I was a faggot, and I had no business living with or sleeping with a woman. That night, I picked up Ricky from the neighbor who was watching him, and after he went to sleep I stayed up waiting for Donna to come home from Your Place.

"You're up late," she said, when she came in the front door, a frosty breeze following her that made me shiver. I had my hands wrapped around a mug of hot chocolate, wearing long johns and a flannel nightshirt, and I still wasn't warm.

"Wanted to talk to you," I said.

She started pulling off her layers. "You could roast a chicken in here," she said.

"I've been thinking, and I want to move on," I said. "Get a divorce. Move down south."

"You won't get an argument from me," she said. "I've already got me a real man to replace you."

Maybe she was expecting to get my dander up, start some kind of battle over who got to claim her, but if she was, she was disappointed. "Guy from Your Place?"

"Jerry. The night bartender. He's been saving up, gonna buy the place when Ethel gets ready to retire and sell it off."

"Good for you," I said.

"And I won't have to worry about him sucking dick at rest stops, either," she said.

"You never know."

She slapped my face then, and I suppose I deserved it.

By the time Red pulled back into the truck stop the next Saturday, I'd sold my truck and given away everything I couldn't pack into a single suitcase. "You be careful not to end up like your dad," was all Donna said when I left the house the last time.

As the cab pulled away, it finally dawned on me that my father'd been a faggot too, and that's why he'd left my mother. Poor Ricky, I thought. Only a year old, and his dad was already bailing on him. But maybe this bartender Jerry would be a better influence on him. I might have gotten out of his life just in time.

The company Red drove for had a strict policy against picking up hitchhikers, so I left the hospital with nothing but a set of clothes, a pocketknife that had survived the truck fire, and bus fare to the homeless shelter. Instead of getting off there, though, I stayed on across the causeway to South Beach, where I'd heard all the faggots hung out.

It was just nightfall, the lights on Lincoln Road coming on. I walked past the funky stores and fancy restaurants until I came to a gay bar I'd seen advertised in a newspaper I'd read at the hospital. I pulled off my shirt and slung it over my shoulder, letting the pants, which were too big on me anyway, ride down to my hips.

I leaned up against the wall outside the bar, and I hadn't been there more than fifteen minutes when this guy came up to me. Maybe thirty, thirty-five, fat as a Thanksgiving turkey, wearing one of them short-sleeve shirts with the little horse and rider on his chest, and a Rolex on his wrist.

What kind of asshole wears a Rolex to a bar where he wants to get laid? That's just asking for trouble, in my opinion. "What's a good-looking guy like you doing hanging out here?" he said. "The action's all inside."

I put on my best innocent look. "I was a little nervous about going inside," I said.

"Come on in with me," he said, putting his arm around my bare shoulder. "I'll take care of you."

I followed him inside, where he bought me a series of drinks, and I started to feel that pleasant sense of freedom that alcohol had always brought me. The music was fast and loud, a sexy Latin beat that made me horny. I put my finger in my mouth and got it all juicy, then pressed it against the crotch of his khaki pants so there was a wet spot there. Against all the soft rolls of fat I could feel him getting hard. I licked my lips and made a five-zero out of my hands.

He was panting for it. "You got a place we can go?" I yelled into his ear.

He grabbed my arm like he was afraid if he let go he'd never get blown again, and I followed him out of the bar and into the parking garage just behind. The dude drove one of those big Land Rovers, and I regretted that I couldn't just knock him on the head and leave him naked and quivering in some dark corner of the garage.

We climbed into the front seat and he started fumbling with his zipper. I'd worked enough of them in my life to know what to do, so I took over. When I was finished, he was panting for air, thin lines of sweat dripping down his cheeks. "Damn, you're good," he said.

"Worth every penny of the fifty bucks," I said.

"Fifty bucks!" he said. "What do you mean!"

I reached over and caressed his limp dick, then grabbed hold and squeezed. "I mean you owe me fifty bucks."

The dude was strong for a fat fuck. He grabbed my arm and twisted, and I yelped in pain. "Wrong move, dude," I said. I flipped open my knife, and with a quick movement I'd slit his fancy blue shirt from neck to waist. "Next move you make is to your wallet."

"Take it," he said, pulling it out and thrusting it at me. "Here, take the watch, too. Just don't cut me."

I'd only expected the fifty bucks I'd asked for, but I wasn't in any position to turn down a gift. I opened the wallet and pulled out the cash, then shoved it back at him. I kept the watch, though.

I scrambled out of his car. "I got your license plate, bud, so don't even think about calling the cops. I'll find out where you live, where you work. You don't want to mess with me."

"No, sir," he said, and he backed that car out so fast you'd think he was in training for the Indy 500. I liked the way he called me sir.

It scared me, too. I'd come to Miami to live out in the open, to give up the kind of soul-draining truck stop sex I'd been having in Albany. But here I was blowing a guy in his car. This wasn't the way I'd intended to start my new life. I started walking around, keeping to the shadowy side streets, thinking about what I could do.

After ten or fifteen blocks, my head cleared and the adrenaline rush dissipated, and I realized that I needed to get a real job. In quick succession, I found a pawn shop, where I got a few hundred bucks for the Rolex, and then a bus stop.

Back across the causeway, I rented myself a room for a week in a run-down fifties motel on Biscayne Boulevard. The next day was Sunday, and I went through the classified ads, looking for construction work. Monday morning I made the rounds, following the line of cranes down Biscayne Boulevard. Every place I got the same story, though. No Spanish, no job.

"Got to be able to speak to the rest of the crew," one foreman told me. "They got jobs up in Lauderdale, everybody speaks English. Try up there."

The last place I went, I walked out of the trailer in disgust, then stood behind it to smoke a cigarette. "Damn!" I said out loud. "Who does a faggot have to blow to get a job in this town?"

The superintendent, Cuban guy who'd been nice enough but had nothing for me, stuck his head out the window above my head. "I hear you right?" he said.

I looked up at him and licked my lips. "You heard me right, brother," I said.

He ducked back inside, and then a moment later appeared again, this time holding a sheaf of papers in his hand. "Fill these out and give them to the girl out front," he said. "Be here tomorrow morning, seven thirty." After I took the papers he said, "You better know how to hang drywall, too."

"Yes, sir," I said.

The next couple of days, I felt him watching me. His name was Alberto, though the guys all called him Señor Berto. I did my best to work hard, keep my nose to the grindstone and all that. We were building out some office space in a new high-rise, a warren of small cubicles framed out with studs. The electricians were working one bay ahead of us, running their wires through the walls, and then our crew would come in and drywall. The painters were right on our asses, and there wasn't much time to fool around.

Friday afternoon, Señor Berto asked me to stick around for a few minutes after the rest of the guys took off, and I knew what was coming.

But that's the way it is in this world. You take your breaks where you can get them, and you pay what you have to. When the rest of the guys left, I found Berto on his cell phone, standing in the lobby of the building, in front of this marble desk where I guessed the receptionist was going to sit. He waved at me and I stood there, my eyes zeroed in on his crotch.

He saw me looking there, and his dick began to stiffen against the denim. Finally he finished his call, and I moved over and put my hand on his crotch. It was warm down there, and I figured I'd drop to my knees right there, blow him, and then get on with my weekend.

Instead he motioned me to follow him to the men's room, where he leaned up against the vanity, no sinks installed yet, and unzipped his pants.

It became a regular routine, every Friday afternoon, kind of like some mobbed-up thug coming by every week to extract a payoff. But in the meantime, I was earning good money, cruising the gay bars on the weekend like a regular guy. I had a lot of sex, some of it good, and never collected a penny. If I didn't like a guy's looks, I just moved on to the next offer.

The office project finished, and one of the guys I worked with told me about a new crew I could join—one where I didn't have to suck dick every Friday afternoon. I said good-bye to Señor Berto and what I'd come to think of as his weekly payoff. I was becoming a regular working stiff, living a clean life in the hooker motel, even saving up some cash to help in my transformation to a productive member of society.

The summer in Miami was hot. Up to the nineties most days, enough humidity to keep your shirt stuck to your back. I didn't mind a bit, though a lot of the guys complained. There was plenty of hunky eye candy, though I kept my zipper closed and my nose clean.

I met Frank on a Friday night in July, jammed into a tight space on the dance floor at the very Lincoln Road club where I'd picked up the Range Rover jerk a few months before. Frank wasn't the kind of guy I usually looked twice at, maybe ten years older than me, and losing his hair. He had a trim figure, though, and the guy had some moves on him.

We were dancing to some shitty Madonna remix, and I liked the way he was totally absorbed in the music, his hips swiveling to the beat. When the song was over he caught my eye and smiled, and when he headed to the tables out on Lincoln Road I followed him.

"I'm Francisco," he said, reaching out to shake my hand, when we were far enough from the music to speak. "But everybody calls me Frank."

"I'm Sean."

"But I'll bet everybody calls you sexy." I liked the way his eyes smiled as much as his mouth did.

"Only the guys I think are sexy, too," I said.

We sat outside and talked. I learned he'd come to Miami as a kid, part of the Mariel exodus from Cuba, worked his way through college and dental school. I told him a few things, all true, but there was certainly a lot I didn't mention.

Around three in the morning, he yawned. "Sorry," he said. "Had to get up early this morning for work."

"Me too," I said. I rubbed my foot against his leg. "I guess I'm ready for bed."

"For sleep," he said. "But I'd like to see you again. Can I buy you dinner tomorrow?"

It was the first time I'd been asked out on a date. Every other guy I'd gone to bed with was one I'd met in a club, sometimes fooled around with in a men's room or an alley. Once in a while I'd end up at somebody's place, even brought a couple back to my room at the hooker motel, too. But Frank was the first one who'd wanted to wait to get in my pants.

That got me hard, a guy who wanted me for something more than just a quickie. "Sure," I said. We exchanged phone numbers, and he offered to pick me up at eight.

He was just the kind of guy I'd been hoping to meet. Stable but sexy. He worked at a dental clinic in Little Havana, making good money, and he already owned his own town house in Kendall, a nice suburb south of the city. "It's nothing fancy," he said. "I'm helping out my folks, and putting my little sister through graduate school in social work. But I'm hoping to get into a house soon."

We had a great dinner at a nice restaurant on Ocean Drive, and after we ate we walked along the sand. I wanted to hold his hand. Me, the biggest truck stop whore in Albany, New York. I was falling in love.

When he pulled up in front of the motel, I asked him if he'd like to come in. "I'd like that," he said.

The next week, I met his dog, a chocolate Lab called Azucar, which he told me meant "sugar" in Spanish. I liked her immediately, and she was all over me with big slobbery kisses. "Azucar, no!" Frank said.

But I said, "I don't mind. She's a sweetheart." When Frank and I went to bed, she sprawled on the floor at the foot of the bed. I thought I'd fallen into the perfect situation.

A week later, I'd moved out of the motel and in with Frank. I bought a used truck and started working with a crew in Kendall, only a couple of miles from home. Frank walked Azucar in the morning before he left for work, and then I took her out in the afternoon when I got home. She and I were perfect pals, her trailing around after me while I hung out, surfed the Internet with Frank's computer, and fixed dinner for him and me.

Everything was going along smooth, until the super I was working for got transferred to another project, and the company brought a new guy in.

Señor Berto.

He talked to the crew for a few minutes on Monday morning, basically saying the same kind of shit supers always did, you work hard for me, I'll take care of you. I knew what that meant. Berto expected me to start taking care of him again. But I was done with all that.

He kept giving me these looks whenever he saw me, and I'd try not to look back. But maybe there was something inside me that didn't like the happy little suburban life I'd begun to build with Frank, and by Wednesday when he looked at me my dick started to spring to life.

I'd never told Frank about whoring around before I met him, and I'd certainly never told him how Señor Berto had given me my first break in construction in Miami, so I couldn't tell him what I was feeling. He knew something was up, though. Thursday he said, "Is something wrong, Sean?"

"What do you mean?" We were sitting at the kitchen table, eating a roast chicken I'd picked up at Publix. Azucar was sprawled behind my chair, locking me in place. I started to feel like Frank was doing the same thing to me, locking me in someplace I didn't really belong.

"You've been in a bad mood all week."

I shrugged. "New super at work. He's kind of an asshole."

"Get another job, then. You've got skills. You can find work anywhere."

"Not that easy," I said. "No *Español*, remember? When I came to Miami I couldn't get a job to save my life because I couldn't speak the lingo. Only way I keep working is to follow the same crew around, guys that know what I can do."

"I can teach you," he said. "We'll have a basic conversational

Spanish class right here." He smiled. "Starting with *pinga*. You know what that is, don't you."

"Yeah, dick," I said. And I said it so he'd know I was calling him that. "I'm going out," I said. I backed my chair up fast, startling Azucar, but I didn't care.

I got in my truck and started driving. I got on the highway, heading for a truck stop I'd read about on the Internet. But halfway there, my interest faltered, and I turned around and went back to Frank. He was already lying in bed, reading a dental journal, when I came in.

He had the air-conditioning cranked up to frigid, something I hated, but I didn't say anything. Instead I stood at the foot of the bed and stripped down, watching him watch me. Then I jumped him and we had ferocious sex.

The next day I was determined to resist Berto—but at the last minute my willpower evaporated. I followed him into another unfinished men's room, just like the first place, and blew him. "*Ay, coño*, I miss you, Sean," he said. "Nobody suck like you."

After work, I drove out to that truck stop, and this time I didn't turn around. I blew three truckers before I finally gave up and headed back to Frank.

I started to spiral out of control. I'd hit a straight bar after work, determined just to get shitfaced and then go home, but instead I'd end up at some sleazy bookstore or truck stop or men's room, and by the time I got back to Frank's I'd be drunk, stinking of sex and beer.

He finally confronted me one Friday night, after I'd blown Berto, drunk a six-pack in my truck, and let two different truckers fuck me. "Why are you doing this, Sean?" He stood in the living room, waiting for me to come through the front door.

"What?"

"This." He waved his hand at me. "You're drunk. And I'll bet you've been fooling around, too. I think you ought to move out."

"Come on, *Papi*," I said, moving toward him. "I'm sorry. Let me make it up to you."

"Get away from me." He turned and stalked away, going into the bedroom. Even the dog followed him as he slammed the door.

I went into the guest bathroom, stripped down, and showered. I let the hot water stream over me until I felt my back burning. Then, naked, I walked to Frank's bedroom door.

"Please, *Papi*," I said. "I promise I'll do better."

There was no answer. Suddenly I saw everything I'd worked for going down the drain. I was never going to have this kind of life again, living in a nice place with a guy who loved me, a good job and a dog. I was damaged, broken. I started to cry, and I slumped down against the door.

It was freezing, too, the air-conditioning cranked up to high, but I couldn't do anything—I couldn't even get up to put some clothes on. I started shivering while I was crying, and after a while Frank opened the door and found me there.

"Sean," he said. He stood over me for a minute. "Come on, get up."

I just hunched over my knees, still crying. He squatted down next to me. "Come on." He lifted me under the arms, and I let him. He led me into the bedroom and got me under the covers. Then he left.

I must have dozed off, but I woke up when he came into the bedroom later. He slipped in next to me, and I tried to cuddle up against him. I was still chilled, and I needed his warmth to help me get back to where I hoped I could be.

But he turned his back to me and scooted off to the edge of the bed.

A wave of despair swept through me. My life sucked, and there was nothing I could do to make things better. And Frank, the fucker, wouldn't even help me warm up. Jesus, I'd moved to Miami to stay warm, not to live inside a goddamned air-conditioning unit.

I sat up in bed and looked over at him. He'd fallen asleep, his chest rising and falling, low snores ripping out of his mouth. Suddenly I couldn't stand to hear him, to have him there next to me. I picked up my pillow and stuffed it over his face.

He started coughing and gasping for air, struggling against me, but I'd built up muscles manhandling those big sheets of drywall. He kicked and waved his arms, desperation fueling him, but I held on. I don't know why I did it; it wasn't Frank's fault that I was so fucked up. It was just another stupid thing I did, after a lifetime of stupid things.

After a while, Frank stopped struggling, and then I pulled the pillow off his head and put it back under my own. I pulled his body close to mine. There was still some warmth there, though it was fading. I held him next to me, knowing I'd probably never feel warm enough again.

MISS TRIAL
ADAM MCCABE

Everyone expects a dick's life to be exciting, but for the most part, my life's been a litany of divorce cases and past due notices. That is, until this case walked into my office. This case had excitement and suspense, a little bit of something for everyone—except for me.

It had started with a phone call from a lawyer friend of mine, Jack Davis. We'd hooked up several years ago, and it must have been good for him. He sent clients my way whenever they had a problem that needed a detective. This case was a little different than most. It was murder.

Davis greeted me at my door with a kiss to the cheek. I was a bit startled by the move, as we normally shook hands with business dealings. He smiled as I pulled away, surprised, and put out his hand. "How are you doing, Logan?"

I brushed off the intimacy and focused on the stack of file folders that he carried. I'd read about the case with some interest. The accused killer was Steve Duerr, a local businessman who had contributed heavily to gay causes in Cincinnati. That was not a popular stance here, and he'd made a fair number of enemies in the local elite and conservative groups that cover the city like a layer of manure. Rumor had it that Duerr was preparing a test case for the courts to overthrow Ohio's draconian defense of marriage amendment. He had a partner and deep, deep pockets.

Duerr's family had made their money in beer, literally. They had owned one of the local brands for nearly a century, until Duerr's father had sold controlling interest to a national brand back in the 1950s. Duerr was the only child and last male heir in the family. Given his orientation, it wasn't likely that there'd be another generation.

I'd only read about the case in the newspapers. I wasn't in the rarified caste that Duerr ran in. I was merely a working stiff. Still, to the detective in me, the story just didn't jibe. Duerr had been taking a shower when he'd heard their two dogs barking. He'd waited for his partner, Rick Lambert, to do something about the dogs, since Lambert had told Duerr that he thought he was developing a migraine.

The barking went on for a few more minutes before Duerr had stopped the shower and gone, naked, to the entryway, where the dogs stood over Lambert's dead body. Duerr had put on some clothes, called the police, and been arrested for murder within the hour.

Duerr's story had been that the front door was open and that the storm door was unlocked, two things that never happened in their house. There were no signs of a break-in, no signs that the dogs had tried to protect their owner. However, Duerr's fingerprints had been found all over the handles of both doors. No other prints had been found. No shoe prints in the blood. No plausible motives had been produced. It seemed as though they had been alone, with only one person standing at the end of the encounter.

Davis was heading into his third trial for this case. The first jury had come back with a verdict of guilty; however, it hadn't stuck. One of the jurors came forward within a month and announced that another juror had quoted Bible verses at the rest of the jurors about the evils of homosexuality and had encouraged them to vote guilty since Duerr would spend eternity in hellfire anyway. The verdict was thrown out, and a new trial was ordered.

The second trial had resulted in a hung jury. The lack of physical evidence combined with the lack of motive had stymied the jury. They agreed that Duerr had opportunity and means, but without motive and stronger ties to the crime, they couldn't find him guilty.

With the third trial getting ready to start in a month, Davis was coming to me, looking for that Holy Grail for his client, a reasonable doubt. Davis wanted me to find a plausible, alternative theory to the crime. I thought it was a long shot, but since Duerr had deep pockets and I had office expenses, why not?

Davis dumped the files on my desk and plopped down in one of the chairs in front of my desk. "Long day."

"So what exactly do you want from me?" I fanned the files out like playing cards in a stacked deck. "I can't pull something out of my ass. I know you've had other detectives on this already."

"They were corporate. They were straight. It wasn't until now that Steve decided to let me use a gay PI. He thought it would look bad."

"And murdering your partner doesn't?" I made a mental note that Davis was calling his client by his first name. It was personal. In all the cases I'd looked into for Davis, he'd always kept it on a last-name basis, to keep some distance from the client.

Davis cleared his throat. "Yeah, well. He didn't do it. You'll just need to check the angles that a straight PI wouldn't."

I picked up a file and started reading. "So what can you tell me that's going to make this easier? What was the COD? I forget."

"Cyanide poisoning." Davis pretended to be fascinated by something out the window. This was not good. He always did this when he didn't want to talk about something. Maybe the papers hadn't printed all they'd known about the case.

"In his drink?" I knew that Duerr had a reputation for drinking, something that had not exactly been discouraged given his family's previous profession. I'd heard about a scene he caused at a fund-raiser last year. I hadn't been invited. A hundred dollars was a week's groceries for me, not a single dinner with a bunch of other rich guys.

"Um, no, injection."

"Injection? Sounds very personal. I understand a little now why the police liked him for the crime." I winced a little, thinking of a syringe filled with cyanide. I hated needles. "Did they find a syringe?"

"Down the street, wiped clean of prints. I don't think there's a lot to look at in that direction. The police tried as hard as they could to link Duerr to the cyanide and the needle, but they didn't have any luck."

"Well, if they couldn't do it, it's doubtful that I will. So exactly what did you have in mind?"

"I hate to sound cynical, but I've been at this long enough to want you to look at the marriage angle. There were some pretty pissed people when they learned that Steve wanted to float a same-sex marriage test case." Davis pulled one of the files from the stack I held and put it on top of the others.

"Mad enough to kill?" I flipped open the manila folder and looked inside. It had affidavits, four of them. Davis didn't speak, giving me time to digest the contents. Each one had been the testimony of a witness that Duerr and Lambert had gone to the courthouse in Cincinnati and been denied a marriage license by the clerk there. The civil servant had been verbally abusive, and a few photos of the event were paper-clipped to the back cover of the folder.

"Convinced?"

"What? That the clerk knew he was being set up and blew a fuse?

Nah, happens all the time. You're going to need a lot more than that to make a conspiracy case stick." I closed the folder and threw it on my desk, deciding that I wanted to keep it for another look when Davis wasn't staring over my shoulder. I played it low-key with the client, especially one as high-maintenance as Davis. He'd want results within a week, if not less. I wanted to make it seem like a long shot.

"Well, get started. We don't have time to waste." Before I could speak, Davis was out the door, and I was alone with a new case.

❖

I started by pulling a CD from the marriage folder and sliding it into my computer. I doubted that Davis had just decided to give me music to solve a case by, so I wanted to see if it was documents or notes.

Instead a full-screen image appeared and began to play. Someone had filmed the scene at the courthouse. Duerr and his partner came into view, both dressed in tuxes and carrying a manila folder of paperwork. The marriage clerk came to the counter, looked at them and walked away. Duerr was having none of that. I assumed that his name typically opened doors, not closed them, especially by not-so-civil servants.

The clerk brought another man with him, and they proceeded to read Ohio constitutional law 15.11, which banned marriage and civil unions in the state of Ohio, peppered with a few choice words that I figured probably weren't in the statute. Duerr tried to get the other man to sign a paper stating that he wouldn't marry them, but the man balked at signing. Duerr kept pushing until the two civil servants went back behind the glass wall again and the area was silent.

I started to click it off, but I noticed another thirty seconds of time left on the file. I kept watching. The camera scanned the small crowd that had congregated during the confrontation. At first, I couldn't see the significance as the clip went to black, so I backed it up and played it again, this time zooming in on the faces of the crowd.

It took me a third time, but I found what Davis had wanted me to see. Paul Greer, the head of Traditional Marriage Now in Cincinnati, was standing in the back row, face as red as my monitor would show, watching the whole thing. There was no way that it could have been a coincidence. Greer had been married for years, even though the rumors had swirled around him like pixie dust. He had no reason to be outside a small office in the courthouse unless someone had tipped him off. That meant a leak in Duerr's group and a possible motive for murder.

I decided that I needed to arm myself before taking on Traditional Marriage Now. I called an old buddy of mine, Aaron Wolf, to get some information. Wolf and I had been on the force together about ten years ago. He was still there, and I was in business for myself. Times change.

He agreed to meet me, and twenty minutes later, we were having a drink at Donnelly's Pub, down the street from my office. Donnelly's had been in and out of trouble for years, nearly getting their license yanked last year, but they still served the best martinis in town, and I was convinced I'd need more than one to get through this case.

Aaron Wolf had been my partner for almost twelve years, and in all that time, he'd never put on a pound, no matter what he ate or drank. He was still rail-thin with short blond hair that looked like a bristle brush. His eyes were an intense brown that made you feel as if you were the only one in the room, a great interview quality that had made more than one perp spill all.

"The Duerr case? What possessed you to get involved in that fiasco?" Aaron waited for my response by pounding back his beer.

"Five hundred a day and expenses, plus the need to eat and pay rent." I looked around the bar, trying to see if I knew anyone. Not a soul. There was a blond at the end of the bar I wouldn't mind getting to know, but not with Aaron here. He was fine with me being gay, but a bit of a prude about sex outside of relationships.

"Good luck with that. He's guilty as shit, you know?"

"And just how guilty is shit? I've always wondered." I took a sip of the martini and felt the vodka warm me on the way down my throat. I set the drink down after one sip, thinking that I should be more interested in what was being said than what was being poured.

"Still got that mouth on you? Guys probably like that, eh?"

"Adore it. So spill, what do you know?"

"Logan, you and I know that I can't talk about an open case. He's going to be retried again for the murder in a couple of weeks."

I winced, knowing that it was only a week and I had to get something quick. "For old time's sake? Like the old days."

He grunted and looked over his shoulder. "Geez, don't get all weepy on me. It's like this. Just the two of them in the house. One dead, one in a towel. No signs of forced entry, doors unlocked, alarm system intact but not armed. Dogs barked but nothing more, according to Duerr. Neighbors didn't see anyone suspicious running around the neighborhood. Who else could it have been?"

"That's what I'm asking you." I had Aaron now. I knew the smart-ass routine always got him talking, even when it was against his best instincts.

"Shit, why wouldn't Davis tell you this? He's been through two trials. He knows everything I know."

"That's not how I work and you know it. I'm the one who wants to find out for myself, not from the client or his lawyer. Too many reasons for them to lie." I'd caught Davis in a lie on another case I'd investigated for him about five years ago. He'd given me an alibi for the defendant and I took it at face value. Two days later, I blew a hole in it without breaking a sweat. We had a very tense meeting over that, where I pointed out to him that if I could do it in two days, the entire PD could break her alibi in less than an hour. He changed the defense, but never bothered to apologize.

"Fine. We always liked Duerr for it. We found witnesses who heard them fighting. One old lady who lived down the street saw someone come and leave Duerr's house a couple of times late at night. Ninety-year-old woman tells me that he's getting booty calls. Her words."

I laughed. Aaron could barely talk about sex with his buddies. I didn't know how embarrassed he'd have been discussing it with someone old enough to be his grandmother. "So no other suspects? At all?"

"Don't you think Davis would have pulled them out of his ass by now, if there were? No, not a one." He took another hit off his beer. "What are you getting at? You've got an idea. I can tell."

"Paul Greer. He was at the courthouse the day that Duerr and Lambert tried to get married."

"And you think it was more than just a coincidence?"

"It had to be. Which begs the question, how did Greer know when to show up?"

Aaron downed the last of his beer and stood up. "You're a good investigator. You need to find the answer to that question and the other things will fall into line." He left and I watched the blond play pool with his friends. He never left them, and I finished the rest of my martini and went out into the frigid night air by myself.

❖

I managed to get in touch with Davis before noon the next day, something of a miracle for him. I knew the case had to be weighing on his mind if he didn't follow his usual regimen of socializing until two a.m. and sleeping in until ten.

He sounded a bit frazzled when I got through to him on his office phone.

"I need a way to get to Paul Greer. I have some questions for him about this case."

Davis cleared his throat and paused so long that I took a look at my cell to see if the call had been disconnected. "Why exactly do you need to see him?"

I quickly outlined what I'd seen in the video and what I suspected.

"I might have a way, but I won't be able to tell you until later this afternoon. I have to go to the justice center first. Our client is back in jail."

I felt a cold shot run down my spine. "What did he do?"

"Parole violation, of all things. He went to the casino boats in Indiana and didn't notify anyone that he was going out of state. The police were tipped off and met him at the docks in Lawrenceburg. He's been there all night."

I grunted, thinking that Duerr was dumber than I'd thought or perhaps someone else was. This was the second tip that I'd seen in this case, the second time someone had played God. I was still mulling the possibilities when I heard Davis talking still. "Are you there?"

"Uh, yeah. Sorry. So call me back?"

He assured me that he'd call back soon and hung up. I began looking at the website for the Lawrenceburg police, hoping to catch a glimpse of someone I knew and could pump for information, but no luck. I decided to keep on with my Google quest. I looked up Traditional Marriage Now and started reading through the site. Greer had started the organization back in 1996 when only Hawaii might have been interested in gay marriage. The group had been funded by religious organizations who funneled millions to them. Greer had taken some of that money for his own perks, not that it mattered to me. The less he used for his smear campaigns, the happier I was. Even though I wasn't exactly in favor of me getting hitched, I didn't think it fair for me to deny it to others.

I'd printed a few pages off when the door to the office opened and Davis stepped in. His eyes were bloodshot and his hair was blown around in a way that wasn't planned. He had stubble on his chin and a small stain on his tie. He looked more like me than I normally did. He threw two tickets on the desk and started to walk out.

"What are these?" I called after him. He turned to look at me.

"Tickets to a TMN fund-raiser tonight. Four hundred dollars a ticket, so feel free to take someone who drinks a lot."

"Damn, we're supporting the wrong side to the tune of eight hundred bucks?"

"It's all for a bigger cause. We are trying to free an innocent man. Justice comes in many forms, and sometimes one has to trump another."

"So I'm guessing that taking another man with me would be out of the question?"

"If you want your precious answers, definitely. You'll be undercover tonight. I got another client to buy these for me under his name."

I went home, showered, and changed into my only tux. I was sure Davis had several and Duerr had even more. They were part of a crowd that I wasn't, and as I squeezed the tie around my neck, I was damned glad that I wasn't.

The soirée at the Phoenix downtown was about what I'd expected. I'd come stag, thinking I had the best chance to get in, learn what I could, and leave without someone else slowing me down. The room was opulent, high ceilings, loads of architectural details; the staff was dressed as well as I was. Champagne flowed and heavy couples showed their wealth with the girth. No gym bunnies here.

I scanned the room and recognized a few lawyers from my days as a cop. No one who used my services now. They couldn't be bothered to work with a working-class guy; they only worked with the heads of the bigger investigative agencies, which is why I thought I'd be able to pull this off. I tried to look constipated, so I'd fit in with this crowd, and began to mingle.

I was on my second glass of champagne, and there was no sign of Paul Greer. I was about to mark this up as a wasted evening of Duerr's money when I saw the blond from the bar across the room. His trim figure and gentle features seemed as out of place here as I felt. He was talking to two older men, both of whom seemed overly attentive to him. One fetched him another drink while the other listened raptly to his story, never taking his eyes off the boy. From his stance, I could tell that he was aware of the attentions and enjoyed it immensely.

He put his hand on the older man's arm and then stepped away. He headed for the restroom, and I decided to follow him. I was at a point where any coincidence was too much for me. I wanted to know why Greer had shown up at the marriage ceremony, and now I wanted to know why this boy was here.

I turned down the little hallway to go to the restrooms, when I felt hands grab my arms. I tried to shake them off as a natural instinct, but they spun me around. I was looking at two apes, both sporting buzz-cut brown hair and tightly fitting tuxedos. The one on my right poked me in the solar plexus before I could object, and the pair dragged me out of the ballroom as if I'd had too much to drink.

I had no choice but to be lead along while trying to catch my breath. They had to be familiar with the hotel, because we were at the freight elevators before I could stand upright. I hadn't thought to bring my gun tonight. It seemed innocuous and I hated the bulge it made in the coat. Even dropped in the pocket, it threw off the lines of the jacket.

So I'd let fashion trump prevention, and now I was squished tight between two goons in the elevator. With my first breath, I asked, "Who do you work for? I want to talk to them."

"You weren't invited. We don't need your type around. We're more than happy to see Duerr fry."

I paused at the amount of information they already had on me. Who had set them wise? My orientation was not immediately apparent to the people around me, so they knew enough to know who and what I was.

One of the apes pulled open the service door to the alley behind the building. Before I could make the step down to the asphalt, something came down hard on my head. I felt my knees buckle and I saw the pavement coming up to greet me more cordially than my host had. I hit with a thud and lay there.

I got up on one arm, but a shoe to the groin took me down again. The kicks started and I lost count of how many came in the next few minutes. Probably because I lost consciousness. I woke to the sound of a rumbling garbage truck coming down the alley. The driver looked a bit concerned but didn't speak. I got up and looked around. No one was in the alley except for me and the trash guys. I checked my watch, but the crystal had been broken by the goons. I couldn't know how long I'd been out or what time it was now.

I limped to the corner. My left leg was sore and the tux pants were ripped. I cursed the whole case and wished I'd never agreed to do this for Davis.

The sky was still a hazy gray that told me I still had time to get home and grab some sleep before I had to be at the office. As I moved down the street to where I'd parked the car, a figure stopped in my path. I cringed, thinking it was another attack from the goons or an aggressive panhandler, but I looked up to see a 6′4″ drag queen. She had mounds of brown ringlets brought up over her head and a wide-brimmed hat that coordinated with her hoop skirt. I started to say something when she pressed a card into my palm. "I don't want to be seen with you here, but we need to talk—today. Find me at the bar and I'll tell you enough to blow this case better than a toothless whore. Duerr was cheating on his partner, you know that?"

"What's your name?" I asked, trying to delay the first real break in the case from leaving me alone.

"You can call me 'Miss Trial.'" She sashayed down the street before I could say another word.

❖

It was nearly noon by the time I'd rested, shaved, and made myself presentable enough to see clients. The right side of my face was complementary shades of red and purple with my eye closed in a permanent wink. I'd tried to make it look better, but I'd only succeeded in drawing attention to my face. My only plan of attack today was to track down Miss Trial and find out what she knew.

I tried Simon Says, a hole-in-the-wall bar on Walnut, but no luck. No one recognized my description. She'd be hard to miss at that height in a hoop skirt. Someone should have noticed her.

I decided to try another part of town, thinking she should stand out. I went to Bronze, thinking perhaps someone knew her there. Northside was a trendy neighborhood, one that lived and let live. I figured she would fit in there. The bar was empty when I went in, and I could see the bartender from behind as he counted stock in the back of the bar. He finally returned to the front and apologized for his absence. I ordered a drink, a double only because I doubted that he'd serve me a triple. The dull throb in my cheek had not subsided, and any painkiller would be helpful at this point. He brought it back and set it in front of me.

I sipped the vodka tonic and asked about Miss Trial.

"I know a drag queen that fits the description, but not by that name." He turned and poured me the drink. "She do that to you?"

I shook my head slightly, trying not to bring up any more pain. "She saw who did. I need to ask her a few questions."

"She's a lunch hostess at the Universal Grill. She still might be there."

I downed the drink and headed off to try the bartender's suggestion. She wasn't at Universal Grill either, and it took two more drinks and nearly an hour to get her home phone. I did a reverse look-up and found that she lived a few blocks from the restaurant. I made my way there, taking care of the leg that had been hurt last night.

It was an old brownstone on Fifth Street, and of course, she lived on the third floor of the walk-up. I made my way slowly up the stairs and knocked on the door. She didn't answer, so I tried again. The door had a funny quality to the knock, so I gave it a push. It swung open. I didn't have to walk inside to see the mess.

Blood had been smeared across the entryway wall. Lamps and jars were smashed on the floor, and the trail of blood oozed across the tile floor into the living room. I followed it like the corpuscles and saw more wreckage. Her body was on the floor, twisted and beaten as mine had been last night. She lay there, uttering a soft moan, and I knelt down beside her. The blood from the carpet dampened my knee through my pants, but I tried only to focus on her.

"Who did this to you? What happened?" I pulled out my phone and dialed 911. The operator came on and I reported the beating.

Her eyes fluttered and she opened one eye, but it drifted. I wasn't sure if she was seeing me or something else. "Ddddd" was all she could say.

"Duerr did this? How? He's in jail."

Her head tipped back and nothing more would come from her ruby lips. I started to stand up, seeing the blood on the knee of my pants.

A shriek echoed from the doorway. I looked up to see an old woman standing at the door, her walker blocking my exit. The cry from her lips sounded like the wail of a siren, intermittently loud and soft, but never wavering in intensity.

I started to move toward her, but she screamed louder. The window on the far side of the living room was open, and I moved toward it. The fire escape hugged the building on this side, and I decided that my best move now was to beat it. I scrambled down the stair, cutting my palm on a rusty bar that had broken away from the rail.

I'd been on foot all morning, but decided to return to my car and try to figure out a place to wait this out. I'd barely gone two blocks when I saw the blond boy walking east on Seventh. I couldn't follow him because of one-way streets, but I circled a few blocks to catch sight of him as he made his way across town.

I circled around Main Street and watched as he entered the justice center through the visitors' door. The requisite families were outside, holding up babies for the inmates to see and waving at parents or spouses. Sometimes they flashed the inmate, letting him know what he was missing behind bars.

My cell rang before I turned onto Court. My mind was racing at what I'd just seen. There could only be one person that the blond had been going to visit: Steve Duerr. What connection did he have with an accused murderer, and what tie-in did he have to Paul Greer? He could be the missing link that provided me with a plausible alternative theory and a fat paycheck.

"Aaron Wolf" flashed up on the screen and I decided to answer. I figured that if I didn't, he'd just track me via GPS anyway. Aaron wasn't known for being shy about getting what he wanted.

"Yeah?"

"Hey, thanks for the lead. We in the CPD appreciate it." Even over the phone, I could see his shit-eating grin at this moment.

"What are you talking about?"

"That blond you've been tailing all over town is Paul Greer's son, Max. He just went into the Justice Center for a tête-à-tête with Steve Duerr. We'll have tape at eleven, if you're interested. He's not a lawyer, so it's all fair game."

"Jesus, you got people following me?" I looked around but saw no signs of a tail. CPD cars were thick as syrup around the courthouse, so it would be hard to spot just one car that had taken an interest in me. I was slipping if I hadn't noticed it before.

"You seem to be on to something here. This case has stagnated for a year, and in two days you've managed to get yourself beat up and a drag queen killed. Care to comment about that?"

"I'm not sure I've uncovered anything. Just pissed off the wingnuts." I turned the wheel and headed back to my place.

Aaron laughed. "Meet me back in your office in twenty and we can go over what you saw at the drag queen's apartment. The ME is putting the time of death way before you were seen in the room. I'm fairly satisfied that we're not after you."

I blew out all the air in my lungs until I felt almost as light as a twink. I hadn't realized how concerned I was about the possibility of being accused of that crime, even though I knew I would be exonerated eventually. I lived too close to the edge of my paycheck to lose cases while I defended myself against a bogus charge. "She kept trying to talk, but all she could say was 'D.'"

"For Duerr, I guess, but he's in jail, so it must have been a more involved message than that." I turned onto Vine and drove back toward Clifton and my office. We were still discussing the details when I pulled into a space on the street in front of my office.

Davis was sitting in my lobby when I got upstairs. He was dressed in a suit and bulky overcoat. "I've been waiting for you. What do you have for me?"

I explained the situation with the Greers and where the younger Greer was at the moment, providing a link between the client and the marriage crowd. I didn't mention Miss Trial, thinking that Aaron had probably told me more than he should have about the murder. "So he's gay and upset with his father? Perfect. He must have been feeding information to his father. He'd kill to keep quiet about his own orientation and so would Greer. This will go over great at trial."

I sighed, thinking of what I'd probably done to this boy's life, just because he seemed to have the hots for Duerr. It hardly seemed fair.

"Is there anything else? Remember, Duerr is in jail until we can prove he's innocent." Davis's question made the hair on my arms stand up. Maybe I was being paranoid, but it seemed as if he already knew about the drag queen's murder.

"Nah, that's it for now. I should be able to get you more details in the next week to use at trial, but I'll have enough to give you a few other suspects for the jury to think about."

Davis slid his hand into his pocket. "No need. I think that after today we have more than enough evidence to make them take notice." His hand flew out of his pocket and onto my leg. I felt a sting and looked down to see a syringe hanging out of my thigh. His thumb pushed the plunger down all the way.

"What?"

"Cyanide. Just like Rick Lambert. When the PI researching the case dies in the same manner as Lambert, the police will have no choice but to reopen the case. Then Duerr and all his millions will go free. It's not every day that a millionaire proposes to make you his next spouse. All I had to do was get him free, which I've done thanks to you."

I yanked the syringe out of my thigh and reached for the phone but Davis grabbed the syringe and ran toward the door. "You can't call. I unplugged the phone and snapped off the jack. You'll be dead before the EMTs get here."

The door slammed, and I slumped against the wall. This was it. The door opened again, and I expected further gloating from Davis over his future as I faded to black, but it wasn't. Aaron Wolf stood in the door frame. "What happened?"

I managed to outline the entire case to him in the minutes remaining. He radioed for a bus, but I knew I'd never make it. At least Duerr wouldn't either.

Last Call
Mel Bossa

W ho killed Easy D?"
Jitters, filtered cigarette pushed to the lip, tossed a Hefty bag over the greasy ledge of the Dumpster. "I mean, shit," he said, his buggy brown eyes shifting nervously to the recesses of the back alley. "It just ain't right Shield. Just ain't right."

Right? Shield thought. What did Jitters really know about basic moral codes? The guy was dealing weapons out of the Detour Club's kitchen. Between orders of prosciutto platters, Jitters—Detour's nimble-fingered cook—was slipping Hank's boys machine guns "to go."

"Well, I don't buy none of it," Jitters said, his face pinched with consternation. Or maybe it was heartburn. "Easy D was no rat. No sir." Jitters's eyes glistened yellow under the watery neon light. *Detour Club*, the faded pink sign twinkled. Jitters shook his head as if to rid himself of a nasty image and sucked hard on his cigarette. He didn't seem to notice it was burned to the stub. "Tell you what, if Easy was a snitch, then that four-eyed bastard deserved to have his throat sliced." He tossed the cigarette into a rain puddle. "Hank's boys sure did a number on him, huh? Rumor is, they couldn't even identify him, except for his teeth or something."

Shield nodded slowly, keeping his eyes on the front street. It was presently empty, but they were coming. Steady and dependable, the club's usual crowd would start rolling in at any time now. It was Friday, and the electricity in the air made him set his jaw. It was going to be one of those nights, and he was the only doorman on call. The other men had all quit before their trial period ended. Something he *should* have done three years ago.

But he couldn't leave this place.

Can't leave *him*, you mean, Shield silently corrected himself.

He turned up the brim of his double-breasted jacket. "Sugar in yet?" he asked casually. The mere sound of Sugar's name on his lips made his heart skip a beat or two. He'd spent the morning with the ravishing bartender, rolling around with Sugar under the boy's silver satin sheets. As usual, Sugar had left his luxurious apartment before Shield had stepped out of the shower. Sugar had left the coffee on for him with a note, which Shield had crumpled without reading. The notes were always the same.

Stay out of the rain, big boy. I'll see you tonight. Had a fantastic time.

"He's in Violet's office," Jitters said. "They're hollering like Armageddon in there." He looked around, his eyes narrowing at the shadows, and wiped his hands down the front of his loosely tied apron. "If Easy D sang, we're all gonna be in—"

"Easy was no rat." Shield's tone ended the debate. He cracked his knuckles and met the cook's uneasy stare. "Why don't you go back inside," he said, with a natural authoritative air. "You're breaking into a sweat over this."

Jitters's features coagulated like melted wax. Begrudgingly, he stepped back into the kitchen's pantry without a glance up.

The cook hadn't gotten his nickname for nothing, Shield mused. The little man was jumpier than ever this evening. But in all fairness, they all were—from the busboys up to Violet, the owner. Because no matter how much they went about their usual business in a phony, carefree manner, they all *knew* something had gone terribly wrong. Shield could feel it in his bones, and his stomach tightened with a growing sense of dread. He leaned his head back on the concrete wall, allowing the cold surface to cool his senses. For the last two days, he'd tried to appear unaffected, but ever since Easy D's body had washed up on the river's east shore, his thoughts had been doing damage to his conscience.

Easy D was the club's bookkeeper. Easy was the kind of quiet man who wore cardigans matched with neatly hemmed slacks. All math. No glam. No games. He never rushed anybody, and never stayed past midnight. He never touched the liquor, not even on Christmas Eve. Easy was a stand-up guy.

And he also knew every single sleazy deal that took place inside Detour's walls. Word on the street was that Easy had kept two kinds of books: One in which the club's activities were on the up-and-up.

And the other?

The other was a lengthy, revealing tab of the club's money-laundering racket. A record of the names of every cop on the payroll and every free bottle of liquor Violet passed under the blind eyes of the commission.

Yes, and every brown envelope Sugar carried out on Saturday mornings.

Easy D had been a very observant little man.

But why would Easy turn on them? He'd been nothing but a small-time accountant before the Detour Club. And because of Detour, Easy had moved his growing family to the 'burbs, bought a Cadillac and a time share in Boca Raton. All this paid for by Violet's generosity.

So why had Easy risked his life?

Well, it didn't matter. Hank's boys had made sure Easy D wouldn't be flying south anymore.

Shield couldn't get this queasy, sick feeling to quit. Hank's boys were brutes. Everyone knew the boys were hired help, tolerated only because they took on the jobs no "civilized mobster" would.

So if they'd slashed Easy's cleanly shaven throat, someone had paid them to do it.

And the death sentence had to have come from the one man who had the most to lose—the man who was the most ambitious of the lot.

Heat filled Shield's wide chest, leaking steadily into his every limb. His face flushed. He swallowed hard, dispelling the thought, which flashed feebly from time to time, like a dying bulb. He wouldn't consider it. *No way.* Sugar was a good boy—just a little too caught up in all this. Sugar liked the bartending money, the small claim to fame the club provided him, and who could blame him? Three years ago, the boy had been surviving on the charity of the local Baptist church—a play toy to its closeted pastor. Today Sugar lived in one of the city's most prestigious apartment buildings, and if anyone wanted to *play* with him, they'd better be prepared to dish out. Sugar was going places, and any man who wanted to tie him down, had better do it with "golden chains." But behind his stone-cold facade, there was still a naïve, blue-eyed farmer's son. Shield just knew it.

And Sugar would come to see how much he could offer. How deeply he loved him. How much he suffered for him.

Shield stepped out of the back alley and shook the rain off his hat. He had to get a grip. Tonight was not the night to go to pieces. He walked slowly, his arms loose at his sides, scanning the side parking lot and the front of the club. A few men had gathered under the street lamp. He recognized two of them. Regulars. No one important. The taller man looked over and raised an eyebrow in greeting, but quickly looked away. The men huddled, talking from under their turned-up collars, casting sidelong glances to the main door. They were reluctant to enter. Like men who were the first to arrive at a funeral.

Who'd take the first step to the open casket?

Word of Easy's death had rattled the customers a little. They acted like they'd caught sight of the sky's chipped blue paint, realizing they'd been duped. The Detour Club was a place where every drink came with a side order of silver-screen dreams. Every night, boys, straight off the cross-country bus, piled up at the bar with fresh, open faces. While Sugar dazzled them with his tricks and knock-your-pants-off smile, their eyes soaked in the light like bottomless wells. And as the night spread thinner and thinner, they leaned in closer and closer, swallowing every promise, every whispered compliment. Meanwhile, the vultures—washed-up film directors, talentless photographers, and bankrupt playwrights—filled the boys' glasses with watered-down booze and their pretty heads with cheap ideas.

The club was a haven of corruption.

The only thing it could really do was break your heart.

Shield folded his gloved hands together, watching the wet street glimmer, his throat clamping up tighter by the minute.

He had to get Sugar out of this place.

❖

Nine thirty. The night had crept up on him. Shield blinked, shifting his weight from leg to leg. He'd been standing at his post by the main glass door, watching the clusters of boys entering but without discerning their features. He was on autopilot, a dangerous state to be in tonight. He tried remembering what his mind had been on for the last two hours, but couldn't bring himself to care. There was only one thing he cared about—his urgent need to be alone with Sugar. If he could snatch Sugar away from those leeches at the bar, just for one minute—

"Hey, did you hear me?" A thin young man with an anxious face waved a bony finger in his face. "Is Ms. Kissme Deadly singing tonight?"

Kissme was Shanghai's drag queen persona. The boys loved her.

She was everything Shanghai, the main waiter, wasn't—tall, loud, and deliciously obscene.

"She's on at eleven," Shield said. "Let me see your ID, please."

The boy winced as if Shield had flicked a lit match at his skin. "You're kidding me, right?" The boy's lips stretched into a mocking, self-satisfied smile across his plain face. "Here's my ID." The young man flipped his wallet open and produced a hundred-dollar bill.

Shield averted his eyes from it as if the boy had shown him a pubic hair. He stared straight ahead.

"Oh, that's grand," the young man snapped, "you're gonna play high-and-mighty with me? You and me both know there ain't nothing money can't buy here." He stepped up to Shield's face, breathing out the scent of cherry cough drops. "Not even the law," he added boldly.

"Step away from my face." It was a command, not a threat. Shield knew these types—they got their kicks out of aggravating the doorman.

"Look, I came here all the way from—"

"No kid, *you* look." Shield turned his eyes to the boy, noting the dullness of his face. "I'm in no mood for your pestering. Get back on your tricycle and roll on out of here."

"You'll regret this." The young man's features blanched with anger. For a moment, Shield expected the boy to slap him, but he retreated, backing up to the sidewall. "I know somebody who works here. Didn't wanna bother him, but I will now. Oh yes, I will."

"Yeah? Why don't you do that." Shield crossed his hands over his waist, closing the conversation.

What did it matter anymore? He and Sugar were going to be busting out of this hole soon enough. He'd whisk Sugar away to some place golden, and they'd spend the rest of their lives drinking Manhattans under a foreign sun. After all, everything he'd done in the last three years—all of the trespassing he'd allowed on his integrity—he'd done for Sugar. He'd guarded this door for him only. He'd spent his nights in the cold for him. Always Sugar. Yes, Sugar was involved in Violet's racket, but only because of his vulnerability. In a world where beauty was the currency, Sugar had offered his to the highest bidder.

He would change that.

He would set Sugar free.

The wind lifted the dead leaves out of the gutter, and Shield shivered.

Time for a break.

❖

Shield made his way through the thickening crowd of men, his stare burning every face he passed. Behind the bar, Shanghai busied himself with fixing a Blue Lagoon. Shield leaned on the smooth, polished bar top, heart racing. "Where is he?" he said, trying to be heard without yelling.

Shanghai raised his slanted black eyes and shook his head. "Forget Sugar right now. Violet wants to talk to you," he said over the sound of the music. "She's in the office upstairs." He tossed his delicate chin up, looking intently over Shield's shoulder. "You should have let that skinny boy in. He's connected, I think."

Connected. Everybody in this joint was. Shield turned in the direction of Shanghai's pointed stare, knowing he'd meet a familiar pair of dumb eyes. Indeed, the thin, dull boy grinned at him from the back table, lifting his martini glass. "He isn't legal—" But Shield stopped himself. What's the use? he thought.

"Look, Shield, I don't know if you've noticed or not, but everyone's a little on edge." Shanghai pushed the vivid blue drink over to a slouching man in a badly tailored suit—a writer, most probably—and leaned in closer. Shanghai wore the club's uniform, a black shirt and white necktie, but on his frail frame, the clothes looked more like a disguise than classic attire. "Violet thinks someone's been playing her."

"Yes, and that someone's got a toe tag."

"She doesn't buy it. She doesn't think Easy D's the canary." Shanghai closed his eyes and touched his lips with two fingertips.

"But they went through his books," Shield replied flatly, his gaze scouring the ill-lit bar for that face, that beautiful, perfect face. "Anyway," he added more strongly, "maybe Easy wasn't gonna feed any of this to the boys downtown. Maybe he was keeping the information, you know, saving it for a rainy day."

"You mean blackmailing." Shanghai gasped unconvincingly. "Easy wasn't that smart. He didn't have the balls for extortion—"

"What do we really know about him?" Shield leaned back, skimming the counter with the side of his thumb. "What do we really know about anybody here anyway?"

Shanghai seemed to ponder this. Slowly, he nodded his head to the back room. "Speaking of deceit, Sugar's in there, going over some numbers, but he asked not to be bothered."

Shield glanced back at the main door, knowing he should head back to his spot. "You don't know Sugar," he said. "He's not like the rest of them." He believed it.

"Shield, it's not too late for you. You could quit this. You could disappear."

"I can't. I won't." Shield stepped away.

"I told you once, the minute you get a taste of Sugar, the tramp gets into your system, and you're hooked for good. I wish you'd listen—"

"Tell Violet I'll see her in a minute." Shield watched the back room's closed door. Behind it, his drug of choice awaited and he was aching for a bump.

To hell with all of them.

He needed to see those baby blue eyes.

❖

Shield knocked on the back room's metal door and pressed his ear to it. The music drowned out all other noises and he strained to hear any voices seeping through. Heart in mouth, he pushed the latch down and cracked the door open a peep.

Clad in his uniform, Sugar stood quietly in the middle of the cluttered room, his back to the door. He appeared to be watching the sky through the windowpane. All around him were scattered papers, and on the desk were five stacks of money, wrapped with brown elastic bands. "Go away," he said, waving a hand up dismissively. He didn't turn around. "And close the door."

"It's me, baby."

"Oh." Slowly, Sugar spun around. Under the naked lightbulb, his ashen locks shimmered. "You shouldn't be here," he said. His voice was dim. He glanced around and over Shield's shoulder. "Violet wants to see you." His eyes were clouded, his movements were tense. "Drink?" he asked, plucking an Eagle Rare bottle off the shelf.

Shield entered and shut the door behind him. His pulse raced. His mind had flown into chaos. He only wanted to put his hands on Sugar. There was only that.

"You know," Sugar said, smiling wanly, "Edward Fairmont is here." When Shield didn't react, Sugar rolled his eyes. "The famous director."

"So what are you doing hiding out in here?" Shield moved in closer, accepting the drink Sugar handed him. "You should be out there, charming him."

Sugar frowned. "How much money do you have put away?"

Shield's chest constricted. He sipped his drink in hopes of steadying his nerves and set it down gently on the bookcase. "Planning to go somewhere?"

"I might have to. I don't know." Sugar drank the contents of his glass and looked over at the money. Shield could plainly see Ben Franklin's face staring back at him. Sugar touched the first stack lightly. "Violet's testing me. She wants to own me."

"But you won't let her."

"I won't?" Sugar laughed. Despair glimmered deep inside his eyes. "And why wouldn't I?"

"Because you're better than them."

"I need to think." Sugar turned away from him. Black rain lashed the glass.

"I love you." Shield felt the words leap off his tongue, and a wave of nausea rolled over him.

Sugar swirled around. A bloom of red heat colored his cheeks. "Have you lost your mind?"

"Go away with me. If it's money you want, I'll write you a check—"

"Don't." Sugar regained his usual poise. He adjusted his necktie and wet his lips. "Don't go tender on me. Not now."

"Are you in trouble?"

"Look around you, Shield. We're standing in the flames and you're asking me if I feel hot."

"Then come with me. Tonight." Panic crept up Shield's back, and he grabbed hold of Sugar's hands. "We could book the first flight out of this city and no one would ever find us—" The look in Sugar's eyes snuffed out the rest of the words.

Sugar stood close, his hands rigid inside his. "No."

Shield shrank back, bruised.

"I don't want you to get hurt," Sugar said, dodging Shield's searing stare. "I never wanted you to get so close."

The room blurred around them, and Shield wiped his eyes. Nothing had ever stirred him to tears before. "I always thought you played along. Always thought this was just a game, and you'd fold when it was time."

"I play to win, Shield." Sugar turned his face to the window again. "But you knew that already, big boy."

Shield heard his own sharp intake of air as he held back a cry. Yes, he'd known all of it. He'd almost written this scene in his mind, word for word, many times over. From the moment he'd caught a glimpse of Sugar's eyes, he'd known how the movie would end.

"You used me, Sugar, didn't you?"

"Don't, Shield. Don't desecrate what we had."

"Desecrate?" Shield's voice boomed through the room. "I've been standing outside every one of your doors for the last three years. I lied for you. Broke all the rules for you. My rules!"

"It was your choice. I never asked you to."

"How can you say that to me?" Shield stepped closer. "Look at me. Why won't you look at me?"

Sugar flinched, but his eyes never left the storm outside the window. "I'm sorry, Shield. You don't belong here. Never did. You should sell everything you own and skip town." There was a fragile tremor in Sugar's words, but his body remained sealed from Shield. His face fused with the shadows. "Tonight, before the dirt starts sticking to you."

"I won't leave without you."

"Then you're stupider than I thought. Can't you see? I needed you, and now I don't. It's simple, really."

"You don't mean it. You're scared." Shield raised his hand to Sugar's shoulder, touching it lightly. "I know you—"

"You're a fool, big boy." Sugar swept Shield's hand off. "Everyone here knows it. You were so busy watching me, you were blind to everything else. Why do you think Violet kept you on?"

"I'm not blind. I know what's going on—"

"You know nothing!" Sugar screamed, his eyes blazing. "And don't you tell anyone any different, you hear me? You're a pawn, nothing more. A dumb brute!" He slapped his palm against Shield's chest. "Now get out! You're dead weight to me now. I want you to disappear!"

This time the cry Shield had been fighting tore out of his lips. It seemed to echo even as he stumbled out of the room, into the crowd, past Shanghai's concerned face, and into the heavy rain. "Whore!" he could still hear himself scream. When Violet stormed out after him, calling out his name in fury, Shield jumped over the puddles, skidding on dead leaves, and never turned around.

❖

Who killed Easy D?

Shield sat in his car, smoking his last cigarette.

Who gave the order? Who delivered his death sentence?

You know nothing, you dumb brute.

He flicked the ashes at the floor and leaned his head back on the seat. He'd turned the headlights off and parked across from Sugar's apartment building.

He closed his eyes, recalling the image of Sugar's elegant fingers— the way they'd grazed, *yes*, almost caressed, the stack of hundred-dollar bills.

You're dead weight to me now. I want you to disappear.

Shield glanced up to the rearview mirror. The gray Oldsmobile was still parked a few spots away, Hank's boys sitting inside in the shadows. They'd followed him out of the Detour's parking lot, staying three cars behind but always in plain view. For a moment, he debated about confronting one of the roughnecks, but decided on caution. One of the men might have been trigger-happy, and having his heart blown to pieces was enough for one night.

There was no need to get a matching set of spilled brains.

Shield stepped out of the car and tossed his cigarette into the street drain. Inside his jacket pocket, his fingers stroked a set of keys— Sugar's house keys. Last spring, Sugar had insisted on giving them to him. "You never know when it'll hit you, big boy. And when it does, I want you to come to me. I'll give it to you, when you need it."

Shield pulled his hat over his eyes, and crossed the quiet, uptown street with long strides. He was greeted in the vacant lobby by Paul, the live-in concierge.

Paul gasped. "Is something wrong? Did something happen to Sugar?"

"No, but I need to get something out of his apartment." Shield jangled the keys and tried to smile as best he could. "I'll let myself in."

"Of course." Paul made an effort to conceal a burp, but everybody knew the old queen never missed a date with his Jim Beam. "I'll be sending out a car for him as he requested."

Shield stopped short. "Right. Yes, please do. Three a.m., was it?"

"I believe it was two, but I may be—"

"No, no, you're right." Shield's heart pummeled inside his chest. "Two is correct. We wouldn't want him to miss his flight."

"I thought he was visiting his aunt."

Sugar, you cunning little bastard.

"I'm sorry," Shield said, feeling his features knot into a fist. "I'm confused. Long night, you know."

"Is there any other kind?" Paul settled back into his chair and resumed his nap.

❖

Shield flicked the lights on in Sugar's apartment and went to the window. He caught sight of the gray Oldsmobile and pulled the dark velvet drapes shut. Let Hank's boys sit there and stew.

He looked around. What had he come here for? What did he expect to find?

Plane tickets.

Or a suitcase full of money.

Some clue to Sugar's destination.

He went to the bedroom first and pulled on the lamp's string. The sheets were tangled, the bed still undone. He wanted to press the pillow to his nose, but refrained from torturing himself. Instead, he opened the top drawer of Sugar's oak cabinet, fumbling through underwear and socks.

"Fool," he said under his breath, snatching a pair of Sugar's white cotton briefs out of the neatly organized drawer. He held the clean cotton up to his face and sneered. "He played you like he did the others." With shaky fingers, he folded the underwear and carefully placed it back in its place.

He rid himself of his heavy wool jacket and threw it on the bed. He glanced frantically around the room, fuming. He'd given Sugar *everything*!

And while they were rolling under those satin sheets this morning, Sugar had been planning to leave tonight. Without a word.

Shield's throat stung and he picked up his jacket. What now, my love? he thought. What now?

Maybe it was time to hit the road. Maybe Shanghai was right. He'd slip Hank's boys a note. Something like, *Left town. Won't be coming back. Keep the change.*

Violet would be relieved.

The desire to survive Sugar began to rise inside his chest, and Shield held on to that brittle hope long enough to make it out of Sugar's bedroom and into the living room. If he could get out of this apartment without having a meltdown, he could get in his car and follow the little tramp's advice. He'd drive until the tank was empty and think about everything else then. But even as his clammy hand turned the front door's golden knob, he could feel the town's black tentacles closing in around his ankles, his waist. The city was inside him; it beat alongside his heart, and no matter how far he drove, he could never leave it.

Well, he'd try.

Shield opened the door and peeked out into the wide carpeted hallway. He stepped out and turned back to take one final look at Sugar's home.

The place he'd once secretly renamed Heaven's Candy Shop.

His eyes moved over Sugar's sumptuous furniture, and his heart jumped. On the sideboard, wedged between two tabloid magazines, he caught sight of an envelope. Adrenaline surged through him.

It had already been neatly opened, and he pulled the thin white paper out of it. Now his eyes raced across the tightly written words addressed to his beautiful, double-crossing lover.

> *Sugar,*
> *This is your last chance. You won't talk to me. You won't look at me. I am insane with love for you. It's done. I went through with it and there is no turning back. I need you, Sugar. I've arranged everything. Don't fret over anything. Come to me. Before it's too late. There is nothing I can do for you if you choose to stay.*
> *Forever yours.*

No. Not this. Not this. Shield clutched the letter between sweaty fingers. How could you? Sugar, you've done it now!

He read the letter again, slowly this time, letting the words scald his eyes. Ah, his darling blue-eyed man was in the midst of a getaway. Where was Sugar running off to? And who was the bleeding-heart fool arranging it all? If he could get his hands on this stranger, he'd tear his—

Enough. Hold on, big boy. Shield stuffed the wrinkled letter into his pocket and bolted out of the apartment, slamming the door behind him. He was going back to the Detour Club to blow the lid right off

Sugar's kettle of lies. If this was a game to Sugar, then the stakes were about to get higher. Shield flew down the stairs instead of waiting for the elevator.

As he swung the lobby door open, he was welcomed by Paul.

"Sir," Paul said, his eyes shining like new shoes. "A call for you. I put the gentleman on hold, and oh dear, I seem to have forgotten about him. I do apologize, I—"

"No need," Shield mumbled, heading quickly to the reception desk. He picked up the phone, gripping it hard. "Hello?"

"Is this—" The voice on the line broke up, and Shield heard the man fiddling with papers. "Well, he calls you Shield, right?"

"Who is this?"

"I need to talk to you. This is urgent. It can't wait any longer."

Shield glanced over at Paul. He was nodding off in his antique velvet chair.

"Talk."

"No, not over the phone." The man's voice was young. Smooth and clear. "Meet with me."

"No." Shield could barely keep still. "I've got too many problems as it is. I'm not adding you to the list."

"It's about Sugar."

Shield's knees buckled. "Where are you? Who are you?"

"I'm at the Brickle Inn. Room number six."

Shield knew the motel. It was a desolate place in one of the grittiest neighborhoods in the city. "Nice place," he said grimly, rubbing his tired eyes. "And why should I jump through this hoop? Listen, I've got a tag on my heels and—"

"Please come. Just lose them and meet with me." The man gulped in air and pressed on, in a voice thick with panic. "There's something you need to know about Sugar, and you need to know it now."

He nodded. Yes, he'd come. Yes, he'd take this dumb risk. For him. For Sugar.

❖

"All right, boys, let's go for a little stroll." Shield turned the key in the ignition and flicked his eyes to the side mirror. "Let's see if you can handle my driving."

Pedal to the floor, he raced out of the quiet neighborhood straight into the glistening streets of the city, Hank's boys close behind. He turned onto the boulevard, zigzagging his car between the late-night drivers. He rolled down the window and stretched his arm out, letting the wind blow rain on his face. He was exhilarated. He was in motion.

To hell with standing still.

Around him, the strip flashed its pretty lights like a hooker on her last trick. Neon invitations to wine and dine twinkled in the rain, beckoning him to *stop, think, be reasonable.* But Shield drove on. No—there was no coffee black enough, no whiskey smooth enough, to coax him from his path. He was going to the Brickle Inn, and he was going there alone.

When he reached the end of the boulevard, the light was green, but he slowed down and glanced up at the rearview mirror, watching the Oldsmobile.

It was 1:23 a.m. The last East Train was rolling in. Shield had spent his life riding the E-Train; he knew its schedule like his own scars. At his right, a city bus approached the intersection, and Shield braced himself. As the light turned red, the bus pulled into the road and accelerated. Shield floored it, speeding across the intersection, avoiding the nose of the bus by a hair. He crushed the brakes and brought the car to a screeching stop. As the bus rolled past with its driver honking and waving a fist at him, it shielded him from Hank's boys' view. Shield jumped out of the car and into the dark mouth of the subway stairs. He'd left the keys in the ignition and a note he'd scribbled on a pack of matches for the boys.

> *Please have the car cleaned, thanks. When you're done, you can leave it in my driveway. Tip is inside the glove compartment. I figured ten apiece would do it.*

He shot down the stairs and even had enough time to drop a coin in the turnstile.

When the train reached the platform, he looked over his shoulder and stepped into an empty coach. As he settled himself into a seat, his eyes adjusting to the bright light inside, one of Hank's boys slammed his fist against the wagon's window. Shield leaned back with a smirk, drawing his damp hat over his brow. It was a forty-minute ride to where he was going. If he didn't try to sleep, he'd start to think about Sugar. About Sugar's mouth on another man's skin.

So instead, he closed his eyes and listened to the E train's metal wheels grinding along the rail.

❖

The Brickle Inn looked exactly the way it did when he'd seen it last. Shabby, and about as welcoming as an outhouse.

Above the reception office, the word "Vacancy" shone permanently. There were two cars in the parking lot. One of them was missing a tire.

Shield walked across the lot and knocked on door number six. He glanced around. The wind had died down and left everything silent. Clouds of mist danced around the street lamps. This place could have sunk to the bottom of the deepest sea and no one would have noticed.

The door opened. Before Shield could get a good look at his mysterious host, a warm hand pulled on his wrist and the door shut behind him.

"Turn on the lights," Shield ordered, but his voice wasn't as steady as he'd have liked.

"Sorry, I didn't realize I was sitting in the dark." The man's black silhouette moved across the room. There was the sound of the switch, and artificial light flooded the room. "Gosh, I really didn't think you'd come, but I"—the man paused, scanning the room nervously, nibbling his bottom lip—"Cigarette?" he finally asked, reaching for a pack of Marlboros left open on the bed. "I only have three left. I've been smoking myself sick in here."

Shield declined. The man pacing the room was neither tall nor short, and there was nothing extraordinary about him. His clothes were plain, his dark hair disheveled, and his shirttail hung out of his brown pants. His green eyes were intelligent and bright.

"Who are you?" Shield asked, getting his wits back.

The man lit a cigarette and blew out the smoke. "My name is Edward." He extended his hand, but Shield didn't take it. "I'll get right down to it, I suppose." Edward lowered his hand and blushed slightly. "Boy, I really don't know how to say this, but here it goes. I'm Sugar's…well, I was his, well we"—smoldering ashes tipped over on the man's hand and he waved them off—"had an affair. It was so silly of me. So silly, really."

Silly?

"You and Sugar had an affair?"

Edward knit his eyebrows. "You're very calm. I thought you'd—"

"Don't be fooled by appearances. And get to the point."

"All right. I'm married. You understand? I have children. I'm, I'm in charge of commercial loans at a bank. A very prestigious—"

"But that didn't keep you from climbing into Sugar's warm bed, now did it?" Shield made a conscious effort to keep on a poker face, but inside, his heart thundered. Images of Edward and Sugar tangled in sweet, but compromising positions, raced through his mind.

"No, you're right, it didn't," Edward said meekly. "I have no excuse for it. I don't know what got over me."

I have an idea, Shield thought.

"But what Sugar is doing is loathsome. I won't stand for it." Edward crushed his cigarette hard against the glass ashtray. "He wants twenty thousand dollars from me or he'll tell Martha everything."

Sugar, oh Sugar, honey boy. Shield winced a little, but stared at Edward's flushed cheeks.

"And all because of this Violet woman. This," Edward shook his head in disgust, "conniving bitch."

"Go on."

"Sugar's unhappy. He's stuck between a rock and a hard place. He wants out, he says. And I tried to talk some sense into him, but…I guess I don't need to convince you. You know him, don't you?"

Shield didn't answer.

"Sugar is going to hang me out to dry. Violet runs a money laundering racket through the Detour Club, he swears. She has cops on payroll. She gets half of her liquor for free from a contact at the commission, and she's in deep with the Polish mob." Edward paused, his gaze sharpening on Shield's face. "I don't know if he's lying. I don't know what to believe anymore." Edward appeared to deflate like a popped balloon, and he plopped down on the edge of the bed, burying his face in his hands. "Is is true?" he asked in a pleading voice. "Is Sugar really in that much trouble?"

"It's true," Shield said. "Sugar may have lied about many things, but not about the Detour. Not about Violet." The words rushed out of him. "Violet runs the scam with a couple of no-good thugs they call Hank's boys, and she has her hand in everyone's pocket. Sugar got tangled up in it, but he's not a bad boy. He just doesn't know his true worth." At these words, Edward's eyes seemed to veil with emotion. Shield pressed on. "The Detour is corrupt. It's all a sham. All of it. Sugar is just trying to survive it."

"It's true, then. All of it." Edward hung his head. "Everything Sugar said. The fraudulent transactions, the guns, everything."

"Yes," Shield said. "All of it. But that doesn't give Sugar the right to—"

"Okay, Shield." Edward's jaw tightened and he got to his feet. "Turn around and put your hands behind your back."

Shield scowled. "What's going on?"

Edward flashed his badge. "I don't wanna draw my weapon. Please. Turn around and breath deep. It's over, Shield." He produced handcuffs out of his pockets. "Easy D swore you were our man."

"Easy D?" Shield shrank back. "He's dead, he—"

"Turn around." Edward firmly forced Shield's arms back and shackled his wrists. "Easy D is sitting in a hotel room downtown. He jumped the fence three months ago and knocked on our door." Edward checked the handcuffs' grip and turned Shield around. "He handed us Detour's books two weeks ago."

"But—" Shield's voice was strangled. *No.* He'd sworn to protect Sugar, and instead he'd sold him out. "Sugar didn't have a choice," he almost moaned, spinning around to face Edward. "He's clean. He's a good—"

"Well, that's what Easy says." Edward picked up the phone and punched in a number. "I got it," he said to the interlocutor. "I got it all." He opened the nightstand's top drawer and pulled out the tape recorder. He pushed the stop button down.

"Whatever you do, don't drag Sugar into this—"

"What is it with this boy anyway? You men seem to lose your marbles around him."

"Easy D is alive," breathed Shield. "I don't get—"

"Look, Shield, Easy's books had a price, and we paid it."

"Immunity."

"You're smarter than you look." Edward peeked out the window. "That's right. Immunity and a nice lifelong vacation to an island called the witness protection plan." He opened the door and signaled to someone outside. He turned his bright eyes to Shield. "Him and Sugar."

The car. The letter.

Sugar, oh Sugar.

Two men walked in. "This him?" the older of the two asked.

"That's him." Edward pulled Shield up by the arm. He stuffed his loose shirttail into his pants and threw on his navy blue jacket. "The boy?"

The older man's face twitched and a faint blush of pink rose above his neatly starched shirt collar. "Gone," he said. "Vanished into thin air."

"What do you mean, gone?"

Shield's eyes darted to Edward's blank expression and he knew. *That's right, boys. Gone.*

"I don't know," the old cop said. "But when Easy's car, I mean, when the *informant's* car showed up, the boy was gone."

"They searched the joint, right—"

"Yes, but he was gone, I tell you." The man swallowed noisily. "Most of the money, too."

Edward—not so gently now—jerked Shield forward. "Did he tell you where he was going? He must have told you. Come on, spit it out."

Shield remained limp, watching the sky turn pink. "We had a fight. He didn't say anything."

"Goddamn it, without the boy we don't have a deal." Edward pushed Shield out of the room, to the unmarked car parked sideways by the door.

"What are you saying?" the younger cop barked, his face twisting into a grim expression.

"I'm saying, Easy will deny everything. He'll call those books a hoax. It was Sugar or nothing."

And wasn't it always so?

Shield let Edward lead him to the car and slid into the backseat. He leaned his head against the leather and tried to get his body into a comfortable position.

"You find that boy!" Edward cried, circling around to the front seat. "I don't care if you have to comb through every city and cornfield across the country!"

Through the rain-streaked window, the sun's first rays grazed Shield's face, and he closed his eyes, sinking back into his seat. Last call, boys.

He smiled.

The bar man has left the building.

THE CASE OF THE MISSING BULLDOG
JOSH ATEROVIS

I knew it was a mistake saying I was a private dick in my online dating profile, but hey, it never fails to impress. I'd already gotten several dates off that alone, and now it seemed I had a case, too. Sure, I could have turned it down, but I've always been a sucker for a pretty face and a perky ass.

Which would explain why I was following that ass through the back door of a run-down Baltimore row house in the dark hours of the morning in a neighborhood I'd usually avoid after sunset.

Did I mention we had to duck under police tape stretched across the doorway?

I paused just inside. "I feel compelled to point out that I could lose my license for this. Why are we here again?"

He stopped, glancing over his shoulder. "Because this is what I was telling you about."

"You haven't told me anything. You said you needed help."

"I do. And this is why." He flipped a switch, and the fluorescent overhead light flickered on, illuminating a dingy kitchen—complete with crime scene. The police had been in and done their thing, but Mr. Clean had not yet made an appearance. Dried blood splattered the bank of chipped enamel cabinets that might once have been white, but had long since settled into the grayish color of neglect. Something had been dragged through more blood on the grimy, cracked, and curled vinyl floor. A smeared bloody handprint on a dented refrigerator added a nice touch.

I raised an eyebrow and turned to my guide. His face was drawn into an expression of disgust, but otherwise he didn't look overly upset by the scene. He certainly didn't look like a cold-blooded murderer, either.

He looked every minute of his nineteen years and not a second more. The boy was model gorgeous: dark curly hair, almond-shaped eyes, and lips just begging to be kissed long and hard. His ass was high, round, and made to fit perfectly into my palms.

I stuffed my hands into my pockets to keep them from testing out that theory. "So what's the story?"

"The police think I killed my grandfather."

"Good story. Why would they think that?"

"Because I hated him."

"Good reason. Did you do it?"

"Would I be talking to you if I had?"

"I dunno. Why are you talking to me?"

"I told you, I need help."

"Help with what? Obviously they don't have proof or you'd be sitting in a cell, not giving me the Halloween tour of the family manse."

"They didn't find him, just…this." He gestured toward the mess. "They couldn't keep me since there's no proof of a crime at this point."

My fingers twitched. A cigarette would have been fantastic right about then, but I'd quit a couple of months before. I'd have settled for a shot of something strong and undiluted. "I charge extra for moving bodies."

The boy frowned. "I didn't kill him."

"When do they think this happened?"

"Last Friday night."

"So a week ago last night?" He nodded. "Where were you?"

"Staying at a friend's house in Fed Hill."

"Can your friend vouch for you?"

"My friend went out. I stayed in to work on a big paper that was due last week."

"Anyone else see you?" He shook his head. "Of course not. That would be too easy. So you have no alibi, and you have motive. Tough break."

"That's it? Tough break?"

"Calm down, kid. I'm still here, aren't I? Why don't you show me around the house while you tell me more about your grandfather."

"It's a long story."

"What else are we gonna do? Stand here and look for shapes in the bloodstains? I think that one looks like a kitty. What do you see?"

He frowned and stalked away through a narrow doorway. I turned off the light—the less we advertised we were in the house, the better I'd feel—and followed him into a room that smelled of stale cigar smoke. He snapped on a lamp to reveal a shabby living room matching the dreary kitchen.

"*Abuelo* wasn't too concerned with cleanliness, as you can tell," he said with a dismissive wave toward the dirty, mismatched furniture.

"I'm sure he wasn't expecting guests. What did he do?"

"For a living? He was an immigrant. He's from Argentina. He worked odd jobs mostly, sometimes as a handyman or carpenter here and there—whatever he could find."

"What about your *abuela*?"

"She died before I was born."

"Did he always live in Baltimore?"

"No, he moved around quite a bit."

"What about you?"

"I was born in New York. My mom moved here when she and my dad got divorced."

"So he's your mom's father?"

"No, my dad's." He picked up a framed photo from a nearby table cluttered with an overflowing ashtray, dirty glasses, and unopened mail. He handed it to me. "That's my dad and grandfather."

The photo showed a short, barrel-chested, middle-aged man standing next to a handsome younger man, two boys at their feet. I didn't see any family resemblance. The kid obviously took after his mother.

"Who're the boys?"

"Me and my brother."

"Who's older?"

"He is by two years."

"Were you close to your grandfather?"

"Not at all. I didn't even know him until a few months ago. My parents split up when I was about four. My mom is from Puerto Rico, so she moved me and my brother back there to live with her mother. We were there for a few years, then Mom sent for us after she was settled here. I saw my dad maybe once every few years, and never saw my grandfather at all until he showed up in town back in August."

"How'd the happy reunion go?"

"Not so great. My mom didn't want my brother and me to have anything to do with him."

"But you did anyway?"

"I did. My brother didn't."

"Why not?"

The kid turned without answering and walked out of the room. I switched off the lamp and followed him into a cramped, cell-like bedroom with no windows. A double bed, stripped to the bare, stained mattress, was shoved against one wall. Some of the stains were more blood. I assumed the sheets had left with the police in evidence bags.

A beat-up dresser leaned against the opposite wall. I wasn't sure if the wall was holding it up or vice versa. On top of the dresser lay a scattering of loose change, a small mountain of receipts, a cast-iron bulldog, and a watch.

He pointed at the dresser. "His wallet was there, too. The police took it with them. They said it still had money in it."

So robbery wasn't the motive. I walked over to get a closer look at the receipts. A couple came from cheap local restaurants, several were from bars of the dive variety, but the majority were from a nearby strip club known for being particularly gritty. The deceased wasn't going to be up for any grandfather-of-the-year awards. "What's with the bulldog?"

"That was his nickname, *Dogo*, because he was like a bulldog."

"Ah." I recalled the photo the boy had shown me and I understood why he had earned the nickname Bulldog. "You still haven't told me why your brother didn't get cozy with grandpa. Or why you hated him."

"I'm getting there."

"Hurry up. I charge by the hour."

The kid hunched his shoulders. "My brother would have nothing to do with him, but wouldn't say why—only that he was bad news. I decided I wanted to get to know him anyway."

"Why?"

"I...I never really had a dad. My mom's father died when she was a teenager, and she was an only child. I have a few uncles on my dad's side but I never knew them. I guess I liked the idea of having a man in my life for a change."

He looked like a little lost boy, and I fought the urge to put my arms around him. No need to get distracted. "I take it that didn't work out so well?"

"No."

This interview was starting to feel like pulling teeth. "Are you going to tell me what happened or are you going to make me guess? Can we at least play charades? How about twenty questions?"

"He tried to have sex with me, okay?"

That brought me up short. My tobacco craving went into overdrive. I actually scanned the room for a spare cigar, even though I never touched the things when I was still smoking.

I turned my attention back to the kid, who was busy staring at the floor, his hands balled into fists at his side. "Care to elaborate on that?"

"At first, everything seemed great. He was good to me. We cooked dinner together, he gave me beer, he told me stories about my dad, said how much I was like him. It was nice, you know? I hardly know my dad. It almost felt like I had a real family for a change. For a little while, at least. Then…"

I felt like a jerk for asking, but I needed to hear the whole story. "Then what?"

"He got drunk one night. Got me drunk."

"And?"

"And he started telling me I was pretty. He kept hugging me and rubbing my back. Then he touched my butt. I tried to pull away, but I'm not very big. He was stronger…"

"Did he…?"

"Fuck me? No. He touched me, told me how much he wanted me. I punched him in the face and ran out when he let go of me."

"What did you do? Did you tell anyone?"

"I went to my brother's. He doesn't live that far from here. I was crying. I told him what happened, and he got really mad. He said…he said our grandfather used to do stuff to us when we were little. I don't remember, but he did. He said that's why Mom left our dad. She found out. That's why she sent us to Puerto Rico. She was trying to keep us away from him. I didn't know." He broke down, tears spilling down his cheeks.

I wanted to comfort him more than ever but kept my distance as he swiped angrily at the tears. "You were little. Not your fault. What happened next?"

"My brother told my mom."

"How'd she react?"

"She…freaked out. She said…"

"What did she say?"

"She said it was probably his fault I'm gay."

I really wanted a cigarette. "What do you think?"

"I don't think it works like that."

"Smart kid. Did she say anything else?"

"She…" He stopped and stared down at the bare floor.

"Spit it out."

"She said she should have killed him years ago."

Interesting twist. "So why isn't she a suspect?"

"She was out of the country visiting my *abuela*, her mother."

"And your brother? Is he a suspect?"

"He was home with his wife and new baby."

"So that leaves you?"

"I guess."

"Is there any more reason for them to suspect you other than process of elimination?"

He shrugged. I had a suspicion I wasn't getting the full story. "You gotta tell me everything. I still haven't decided if I'm going to help you or not, but I'm sure as hell not getting involved if you're holding out on me."

He sighed shakily. "My fingerprints were on the knife they found in the kitchen."

I felt both my eyebrows fly up.

"Oh, come on. Not you, too. I was over here all the time for a while. I helped him cook dinner. Of course I touched his knives."

"When did he…get inappropriate with you?"

"About a month ago."

"And he didn't wash his knife since then?"

"You see where cleaning fell on his list of priorities."

"Not sweeping or emptying an ashtray is one thing; not washing your dishes for four weeks is something else altogether."

"So you think I did it, too?"

"Well, you haven't said you didn't."

"I didn't kill him," he shouted. "Why would you be here if I did? I want you to prove I'm innocent."

I shut the bedroom door. If he was going to start yelling, I didn't want the neighbors to hear. "And how do you want me to do that?"

"Find who did kill him? I don't know. That's what you're here for."

"You're not giving me much to work with."

"What more do you need?"

"For starters, whatever it is you're still not telling me."

He deflated a bit as he ran out of bravado. "I came back."

"When?"

"Last week. The night he was killed."

"Why?"

"I was angry. He was acting like nothing had happened, calling me all the time, inviting me over for dinner. I didn't answer, but he kept leaving messages on my phone."

"What did you do when you got here?"

"Nothing. I mean, I yelled at him, told him he was a sick bastard. I told him I knew what he used to do to me and my brother when we were little kids. I warned him to stay the hell away from me or I'd go to the police. I...I just wanted him to leave me alone."

"Did anyone hear you?"

"I don't know. Maybe. It was warm last week, so all the windows were open. One of the neighbors could have overheard." He looked away. "I guess someone did, because they must have told the cops. When they took me in for questioning, they asked me about the fight."

"Where were you yelling?"

"In the front room."

"And the knife?"

"He...he came at me. I was afraid. I ran into the kitchen and grabbed the knife. It was on the counter. I told him to stay away from me." He choked back a sob. "I swear I didn't kill him."

"What did he do?"

"He left."

"Front door or back?"

"Back."

"Then what did you do?"

"I left."

"Front or back?"

"Front. Why?"

"We'll get to that. And the knife?"

"I left it there."

"On the counter?"

"I guess. I don't really remember. I was pretty upset."

He was still pretty upset. Tears kept on rolling down his cheeks. I finally couldn't take it anymore. I moved toward him, and he practically threw himself into my arms.

While I stood there holding a crying kid, I tried to work through his story. My gut told me he was telling the truth, but some things still didn't add up. Someone could have easily heard the kid yelling at his grandfather, seen the kid leave through the front door, and…what? Plotted a murder to frame the kid? With the knife he'd conveniently left his prints all over? Too easy. Too pat. It was much more likely that whoever overheard the fight just called the police.

Maybe the kid really did off his *abuelo* and was just using me as a patsy. That didn't make sense, though. As he kept insisting, if he'd done it, why involve me at all?

Most importantly, where was the stiff?

That was the strangest part. Why leave a bloody mess all over the house but hide the body? Sure, it's harder to prosecute without a corpse, but it's happened.

A slight scraping noise from the other part of the house suddenly distracted me from my thoughts. The kid, still sniffling into my chest, didn't seem to hear it. I pulled away and placed a finger over his lips before he could say anything. He gave me a confused look. I jerked my head toward the door, and comprehension and fear flooded his face.

Before I could formulate a plan, the doorknob started turning. I left the kid standing wide-eyed in the middle of the room and flattened myself against the wall behind the door.

Someone came into the room, and the kid gasped. "Wha…what? I thought…"

"You thought I was dead?" The man took another step into the room, and I saw him clearly for the first time. He'd aged, his hair had turned iron gray, but I still recognized the missing Bulldog I'd seen in the photo. "Sorry to disappoint you."

"But…what? How?"

"It takes more than a coupla cuts to get rid of me." He chuckled, but it was a dry husk of a laugh, no humor or warmth to be found.

"But there was so much blood…"

He snorted. "I guess I'm a bleeder." He held up his hands, which were wrapped in dirty bandages. "So are you here to finish the job, or did you decide to come back for more?" He rubbed his crotch suggestively, and my stomach turned.

The kid hadn't been completely honest with me. Maybe I should've figured that out, but I certainly hadn't seen zombie grandpa coming. So far, he hadn't noticed me, which was just how I wanted it.

Grandpa took another step forward, and the kid inched away until the bed caught him behind the knees and he fell onto the dirty mattress.

Grandpa chuckled again. "Right where I want you. This time we'll finish what I started."

As he advanced on the cowering boy, I scooped up the cast-iron dog and clobbered the old man on the head. He dropped like a sack of potatoes.

I stood looking down at the unconscious *abuelo* and shook my head. "This is going to be a mess to explain."

❖

Much later that morning, I was still enjoying my afterglow as the sun started lighting up the sky with its own glow. We'd spent hours at the police station explaining our way out of the situation. There was a small chance the kid might get charged with assault, but since it was a clear case of self-defense, nothing would come of it even if it happened. Even a trained monkey would be able to get the case dropped—not that most of the public defenders in this town were much better than trained monkeys.

We'd celebrated our release by heading back to his apartment for a little release of our own. I was completely exhausted and ready for nothing more but to fall asleep, but I realized the kid was staring at me, his head resting on my bare chest. Nothing good could come of this.

He ran a hand through my chest hair. "Any chance this won't be a one-night stand?"

I groaned. "Nope. None."

He poked his bottom lip out, and I thought about biting it again. "But I like you."

"Thanks. I like you, too."

"Then why can't we at least try dating?"

"Ah, hell, kid. Can't you find anybody your own age to play with?"

"You're not that much older than me."

"I'm old enough to be your"—I did some quick math in my head and didn't like the results—"your much older brother."

He sat up. "You can't deny the sex was great."

"I'm not denying anything. Why would you even want to date someone my age?"

"I'm tired of younger guys. They're all so…immature. All they want is sex. You're older, wiser, and stable."

"You got one right, at least." I slipped out from under him and started to pull on my pants.

"Where are you going?"

"Home. Have a great life, kid."

"But—"

"Don't worry. I'll send you the bill. I accept all major credit cards."

He tried pouting again, but it wasn't working anymore. Not too much anyway. When I started buttoning up my shirt, he rolled his eyes. "Fine. What about cash? Will you take a personal check?"

"Look, kid—"

"Or I can think of a few other ways to pay off my debt..." He pushed the sheets down a little lower, and I missed a button. "Come back to bed. I'm sure we can work something out."

I know a decent offer when I hear one.

IMAGO BLUE
FELICE PICANO

When he opened his eyes upon a seamless, all-enveloping, pale lilac light he immediately realized that he knew for certain these four things:

He was alive.

His name was Blue Andresson.

His official vocation was Investigator: privately established, financed, and (as a rule) client-paid; specializing in Difficult Interpersonal Relations and Potentially Criminal Conflicts.

And lastly, if he reached his hand out he would encounter—while his elbow was still slightly flexed—the surface of a soft, protective Heal-All within which he had been enclosed, and which had served to return him back to full physiological health over an unknown period of time, while he was seriously injured or chronically ill, and which a thrust-out fingernail would easily rip open.

There was one other thing he wished he knew but did not: What was he doing inside a Heal-All in the first place?

There would be time enough for that. His sense of his body odor was growing stronger by the second from long enclosure and he must get away from it. He reached out his right hand, struck the smooth surface, tore at it, and it collapsed all about him with a soft hiss.

Instantly a soft chiming began somewhere below the plinth upon which he lay.

He tried to sit up and found it difficult: His muscles wouldn't work, not even supported by his hands. He tried again and felt slightly nauseated.

The room around him was an even softer lilac color, nearly pearl; its surfaces were smooth, indistinguishably similar, at least from this level and position.

He tried to sit up again and this time achieved an inch or two of head height. His body was unclothed and the Heal-All's therapeutic dews were quickly drying in the ambient warming air. His chest hair was sparse, golden; his abdomen flat, muscled, his legs were long and also golden haired, his feet were large and personable.

A fourth attempt to sit up got him onto his elbows facing his large perfect toes, and what he now saw, since it slid open with a whoosh, was a door, through which three completely clothed and hooded figures stepped and immediately came to his side.

"You're awake, Mr. Andresson? How do you feel? Not too disoriented, we hope?" said One.

"You must be thirsty. And hungry too, I'm guessing," said Two.

He was. And nodded so.

"Your personal secretary has been notified," said Three. "You're unexpectedly early and she is out of town on her own business and can be here in a few hours. Should we contact her? Or a friend or relative? Your mother is listed as next of kin. There is as well as a relationship that might have been as close as fiancée before your injury."

A slight transparent tube arrived from out of nowhere right at his lips and he received a delicious cold drip of water that he then sucked at greedily. After which he said, "No. Thank you, don't bother anyone," somehow surprised by the deepness of his voice (was it because of this resonant little enclosed chamber?). "In fact, my secretary need not hurry back if she doesn't have to. I'd prefer her to finish her business already begun."

What he wanted more than anything else was time, he'd already decided. Because now there was another unanswered question: "How long have I been here? In the Medical Cocoon?"

"Close to a year": One.

"Don't worry about it, Mr. Andresson, you were very seriously injured": Two.

"You're fine now. Perfect, in fact": Three.

No, I'm not, Blue thought. I don't remember things. Things I believe I ought to remember.

The plinth tilted slowly and a shelf came out at his feet. He realized he was being stood up.

An opposite wall mirrored over and he could see himself in it.

"You see. You're perfect": Three, again?

He was in fact, physically perfect. Medium-height, handsome in a square-jawed, straight-nosed, blue-eyed way, with thin lips and a facial fuzz of light hair. His upper body was strong and muscular, with well-developed arms and legs. No scars apparent anywhere, naturally; the Heal-All would have gotten rid of any. No sign of any kind of deformity. Everything looked size appropriate, except maybe slightly larger than normal genitals. He figured he must be about thirty years old.

Why did all this seem ever so slightly, although by a mere hairsbreadth, off? Blue wished he knew.

There was more chiming now and One said: "Contamination is nonexistent. Quarantine off!"

Their masks melted off the medicals' faces and two were revealed as females, one male.

"We're going to stand here and help if you need help walking. Take one tiny step," Female one said.

She and the male medical held out supportive arms for him to lean upon. Blue did put out his hands and he was able to stand away from the plinth for a few seconds before total exhaustion set back in.

"Excellent start. Your physical rehabilitation will set in later today," female number one assured him. "It will be constant, and, I'm afraid, rather annoying at first."

"But it's necessary," the male said. "If you're to get on your feet and be a full member of our community again."

"We think you can do it in a few days. Less than a week," she added.

He lay back on the plinth and it slowly angled back so he was in a partially sitting position again.

They left and Medical Number Three arrived again with a tray in which he could smell simple food. Eggs, toast. He was ravenous.

The tray attached easily to the extensor sides that he just now noticed were part of his plinth-bed, and he could reach out for the transparent bulbs of food.

"We'll begin therapy with you reaching," Three said. She was the least attractive of the three medicals and the nicest.

"We'll also be exposing you to visual, audio, and then intellectual stimuli," she said.

A Vid-set suddenly turned itself on where the mirror had just been, with soft-focus moving pictures of the outer world: a countryside, a pond, an ocean, along with music he almost recognized.

"All you say is 'more' and it will provide you with stories, newscasts, weather, sports, specific information, whatever you ask," she added. "You can also ask it to repeat. Or to be only music, or only voice."

"I understand," Blue said. "I can control it by my voice."

"There is an important intercontinental air-race final taking place," she suggested.

His hands could barely grasp and hold the bulbs containing 1) a poached egg 2) a fruit juice concoction 3) a weak herbal tea. When he dropped the last one it bobbed right up and floated toward his hand again as though somehow attached.

He could do this, Blue decided.

Three fussed about him, covering his body with a light sheet, tucking it in, beneath. As she was leaving he asked:

"What was it?"

"What was what, Mr. Andresson?"

"My serious injury?—I can't seem to recall it."

"You really can't?"

"Not at all. No."

"That's probably because you were shot in the brain."

"I was shot in the brain?"

"Yes. Twice. Once in each lobe. In the brain twice and once each in the kidneys, the liver, and the heart."

With that, she sailed out of the room, humming to herself.

❖

Andresson Investigations inhabited a stylish three-room suite on the ninety-eighth floor of an upscale bronzed glass building at the northwestern transportation-hub edge of the city. The rooms were spacious, comfortably lighted with diffused and slightly dimmed afternoon sunlight, and with built-in storage areas. His own office appeared to be the most functional and most characterless of the rooms.

Another, slightly smaller office, had been converted by his secretary for use in her new part-time business, which as far as he could figure out involved stock option bids on speculative off-world futures. It was filled with computers and printer-scanners, all merrily chugging away by themselves, accessible to his secretary he assumed through the Vid-net. The third room, the outer waiting area, had received the most attention of the three in terms of design and expense—fine carpets, posh furniture, gleaming coffee tables, sculptures of lighting, individual framed artwork, etc. It all showed Andresson Investigations to be a successful business—to have been once successful.

It was six days after he'd awakened and Blue was just too bored and itching to do something, anything, to remain in the Heal-All Center. When he'd checked out, he'd been warned by Medicals One and Two there that he was still only at about seventy-four percent of his required physical capacity to continue his vocation as usual and that he would have to continue therapy for weeks more.

He'd noted with satisfaction in the downstairs lobby of this edifice that a new health club had opened twenty-six stories below. He'd sign up later today.

His secretary, a woman approximately forty-five years old, had not yet appeared except by Vid-screen phone. When she did, she remarked that although his vocational insurance had covered all the expenses included in keeping the agency afloat for six months, that she had become quickly immersed in her own sideline, and that she'd begun showing profits early enough in that sideline that she took over the suite's lease, utilities, and other incidentals for the following five and three-quarter month period.

She told Blue she was prepared to share the quarters with him for as long as he wished. She had no interest at all in his line, she stated rather bluntly, being a "fearful type, unlike yourself," whom she characterized as "curious and adventurous." She had referred his newer clients to a competitor at the other end of the city who was prepared to refer clients back as soon as Andresson was once again in business. She doubted that he would need a secretary for another few months yet, and she agreed to hire one for Blue when he did.

I'm an investigator," Blue had thought, the first time he'd clearly been able to think about his past and future in the Heal-All Center. "I'm privately established, financed, and client-paid. So I must have been pretty good. And I specialize in 'Difficult Interpersonal Relations' and 'Potentially Criminal Conflicts.' So I must have been very good."

It wasn't lost on him also that he couldn't have been all that good, or at least all that lucky, since he'd ended up so seriously wounded that it had required almost a year to return to health. Surely something or someone he'd been investigating had been responsible for putting those five bullets into fatally strategic spots of his body.

As an investigator it was his job to find out how that had happened—and why.

But right now it was his job to find out who he was, since that also remained alarmingly unfilled and in fact mostly blank.

His desk had six drawers. Two locked, one with a touch-print, the other with a key and vocal recognition. He had the key, and while the drawer's primitive system hesitated at first, it must have been voice-keyed because it did open upon the second utterance of a simple sentence, "Open up for me. Go on, open!"

In the first were leather billfolds filled with cheques and cash cards. Confirming that he was quite well off in business. The other drawer held six files that had still been "open" at the time that he was so seriously injured.

He began reading them.

Looking for a stylus to take notes with, he rummaged in a bottom drawer and there Blue came upon a small leather woman's purse. Inside it, no ID. but the expected articles: lipstick, compact and powder, breath mints, eye shadow, etc. Presumably, he thought, it belonged to the fiancée who had been mentioned in the Heal-All Center twice, but who had made no attempt to see Blue while he'd been there.

No surprise. He probably wouldn't have seen her if she had tried to contact him. The reason being, he didn't remember her at all. Didn't remember any kind of close sexual or affectionate relationship with a woman. He could bring up no face, voice, nor perfume that was at all familiar.

Some other faces did come up as he remained awake and pensive, if very slowly: his mother's (after four days) and just barely, and actually just before he accepted a Vid-screen phone call from her, confirming that's who she was. She rather looked like a much more refined version of himself, at least from the neck up, with a porcelain complexion and a darker version of his light hair. She also had a familiar-sounding voice, but Blue didn't truly recognize her, and he didn't hide that fact, and she was sweet and accepting about that fact, saying twice how she'd been certain he'd never awaken and certainly not with a full memory, not after what the medicals had told her when he'd first entered the Heal-All Center.

Once Blue had seen some Vids of her, his former secretary also seemed somewhat if again not deeply familiar. She'd been fairly new anyway, he'd been told, having only worked for him for four months before his shooting, so there was no big surprise there.

In what little there was of Blue's memory beyond the cognitive, the practical—i.e., what the brain surgeon-bots had hurriedly worked on getting reconnected before sticking him into the Heal-All cocoon a year before, there had been traces of memory of a male his own age, or thereabouts, nice-looking, darker-haired, slender, named Bern or Burn, something like that.

A relatively strong trace memory of affection was connected with him. Perhaps they had been boyhood pals who'd remained friendly after they'd grown up. That would be okay. He would probably be trustworthy—if anyone could be considered so in a life that had nearly ended, violently, explosively, like his almost had. No word from this friend, of course, and frankly Blue hadn't trusted his "mother" or his own memory sense of her well enough to ask her who this male friend might be.

But he had no trace memory of any woman. So whom did this purse and this make up belong to?

"Face it, Blue," he said to his bathroom mirror, shaving before leaving the Heal-All Center, "She could be anyone. You're a hot and handsome man." Medical Number Three had slipped in while he was napping on Awake Day number two and made her own investigations of certain lower body areas of his physiological condition. When he'd joked about it to Medical Number One, she'd asked, "Would you like that to stop? Or continue?" He'd said "continue, please" and she had replaced the lower-status doctor with herself. This also had not been surprising. As far as he could figure, his personality structure was undoubtedly that of a person who'd had great looks and who'd used them to get what he wanted and needed. Except...

Odd, this memory business.

Now Blue recognized that he had the most difficult job of all: finding out which case had come so close to doing him in. He'd need to know that. He hadn't decided whether to avoid anyone and anything connected with it in the future or not. Maybe, some little mental itch suggested somewhere in the periphery of his mind, maybe he might also figure out why he'd been targeted.

❖

It was later that afternoon that the downstairs auto-desk called and told him he had a visitor. A Vid showed her to be a woman in her mid forties, made up rather severely, dressed carefully, and surprisingly ethnic looking, perhaps from off-world? He knew from the Vid-channels he'd been watching that very few people chose to highlight their ethnic origins by retaining inborn characteristics. Especially when it was so easy to lose them. The name given for her was Dusk Martila, with no matronymic or patronymic supplied, and which meant nothing to him.

Naturally Blue asked the auto-desk if she'd been to his office before, and it named the date he'd been told he had been killed. Negative. Several weeks before then and once since, the auto desk said, so Blue let her come up. The auto lift CT scanned her for metal and other types of weapons or powders or explosives. Negative.

"What can I do for you?" he greeted her at the door. Close up, Martila was taller, and more prepossessing. Her voice was somewhat guttural, too, with a slight and difficult to place accent, so she'd not had vocal cord reparation either. On purpose, it must be, as she dressed well-to-do to be able afford the simple operation.

"Blue Andresson?" she asked, slightly surprised.

"We've not met?" he asked. Then added, "You heard of my Heal-All experience?"

"We have met, yes, but you are—changed," she said.

"Only physically," he assured her. "You didn't take Davis's suggestion to go to my colleague, Mr. Chango Lock?"

"I did. We met. I didn't trust him. Not like you," Martila said, not looking to be all that trusting in Blue either; at least not at the moment.

They sat and his work screens brought up her case and the work done so far, and in seconds they were discussing the business she'd come for: which had apparently been held in abeyance for almost a year. It was a Missing Person: and both a Difficult Interpersonal Relation with a Potentially Criminal Conflict. Her first husband had vanished three years previously, mysteriously, from his place of business, which he shared with his wife. Through Blue's earlier efforts, she had already received permits to continue operating the family business in full sole authority, and even sell and or lease it out. But now she had met a countryman, she said, and he wanted her to get a more permanent declaration so they could unite their businesses and "other matters," which Blue took to be interpersonal and probably marriage. "Also," she added, "before you ended up in a Heal-All, you left a message saying you thought you had an idea where my husband might have gone to. I took it you were looking into that idea."

Blue didn't recall that at all, of course. And if he had, he had left no clue to himself among these screen files on the case.

Martila renewed the bank number where money could be deposited into his agency's account and left. For the next half hour, Blue listened to his many notes on the case as the auto-Vid played them back to him. To his surprise, he made a mental connection that the pre-Heal-All Blue had never made before, concerning a bank account and an important client.

He caught Martila by pad-phone in her private vehicle, not very far away from his office, and checked the information. The minute Blue mentioned it, she grew excited.

"Yes," she said, darkly, "this I can well believe of this person," and she used some kind of foreign obscenity. Blue said he would need as much information as she had on the new suspect, and he would delve into it more deeply.

Feeling renewed, and suddenly comfortable in his new skin now that he had proved to himself that he was useful, he strode over to the floor-high windows and stared out through the triple-paned, multiply tinted glass. The blue-white sun was setting, quickly falling behind the artificial-looking skyscraper scrim of the city's far horizon. Only the dull orange sun still hung in the crepuscular sky, casting a warm evening glow.

❖

"It was a lovely funeral, Blue," Andre Clarksdotter gushed. "I spared no expenses. After all, you're my only child. Our life insurance was all paid up and it had accrued so well; it's been decades since anyone has died and I decided to do it up full scale. Everyone came. Family, of course, they flew in from all over. Many of your school friends, and even some of your clients."

She'd pre-fed the Vid-screen before arriving at his flat and it now showed moving Vids of the ceremony—sound turned down—and afterward at the celebratory feast. He could clearly see sitting next to his mother the very same young man who'd popped into his memory upon awakening, and who appeared at least as upset as she was. Then the Med Center people arrived and Blue's inert and by then fully cocooned body was ceremonially placed in the Heal-All, people said their good-byes, and it was floated out.

Andre already knew of Blue's memory loss and couldn't have been sweeter or more explanatory as he asked who each person shown was. When he reached the bereft, handsome young man with the dark curling hair, she said, "Bruno. Of course."

"Bruno?" He tried it out and it sounded right.

"Bruno Thomasson, your adoring fiancé. He hasn't found anyone else, you know, in all the months since. In fact, Blue, from what he was saying the other day when I called to tell him of you, I do believe he wants to try to see you again."

"Bruno?" Blue now asked, stunned. "Then I was…"

"A woman. Yes, Blue. Didn't anyone explain it to you at the Med Center? We seldom come back the second time as the same gender. Your aunt/uncle Clay Clarkson? the one who died in that fall, climbing the Capsilian Mountains? She once explained all the complex genetics of it to me, but you know how dense I can be about scientific matters."

"So that's Bruno!" Blue now said, not Burn, of course, and looked at the Vid-screen as the compelling figure was highlighted and zoomed in on, the large dark, misty eyes, the downturned full lips and picturesquely sunken cheeks.

"You don't have to see him, you know, if it makes you—nervous," Andre settled on, and changed the subject back to those in the family she would never speak to again because they simply never even acknowledged Blue's death, never mind Andre's grief.

It all began to make sense now: the purses in the office and at Blue's flat with no ID in them. The scarcity of male clothing in the closets: two suits—both new looking. Scarcely anything in the way of male accessories. Only the most basic toiletries in the bath. It also explained the rare photos: all of them of other family members, not one of them showing Blue.

He had to ask, "Mother? What kind of woman was I?"

Andre only wavered a second. "Frankly, Blue, you were a complete pain in the ass. You were a physically tough, emotionally cold, adventure-loving, overconfident, thoughtless, hard-living, self-absorbed egomaniac to almost everyone but Bruno. You drove me crazy as an adolescent. I needed most of the family and sometimes City Services, too, to help raise you. In truth, you were such a bitch to most of us that it was a constant wonder that someone didn't kill you years ago."

As Blue absorbed that, Andre added, with a nervous little laugh, "We're all hoping that those qualities will fit you better—now that you're a male."

When Blue chuckled, Andre added, "You know, Blue, while it's a difficult adjustment for many, some people only begin to really find themselves when they're second-born."

❖

Chango Blocksson's Vid-screen image was of an older man, but his voice was older than his appearance and Blue was forced to conclude that he'd done at least one expensive voluntarily short period in a Heal-All age-proofing himself. Blue's mother had done two of those herself and looked almost Blue's age.

Two of the cases Blocksson had taken from Blue's six had been solved. Cases closed. Two of the clients, Dusk Martila and another woman, had chosen to not to accept Lock's services. And two cases remained in progress: one a long-term private investigation by two wealthy brothers of their industrialist father's concerns: "Very straightforward and utterly paranoid," according to Chango. "They think he's hiding their eventual heritage." Another, an equally long-term search for an amateur pilot, a playboy, lost over Oceania, whom his family needed declared dead—or alive, and non-compos mentis, they almost didn't care which.

"I don't buy anyone involved in these two cases as even possessing a weapon, never mind using one on you," Lock declared. "Their motives aren't impelling enough," he added, even before Blue could ask his opinion. But it confirmed Blue's own surprisingly strong investigative intuition.

"This Martila woman, however…well, her I just don't know. They're off-worlders, you know: Albergrivians, and whatever those people do is weird and mixed up with that cockamamie religion they've got."

"The sixth case?" Blue asked. "Did you look at that long enough to see if it was more than a simple potential female infidelity?"

"It looked like a simple female love triangle. By the way, you look terrific," Chango added. "And I've got to thank you. I met my fourth wife at your funeral. A second or third cousin of yours who came along with others. We're married five months: So we're now distantly related. She says you should come to dinner. Bring that guy Bruno, too, if you're still seeing him?"

"Should I be?" Blue asked.

"Everyone at the funeral seemed to think so. He was all busted up. But of course things may be a little iffy between the two of you."

After Chango signed off, Blue made a Vid-call to Bruno. Luckily, he wasn't in and asked for a message to be left. This close up, Bruno's photo made a very strong impression. Shaken, Blue left no message at all, even though he knew the Vid would take a trace of his call.

All the rest of the day, Blue threw himself into the Martila case. Leads had developed in the year since he was gone, and suddenly they began edging out into possibilities.

One lead directly shot into a Albergrivian Benefit Society, and its president, a publicity-shy character named Aptel Movasa who had moved the organization out of downtown to a local Civic Center hub, only a few streets from Blue's office. Perhaps a drop-in visit was in order?

Blue had used the transportation hub stations there but he didn't recall ever going beyond the little concentration of public buildings another two streets over to the commercial area, which, now as he walked that way, was clearly evident by the increased pedestrian traffic.

The familiar, male-female, two-headed bust stood at one end of a pedestrian-only street, and it was also marked that it tolerated none but ultra-light, public, surface vehicles. The second thing Blue noticed were several storefronts given to inter-world transport, inter-world freight, and inter-world currency conversion. In each window, the strangely square script of the reformed Albergrivian alphabet translated simple phrases.

The north side of the street, for most of the block, was given over to what seemed a modern enough looking hotel named Rha Cantrobergle and described as an "Alberge for Off-Planet Travelers." Sure enough, across the street, the next half dozen shop fronts on the southern side were given over to Albergrivian ethnic food specialties, what appeared to be native clothing and other dry goods, and what might be a combination tea room and Skimko parlor.

His phone-pad went off and he read the tea room's address as the same as last given for Aptel Movassa.

He knew he would look out of place the second he stepped in the door, so he didn't attempt to be anyone but himself.

Through the haze of Spital-Leaf smoke, only one person of the dozen or so elderly Albergrivian gentlemen seated around floor-mounted smokers looked up from the games at their complex Skimko boards.

"Zha Andresson," Blue introduced himself to a clerk. "Seeking

Zha-Kas Movasa." The ethnic honorific got a few more heads turned his way.

"Does Zha-Kas know the Zha?" the tea-counter clerk asked. He was young, thin, typically unattractive, and given his awful complexion, unquestionably addicted to carbonated drinks.

"Unfortunately, this Zha has not had the pleasure," Blue said. He knew he was being scanned from another office or at least being checked out by some minion just making a Skimko move at a table nearby.

The clerk caught a nearly invisible signal and brought one refill to a pair of ancient players, and a barrage of Albergrivian chatter ensued. The clerk bowed away, taking the used cartridge with him.

"Zha-Kas Pirto remarked how more lovely than an Albergrivian woman are the young men of this world," the clerk tittered.

Blue turned and bowed to the flatterer, who curlicued an age-spotted hand in response, without looking up from his complex, three-level game.

Behind his counter again, the clerk apparently read off a message, because he said, "Will the Zha follow, please."

Behind the back wall curtain of red-reed, a small elevator slid open and Blue stepped in.

Just as the doors closed on him, Blue heard a baritone shout he was certain was directed at himself; too late for him to worry how hostile it might be.

The lift flew up twenty-five floors and flashed open onto what seemed to be a rooftop garden with a central fountain. Beneath an awning, a standard desk much altered by colorful ethnic throws and runners, and behind it was an elderly Albergrivian, almost hidden within a throne-like chair constructed of the same red-reed, this time twisted into arabesques.

Blue bowed slightly three times approaching and used the correct honorific and Movasa waved him to a seat. A slender youth almost identical to the clerk downstairs immediately brought them wide-mouthed mugs of a fragrant purple-tinged tea, and vanished. Movasa quickly sipped his, to show it was harmless and tasty.

Blue followed and presented his credentials.

"A simple case of a vanished businessman," Blue explained. "It eluded my predecessor. She apparently was unaware of the wide-ranging knowledge of the Zha-Kas."

"To the contrary," the soft-voiced, unattractive old Albergrivian said. "She sat where Zha Andresson now sits, and she lacked all the social graces. How could a person speak to her?"

"How indeed! Apologies."

"She might have been a sibling to yourself, Zha."

"We never met," Blue truthfully said, couching it so that if lie detection were built into the table or chair he would not be suspect.

"She was lovely, like the women of this world. But she could not equal yourself, Zha. Already in the tea parlor below they are replaying the Vid taken during your brief visit and perhaps saying and doing unclean things…in your honor, Zha."

Blue had done enough homework on Albergrive society to believe this might be taken either as a provocation or as a compliment: he decided to take it as a compliment. He smiled.

"Worse than her attitude, Zha," Movasa went on, "Was her ignorance of proper manners."

"The Zha who wishes to"—Blue purposely used an Albergrivian word that could either mean "crucial conversation" or "sexual intercourse," depending solely upon its tonal inflection—"with a Zha-Kas must acquaint himself with proper manners."

Movasa laughed at the double-edged witticism.

"Tell, me Zha Andresson, how may this old Zha-Kas be of help?" Movasa asked.

"An attractive woman client"—and here Blue used the Albergrivian term he'd especially learned to describe one who was both widowed and yet not—"seeks her husband long missing." He produced his phone-pad and flashed the most flattering videos of her he could locate. "This Zha naturally believes the Zha-Kas would be able to assist. Her name is Zhana Martila. She wishes to now be Zhannia Martila," making it clear that she wanted to be single again.

"To remarry a Zha of this world?"

"Indeed not. To marry an Albergrivian. But," Blue quickly added, "I believe one who is mainstreamed into this world's society and work."

"A lad ignorant of the ways of his people," Movasa said.

"Or one who is knowledgeable and…uninterested."

"More and more such Zhaos exist," Movasa sighed, using a term unfamiliar to Blue. "Perhaps seduced by love. And Zhanna Martila? What does Zha Andresson think of her?"

"We have only met once, briefly. But she is honest, and she seems without external motive. Three years her husband is gone. The Zhana seems to be beyond anger, reproof, or even revenge."

"On our world, one favor gives birth to another," Movasa said.

"This Zha will of course be in your debt in the future," Blue admitted. He suspected this was how the old power-broker worked anyway.

"This Zha will put out a"—here Movasa used a word meant to signify query but also demand—"for this missing Zha Martila. You will hear from me in three double sunsets."

"Whatever future, non-illegal, request you make of this Zha will be yours," Blue assured him.

They sipped their tea and watched the blue sun prepare to drop below the horizon. The sky flashed green several times, then settled into dull orange.

Movasa was called indoors, and Blue stood up and began bowing to leave, but the old man pulled him over and gave him a kiss on his cheek. "So lovely, these males!"

As Blue stepped into the elevator, Movasa looked out of his office and said, "This will take you directly to the street. That way you may avoid disrespectful words."

"You mean like those words I heard as I stepped in before?"

"Those words were not so much disrespectful as they were descriptive—if crude." Movassa smiled.

Bruno Thomasson looked far better in a video than he did even in still photos. Blue found himself reminded of what the Albergrivians had said several times about the "lovely males" of this world. No wonder women like his mother worked so hard to keep up.

When he'd returned to his office after the meeting with Movasa, Blue had immediately taken a "crash-course" in that paired planet's people's interpersonal relations, with an especial look into their sexuality, a topic he'd ignored totally before going to meet Movasa, if not exactly to his peril, at least to his slight discomfiture.

He was surprised to see that same-sexuality was a fairly recent development among those off-worlders, and one that had only taken fire when the two planets had once made contact. Even now, it was not much practiced on their home world, and it seemed to be chiefly a cross-cultural phenomenon, actually more spoken of than acted upon, even here in the City, among those who visited or had immigrated. Among Albergrivian women it was all but unknown at home, and it was rare here; however, it seemed widespread among Albergrivian men who had relocated. But even among those newcomers, the author of the short documentary Blue watched believed, it was more spoken of and written about than actually practiced. Acceptable mostly because of some ancient Albergrivian texts and poems that everyone learned at school in their early years, detailing the legendary loves of great warriors and their teen male lovers.

Blue's world's athletes and male celebrities were the main fantasy choices of both younger and older Albegrivian men, who filled out their fan clubs and paid astronomical sums for porn-Vids of their idols (a few of whom seemingly and quite callously produced them specifically to cash in, ruthlessly locating and exploiting the very few existing Albergrivian beauties for their videos).

Blue wondered if he might bring this topic up later on at dinner, because at long last Bruno Thomasson had called back and left a message asking if they might meet for dinner.

Blue would have to see. He tried to recall what his mother had said about Bruno, besides the fact that he'd been smitten with Blue as a woman enough to propose marriage. Given the vast Thomas family holdings, its long and colorful history, and its political and financial status in the City, Bruno must have been crazy about such an unlikely mate for him as a tough woman investigator. So Blue was gracious as he could be on the Vid-screen responding and said he was "looking forward" to "seeing Bruno again"…

The restaurant Bruno chose was an expensive one, so he wasn't hiding this meeting from his clan. In honor of such a classy date, Blue dressed as well as possible.

All the more of a surprise then when the maitre d' showed him to a private table set apart from the rest of the diners by floor-high mirrors and metal panels.

However, at it sat not Bruno Thomasson but two strangers. They introduced themselves to Blue as Thomas family attorneys, and immediately asked if Blue would sign a quitclaim on the family.

"That's not legally needed," he said, only half surprised by this tactic. "As a Bi-Vivid I have no claim whatsoever upon Bruno Thomasson no matter what prearrangements were made."

"Agreed. This quitclaim, however, provides you with the following sum"—the female of the two pointed to the line and the large amount—"but only if Bruno Thomasson also signs it."

Meaning that if Bruno wanted out after this date, buying Blue off would be more or less legal.

"I'll sign. But I may not ever claim the money. Wealth is so… boring! Don't you think?" Blue asked, sipping his cocktail. He scrawled a signature almost as an afterthought.

Evidently they didn't agree it was boring, because they got up and left without another word.

"That's *not* something the old Blue would have done," Bruno said. He'd been behind a panel or mirror observing and stepped forward now. His voice was velvety and higher than Blue would have expected. He was taller, too. Beautifully dressed, of course. "Or something *she* would have said," Bruno added.

Blue smiled politely and held out a hand, saying "Blue Andresson. The Second." He offered the cocktail already delivered to the table.

Bruno gestured, and Blue invited him to sit.

"Also, Blue the First would have phoned me immediately upon awakening from the Heal-All," Bruno said.

"A year in a Heal-All does not, despite the popular myths, provide full memory retention," Blue said. "And then there is the natural awkwardness of the situation."

"You mean with the attorneys. Not my idea at all. I assure you, Blue."

"I believe you, Bruno. But no, the awkwardness I meant was that both of us now use the same restroom facilities. My predecessor's very flimsy personal file on Bruno Thomasson did not include or highlight… personal flexibility," he ended up saying.

"Very flimsy file?" Bruno asked.

"Extremely flimsy…for such a professional investigator," he admitted.

"Maybe she kept it all in her head?" Bruno suggested.

"Unquestionably."

"Whereas she was herself quite flexible," Bruno said, and smiled a bit.

"Your eyes are pale green," Blue said. "That doesn't show in photos or videos. There they look gray or blue. Is that color natural?"

"Completely," Bruno said. "Do you like green eyes?"

"On you, yes."

"You are the same size and general muscular build as the First."

"Does that satisfy you?" Blue asked.

"Yes."

"Let's order," Blue said. "I'm hungry."

Again Bruno's smile. Blue's predecessor had been as frank.

The dinner proceeded with discreet little references back and forth. Before dessert, Blue said, "I meant it before. I have no claim on you or your family at all. I died. And the fact that I'm alive again is merely a product of our inborn physiology, and has nothing to do with your previous engagement."

"So you believe that theory that existence under double suns provides for double lives," Bruno asked. "Bi-Vividism, you called it."

"It seems irrefutable, at least among the higher vertebrates. And it seems to apply both to us and to the Albergrivians."

"How scientific and how philosophical of you."

"Isn't it? So if you leave after dinner and I never hear from you again…well, that's fine with me."

"Is it, truly?" Bruno asked.

"I said it was."

"Except, my dear Second, the spy camera my attorneys had placed under the table to ensure that you carried no hidden weapons also reveals something else." Bruno froze the picture and passed the phone-pad to Blue.

"Oh that! Well, I've got an excuse. This body is new, and I never exactly know how it will respond to *any* specific stimulus."

Bruno did something with a foot under the table and then froze that and passed the phone photo to Blue.

"I, on the other hand, have been in this body for many years. And I'm even more surprised to see *this* reaction."

The photo he showed now was of his own lap.

Their desserts arrived: tottering cream and cake towers of deliciousness threaded with platinum candy.

"As my predecessor might say," Blue looked at Bruno closely, searching for anything resembling an imperfection, "I'm pretty much ready for anything. Lead the way."

"You see, Second. *That's* new," Bruno said. He picked up Blue's hand and brought it to his mouth, where he nibbled on the edge of Blue's palm before saying, "Your predecessor would have *led* the way…I think I'm going to like this change."

❖

The address Aptel Movasa had sent over was in the River Heights section of the City, and quite upscale. The Lanscro Vidis Air-Skimmer Showroom was a sixtieth-floor penthouse, all the better for off-the-roof test-drives, Blue assumed. It was quietly posh, with the fountain and gardens he'd come to expect with well-to-do Albergrivian business offices. A dozen of the luxurious Black Hawk and Silver Hawk models were strewn about the lawns and flower beds: ranging from the sportier four-seaters to the deluxe seven-door, fifteen-window limos with separated brougham-style driver pods, only available in muted colors. Blue's eye, however, was immediately drawn to a tiny, quietly glowing, low-cut, cobalt blue two-seater, identified as a Thunder Hawk.

"The upholstery matches your eyes," he heard behind him and turned to the voice belonging to a middle aged Albergrivian gentleman who was taller, stouter, and better looking than any off-worlder he'd ever seen.

"Zha-Kas Lascro Vidis?" Blue asked.

"None of that is needed. It's *Mr.* Vidis to you. What do you think? Stunning, isn't it? Brand new. We have the first three Thunder Hawks off the robo-assembly line in the entire City." He continued on with specifications, speeds, handling and maneuverability reports. "Mr…?"

Of course the Vidis dealership would have the first three of the model. This was probably the highest-end and most successful air-skimmer dealer in town.

"Andresson."

"Mr. Andresson. Well, should we wrap it up for you, Mr. Andresson?"

"Let me think about it. Meanwhile, I have come on a slightly less mercantile matter."

"Ah."

He immediately turned Blue away, heading him toward a two-story-high glassed-in office area.

"Zha-Kas Aptel Movasa believes you might be able to help me in locating…someone."

"Aha. You see, my dear." He turned to a woman in her late thirties, less slender than most of her race, with bright eyes and the typical straight black hair. She was dressed well, if very quietly. "I was telling my wife, Mr. Andresson, the minute we noticed you arrive, that you would be someone special. You know Movasa?"

Blue reached to take her hand but she bowed slightly and moved backward out of reach. He noticed she wore dark laced gloves. "Pleased to make your acquaintance," Blue said.

She immediately and wordlessly withdrew as the two men sat on facing if not matching love seats, but she seemed to Blue to hover, and even listen in on their conversation. For all he knew she might even be recording it.

Blue explained his purpose and said that Movasa had somehow or other gotten word that Zha Martila might have worked in some capacity for Vidis.

The Albergrivian denied it, politely enough, and turned to just behind Blue to ask his wife if she remembered any such named worker either here or at their other showroom. Evidently not. She then said something and Vidis told Blue she had another appointment.

Blue then explained why he needed to find Zha Martila for his client. Vidis sympathized and assured him he would put out the word among those who worked for and with him for this fellow off-worlder.

They drank more of the purple tea, iced this time, with little pale yellow flowers crushed over the surface for a slightly spicy flavor. It was a pleasant, if inutile half hour, and Blue left relaxed but frustrated. Of course Movasa had promised, but then perhaps that promise was less substance than off-world formality.

Even so, as he stood in the lift dropping through the open courtyard of the center of the building, Blue felt odd, as though something were not quite right.

He'd come to realize in this short period since his renewal that his intuition was actually quite useful. It had worked with the meeting with Bruno last night; it had worked with Movasa, and now he explored it a bit more.

The problem wasn't Vidis, who seemed about as straightforward an Albergrivian as any he'd encountered—one reason, Blue guessed, for his success in the City. The problem was Mrs. Vidis. She looked slightly off; she acted oddly, and those black laced gloves... Definitely something wrong.

He'd begun going to the exercise club in his office building, so he was both confident and ready for most anything when he stepped out of the lift and into what he only now saw with one step out was not the glittering lobby he'd entered from before, but instead a lower floor, possibly a basement.

One glance at the lift's inner panel showed him he was two floors below the street. Not where he had signaled: so someone had brought him here.

Blue immediately flattened himself to a side wall, and thus missed the thrown kris that embedded itself into the lift's back wall, as the doors closed. He dropped down and tumbled to the other side of the little corridor while a second kris embedded in the wall he'd just been at, and he rolled forward in a zigzag pattern hearing two blades more whizz by him.

He was inside a shallow doorway when he saw a figure in his peripheral vision and dropped down to miss the fifth and he thought last blade, then he exploded out and into the corridor, where he used his martial arts knowledge to jump atop the figure, wrapping his legs around its midsection, pummeling it with the sides of his hands as the figure fell down sideways and tried to escape.

It was Mrs. Vidis, as he'd suspected, And as she lay upon the corridor floor, he held down first one hand, then the other, and tore off the lace gloves.

Each thumb was deformed, thinner than normal, and artificially padded: often the sign of a recent, voluntary, Heal-All experience.

She turned to him, her eyes blazing with fury. "How could you possibly know?"

Blue wrapped her hands in a silk handkerchief and knotted it twice, then stood up and pulled her to her feet.

"Know what, Zha Martila?" Blue asked. "That you were my murderer? Or that you had undergone a gender transformation in a Heal-All?"

"Either," she said, softly. "Both?"

"Surely you've already learned what an advantage it is being both genders? Take you, for example, ruthless as a man to hide your secret, and yet in the end with inefficient upper body strength to throw me off just now. Your trade-off worked against you, Zha. And mine worked for me."

"Stop calling me Zha!" she pouted, not prettily at all, then said, "So now what? You turn me in?"

"Not necessarily. After all, I'm coming to like this body. Like your own new body, it feels a lot more natural to me than the other one ever did. I take it Zha Vidis knows nothing of this?"

"Nothing at all. He only knew that I needed an operation before we could marry. I paid for it myself."

"I have recorded this entire encounter, Martila. This is what I'll need, to keep your secret." Blue outlined it: 1) a death notice for Dusk Martila. 2) a signed confession for the murder of Blue Andresson, the First, and 3) "appropriate compensation."

"The confession is so that I won't ever try this solution again?" she asked. "Yes. Yes. Of course, yes to all three of terms."

❖

He'd heard about and once, too (in another life, he believed), had even seen videos of the Bruno's family's in-City estate. It covered the rooftops of three buildings, in a giant L, those connected by various hundred-story-high transparent, enclosed galleries.

He'd driven into a large lift and had been lifted to a valet at a parking area, one floor beneath the penthouse itself opening to a large open to the sky garden. A young usher checked his face against the list, seemed impressed, and handed him off to an usherette, all of them clad in the bronze and teal family colors. She brought him to a raised deck opening onto several four-story-high, half-open rooms: scene of Bruno's birthday party. People he assumed were family members were streaming across the galleries from other buildings onto the deck. Blue immediately spotted the two attorneys from last week, both of whom smiled, and one of whom even raised a glass in a toast.

As he stepped onto the top step of the deck and stood looking over the hundred or more guests, he heard a voice speak out, "Blue Andresson. Fiancé to Bruno Thomasson." All heads turned to him, and a stylishly slender young woman with dark hair, closely encased in a platinum-threaded gown, sprang to take Blue's hand, saying, "I'm Claudia, Bruno's younger sister."

When the meetings and greetings died down, Bruno appeared, casually dressed, unlike the others, in an iridium-threaded open-necked blouson and slate gray slacks. He was barefoot and bareheaded and he cut through the crowd to kiss first his sister and then Blue. Applause greeted him and even greater applause greeted these gestures.

An hour later, Blue had met most of the immediate family as well as a score of nephews and cousins and great aunts. He felt enveloped by all but perhaps Bruno's mother, the family matriarch and current CEO of most of its holdings. She'd been polite but cool, and Blue thought he could live with that.

They had come to the toasts and well-wishings and the gifts, when they were all startled to see a Thunder-Hawk air skimmer approach and settle upon the roof, just beyond the deck. Its large, multicolored ribbons signified that it, too, was a gift.

Partygoers dropped down to look it over, and it was wonderful to see.

Blue heard the matriarch, Marcella Thomasdotter, saying to someone, "It's not from me! I *wish* I'd thought of it as a gift for him."

Bruno pulled Blue along and over to the skimmer, where someone had found a tiny gift card. He immediately turned and threw his arms around Blue, kissing him again and again. The applause rose and died down.

Sometime later on, Blue was just coming back to the party after a visit to freshen up when an usher intercepted him and led him to one edge of a large chamber where Marcella was seated. She swanned out a hand, which he took and kissed and then sat down across from her.

"I didn't like you the *first time* I met you," she said.

"I'm afraid I can't remember that meeting, although I've tried," he honestly told her.

"His adjustment is a wonderful proof of his continued commitment," Marcella said.

Bruno, she meant.

"Yes, it is. And I'm grateful."

That somewhat mollified her.

"And the bauble?" she waved in the direction of the air-skimmer. "I hope it didn't set you back too much? That would be imprudent."

"No. Not at all. It turned out that someone owed me," he said with a casual shrug. "It was merely a piece of business."

"He looks good in it," she said; Bruno was in the driver's seat and waving to them indoors.

"Diamonds always shine brighter for their setting," Blue said. "That was one thing I learned—the first time around."

"Live and learn. Then live again and learn even more," Marcella quipped. She stood, and when he did, too, she took his arm and began to lead him out to the party. "Of course you'll both live here in one of the residences when you're in-City. But we really must find something unique for you in the countryside. Do you like the beach?"

"Does Bruno?"

"I think we're going to get along, just fine, Blue. Just fine."

THE COCKTAIL HOUR
JOHN MORGAN WILSON

The phone rang a few minutes past three. Morning, not afternoon. You know the sound: that unexpected shrillness in the still of the night that jolts you awake and drives fear like a drill bit into your nerves. That is, if you're asleep at three a.m. like ordinary people, which I wasn't.

For a guy like me, pushing fifty, with too many bad choices behind him, sleep was just another ghost to chase. I was sprawled on a lumpy mattress in a weekly rental, skimming a second-rate thriller the last tenant had left behind, wishing I had a book in my hands that didn't remind me of a few hundred I'd already read. Even awake, I was jangled by that insistent phone, worrying who might be at the other end. When you've got more enemies than decent shirts, a phone call in the lonely hours can do that to you.

When I finally picked up and the caller spoke my name, his voice was unmistakable.

"Jack?"

It triggered a rush of old feelings I'd long ago discarded, or tried to.

"Hello? Jack, are you there?"

"Yeah, I'm here."

"It's Randy, Randy Devlin. Remember?"

"Sure, I remember."

"So, how are you, Jack?"

He'd be in his mid-thirties now but sounded just like he did seven years ago, the last time I saw him: engaging, upbeat, brimming with youthful enthusiasm. Just my opposite, which is probably what drew us together, before it drove us apart. I'd often asked myself what he'd seen in a hard-bitten loser like me, a washed-up jock who'd acquired nothing of distinction in his life but an unfinished novel and a broken nose from one too many brawls. Hearing from him now made me wonder even more.

I carried the phone to the lone window in my little room and looked down on a Hollywood side street not fit for regular people until the sun comes up, and maybe not even then.

"How did you find me, Randy?"

"You always holed up in that cheap hotel when you were down on your luck."

"I'm a creature of habit, I guess."

"A few bad habits, as I recall."

He laughed as he said it. Chiding but playful, just like before.

"I've lost one or two," I said.

"Which would those be?"

"I gave up booze and anything else addictive, like hot young men."

"That's it?"

"I haven't put my fist into anyone's face in a while, if that's what you're getting at."

"That's an improvement."

"You were a big help."

"How's that?"

"You had me arrested, remember?"

"You deserved it."

"No argument there."

"You sound different, Jack. Sadder but wiser, maybe?"

"Look, I'm not proud of what I did. Using someone for a punching bag and blaming it on booze is spineless at best. A year in County helped me understand that. Later, the Twelve Steps. Anyway, it's all in the past. Like a lot of things."

"So, how long has it been, Jack?"

"Since we were together?"

"Since you had your last drink."

"After I got out, it got worse. You were gone. It was just me and the bottle. The cocktail hour kept getting earlier, until it arrived around breakfast time."

"Sounds like it got pretty bad."

"Bad enough that I finally quit, five years ago this Friday."

"I guess I did you a favor, then, splitting like I did."

I heard spite in his voice, buried deep; I couldn't blame him.

"So what's on your mind, Randy, calling me after all these years?"

"I can't hear you, Jack. I think I've lost you. Can you hear me?"

I told him I could but he said I still wasn't coming through. He gave me a number with an unfamiliar area code, asked me to call him back. I thought about it for a hard minute, then made the call. He picked up on the first ring.

"I wasn't sure you'd get back to me."

"I did. So why don't you tell me what this is all about."

"I was thinking about you, that's all. Wondering how you've been."

"At three in the morning?"

"I haven't been sleeping well. I needed someone to talk to."

"You've got no one better for that than me?"

I couldn't imagine Randy single. He'd never liked being alone, and attracting men had never been a problem for him. Not for a guy with his looks, dark and slender, Caravaggio face, and more charm than a puppy dog.

"I'm in a relationship, if that's what you mean."

"Who is it this time?"

"His name's Arthur Cavendish. We've been together two years. An older guy."

"No surprise there."

"A lot older, Jack. He's in his late seventies, retired businessman. Has some health issues. He's getting frail."

"That can't be much fun."

"For him or for me?"

"You tell me, Randy."

"I love him, Jack, I really do. He's been good to me. We live on a ranch, up on the Central Coast. We've got ocean views, and mountains behind us."

"Lucky you."

"Arthur bought me a horse, a beautiful mare. You know how I love to ride."

"I'm getting hard just thinking about it."

"Very funny."

"So old Arthur can't get it up. It's three a.m. and you're wishing you had a stallion to mount who can take you to the finish line."

"That's not why I'm calling, Jack."

His voice quavered, and it got to me. Despite his age I could still hear some boy in him, searching for that elusive father figure, never quite finding the right one. The way it had been with us on our three-year roller-coaster ride.

"I'm listening, kid."

"I'm lonely. I don't have any friends up here. Arthur has his own circle, gay couples his age, been together forever. He tries, but—"

He broke off. I thought I heard him choke back tears. When he spoke again, there was a plaintive quality to his voice that tore into me a little more.

"I need someone to talk to, Jack. Someone who understands me, who knows me the way you do."

Down in the street, a lanky dude in sharp clothes stepped from the shadows and sold a taste to a white guy in a fancy car. As it pulled away, the dealer retreated, back into the crevices. The street was quiet again, empty. Sometimes, I felt destined to die on a dead-end street like this one. A chill ran through me, as if the desolation below had crept up the walls and seeped into my soul.

"What are you suggesting, Randy?"

"If you could just visit, it would mean a lot. Maybe you could find work up here. Arthur could help. He knows people down in town."

"What makes you think I need work?"

"You've got felonies, including one for violence. Maybe more, after I took off."

"Not even for jaywalking. I'm clean, kid. I plan to keep it that way."

"Still, it can't be easy, finding a decent job. Not with your record."

I felt myself softening, not a condition I'm comfortable with. But Randy was right, I did need steady work. Hell, I needed more than that, a lot more.

"Arthur's a writer," Randy said. "You wanted to be a writer once, Jack."

"That was a long time ago."

"You took a couple of writing classes, before you quit college. Whatever happened to that novel you were working on?"

"Drop it, Randy."

"Seriously, I think you two might hit it off. I helped Arthur get his novel published last year. Maybe I could do the same for you."

There'd been a time when getting a novel into print had been the most important thing in my life. But I was one of those dreamers who couldn't keep his butt in the chair long enough to finish anything or be any good at it. Not my novel, not anything else. Now this phone call. Like a gift, a second chance.

"This Arthur," I said, "he won't see me as an intruder, sniffing around his pretty young man?"

"I'm not pretty."

"Yes, you are, and you know it."

I laughed, so did Randy. It was almost like old times. Almost.

"Will you come up?"

"Just friends," I said. "That's it?"

"I'd hate to think we can't at least be that."

"I don't want to get between you two. I can't afford trouble."

"I understand. But it would be a shame if—"

"If what, Randy?"

"If we never saw each other again."

That one hit hard. Every voice inside me—and there were plenty— urged me to tell him no, to leave the ashes undisturbed. But loneliness and longing can turn a strong man weak, and hope can knock him to his knees.

"Tell me where you are," I said, "and how I get there."

❖

I got a late start the next day—engine problems—and drove up the 101 in my '74 Dart, hoping the gaskets held.

It was late afternoon when I took the cut-off for Mira Costa, the little town along Highway 1 where Randy and his sugar daddy had settled down to play house. It was a pretty spot, set at the foot of rolling hills developers had turned into a manicured landscape of vineyards and horse ranches for comfortable pensioners who like to pretend they're living the rugged outdoor life. There was a main street of pricey cafes and shops that overlooked a small bay where surfers carved up waves that flung off sparkles of light. Scenic, charming, idyllic—those were the words the tourism brochure would have used, leaving out the dirty parts that money always hides.

I followed Randy's directions up to the house, winding along a paved road that took me high into the hills, past expansive properties cleanly defined by white rail fences. Near the top, I saw open gates under a wrought iron arch formed by two mustangs rearing up on their hind legs, their front hooves clashing. On a post was a number I'd been told to watch for. Coming out was an old pickup with a saddle in the bed. Behind the wheel was a leathery Hispanic man wearing a cowboy hat that had some years on it.

I turned in, kicking up pea gravel. A pleasant breeze stirred the sweet aroma of yellow roses that clung in blossoming bunches to the long fence rails; somewhere in the mix was the pungent smell of horse manure. From the west, the sharp sunlight slanted across a sky of scattered clouds; the ocean lay in an endless gleam. Not a bad place, I thought, to spend one's golden years with a beautiful young man who didn't mind liver spots and sagging flesh and being owned like a chrome-plated trophy wife.

Randy was waiting in front of the house, and the sight of him sent my blood pumping to all the right places. He was dressed in sandals, shorts, and a tank top that showed off his lithe frame but also firm muscles he didn't have the last time I saw him. He was more handsome now than pretty, with a hard, defined chest tautening the tank and a coarser beard adding some character to his narrow, boyish face. The brown eyes were as wide and warm as I'd remembered them, the grin as heartbreaking as ever. He was the kind of man, I thought, who would look good for decades if he took care of himself, turning heads and causing cocks to swell, as mine was doing now.

He waited where he was as I climbed out, making me come to him.

"Jack. You made it."

We hugged briefly. Touching him again caused me to lose my sense of time and place for a moment. I let go reluctantly, my fingers lingering on his bare arms, on his sun-warmed flesh.

"We're about to fix drinks," he said. "I know better than to offer you anything with alcohol."

I glanced at my watch. It was half past five.

"The cocktail hour," I said.

Randy shrugged. "Arthur likes his martinis."

"I'll take an iced tea, if you've got it."

"Whatever you want, Jack."

He met my gaze head-on for a long moment. Then he turned toward the house, hollering a name: Liselle. A middle-aged woman appeared at the doorway, straight-backed and severe, graying hair pulled tight in a bun, white apron over a plain dress.

"Yes, Mr. Devlin?"

"Iced tea, please, for the two of us."

"This is the gentleman you spoke of?"

"Yes, this is Jack."

She studied me with cool eyes. "Will he be staying for dinner?"

Randy faced me again. "Will you, Jack?"

"If I'm welcome."

"I suppose we could set another place."

He made it sound like an imposition. But his back was to Liselle and he winked as he said it.

"We eat at seven," she said curtly, and turned back inside.

❖

I followed Randy into the house for the obligatory tour, preparing myself to meet the man he now shared a bed with, or at least a home.

It was a rambling, one-story place, faux Santa Fe, right down to the terra-cotta lamps, howling wolf sculptures and potted cacti that almost looked real. Arthur's study occupied a far corner of the house, its shelves laden with Wild West paperbacks. A vintage Underwood sat on an antique desk. Next to it was a tall stack of white paper with a hand-typed title page on top.

BLOOD ON THE TRAIL
by Arthur Cavendish

"He still works on a manual typewriter?"

"Insists on it," Randy said. "Says it's more pure that way. Personally, I think he's intimidated by computers. He doesn't even use the Internet."

"This is the novel that was published?"

"No, that was *Bullets on the Trail*." Randy grimaced as he spoke the title, as if in apology. "This is the new one."

A gruff voice boomed behind me.

"He keeps telling me it's not ready! Says it needs more work!"

I turned to see a stooped and wrinkled man in the doorway, using the frame for support.

"Second novels are often more difficult for a new author," Randy said gently. "If you'll just keep at it, darling, I know you'll get it right."

Arthur Cavendish was nearly my height—six feet—but looked

bent and shrunken, as if he'd once been inches taller. He was on the stringy side, deeply tanned, luxuriant white hair worn long and brushed back, blue eyes that had gone rheumy. Even in his feeble condition he was a striking man, I thought, although he looked a bit silly with his snakeskin boots and a silver belt buckle the size of Texas.

Randy introduced us. Arthur gripped my hand with probably all the strength he could muster, which wasn't much.

"He tells me you're a writer, too," he said.

I smiled uncomfortably. "Pipe dreams, that's all."

"Just the same, I need a second opinion on this manuscript." He picked it up with palsied hands, struggling with the weight. "This one's my masterpiece. Randy keeps at me to do more with it. I need feedback from somebody who knows something about writing." He thrust it at me. "Read it, tell me what you think."

"I'm not sure my opinion counts for much."

He shoved it harder into my gut.

"Just read the damn thing and give me an honest appraisal, that's all."

I caught a look from Randy and accepted the pile of paper.

"Of course," I said. "I'd be honored."

"I'm glad we got that settled." Arthur slapped me on the shoulder like he'd known me forever. "Now let's do some drinking. The sun's going down, for God's sake."

"Jack doesn't drink," Randy said, but Arthur was already hobbling down the hall, bellowing for Liselle to bring him a martini.

❖

It took about two minutes for Arthur to drain the stemmed glass and Randy to get another into his arthritic hands, brimming with high-octane vodka. Arthur took his martinis straight up, extra dry, the time-honored way for a respectable alcoholic to get a fast evening fix without looking like a cheap drunk, a discretion I'd never bothered with.

We all sat on the terrace in the sunset glow, Randy and I sipping iced teas while Arthur anesthetized himself with a third hard one and I fought the urge to join him. The wind had kicked up and Randy brought jackets for both of us, one of Arthur's L.L.Beans for me and a western-style leather model with fringed sleeves for Arthur, along with a fancy Stetson that must have set him back a few hundred bucks. Then we left for a stroll along a path at the north end of the property, Arthur leaning on a cane.

The narrow trail ran along the edge of a ravine whose steep slopes descended to a boulder field and a dry creek. Between us and the rim was another stretch of white railing. We reached a section of splintered boards that looked like a horse might have heaved into it without quite breaking through. Despite Arthur's grumbling, Randy put himself protectively between the old man and the damaged fence, offering his arm for support. The path took a turn, ending at the stables; beyond were a corral and a grassy pasture, divided by more white borders.

Randy showed me several horses, including his favorite, a muscular black mare he called Dark Streak. Arthur stayed behind, outside the barn; he was uneasy around horses, Randy said, and rarely went in. After a while, we heard Arthur grousing about needing a fresh cocktail, so we started back to the house.

By the time we took our seats in the dining room at seven sharp, the old guy had put down five martinis and had his eye on a bottle of cabernet airing on the table. As Liselle served dinner, she cast a hard look at me like I was there to steal the silver. Randy poured a glass of the cab for Arthur and himself, while Arthur did most of the talking. His conversation swung to his ungrateful children and their spoiled kids, how they never came to visit, how they spoke rudely to Randy on the phone, saying terrible things, although Arthur apparently had never heard any of it himself.

"They know better than to say anything like that in front of me," he roared, while Randy tried to calm him. "I'd box their damn ears, that's what I'd do."

"It's okay, Arthur," Randy said soothingly. "It doesn't matter."

"The hell it doesn't!" Arthur turned toward me, anger flickering in his cloudy eyes. "I'll tell you this, they'll get a surprise when I'm gone. They won't get one red cent out of me, or one piece of my property. It goes to Randy, every bit of it."

Randy flushed.

"Eat your steak," he said, cutting Arthur's meat into small sections. "And your vegetables, at least the carrots. No more wine, though. You've had enough."

"I'll decide when I've had enough," Arthur snarled, reaching for the bottle. When he had trouble getting the wine into his glass, Randy poured it for him.

By the time we got to the dessert, Arthur's speech was slurred and rambling. He went on about the travails of the writer's life, in particular his frustration trying to get another novel finished and out while his first one was still hot, as he put it.

"That's why you want your second book to be your best effort," Randy said, touching Arthur's bony wrist sympathetically. "You need to be patient, sweetheart."

Arthur didn't hear him. He'd nodded off, his head bobbing perilously close to his pecan pie. Randy roused him, got him to his feet and trundled him off to bed, while Liselle glared from the kitchen. A minute later she was clearing the table, working briskly around me like I wasn't there.

"It's nice that Arthur has Randy to look after him," I said, trying to make small talk.

"Mr. Cavendish has other people who could do that," she said sharply, keeping her hands busy and her eyes on her work. "His sister, his children, his nieces and nephews. But that's not likely to happen, is it?"

"Apparently they aren't interested in seeing him."

She sneered.

"They call but Mr. Devlin always takes the phone. He keeps Mr. Cavendish stuck in that room, always writing, then rewriting what he wrote the day before. It never ends. No phone in there, of course. Mr. Devlin claims it would be a distraction from Mr. Cavendish's work. Mr. Devlin handles all the finances, all the correspondence. He makes sure that Mr. Cavendish is cut off from anyone who has his best interest at heart."

I felt the blood rise in my neck.

"It was my impression that it's Randy who feels isolated."

"Is that what he told you? More lies." She snorted. "I knew he was trouble when I first met him. I could see how he corrupted Mr. Cavendish."

"If you're uncomfortable with their relationship, why are you still here?"

"I won't be, after tonight. I gave notice two weeks ago. I can't bear to be a part of it any longer, the goings-on in this house. At least I'm free to speak my mind now, little good it will do that foolish old man."

"I think you've said quite enough."

She turned on me, her eyes fierce.

"And what is it you're after, pestering Mr. Devlin and showing up here where you're not wanted? He warned me about you. At least he has the decency to have you in for dinner, before sending you packing. I'll give him that much."

"I'm afraid you've got it wrong," I said, but she was on her way back to the kitchen, unwilling to hear another word.

❖

She was gone within the hour, taking a check for three month's pay that Randy didn't have to give her. I could almost hear her hissing on her way out.

"She never liked me," he said, after I'd mentioned some of what she'd told me. "Never approved of my relationship with Arthur. Never could accept the idea that a man who'd been married with children for thirty years could be queer."

We were sitting opposite each other in the living room, candles flickering on the rustic wood table between us. Without the background noise of the city, the house seemed deathly quiet. I was surprised Randy had lasted so long up here, away from anyone with whom he felt a kinship.

"She claims you deliberately cut Arthur off from his family."

Randy shook his head, smiled painfully. "The only thing you can believe from Liselle is that dinner will be served at seven sharp, and you'd better be at the table."

I laughed, Randy tried to.

"I've pressed Arthur to revise his trust, to include his family in it," he went on. "But he won't have any of it." His voice was bitter but tears brimmed in his eyes. "If I didn't care about him so much, I'd pack my things and leave. Disappear and let them have everything, even the horses."

After that, he grew pensive and the silence got to me, so I mentioned the long drive and how worn out I was. I got my bag from the car and he showed me my room. When I was alone, I stripped down to my boxers, crawled into bed, and turned off the lamp on the nightstand. I was still awake when I heard a light tapping on the door and switched on the lamp. Randy peeked in, his hair and bare shoulders damp from a shower.

"I just wanted to tell you how grateful I am that you came up." He opened the door wider; he'd drawn a towel around his narrow waist. "It means a lot, Jack."

The moist hairs on his torso glistened in the lamplight, which caught the contours of his cock beneath the towel. Like his plated chest, his stomach was hard with new muscle, framed by prominent hipbones that tapered like perfect sculpture into his lower belly and groin. The towel was knotted low in front, allowing a glimpse of pubic hair, just enough to make me want to see more of him, to touch him the way I once had, when we'd been crazy for each other.

"Sleep well," he said, stepping back and closing the door softly behind him.

I barely slept at all. The image of him standing in the doorway stirred up all the old feelings, sexual and otherwise. A sleepless hour passed, then another. I finally gave up, turned on the lamp again, and did a hundred push-ups, four sets of twenty-five. When that didn't work, I picked up Arthur's manuscript from the nightstand and began reading.

I'd never claimed to be much of a critic, but I'd read enough to know that no reputable publisher would be interested in *Blood on the Trail*, not at this stage. The characters were cardboard, the descriptions flat, the dialogue clunky, the plot ridiculously contrived. Never mind all the spelling and grammatical errors. If this was Arthur's masterpiece, as he'd declared, I was mystified by how the first one had gotten published, and why Randy urged Arthur to keep at it. Even more, it caused me to question my own worth as a writer, and whether Randy's encouragement was equally misguided.

It bothered me enough that I lay awake for hours thinking about it, along with other things. Finally, just before dawn, I settled into a troubled sleep.

❖

Late the next morning, Randy went out riding on Dark Streak, cantering her across the bridged ravine before urging her into a gallop as the land opened up before them.

I didn't mind horses, as long we both kept our feet on the ground. So I stayed behind, admiring Randy's grace atop all that surging power, the way he controlled it so deftly with his light touch on the reins. After he disappeared over a distant ridge, I took a stroll around the property, circling back just as he was dismounting and turning his panting mare over to Jorge, the stable hand I'd passed on my way in the previous day. Randy introduced us but Jorge spoke little English, so our meeting was brief.

Then Randy drove us down into town while Arthur stayed behind, pecking away on his old Underwood. It was a fine day, clear and bright. We had lunch in a small café overlooking the beach, talking about old times, people we'd known. We laughed a lot, something I hadn't done in a while. As Randy paid the check, I thought about what our lives might be like if Arthur wasn't around, and immediately felt sick with shame.

Back on the main street, Randy left me and headed for an office Arthur kept above an art gallery, where Randy handled their business matters. We agreed to meet in front of the gallery in an hour. To kill time I meandered about the town, until I happened across a little bookstore called the Book Nook. Displayed in the front window was the current bestseller list clipped from the *Central Coast Times*, with rankings calculated from sales figures collected from selected bookstores in the area. Remarkably, *Bullets on the Trail* was on the list, still selling well after more than a year in print, at least locally.

Inside, I found three copies sitting alone on a bottom shelf labeled Westerns. I grabbed one and leafed through it, wincing with each new page. It was the same inferior writing I'd seen in *Blood on the Trail*, replete with glaring grammatical gaffes no competent editor would have missed. The publisher, Prospect Press, was based in San Francisco. Coincidence there—ten years ago, when I'd met him, Randy's Los Angeles apartment had been on Prospect Avenue. It was obviously a small press, and one I hadn't heard of, though that didn't mean it wasn't a good one. Still, I figured, even the crassest publisher would have standards higher than this. How *Bullets on the Trail* could still be selling a year after publication was puzzling.

I put the book back on the shelf, browsed awhile, purchased an Annie Proulx collection, and left to meet Randy at our appointed time and place. We grabbed coffee, then took a short trip up the coast for the scenery, Randy at the wheel, while I studied the way the sun caught the mesh of fine hair on his forearms, and felt my longing for him rise in me like a tide I couldn't hold back. When we stopped for a walk on a rocky beach, I took a chance and laid a hand on his slender neck. He let it stay a moment as if he might want more, before he broke away to walk on by himself.

I tried to apologize on the ride back but he told me not to worry about it, and seemed to withdraw into himself, deep in thought. It was almost six when we arrived. Jorge, coming out in his old pickup, stopped at the gate to meet us. He and Randy exchanged a few words in

Spanish. Jorge nodded vigorously, saying, *"sí, sí,"* and then we drove on.

Arthur was waiting on the front steps, bending to his cane and looking irritable. He wanted to know where Liselle was. After reminding him for the third time that day that she'd quit, Randy promised to find a replacement as soon as possible.

"No Mexicans!" Arthur barked. "I don't want to be eating no damn Mexican food. And don't go off and leave me alone again, either."

"Let's get you a martini," Randy said, and guided the old man into the house.

❖

After Arthur polished off his fourth cocktail, the three of us repeated our stroll of the previous evening, along the narrow path above the deep arroyo. This time, Arthur was in his comfy L.L.Bean jacket, the one I'd worn the previous evening, while I was in an old Windbreaker I'd brought that wasn't fit for a thrift shop.

"Tomorrow, we'll find you a nice jacket in town," Randy said.

To my surprise, he slipped an arm around my waist. Arthur, dull with drink, didn't seem to notice. Or maybe he didn't mind. Maybe he was happy to have someone around who might provide what had been missing in Randy's life, to keep him from straying too far, or leaving for good. As we walked on, the three of us, Randy and I exchanged a glance that seemed filled with possibilities.

Dusk was deep now, with darkness not far off. Randy wanted Arthur to see a section of the stables that needed renovation and asked me to go on ahead to make sure all the animals were securely in their stalls.

The horses stood placidly as I checked the latches on each gate. I didn't see anything amiss and was about to turn back when something caught my eye at the rear of the barn. Several bales of hay had become dislodged and tumbled to the straw-strewn floor, exposing cardboard boxes stacked one atop the other and partially covered with a plastic tarp.

Curious, I took a look. Under the tarp and hidden by baled hay, dozens more boxes were stacked against the wall. I examined a few. Each was affixed with a mailing label bearing the name and address of the Book Nook or some other bookstore in neighboring towns. I pried open a box. Packed tightly inside were pristine copies of *Bullets on the*

Trail. Other boxes I opened held the same contents. There must have been hundreds of books there, thousands maybe, sequestered where Arthur was unlikely to ever find them, given his fear of horses.

Yet Randy was about to bring Arthur into the barn now, which didn't make sense. I was pondering that when I heard Randy's voice behind me.

"I guess you've uncovered my little secret, haven't you?"

I turned to find him standing there, stroking Dark Streak's muscular neck as she stood obediently in her stall, her big eyes blinking passively.

"You were gone so long," he said. "I thought I'd better come check."

There was nothing in his voice or manner to suggest uneasiness. If anything, he seemed unusually calm, almost eerily so.

"You've led him along all these years," I said, "encouraging his writing, when you knew he had no talent for it."

"Nurturing his dream," Randy said. "Everyone has a right to dream, Jack."

"You're sure it wasn't to keep him tucked away all day in his study, where he wouldn't be a bother to you?"

"It gives him a purpose, a reason to keep going."

"Then, at sundown, you start filling him with booze so you can get him off early to bed."

"He was a heavy drinker when I met him."

"You created a phony company and published his book yourself."

Randy shrugged.

"Nobody else would. I hid the rejection slips from him. I couldn't bear to let him see them." Randy smiled. "You should have seen his excitement when I showed him the acceptance letter from Prospect Press. He said it was the best moment of his life. I was able to give him that, Jack."

"You bought up all the stock at bookstores around here, still in the boxes. They kept ordering more, happy to play along. That kept Arthur on the local bestseller list, feeding his fantasies about being a big-shot writer."

"Isn't a fantasy preferable, when the truth is so cruel?"

I digested that and then felt a jolt of dread.

"Where's Arthur?"

"Arthur had a bad fall," Randy said.

In that moment, all the questions that had been plaguing me, the concerns I'd tried to rationalize away, were clarified. The hidden books, the way Randy fed Arthur so much hooch, the fact that Liselle was conveniently gone, and that of all the sturdy fencing around the property, only that one section above the ravine had been in disrepair, along the path where Randy and Arthur took their evening walks.

I dashed past Randy, back the way I'd come.

❖

Out on the path, Arthur was no longer in sight.

As I reached the section of cracked railing, I saw that it was broken through, a mess of splintered boards framing a gaping space. A hundred feet below, in the encroaching darkness, I could just make out a crumpled body on the rock pile.

Randy joined me, looking over.

"He was old and frail," Randy said. "He wouldn't have been happy as his health declined."

"You started planning this the moment Liselle gave notice, didn't you? When you realized she wouldn't be around to interfere."

"It was an accident. You know how unstable Arthur is on his feet when he's had a few."

"You didn't need me here, Randy. Why didn't you leave me out of it?"

"But I do need you, Jack. Don't you understand?"

He reached to touch my face. I pushed his hand away.

"I love you, Jack. I want you with me." He swept an arm, taking in the property. "All this is ours now. We'll have more money than we ever dreamed of."

"You think I'm going to be a part of this?"

"But you are part of it, Jack. You must know that."

The conviction in his voice was unfaltering. I felt panic setting in.

"You called me, wanting to get back together," he went on. "I reluctantly agreed to see you one last time, hoping to talk some sense into you. That's what I told Liselle, who can back me up if necessary."

"Jorge saw us together," I said. "You and Arthur hardly treated me as an intruder."

"You wormed your way into Arthur's good graces, played on his insecurities as a writer. He insisted that you stay on, not me."

"You called me, Randy. The phone records—"

"The phone I used to call you was neither mine nor Arthur's. It's deep in the ocean, somewhere between here and Big Sur. Your phone records, on the other hand, will show that it was you who called me, initiating contact. Pleading with me to take you back, until I finally agreed to see you one last time."

"Don't do this, Randy."

"Tonight, I left you and Arthur alone for a moment to check on the horses. I heard a struggle, then Arthur screaming. From the stables, I saw you push him through the broken railing."

"You could have had that railing fixed. You didn't. That won't look good."

"Last week, I asked Jorge to repair it. He's wonderful with the horses but he tends to put off other tasks. I knew he'd take his time fixing it. This evening, as we passed him driving in, I told him to get it done first thing tomorrow morning. I was quite firm with him. Another witness in my favor, Jack."

"Did I do this to you? Did I make you this way?"

"And then there's the matter of your DNA on the jacket Arthur's wearing, which puts you in contact with him."

Somewhere in the distance, a coyote howled. I shivered, but not from the cold.

"There's no reason for any of this to come up, Jack. Really, I've worked it all out. You don't need to get in trouble over this, if we handle it right."

He reached for me again. I could have thrown him over the edge, or strangled him, or beaten him to death. It crossed my mind. But the impulse one needs for that, the burning rage, wasn't in me anymore. Randy kissed me on the mouth and looked surprised when I didn't respond. But I didn't pull away, either. I stood there submissively, accepting his attention, the way Dark Streak had.

Randy scrambled down the slope, no doubt to make sure Arthur was dead. I was waiting as he crawled back up. He must have known I'd be there.

"He was good to me," Randy said. "In a way, I'll miss him."

He took my hand.

"Come, there are things to do."

❖

Back at the house, I sat on the terrace, feeling dazed, numb.

I could hear Randy on the phone, reporting his version of what had happened. His voice was tremulous before he broke into racking sobs. It was a fine performance, a mix of lies and truth. Already, I was having trouble separating the two.

Across the hills, scattered oaks, the ones that had survived the power saw, created twisted silhouettes against a final blaze of orange in the darkening sky. Randy came out and lit a candle in a small globe. He'd brought with him two glasses and a bottle of tequila, my favorite brand. He took a seat, poured two glasses to the half mark, and pushed one in my direction. No lime, no salt. Just pure and straight, the way I'd always liked it.

"You and I were drinking," he said. "Arthur wandered off alone, after he'd had one too many. A tragic accident, but nothing too unusual."

"What were we talking about?"

"What we talked about at lunch today. Don't embellish. Just stick to that conversation, and we should be all right, if it even comes up. Our local police department doesn't look for dirt where it doesn't have to. Hurts property values, you know."

The candle flickered in the encroaching darkness. The cocktail hour was almost over. I stared at the golden liquid in the glass, felt myself tremble with my desire for it.

"You'll see," Randy said. "In time, we'll forget all this. Memory is malleable, Jack, something we revise to help us get through this life. You and I will be a couple, just like before, but with the bad parts edited out. You can start writing again, every day. You'll find the discipline this time, I know you will."

"While you're out riding horses," I said.

"Exactly." He reached across, clasped my hand. "Trust me, Jack. Everything's going to be fine."

He sipped his drink, but I left mine untouched, even though the craving had begun to claw at my insides. From down on the highway, sirens could be heard. They got louder as the patrol cars turned up into the hills.

"I'd better meet them at the gate," Randy said. "It will look better that way."

He left me sitting there, watching blades of grass ripple as the wind moved across the pasture. From the stables came a horse's whinny. It was an agreeable sound, oddly comforting.

Someone told me once that in a wildfire, horses will run back into a burning barn and into their stalls to die in the flames, so conditioned are they to the feedbag and the brush, the bridle and the bit, the illusion of safety. Now I believed it.

PRIVATE CHICK
JULIE SMITH

Don's the name, Diva's the game. That's right, my baby. Born Don Devereaux in Terrebonne Parish, and magically morphed into the *fabulous* Diva Delish, New Orleans's most famous mixologist, sometime drag performer, *and* Mistress of Detection and Disguise. In my business—my second business, that is—you see everything. But what you *don't* usually see? A gutter punk with money to spend. The minute she walked in my bar, I recognized her.

Oh, yeah, I knew her—Miss Thing from down the block. One day her hair's purple, the next day it's green, but tell me somethin'—who else goes *out of their way* to be the worst-dressed chick in the Faubourg Marigny? You know how much competition there is? On this particular night she had cotton candy where her hair should have been and she was wearing this severely clashing yellow polka-dot halter thing that showed off a couple collarbones you could shave your legs with, and the skinniest arms this side of a telephone wire, with brand-new tattoos wrapped around 'em.

The Palace was hoppin'. You couldn't hear yourself above the babble of the crowd and the ravishing caterwauling of the blenders making Miss Diva's ambrosial margaritas. I don't exactly own the Marigny Palace, but I do own the ambience, if you get my drift. And that night I was wearing my Bar Diva hat.

"Hello, Your Pinkness," I said. "Nice slave bracelets. What can I get you? Vodka and cranberry to match that hair?"

But she wasn't in a drinking mood. In fact, she seemed a bit puzzled. She consulted a crumpled piece of cardboard. "Somebody gave me this business card, but…I think I might be in the wrong place."

I knew all about that card. "Oh, not so much," I said. "Let me guess whose card. Does it direct you, by any chance, to the world-famous Marigny Palace, home of Double D Investigations, Devereaux and Delish Proprietors, by any chance?" (My second office is just down a little hall at the back side of the bar.)

All she said was, "*This* is the Marigny Palace?"

Well! I thought *everyone* knew the Palace. They should. The Palace is the quintessence of Neighborhood Bar. It's the size of a couple of double parlors, and it has ten tables, max. Who needs tables? Palace people—and believe me, they are *all* kinds of people—belly up. The whole idea is, it's a lot less barroom than *bar*—a huge, warm, wooden, U-shaped bar you could wrap around two houses. When you're in the middle of that U, which is where I was, you command the universe.

I said. "You're there, my baby. So. You need Diva?"

"Who's Diva?"

Oh, really! Who doesn't know Diva? But I am the soul of patience with my clients. Half a dick's job is being a mom. If you can figure that one out. "Me, my darlin'," I said, the soul of reassurance. "Diva Delish, PI, at your service. Devereaux's the muscle, Delish is the brains. You're Wendy, right?"

"Hey, Delish!" hollered one of my regulars. "Who do I have to kill to get a cocktail around here?"

I passed the buck. "Carlo, take care of him, okay, baby? Pink drink, extra ice. Wendy here's got a problem. How about a little drink for her, too?"

At the sound of her name, Miss Thing looked a little shaken. "Some guy gave me the card. How the hell do *you* know my name?"

All righty, then. Nothing to do but tell her the truth. "Cause I'm gooood," I admitted. "You're the gutter punk kid panhandles over on Frenchmen, right? With her filthy-ass dreadlocked boyfriend. The one who hasn't been there lately? Hey! Hey, don't cry, my baby. Let's just step into my office and you can tell Miss Diva all about it."

She followed me to the back of the bar and into the little hall, her boots clomping, my heels clicking. Barkus heard us and started barking as soon as we crossed the hall to the office. She had to know there was a dog in there. She had two ears, each sporting approximately nineteen piercings, but still, they were ears. But the minute I opened the door, and he rushed her and tried to kill her with kisses, she bellowed, "What the hell is that thing? Get away from me!"

She pushed him away. Actually *pushed* my poor sweet baby with both hands, causing him to land back on four feet, puzzled and whimpering.

I picked him up, administering consoling cuddles. "This is Barkus. Say hello, Barkus."

On cue, Barkus barked once, and I popped a tiny treat in his mouth. He is without doubt the cutest dog in the Marigny.

"I'm, like, a cat person," said Wendy, confusing me with someone who'd care.

All righty, then. Miss Thing was a cat person. Once she got over confusing a long-haired chihuahua with a pit bull, she unspooled her sad little yarn.

The gist? One filthy-ass missing boyfriend. It happens, my baby. Boyfriends come and boyfriends go, and most of them aren't worth tracking down. God knows Diva knows about that noise. I figured I'd give her a shoulder and a vodka and cranberry and send her on her sorry way. But this lost boyfriend story had a little twist to it.

"See," she said, "the guy my boyfriend worked for..."

I interrupted. Just couldn't help it. "That kid *worked*?" I'd been seeing him panhandling for at least a year, white kid with dreads. And it wouldn't take a PI of Diva's caliber to spot a clear aversion to soap and water. God, what a wreck. Why anyone would miss him I had no idea.

Wendy said, "You don't have to be so judgmental. We're not criminals, you know. Geo worked for an artist. A metal sculptor. He helped him...you know...haul stuff. And, like, make, you know...art."

"And?"

"The sculptor was Ramsay Erickson. You know who I mean?"

Sure I knew. Everyone did. "The guy's who's doing that sculpture for Armstrong Park. The one of the giant musical instruments. Real handsome dude."

"Geo was around Erickson's place a lot. He saw things he shouldn't have—if you know what I mean. One day he went to work and just... never came back. I'm just so afraid he..."

Her skinny little face collapsed. I handed over the requisite box of tissues, as much a standard-issue item in a PI's office as a shrink's. Though if you are Diva Delish, yours is encased in a spiffy red holder, with tiny plastic revolvers glued to it.

Between embarrassing displays of emotion, the client finally managed to explain that she thought her boyfriend Knew Too Much. Oh, yeah! Dum de dum dum! Knew Too Much. The most popular murder motive on the third planet from the sun. And the best, babycakes. Hands down the best...but what was there to know about a guy like Ramsay

Erickson? Ramsay had it all—fame, looks, money…what could he be hiding? 'Course, there's always somethin'—look at Diva.

Miss Thing's story was so not ringing true. She'd lived with this guy, God help her! "All right, my baby," I said. "Geo told you he saw things. Who leaves *that* lyin' in the middle of the road? Please do not try and tell Miss Diva Delish you didn't ask him what he saw, or she will have you drummed out of the International Sisterhood of Females Able to Breathe."

"He wouldn't tell me."

Right. "So what could he know? You think Ramsay was casting bodies in the sculptures?"

She actually looked shocked. "You are a sick and twisted person!"

"I try, my baby. You got a little bitty advance for Diva?"

She said the secret word.

All righty then. She might have been a fashion tragedy, but her money was as good as Kate Moss's. So the next morning found me armed with a picture of Geo and risking my Jimmy Choos over at the big ol' compound in the Bywater where Ramsay Erickson had his studio. Only it was more of a factory than a studio. He even had his own fab shop, which, to Diva's deep disappointment, did not mean what it sounded like.

I found Erickson taking a break. He was a lanky dude with shoulder-length brown hair, handsome in all his pictures, but up close he had a layer of "I love me" around him that just wasn't my idea of adorable. He was sitting on a plastic chair in the middle of his dusty outdoor welding area, wearing dirty khaki shorts, caressing a Starbucks cup, and rockin' a half-smile. Evidently admiring his handiwork. At least he was looking at what passed for a sculpture, I guess. Anyhow, it was a giant pile of metal.

I stuck out a hand and prepared to lie. "Mr. Erickson? Diva Delish. This is…ummm…a totally fab set-up."

The half-smile turned self-satisfied. "Isn't it? I never even have to go off the block—I can fabricate everything right here. And I can do casting, too. What can I do for you, Miss Delish?"

Barkus chose that moment to let me know he was tired of riding.

"Excuse me," Erickson said, "but your purse is barking."

"Oh. That's Barkus." I lifted him out. "Come on, my baby, let's get you out of there and on solid ground."

But I guess the barking was about more than being tired of purse-riding. The minute I set him down, my baby set off on a little mission of his own, heading straight for the pile of scrap metal that I had a terrible fear was the sacred Armstrong Park piece.

"Uh-oh! Barkus! Barkus, darlin'!"

Too late. He was giving it the major sniff treatment, which usually preceded something else.

"What's that...*ragmop*...doing?" Erickson actually hauled his skinny butt out of the plastic chair and headed right toward Barkus, like he was going to kick him.

"He's just investigating the, uh..." And then, just as I feared, one tiny rear leg lifted ever so delicately. Erickson stopped in his tracks, no doubt to avoid getting his kicking foot wet.

"Omigawd. I am so sorry!"

"You have *got* to be kidding. He just peed on the clarinet!"

"That's the clarinet? I never saw a six-foot clarinet before. With, uh, pointy things sticking all...uh..."

"It's a *stylized* clarinet."

I could have died. I pride myself on a beautifully behaved dog, a dog you can take anywhere, and this was supremely bad form.

But Barkus was anything but penitent. He'd now taken to barking fiercely at his makeshift fire hydrant, as if...well, as if he thought it was simply too ugly to exist.

Erickson was so not amused. "Get that rodent the hell away from my art!"

I couldn't help it if he was a critic, I was still embarrassed. "Back in the purse, short stuff."

As you might imagine, *that* got us off on the wrong foot. But eventually I'd gushed enough about Erickson's stylized musical instruments, which actually looked more like stalagmites—that I managed to turn the conversation around to his missing employee. "Know this guy?" I stuck the photo in his face.

Erickson didn't hesitate. "Yeah, I know him. That's the kid I had to fire. Lied, came to work loaded, stole money, you name it. He was strong, I'll give him that, but enough was enough."

"You fired him?"

"I just told you I did. I even gave him a few bucks and a ride home."

"Oh, yeah? Where does he live?"

"How'm I supposed to remember that? Somewhere around here. Mazant Street, I think."

"I'll try that neighborhood, then. Thanks for your time."

As it happened, the Mistress of Detection had taken the precaution of getting the client's phone number and address. So I knew Wendy and Geo lived on Dauphine, not Mazant. In the Marigny, not the Bywater. It was starting to look like Miss Thing was onto something. Maybe Geo did Know Too Much. But the question remained, *what* did he know?

A PI's best friend is always the neighborhood mixologist and, as luck would have it, there was a cozy little bar down the block. I walked in, surveyed the joint like Bette Davis in her "what a dump" mode (because that's what I always do), but ended up giving an approving nod. Yeah, baby, it might have been a dump, but it was my kind of dump, a great little Bywater dump with six or eight bar stools and five or six tables. Cozy as ya grandma's kitchen.

The bartender looked like he'd just arrived from Itawamba county, Mississippi, to follow in Tennessee Williams's footsteps. By that, I mean he was pale like he never went outside and he had that look of dazzlement that people from away always wear when they come here to Write. He was short and slightly plump, possessed of ancient acne scars, and way too serious-looking. But he was still cute as a Catahoula. Must have been the adoring looks he was giving me. Like we'd been an item in another life. And come to think of it, he did seem slightly familiar.

Well, given our common calling, maybe he'd extend a little professional courtesy.

"Hi, there, handsome," I said. "I'm Diva. From the Marigny Palace? And this is Barkus."

On cue, Barkus barked. This was going much better than that debacle at the fab shop.

But the cute little bartender wouldn't have noticed if my baby had bitten him. He was too busy giving Miss Diva her due. "Oh. My. God. This is such an honor! Miss Diva Delish at the humble Tavern of Memories. Are you kidding me? Everybody knows Miss Diva! You wouldn't remember *me*, but you've made me so many drinks I bleed tequila some days. I can't even touch your margaritas, you have got the magic touch, but, hey, my mojitos aren't bad. Let me rustle one up for you. I'm Freddie Boudreaux, by the way."

It was coming back to me. He always wore a fedora and smelled of spicy aftershave. "You are the sweetest thing. Of course I remember you. You're the guy always proposes when you get drunk, right?"

"Are you kidding? I don't have to be drunk. Marry me, Diva Delish. I can't even believe you're in my bar. Marry me now!"

Well, he *was* cute. "Next time, bring me a ring and I'll give it some thought, my baby. And remember, darlin', size doesn't just matter, size is everything."

"I'll do that. So tell me something. How does it happen that of all the gin joints in all the world, Diva Delish walks into mine?"

"Thought you'd never ask, my baby. Fabulous mojito, by the way. Well. I was just visiting your neighbor, Ramsay Erickson.

"Oh. The neighborhood pond scum."

Every cell in my body went on info alert. Because in every case there's a moment when you know Lady Luck has just smiled. And this was it in Wendy's. Ever so casually, I asked, "Why would you say that, my baby?"

"You know what, Miss Diva? That guy's got the nicest wife in New Orleans. Not to mention one of the richest—he'd be nobody if it weren't for Mimi Dupuy. Who do you think gets him all those fancy commissions? Have you seen his stuff?"

"Looks like stalagmites," I said automatically, and Freddie said it with me. Maybe we were kindred spirits.

"Ha! Jinx. Anyway, he'd be nothing without her—and he treats her like dirt. I see it all, Miss Diva! My nose gets rubbed in it every day of my life."

"Meaning?"

"In here three times a week with a different little hottie every time—lately. For a while—and this is where it really got bad—it was the same chick all the time. Are you ready for this? It was Miss Mimi's assistant. And so beneath Miss Mimi! Skinny little skanky trailer-trash blonde."

"You might want to take it easy on that blond thing, baby."

"Oh, Miss Diva, you aren't even blond—I think of you more as a flash of silver platinum...uh..." He stopped and searched for the right word.

"Silver platinum what, darlin'? The suspense is killing me."

"Silver platinum *kryptonite*. Able to turn strong men into pathetic weaklings."

I winked at him. "Well, I usually do win in a fight. But that's another story. What else about blondie?"

Freddie winced. "Miss Diva. She had a purple flower tattooed on her face! Come on, who has a tattoo on her *face?* Right on her left cheek."

"Really? What's her name?"

"Violet. What else, darlin'? Never knew her last name."

"And Mimi Dupuy is Ramsay's wife? Would that be Mimi Dupuy from the shipping family Dupuys? The Serious Bucks Dupuys?"

"Yeah, that'd be Miss Mimi. She founded a nonprofit for artists. Guess who's the chief beneficiary?"

"Stalagmite Man?"

"Uh-huh."

So that was Freddie's story. Quite a bit more intel than I bargained for—and I hadn't even showed him the picture yet. I figured Geo worked down the block, he was bound to frequent the neighborhood oasis. I pulled out the photo and asked Freddie if he'd seen the kid. Predictably, he had. Only, one thing wasn't so predictable.

"Sure, I've seen him. He said he worked for Ramsay, but the funny thing is, I never seen him in here with Ramsay. He was always with Mimi."

Oh, boy. Why hadn't this come up yet? I wagged my red-tipped finger at him. "Freddie, you bad boy. Have you been wasting Diva's time? So Ramsay was doing the Big Bone with Mimi's assistant? And now it turns out *Mimi* was on *his* assistant's shaggin' wagon?"

But, appearances to the contrary, that wasn't Freddie's idea at all. In fact, his response was downright puzzling. "Miss Mimi? No way. Not happening. Funny you'd think that. I never thought about it even once. They were always sitting in the corner, talking kind of low."

I was getting impatient. "Hellllooo! And what did *that* tell you?"

"No, there'd be these big fat sparks flyin' between them."

"Uh, Freddie? Sparks flyin'? You feel okay?"

"No, you don't get it. They were always fighting."

I sang him a little song. "'You always hurt the one you love...'"

"It wasn't like that. She treated him like...a kid."

Oh. Well, why was that so hard? I gave him a big fat kiss on the cheek. "Diva thanks you, my baby. Come see me at the Palace, I'll buy you a drink. And don't forget that big ol' ring."

So Erickson's wife had a relationship with Geo. Now *that* was worth pursuing. By all accounts, Miss Mimi was the second nicest lady in New Orleans (after Miss Diva her ownself), so I was sure she'd give me a big ol' welcome. I got in my ancient Jaguar (found online and bought for a pittance) and drove to the Ericksons' elegant Garden District home.

The first thing I noticed was this: Any welcome here would have to be big, to match the house. It had to be the Dupuy family mansion. At any rate, it was definitely a mansion, with practically a city block's worth of land around it, enclosed by a fine old wrought iron fence. They didn't call this the Garden District for nothing.

The house itself was what they call Greek Revival style, the most notable feature of which, in this town, is two regal balconies, one atop the other (if that doesn't sound too naughty). I expected a maid in a starched uniform and cute little hat, but I was pretty sure the person who answered the door was Miss Mimi herself—unless the maid had a thing for Chanel suits.

Because that's what Mimi was wearing, my baby! A pink Chanel suit, pantyhose, and heels at 11 a.m., not a highlighted hair out of place. She looked like somebody about to go to a business meeting, but something told me she was the type that always looked like that.

"Mrs. Erickson?" I said.

"Mimi," she answered. "Just Mimi, please. What can I do for you?" Well, that was quick. Two seconds and we're BFFs. I could see why Freddie liked her. But I also noted a faint whiff of Maker's Mark. It's soooo easy to be nice with Mama's Little Helper. I pulled out the picture, which put an unsightly frown on the lovely puss. "Mimi, I'm a PI looking for a young man named Geo. I understand he might be an acquaintance of yours."

She laughed, but the frown stayed. "Acquaintance? That's no acquaintance. That's George, aka my deadbeat gutter punk little brother. What's he done now?"

"Actually, we're a little worried about him, darlin'. His girlfriend says he's gone missing."

"Girlfriend? George couldn't possibly have a girlfriend! He smells too bad. Look, I haven't seen him in a while either—ever since my husband fired him. Sure, he could be missing, but no one in the Dupuy family would know if he was. Or care. He's been dead to Mother and Daddy after the first fifty thousand they 'lent' him. Daddy's so mad about that he's spent the last five years trying to bust the trust Pa-Pere set up for him. To no avail, I might add. Tell you what, Miss…"

"Delish."

"Tell you what, Miss Delish. Wait another year or so, till George's twenty-eighth birthday, and you'll find George, all right. He'll be strolling into the offices of the family lawyers to sign the papers that will make him a very rich young man. Temporarily."

"Why only temporarily, darlin'?"

"Because George could go through *any* amount of money before you can say Stone Pigman Walther Wittmann."

The law firm, I presumed. "Well. I don't mean to pry, my baby, but it *is* kind of my job…"

"Believe me, I have no secrets about Baby Brother."

"You were seen arguing with him."

This time when she laughed, the notes were high and tinny. "Ha! Recently or when he was in junior high? We've always argued; we're siblings."

"Recently. At the Tavern of Memories. I was wondering what you were upset about."

She smirked. "You seem like a smart professional. What would be your guess?"

"Oh, let's see. He needed money and you didn't want to give him any?"

"Bingo. Remind me to hire you if I ever need a PI."

So far so good. On to the rest of Freddie's intel. "Tell me something, my baby. You ever work with a young lady named Violet?"

"Oh, Violet! My former assistant. She volunteered to help with Dollars for Art, and then one day she just didn't come in. No phone call, no forwarding address, no nothing—and the Dollar Ball two weeks away!"

The Dollar Ball was her foundation's big fund-raiser. No one in New Orleans hadn't read about it, in all its glittering glory. "That was about a week ago, right? So she's been gone about three weeks. Well then. Tell me something else—did she quit about the time your husband fired George?"

Maker's Mark or not, Mimi was a fast one, on top of the answers almost before I could fire the questions. But on this one her eyes widened. Her jaw even dropped slightly, but she caught it before it became unattractive. And she was quiet for a moment. "Let me think. Yes, as a matter of fact, I think she did. They both started at the same time, too. I remember because George asked me about 'the weird chick.' That was what he called her. Can you imagine that? George! Calling somebody else weird. Why? Do you happen to know where Violet is?"

"I'm working on it."

"Well, do me a favor—if you see her, would you kill her for me?"

"There's a surcharge for that, my baby."

That one brought her up short, too—even I knew I'd gone too far. "Sorry?"

"No, *I'm* sorry. Diva shouldn't even joke about things like that. Thanks for your help, darlin'."

Mimi Dupuy was the Queen of Denial if she thought we were talking about a coincidence. On what planet do they make coincidences like that? Excuse me, George and Violet came to work for two halves of the same couple at the same time and then disappeared at the same time? And now they were both missing? I didn't think I was going to have a chance to collect that surcharge from Mimi—my guess was Violet was already dead. Along with Geo.

Time to pay a visit to Detective Clarence Bopp, NOPD.

Bopp and I go back a long way. We met when he was busting some pole-dancer for dealing and I was the featured act at the club. Before he figured out I wasn't your average everyday dancer, he made some moves that could have been embarrassing if Diva hadn't taken pity and clued him in. So now he loves me—plus he's a well-known sucker for a pretty face.

I hoped I didn't embarrass him, barging into the squad room like I did, but probably not. Only one other guy was there, and he was talking on the phone. "Oh, Clarence! It's your favorite private dick. Or should I say chick?"

Bopp was bent over something that looked suspiciously like a racing form. When he looked up, I was touched by the look of unmitigated delight on his world-weary—if pudgy—mug. (Though some might have mistaken his sunny smile for a grimace.)

"Oh, crap. It's the world-famous Mistress of Disguise."

"I didn't get that title by choice, my baby; only because Disguise wouldn't marry me."

"Why buy the cow when the milk is free?"

See how much fun Bopp and I have together? "You calling Miss Diva a cow?" I inquired.

"Moooo!" he riposted. We'd be the bromance of the century if Miss Diva weren't such a lady.

I pantomimed kissing: "MWAH. We both know you love me."

Bopp said, "Yeah, right, Devereaux. How do I pry you outta here?"

I ignored his lively wit. "You got a missing persons report on a kid named George Dupuy? Filed by a Miss Wendy Thornton?"

He lit up. "Promise you'll go if I find it?" And without another word, he started staring at his screen and clicking around. Miss Diva was quiet as a cat.

After a while he said, "Well, I've got a Geo De Pew. Damn close, huh?"

I figured that was no accident. "Yeah, that'd be him. Listen, I've got a pretty good idea where he is. That is, Barkus does. He thinks a certain sculpture stinks. If you take my meaning."

And I proceeded to tell Bopp the whole story, to which he replied...

"Okay, simple. All I've got to do is get a court order to melt down a piece of civic art commissioned by one of our most prominent citizens, who happens to be married to the artist. Sure, no problem. What if there's no body in there? You gonna pay for my retirement party?"

I knew he'd believe me. As usual, he was just playing hard to get. "The nose knows. Barkus is never wrong."

"Yeah, well what about this Violet chick?"

"Get back to you on that."

Oh, yeah. I sure would. Because the Mistress of Detection was definitely putting three and three together. And you know what Diva just hates? Being played for a sucker. Fortunately, unlike Bopp, I do *not* work for NOPD.

Perhaps it would be revealing too much to say exactly what the Mistress of Detection did next—and how. Suffice it to say, the color of the day was basic black and I was forced to trade in my usual fabulous footwear for something a bit stealthier. And then...

Back to that Dauphine Street address Wendy'd given me, an entirely boring two hours waiting for her to go panhandle or drink coffee, depending on whether she was in money-in or money-out mode, and finally—Action Jackson!

Not being Bopp, I could operate freely on the theory that you can't make a case without breaking windows, and in the back, I found a nice one I could kick in with my stealth-boots. I lifted Barkus in first and then followed gracefully. Who knew whether she'd gone for a quick coffee or a slow day of panhandling, so I had to be fast. But no problem, it was a one-room room, as the old joke went. It was going to take about five minutes to toss the entire joint.

Oddly, nothing of Geo's was in evidence. It was clear only one person lived here, and that person was a woman. Wendy obviously wasn't expecting her dearly beloved to come back. Okay, then, drawers, files, suitcases, closet. Right. Check. Good show. A very fruitful search indeed.

All that remained was to find something amusing to read till Miss Thing came home. I settled for her personal papers.

And in about an hour, she returned, carrying a coffee cup—so maybe panhandling first, then sustenance? That would explain the time frame. She found me waiting for her, on a chair she evidently used to catch yesterday's appalling outfit, and the one from the day before that and…hmm, seemingly back through eternity. I'd transferred them all to the unmade bed, and you could hardly notice the difference. In my lap were my faithful dog Barkus and three items of interest.

Quite a reasonable question she asked upon seeing us: "What the hell are you doing here?"

What she'd asked me to do, of course. I said, "Making this case my *bitch*, darlin'. Think I might almost have this thing wrapped up. Doesn't look so good for Geo, though. You were right, my baby. Looks like Ramsay did kill him because, just as he suspected, he Knew too Much. Oh, yeah, Geo knew all about Violet and Ramsay, a circumstance that was gonna cut off Ramsay's gravy train if his very rich wife found out. Geo tried to blackmail him, and…well…Ramsay didn't want to be blackmailed."

"Oh my God! No. Do you mean what I think you mean?"

"Well, it's not all bad, Ramsay *was* going to make him immortal. Until Diva came along. So Geo's now a clarinet, I'm sorry to say. And I'm even sorrier to have to report it's the world's *ugliest* clarinet. But, see, there's another problem. Violet's dead, too. Or let's just say she never existed." The coffee cup slipped unnoticed through her fingers. "Barkus, could you get off the evidence, please?"

My sweet baby jumped to the floor, giving the client a tiny little Barkus-snarl.

I held up the first item in my lap. "Recognize this nice blond wig, Miss Thing?"

"Excuse *me*, Delish, but we're wigs 'r us around here—haven't you noticed? I've got blue, I've got pink, why wouldn't I have blond?"

Hmmm. Very defensive. She definitely saw where I was going. I stayed on course. "Oh, and would these temporary tattoos be yours? By the way, I see you're not wearing your slave bracelets today."

"The last I heard, permanent tattoos weren't mandatory in this parish."

"Well, aren't we petulant!"

"What are you implying, anyway?"

I stood up and got in her face. "I'm *implying*, Miss Thing, that you don't know who you're dealing with, my baby. Diva Delish was a world-famous Mistress of Disguise before you got your first training bra. And what's the first rule of disguise? It's sleight of hand, my darlin', just like magic. Distract 'em—like with a *face* tattoo—Diva's hat's off to you, by the way—and that's all anybody's gonna notice. *You* were Violet, darlin'. Oh, yeah, you and Geo set the whole thing up. You went to work for Mimi so you could hit on Ramsay Erickson and cook up a yummy delicious Blackmail Pie for your boyfriend Geo. Only Ramsay liked his gig as kept artist a lot more than you figured."

"You're crazy!"

"Oh, yeah! Don't ya love it? See, you knew Geo was a trustifarian. And if the two of you could have held on for another year, you would have been rich. But you got greedy and Geo got a hostile makeover. You didn't hire Diva to find Geo, you hired me to find his body. Because unless Geo was officially dead, you wouldn't officially be a widow. And you wouldn't get a dime."

"What are you talking about?"

Holding up the third item of interest, I went into incredibly annoying singsong mode. "Found ya marriage license," I sang, like the worst bully on the playground. This was the most fun I'd had since Mardi Gras.

"Give me that!"

She reached for it, but I was ready for her. Grabbed her arm, spun her around, and pulled up on it, which had to hurt.

But she only said, "Damn, you're strong!" and kicked backward at my knees.

Hmmm. Maybe it didn't hurt enough. I exerted a bit more pressure. Oh, yeah. Better. She screamed, but she still had fight in her.

"Let me go!" she hollered and her other arm came up, the idea being to throw me off balance with a little hair pulling, I guess. But, darlin', since you know Diva's secret, you can guess what happened instead. Wendy ended up with yet another blond wig, this one of exponentially better quality than any she owned.

And there I was in nothing but my basic black burgling suit and a silly wig cap. I caught a glimpse of myself in the mirror and burst out laughing.

"Why, Mrs. Dupuy," I said, using Don's voice for the first time, "you seem to have snatched me bald-headed!"

"You're a guy!" she yelled. "You're the guy who gave me the card." Ah, yes. The card she brought to the Marigny Palace that fateful night.

I filled her in while I applied a pair of simply *captivating* pink cuffs that I got from handcuffworld.com for a mere twenty-one dollars. Bopp was just going to love them.

"Oh, you mean my partner, Don Devereaux," I said, still in Don's voice. "Yep. Don's the name, Diva's the game."

And then I switched back to Diva. "That's right, my baby. Born Donald Devereaux in Terrebonne Parish, and magically morphed into the *fabulous* Diva Delish, New Orleans's most famous mixologist and private... Well! *You* know. Gives new meaning to that tired old phrase, now doesn't it?"

She didn't think it was funny.

CONTRIBUTORS

JOSH ATEROVIS has published four books in the Killian Kendall mystery series. His first book, *Bleeding Hearts*, introduced gay teen sleuth Killian Kendall and won several awards, including the Whodunit Award from the StoneWall Society. He followed up by winning the Whodunit Award again the following year for *Reap the Whirlwind*. The third book in the series, *All Lost Things*, was a finalist for the 2010 Lambda Literary Awards for Gay Mystery. *The Truth of Yesterday*, the fourth in the series, has just been published.

MEL BOSSA is the author of the two novels, *Split* and the forthcoming *Suite Nineteen*. Mel lives in Montreal.

'NATHAN BURGOINE lives in Ottawa, Canada, with his husband, Daniel. His previous short stories appear in *Fool for Love, I Do Two, Blood Sacraments*, and *Tented*. He has nonfiction works in *I Like It Like That* and *5x5 Literary Magazine*. He promises the real Ottawa is not nearly so rainy or grimy. You can find 'Nathan online at n8an.livejournal.com.

ROB BYRNES is the author of four novels—*Straight Lies* (2009); *When the Stars Come Out* (2006; winner of a Lambda Literary Award); *Trust Fund Boys* (2004); and *The Night We Met* (2002)—and has contributed to several anthologies. His next novel, *Holy Rollers*, is being published by Bold Strokes Books in late 2011. A native of upstate New York, he currently lives in West New York, New Jersey, with his partner, Brady Allen. He can be found online at www.robbyrnes.net and robnyc.blogspot.com.

MICHAEL THOMAS FORD is now best known for his charming novels about Jane Austen living as a modern-day vampire, and men falling in love with one another, but once upon a time to pay the bills he wrote dirty stories under various names. Much of his erotic fiction has been collected in the book *Tangled Sheets*. You may visit him at www.michaelthomasford.com.

GREG HERREN is the Lambda Literary Award–winning author of *Murder in the Rue Chartres* and the Lambda winning editor of *Love, Bourbon Street: Reflections on New Orleans.* Under his own name and various pseudonyms, he has published seventeen novels and edited nine anthologies, as well as over fifty short stories. "Spin Cycle" is an adaptation of a radio play originally produced by the Southern Repertory Company, in conjunction with WWNO Radio.

ADAM MCCABE is the pen name of an award-winning mystery author. He lives in Cincinnati with his partner and two dogs.

FELICE PICANO is the author of more than twenty-five books of poetry, fiction, memoirs, nonfiction, and plays. His work has been translated into many languages, several titles have been national and international bestsellers, and four plays were produced. He is considered a founder of modern gay literature along with the other members of the Violet Quill. Picano also began and operated the SeaHorse Press and Gay Presses of New York for fifteen years. His first novel was a finalist for the PEN/Hemingway Award. Since then he's been nominated for and/or won dozens of literary awards, including a Lambda Literary Foundation Pioneer Award in 2009. His most recent work includes the history/memoir *True Stories: Portraits From My Past*, and co-editing *Ambientes: Latina/o Writing Today* with Prof. Lazaro Lima. He teaches literature at Antioch University, Los Angeles. Recent (free) Picano stories, essays, and book reviews are available at www.felicepicano.net.

NEIL PLAKCY is the author of the Mahu mystery series, about openly gay Honolulu homicide detective Kimo Kanapa'aka. They are: *Mahu, Mahu Surfer, Mahu Fire, Mahu Vice, Mahu Men,* and *Mahu Blood* (2011). He also writes the Aidan and Liam bodyguard adventure series: *Three Wrong Turns in the Desert, Dancing with the Tide,* and *Teach Me Tonight* (2011). His other books are *In Dog We Trust* (a golden retriever mystery), *GayLife.com, Mi Amor,* and *The Outhouse Gang,* and the novella *The Guardian Angel of South Beach.*

MAX REYNOLDS is the pseudonym of a well-known East Coast writer. Reynolds's stories and novellas have appeared in numerous anthologies, including *Men of Mystery, Frat Boys, Rough Trade, His Underwear, Blood Sacraments,* and *Wings.*

JEFFREY RICKER is a writer, editor, and graphic designer. A magna cum laude graduate of the University of Missouri School of Journalism, he has had writing in the literary magazine *Collective Fallout* and the anthologies *Paws and Reflect*, *Fool for Love: New Gay Fiction*, and *Blood Sacraments*. His first novel, *Detours*, is forthcoming from Bold Strokes Books. He lives with his partner, Michael, and two dogs, and is working on his second novel and too many stories to keep track of at once. Follow his blog at jeffreyricker.wordpress.com.

JEFFREY ROUND's most recent novel is *The Honey Locust*. His first two books, *A Cage of Bones* and *The P-town Murders*, were listed on AfterElton's Top 100 Gay Books. He has worked as a television producer and writer for Alliance Atlantis and CBC. Jeffrey directed the long-running stage production of Agatha Christie's *The Mousetrap* for three of its most critically acclaimed years. His short film, *My Heart Belongs to Daddy*, won awards for Best Director and Best Use of Music, among others. *Vanished in Vallarta*, his third installment in the Bradford Fairfax Mystery Series, is scheduled for publication in 2011.

JULIE SMITH is the author of more than twenty novels, most of them mysteries, and an Edgar winner. Her most popular series feature NOPD Detective Skip Langdon and PI Talba Wallis. She's also the founder of an electronic publishing group, www.booksBnimble.com.

JOHN MORGAN WILSON is a widely published journalist and fiction writer. His twelve books include eight novels in the Benjamin Justice series, which has earned an Edgar from Mystery Writers of America for Best First Novel and three Lambda Literary Awards for Best Gay Men's Mystery. His short stories have appeared in *Ellery Queen's Mystery Magazine* and a number of literary anthologies, including *Art from Art* (Modernist Press) and *Saints and Sinners 2011: New Fiction from the Festival* (Rebel Satori Press). John lives in West Hollywood, California, where he serves on the planning committee of the annual West Hollywood Book Fair.

About the Editors

GREG HERREN is a New Orleans–based author and editor. Former editor of *Lambda Book Report*, he is also a co-founder of the Saints and Sinners Literary Festival, which takes place in New Orleans every May. He is the author of ten novels, including the Lambda Literary Award–winning *Murder in the Rue Chartres*, called by the *New Orleans Times-Picayune* "the most honest depiction of life in post-Katrina New Orleans published thus far." He co-edited *Love, Bourbon Street: Reflections on New Orleans*, which also won the Lambda Literary Award. He has published over fifty short stories in markets as varied as *Ellery Queen's Mystery Magazine* to the critically acclaimed anthology *New Orleans Noir* to various websites, literary magazines, and anthologies. His erotica anthology *FRATSEX* is the all-time best-selling title for Insightoutbooks. Under his pseudonym Todd Gregory, he published the bestselling erotic novel *Every Frat Boy Wants It* and the erotic anthologies *His Underwear* and *Rough Trade*.

A longtime resident of New Orleans, Greg was a fitness columnist and book reviewer for *Window Media* for over four years, publishing in the LGBT newspapers *IMPACT News*, *Southern Voice*, and *Houston Voice*. He served a term on the Board of Directors for the National Stonewall Democrats and served on the founding committee of the Louisiana Stonewall Democrats. He is currently employed as a public health researcher for the NO/AIDS Task Force.

J.M. REDMANN has written six novels, all featuring New Orleans private detective Michele "Micky" Knight. The fourth, *Lost Daughters*, was originally published by W.W. Norton. Her third book, *The Intersection Of Law & Desire*, won a Lambda Literary Award, as well as being an Editor's Choice of the *San Francisco Chronicle* and featured on NPR's *Fresh Air*. *Lost Daughters* and *Deaths Of Jocasta* were also nominated for Lambda Literary Awards. Her books have been translated into German, Spanish, Dutch, and Norwegian. She currently lives in New Orleans, just at the edge of the flooded area.